FIRESTORM

DESTROYERMEN

FIRESTORM

TAYLOR ANDERSON

A ROC BOOK

ROC
Published by New American Library, a division of
Penguin Group (USA) Inc., 375 Hudson Street,
New York, New York 10014, USA
Penguin Group (Canada), 90 Eglinton Avenue East, Suite 700, Toronto,
Ontario M4P 2Y3, Canada (a division of Pearson Penguin Canada Inc.)
Penguin Books Ltd., 80 Strand, London WC2R 0RL, England
Penguin Ireland, 25 St. Stephen's Green, Dublin 2,
Ireland (a division of Penguin Books Ltd.)
Penguin Group (Australia), 250 Camberwell Road, Camberwell, Victoria 3124,
Australia (a division of Pearson Australia Group Pty. Ltd.)
Penguin Books India Pvt. Ltd., 11 Community Centre, Panchsheel Park,
New Delhi - 10 017, India
Penguin Group (NZ), 67 Apollo Drive, Rosedale, Auckland 0632,
New Zealand (a division of Pearson New Zealand Ltd.)
Penguin Books (South Africa) (Pty.) Ltd., 24 Sturdee Avenue,
Rosebank, Johannesburg 2196, South Africa

Penguin Books Ltd., Registered Offices:
80 Strand, London WC2R 0RL, England

First published by Roc, an imprint of New American Library,
a division of Penguin Group (USA) Inc.

First Printing, October 2011
10 9 8 7 6 5 4 3 2

Copyright © Taylor Anderson, 2011
All rights reserved

ROC REGISTERED TRADEMARK—MARCA REGISTRADA

Library of Congress Cataloging-in-Publication Data:
Anderson, Taylor.
   Firestorm/Taylor Anderson.
      p.   cm.—(Destroyermen; 6)
   ISBN 978-0-451-46417-0 (hardback)
   1. Imaginary wars and battles—Fiction. I. Title.
   PS3601.N5475F57   2011
   813'.6—dc22   2011020485

Set in Minion
Designed by Ginger Legato

Printed in the United States of America

PUBLISHER'S NOTE
This is a work of fiction. Names, characters, places, and incidents either are the product of the author's imagination or are used fictitiously, and any resemblance to actual persons, living or dead, business establishments, events, or locales is entirely coincidental.
   The publisher does not have any control over and does not assume any responsibility for author or third-party Web sites or their content.

To: Mosby. I think she would have appreciated the tactics.

For: The families of the men and women of the United States Armed Forces. Only the sacrifice of those who serve can be compared to that of those who wait and worry for them.

ACKNOWLEDGMENTS

Again, I wish to thank my friend and agent, Russell Galen, as well as Ginjer Buchanan and all the fine folks at Roc. I'm sure they'd all occasionally like to "get me by the neck and choke me" (as someone once famously said) out of frustration, but distance has thus far preserved me. I appreciate their patience and support.

Kate Baker still cheerfully maintains my Web site by means of benign mystical powers I cannot comprehend. As of this writing, she's been honored with a Hugo nomination. Hopefully, by the time this volume is released, she'll be Hugo *winner* Kate Baker! She's a great dame!

Lt. Colonel Dave Leedom, USAFR, continues trying to help me "Keep 'em Flying," and his assistance in this respect (and others) has been particularly helpful this time around. Sorry I missed your change of command, brother, but somebody had to tape your favorite cartoons!

In the past, I've tried to recognize the contributions made by the many great fans of this series, some posted on the Web site, others sent to me directly, but, like the list of "usual suspects," this list has now grown to the point that space no longer allows them all to be named here. That's a great shame, because they deserve recognition. Check out the Web site and you'll see what I mean. Many are active-duty or veteran servicemen and -women—from numerous countries—and their input and service is hugely appreciated.

Special exceptions to this remain: Rebecca, Jennifer, Christine, Nancy, Dennis, Jim, Mark, Syd, Mika, Walter, Michael, Erik, Lynn, Chris, Cliff, Debbie, Dex, Gene, Jeff, Don, Lauren, Pete, Robin & Linda, Paul, Ron, Stacey, Darla, Tom, Carey, Brent, Brad, and Gordon. Some of these represent multiple people with the same names, but all continue to inspire just by being who they are—even Jim . . . in strange, amusing ways. Finally, I must again thank my family. They have to put up with me every day—and really could choke me if they wanted to.

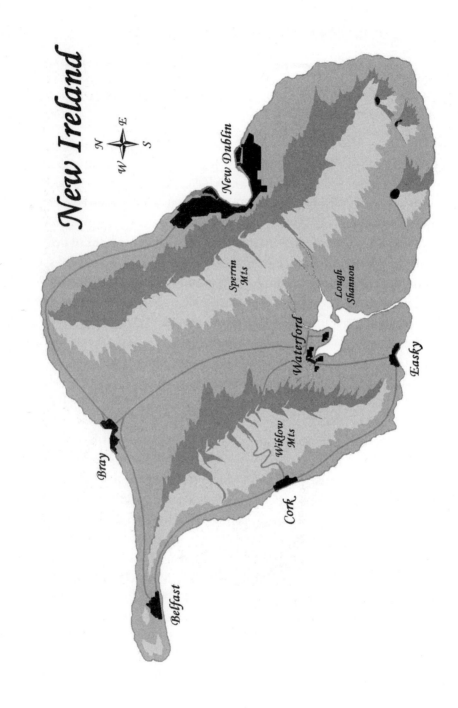

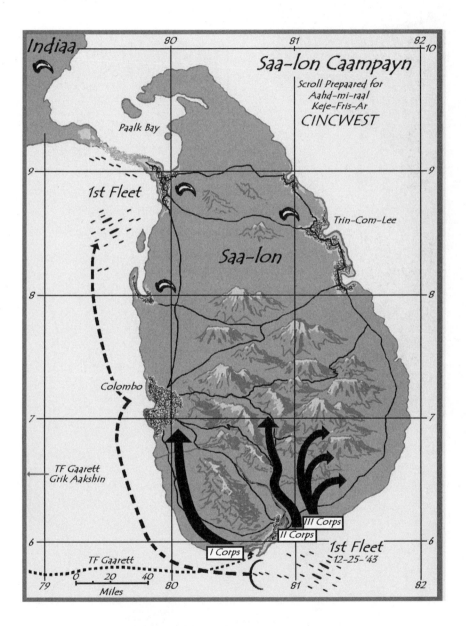

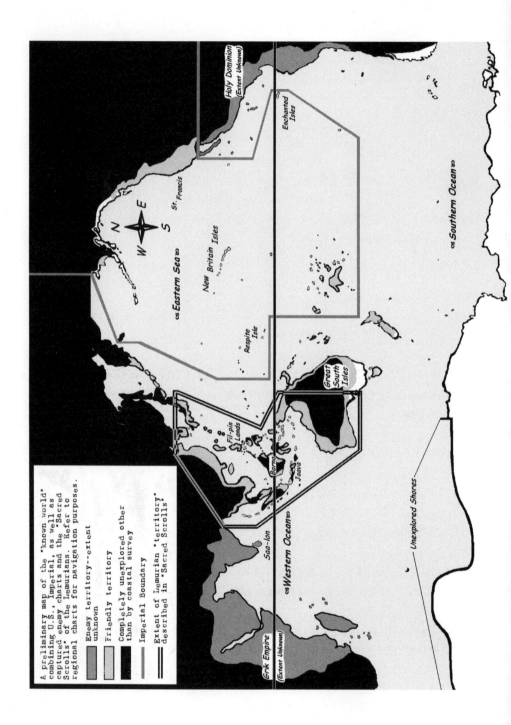

ALLIED SITREP, DEC 19 1943

    X

FROM: CMDR S RIGGS (ACTING CHIEF OF STAFF) LOCATION: BAALKPAN X FOR COTGA (CHAIRMAN OF THE GRAND ALLIANCE) ADAR

    X

TO: ALL STATIONS SPC

    X

    CAPTAIN M P REDDY CINCAAF (COMMANDER IN CHIEF ALL ALLIED FORCES) CINCEAST COMM FLEET 2 LOCATION: EMPIRE OF NEW BRITAIN ISLES

    X

    HER EXCELLENCY SAAN-KAKJA HIGH CHIEF FIL-PIN LANDS X COLONEL T SHINYA LOCATION: MAA-NI-LA

    X

    HIS EXCELLENCY ADMIRAL KEJE-FRIS-AR CINCWEST COMM FLEET 1

    X

    GENERAL P ALDEN X LOCATION: ANDAMAN ISLAND

    X

HIS EXCELLENCY ADMIRAL SOR-LOMAAK COMM TF "OIL-CAN," X LOCATION: EASTERN SEA

X

EYES ONLY DISTRIBUTE AT DISCRETION

X

BAALKPAN: SALVAGED STEAMER SANTA CATALINA AR-RIVED SAFELY UNDER POWER X MAJORITY CARGO OFF-LOADED X WILL ENTER DRY DOCK FOR REMAINDER CARGO REMOVAL X SEAPLANE CARRIER ARRACCA (CV-3) WILL DEPART IN COMPANY NEW BATTLE GROUP AND TROOPSHIPS X AIR WING WORKING-UP EN ROUTE ANDA-MAN X ALLIED COUNCIL CONDITIONALLY ACCEPTS MEMBERSHIP RESPITE ISLAND AND EMPIRE NEW BRIT-AIN ISLES INTO GRAND ALLIANCE X AWAIT REPRESEN-TATIVES XXX

X

MAA-NI-LA: CAPITAL FIL-PIN LANDS ESCAPED SERIOUS DAMAGE FROM TIDAL WAVE CAUSED BY ERUPTION TA-LAUD ISLAND X OTHER FIL-PIN LANDS HOMES SUFFERED GRAVELY X PAGA-DAAN ALMOST WIPED OUT X RESCUE EFFORT INVOLVING LAND AND NAVAL FORCES CONTIN-UES X WILL DELAY DEPLOYMENT SOME ELEMENTS X TF (TASK FORCE) MAKAA-KAKJA (CV-4) AND BATTLE GROUP READY TO DEPLOY X RELUCTANTLY CONCUR NECESSITY TO SEND IT EAST TO AID CAPTAIN REDDY AND IMPERI-ALS X COLONEL SHINYA CAN DEPLOY DIVISION IN LESS THAN TWO WEEKS X WHERE SEND? X SUBMARINE S-19 PASSENGERS AND CREW—INCLUDING SEVENTY-ONE (71) EX-TAGRANESI (LAWRENCE PEOPLE) SAFE IN MAA-NI-LA X WHERE SEND? X NAVY OILER RETURNED FROM RESPITE ISLAND WITH FIRST LOAD HUMAN FEMALES X WHERE SEND? XXX

X

EMPIRE OF NEW BRITAIN ISLES: COMPANY COLLABORA-TION WITH FORCES "HOLY DOMINION" QUASHED ON ALL ISLANDS EXCEPT NEW IRELAND X DOMINION/REBEL

FORCES STRONGLY POSITIONED THERE X NOT KNOWN IF WORD OF HOSTILITIES HAS REACHED DOMINION PROPER BUT PRISONERS SAY HOSTILITIES LONG EXPECTED X FOUNDERS' DAY CELEBRATION JAN 5 1944 IS DATE AFTER WHICH THINGS WILL "AUTOMATICALLY HAPPEN" X GOVERNOR-EMPEROR AND COMMODORE JENKS SUSPECT MOVE AGAINST CONTINENTAL IMPERIAL HOLDINGS AT LEAST X REPAIRS USS WALKER ALMOST COMPLETE X WALKER AND SIMMS REMAIN ONLY US NAVY ELEMENTS IN THEATER X ANTICIPATE ARRIVAL TF "OILCAN" SO CAN COMMENCE OFFENSIVE OPERATIONS X HOPE ECO-NOMIC ADVICE HELPFUL X NEED MORE MARINES XXX
X
ANDAMAN: PORT FACILITIES INCLUDING FLOATING DRY DOCK AND AIRSTRIP NEAR COMPLETE X TF GARRETT REMAINS ON BLOCKADE DUTY X ALL OTHER ALLIED FORCES INCLUDING I AND III AND IV CORPS—FIRST FLEET COMPOSED OF SALISSA (CV-1) AND HUMFRA-DAR (CV-2) BATTLE GROUPS AND TRANSPORTS READY TO COMMENCE OFFENSIVE OPS CEYLON IN MOST RESPECTS X THANKS FOR SENDING CMDR LETTS TO SORT OUT MESS! X HIS PLANE ARRIVED SAFELY YESTERDAY XXX

MESSAGE ENDS XXX

CHAPTER 1

////// *"Western" (Indian) Ocean*

ommander Greg Garrett, former gunnery officer of the old Asiatic Fleet "four-stacker" destroyer USS *Walker* (DD-163), now captain of the sailing frigate USS *Donaghey*, leaned on the starboard quarterdeck rail, staring through his binoculars. The colors of the sea and sky had proclaimed their independence from each other and a yellow-red smear splashed the eastern horizon. The boisterous sea was becoming a tumultuous, toothy, pink-tinged purple. The Lemurian lookout, high in the maintop, had sighted dawn-spangled sails to the northeast with her keen eyes, but Garrett still saw nothing. As he searched, the sun darted tentative beams over the distant, hazy line of the continent.

"What have we, sur?" asked Lieutenant Saaran-Gaani, joining Greg beside the rail. Saaran was *Donaghey*'s exec, her "salig maa-stir," in the Lemurian vernacular. He'd replaced Muraak-Saanga, who'd been recently appointed to command the new USS *Tassat* when Garrett declined the honor in favor of remaining with *Donaghey*. Saaran was a bona fide "Sky Priest," of a southern denomination, so he filled the "sailing master" role without suffering any of the religious resentment that sometimes plagued laymen in his post. More and more Sky Priests joined the Navy these days, surely out of patriotism, but also possibly to help secure their relevance in these strange, transitional times.

Garrett didn't care about that. Saaran was a fantastic navigator, as were most of his order, but like Adar—the "highest-ranking" Sky Priest Greg knew—Saaran was a fanatic for "the cause." Greg lowered his binoculars and looked at him. The oversize, dark amber eyes gazing back were common among Lemurians, but the fine, almost perfectly symmetrical coat of brown and white fur was unusual. Lemurians could be almost any color and were often striped, blotched, or even brindled, but not many had so much white. Greg shrugged mentally. Sky Priests were often odd in a number of ways. In Saaran's case, it might even be his "southern" lineage. He was one of the few 'Cats from the Great South Island, the land humans remembered as Australia, who'd joined "the Grand Alliance" so far. He even talked funny. Word was, some "land Homes" of north and west "Australia," culturally similar to Baalkpan and Maa-ni-la, were forming regiments and might apply for full membership in the Alliance. Garrett hoped they would. This war was a fight for all Lemurians to make—all *people* of whatever race or species.

Regardless of where he was from, Saaran was an aggressive, eager student of naval warfare, and Garrett felt lucky to have him. He scratched the dark hair poking from under his hat with his left hand, while still holding the binoculars with his right.

"Sails," Garrett replied. "Plural. No count yet. Lookout caught 'em in the northeast, probably sailing in column. I can't see squat from here."

"Ah," Saaran said, smiling. "The predawn 'GQ' strikes again!"

Garrett smiled too. It wouldn't be the first time they'd snapped up a Grik ship simply by being on their toes at that critical time of day.

"Maybe. I hope so. It's been a little boring out here lately."

"Boring!" Saaran huffed. *Donaghey* and her sister, *Tolson*, under the command of Russ Chapelle, as well as the newly arrived *Revenge*, were blockading the western approaches to Ceylon and India. Besides the occasional enemy ship, these waters teemed with some of the most dangerous creatures in the known world. They were *packed* with an un-precedented (in their experience) density of ridiculously large and scary predators—some more than capable of destroying ships twice as large as theirs. The Navy had developed countermeasures that worked—when there was time to deploy them—but discovering the threat in the first place was the tricky part. Dangerous submarine creatures, like submarine boats, were difficult to detect and the "blockading squadron" was operating on one of the most nerve-racking stations imaginable.

"Well, maybe not *bored*," Greg allowed, "but there hasn't been much 'business' since we clobbered that east-bound convoy a couple of weeks ago." He shook his head. "As I said before, I think they've figured out that somebody out here is beating up the mailman!"

Donaghey and *Tolson* had been making things rough on the Grik "mailman" for a while now, paired continuously since *Tolson*'s return from a special mission to Tjilatjap (Chill-Chaap) where Russ helped salvage an old freighter—and her impossibly valuable cargo. The two "first new construction" frigates were the last dedicated "sailors" in the Navy besides the dozens of prize "Indiamen" that had been "razeed" into swift, lightly armed corvettes, and they were commanded by the most experienced skippers. Not only were they independent of fuel requirements and able to remain on station longer, they were the fastest ships in the Navy—with the exception of the ship that brought the destroyermen to this "other" earth in the first place: USS *Walker* herself.

Revenge had just arrived in theater. She was a new construction steam frigate of an entirely new—hopefully improved—design called the "Scott" Class. Named for the first *Revenge*, a captured Grik ship whose human-Lemurian crew fought to the last against staggering odds, she was bigger, faster, and more powerful than the first allied steamers. Her auxiliary sailing rig remained, but she was supposed to be almost as fast as *Donaghey* under steam alone. She had a good skipper too. Pruit Barry had been *Walker*'s assistant gunnery officer, and he'd commanded *Tolson* during the Battle of Baalkpan. Although he'd saved his ship, he'd been so sorely wounded that he was just now returning to action. Garrett was glad to have him back.

"Deck there!" came the cry from the lookout above. 'Cats—Lemurians—had strange voices, Garrett reflected again, to carry so well even over such a brisk wind. "Sur-fass Taa-git now eight sails! Eight! Taa-git bearing seero fo fi, rel-aa-tive!"

"Course?" Saaran bellowed in reply.

"West-sou-west!"

Saaran looked at Greg. "Perhaps business will pick up today!"

"Yeah. Tell Clancy to get *Tolson* and *Revenge* on the horn. Maybe we can work it so we can snatch the whole bunch! We'll keep our distance here to windward until we sort something out."

Over the next hour and a half, coded wireless messages clattered back and forth between *Donaghey*, *Tolson*, *Revenge*, and the distant Allied headquarters on Andaman Island. They had no proof the enemy even had receivers, but crystal sets were simple to make, and they had to assume they did. Therefore, all Allied transmissions were sent in five-letter code groups. The Japanese from the destroyed battle cruiser *Amagi*, which came through the same "Squall" as *Walker* and allied with the Grik, had been "reading their mail" from the start, and that memory still stung. Now, even before the plan of attack was finalized, Greg ordered Chapelle to bring *Tolson* north from the southernmost station, and she'd have to move quickly to reach position if they were to intercept the enemy short of the islands to the west. Not only was there a chance the Grik might scatter among the islands, allowing some to escape, but ocean denizens tended to congregate near the rich feeding grounds the islands provided. *Revenge*, with her steam power, cruised closest to shore, and Barry was told to bring her south. Before long, *Tolson* was seen flying north with a quartering wind, shouldering the sea aside. With the plan of attack taking shape as Garrett's squadron assembled, *Donaghey* prepared to turn north herself. If everything went as Garrett hoped, it would be an exciting afternoon. Of course, Greg knew all about how fickle plans and hopes could be.

"Sur-fass Taa-git, port bow, tree hunn-red yards!" warned the lookout. Garrett and Saaran crossed the deck. "Shaark!" came several cries.

Garrett raised his glasses and stared at the fin cutting through the swells. "Jeez," he said, "that's not a shark! It's a B-17 tail sticking out of the water!"

"What's a 'bee-seven-teen'?" Saaran asked.

"Never mind," Greg replied flatly. He raised his voice. "Helm, make your course three, zero, zero. Mr. Saaran, please adjust the sails for speed as you see fit." He turned and looked northeast. The Grik ships were in view now, their column in disarray. He knew they could see *Donaghey*, and probably *Tolson*, but wasn't sure about *Revenge*. He wondered how they'd react. He wondered if they knew *how* to react. Returning to port had never seemed an option for them in the past. Just the same, he'd always tried to bushwhack them far enough out that the Allied ships could chase them down.

"Making my course tree, seero, seero," the helmsman replied.

"Very well," said Greg, looking back at the "shark." It wasn't following them. "Wow," he murmured. There were some absolutely humongous sharks around here. According to reports, there were big ones around the New Britain Isles too, where Captain Reddy and *Walker* were. Greg honestly didn't know whether they were a genuine danger to a ship like *Donaghey* or not. They didn't ram—at least they never had—and the few times they'd "tasted" his ship, they'd left teeth the size of hubcaps stuck in her copper-clad wooden hull. He doubted one of the damn things could sink *Donaghey*, unless it did ram, but he always worried about the ship's rudder. A shark like the one he'd just seen could bite it clean off. He shook his head and returned his attention to the Grik.

"They look like a gaggle of geese on a pond," he said. The column was falling completely apart, beginning to bunch together as if for mutual support. The Grik ships were actually acting less like geese and more like a herd of goats that just saw a bear. Greg grinned at the analogy. He'd seen that once, back home in Tennessee, and it was a funny memory. He hated goats.

"*Revenge* is coming up," cried the lookout. "There blue smoke beyond the enemy."

For another half hour they approached the Grik convoy, and soon the three Allied frigates had closed every route but the one back to port. It struck Garrett that if the Grik had just maintained a cohesive column and continued determinedly on, some might have broken past at least one blocking ship, but these weren't Grik warships, filled to the gunwales with fierce warriors, and evidently that made a difference. The convoy commander was probably some bright, civilian Hij—they knew such things existed now—who thought he could *think* his way out of this mess. His hesitation and indecision were making it worse—for him.

"Sound general quarters," Garrett said, then in the tradition of the sailing Navy added, "Clear for action." A quartet of Lemurian younglings, wearing the blue kilts and white leather armor of Marines, scampered to the waist, and their drums thundered in unison while a bosun's mate rapidly struck the hollow bronze gong mounted near the ship's wheel. The resulting cacophonous combination couldn't be mistaken for anything other than the GQ alarm. Gun's crews ran to their massive weapons, tails high in excitement, and twenty-four eighteen-pounders were run out. 'Cats rigged netting overhead to protect against falling debris, and gunners threaded lengths of slow-match through holes in their linstocks and waited for one of the midshipmen trotting the length of the gun deck to arrive and light the slow-burning match. Marines scaled the ratlines to the tops with muskets slung diagonally across their backs, and others stood near the center of the ship, prepared to move to whichever side they were directed.

The exercise of preparing the ship for battle went off without a hitch, just as it did in the daily drills. Greg was pleased with the professionalism of his almost entirely Lemurian crew, and he knew they were proud of it too. *Donaghey* had a gallant name and history, and she'd already racked up more than her share of battle honors in this war. She prepared each time as if she'd face an enemy at least as powerful as she was—she'd been the first ship surprised by Grik cannons, after all—and the extra attention to detail had served her well many times. Garrett didn't know if any of the ships *Donaghey* approached was armed; in fact, he rather doubted it. They weren't acting as if there were warriors aboard, but he'd never let appearances lull him again. He raised his binoculars.

Weird. The eight Grik ships, so similar in appearance to the ancient British East Indiamen their lines were stolen from centuries before, appeared to have heaved to, almost as if they were surrendering and waiting to be taken! "Get a load of this," he said, handing his glasses to Saraan.

"I don't understand," said the 'Cat, blinking confusion. "Most un-Grik-like. They've never behaved like this before."

Chief Gunner's Mate Wendel "Smitty" Smith joined them. "The main battery's manned and ready for action in all respects," he declared.

Garrett looked at the short, prematurely balding man, once just a green ordnance striker on *Walker*. "Very well, Smitty. We'll probably make a turn to port as we get close, so prepare for 'surface action, starboard.'" He paused. "Why don't you take a look and tell me what you think?"

Smitty nodded and raised his own precious binoculars. There were only two pairs on the entire ship, and the 'Cat lookouts didn't really need them. Russ had brought a crate of the things from his salvage mission to Tjilatjap, but most were scarfed up by HQ. "Looks weird," Smitty confirmed. *Donaghey* was within six thousand yards of the enemy now, closing fast. "Can't tell if they're armed yet, but they're just sittin' there. Say, there's *Revenge*, steamin' up on 'em from the north. She's a pretty thing!"

The distance to the targets continued to dwindle as the morning wore on and evolved into a clear, beautiful day. The heat wasn't as oppressive as it was within the Malay Barrier, and the steady wind kept the humidity at bay. At Smitty's estimate of fifteen hundred yards, something caught Greg's eye. "What the hell? Hey, look at that. There's lizard birds swooping all over those ships, like you see around a fishing fleet—or a big school of fish. They're swarming like flies!"

"You're right," Saaran agreed. "What could be the cause? Perhaps they carry a cargo that attracts the fliers—or fearing capture, they throw it over the side."

"Fearing capture . . ." Greg murmured. "This whole setup makes less sense all the time. Of course, who knows how 'civilian' Grik sea captains act. I guess we've probably run across a few before . . . but they never acted this weird. Hmm." He motioned a 'Cat midshipman near. "Tell Clancy to send this to *Revenge* and *Tolson*: 'Watch out for something screwy.'"

"Ay, ay, sur! Anything else?"

Garrett shook his head. "No . . . just . . . something screwy—and be sure they know to report it if they see anything that fits that description!"

The midshipman bolted down the companionway to the "wireless shack" beside Garrett's own quarters.

"What do we do?" Smitty asked. The range was down to nine hundred yards.

Tolson was closing from the west and *Revenge* was about the same distance to the north of the enemy, steaming into a steady wind on her starboard bow. Greg smiled with appreciation. The new *Revenge* was fast, and only one of the fore and aft rigged feluccas could have matched her course. It was a near-textbook interception, but the Grik weren't acting "textbook" at all.

"Do we sink 'em or what?" Smitty persisted.

"I don't know," Greg ground out. He shook his head. "How do you know if Grik are trying to surrender?" The very idea of such a thing would've seemed impossible not long ago—until an aged "civilian" Grik called "Hij Geerki" surrendered to General Pete Alden and Lord General Rolak during the "Raan-goon" operation. Ever since, the creepy old Grik had been a font of unrestrained information. It was as if, having surrendered, he'd literally, unreservedly, switched sides. Rolak owned him now, body and soul. Greg's skin crawled. Personally, he'd prefer to open fire and sink every Grik ship in view as soon as in range, but he had to think of the intelligence value! They had Grik "captives" of the "Uul," or "warrior-worker class," that understood the Lemurian tongue—back in Baalkpan now—but they couldn't *speak* anything anyone understood. Their "Hij" leaders couldn't speak anything comprehensible either, but many could read and write English, considered the "scientific tongue." All Grik sea captains were "Hij," and the prospect of capturing *eight* more sources of information was a powerful lure.

"Well, let's leave it to them," Smitty said. "We can sink some, and if the others want to surrender, let *them* figure out how."

Saaran shook his head and his ears twitched negation, even while his tail swished with amusement. "That will just frighten *any* out of surrendering—if that's their intent."

"Whoa!" said Garrett, looking through his glasses. "They're really starting to bunch up now, all eight. Shortening sail—and those red pennant-flag things are coming down! They're lowering their flags! They really *are* surrendering . . . Looks like they're taking in all sail and lashing their ships together too. Who the devil told them to do that?"

Smitty snapped his fingers. "The Japs! There's bound to be Japs on Ceylon. They must've told them what to do! Might even be Japs on those ships!"

"When did you ever see a Jap surrender?" Greg demanded, but realized it must be true. They already knew few of the surviving Japanese cared much for their Grik "allies." He shook his head. "Holy smokes. Pass the word for everyone to hold their fire. *Tolson* and *Donaghey* will take a closer look. Signal Mr. Barry to keep *Revenge* back, but close enough to cover us." The range was seven hundred yards.

They began spotting gri-kakka, or "pleezy-sores" at about three hundred yards. The big "lizard fish" were deadly dangerous to small boats, and even feluccas. Ships sometimes sank after striking a large one near the surface. "Look at them all," someone murmured quietly. No one had ever seen such a concentration before, and the closer they moved to the Grik ships, the denser they got—almost as dense as schools of flasher-fish sometimes got—and there were swarms of flashies too! The surface of the sea began to froth as giant fins lanced through the sedately cruising gri-kakka, and bright blood swirled in the water. Gri-kakka reared up, jaws agape, with sharks as large as they were fastened to their bodies, wrenching their heads back and forth. The gri-kakka started turning on the sharks as well.

"What the hell's going on here?" Garrett muttered. "It's like some kind of 'war of the sea monsters'! Better shorten sail, and prepare to heave to," he told Saaran.

A midshipman slammed to a stop beside him. "Sur, Mr. Clancy say Mr. Chaa-pelle on *Tolson* don't like this." The young 'Cat blinked irony. "He say something 'fishy.'"

Smitty was looking through his binoculars. "Skipper! There's Griks over there, throwing junk in the water. Looks like . . . dead stuff! Chunks of meat or something!" He turned to Garrett with wide eyes. "The bastards are *chumming* all these devils up!"

"Prepare to commence firing! Helm, make your course three, six, zero! We're getting out of here before something knocks a hole in us, but we'll blast 'em as we pass! Chumming up herds of dangerous sea monsters is *not* a peaceful, surrendering act!" He looked at the midshipman. "Tell *Tolson* we'll steer out of this feeding frenzy, then paste them!"

The midshipman saluted and started to turn, but then did a double take over Garrett's shoulder. "Sur!" was all he managed. The officers spun in time to see a cavernous mouth rise from the sea a few hundred yards off the port quarter. Water cascaded down the flanks of the gray-black island of flesh, and the thing immediately surged forward, taking Gri-kakka, "sharks," and thousands of flashies into its hundred-foot maw.

"It's a trap!" Saaran yelled. "They have lured forth a mountain fish!"

"Commence firing, all guns!" bellowed Greg. "Port battery'll concentrate on that big fish! AMF-DiC [Anti-Mountain Fish Destruction Countermeasures] will prepare to fire!"

The great fish, seemingly oblivious of *Donaghey*, chomped down on its stupendous mouthful and prepared to take it down to swallow. They all knew it wouldn't go away, however. It would be back to feed and feed until the entire smorgasbord above was consumed, or managed to flee. *Revenge* might get away, but *Tolson* and *Donaghey* were doomed—if they couldn't scare the creature away. The eight Grik ships were doomed as well, and their crews had to know that. The significance of that didn't occur to Greg just then. He looked at the Grik, just over a hundred yards off the starboard beam, hoping they didn't have any "Grik fire" bombs. *Tolson*'s guns opened up, and a moment later, *Donaghey* shuddered with the rolling broadside that thundered out from both sides.

Smoke gushed, choking Greg and Saaran on the quarterdeck until it passed. Smitty was gone, directing his guns. There was a momentous writhing splash to port, accompanied by a deep, bass, bone-tingling, moaning roar. The splash launched a wave large enough to heave the ship on her beam ends, and they saw the mighty flukes of the titanic monster rise in the air.

"Y guns!" came Smitty's roar from forward, calling on the crews of the mortarlike contrivances that launched "depth charges." They were the primary, most effective aspect of the AMF-DiC system. They weren't necessarily meant to harm a mountain fish, but the acoustic assault they created was known to discourage the mammoth creatures. "Drop them a hundred yards off the port beam!" Smitty directed.

Greg turned aft. "Depth charges!" he cried. "Set depth for one hundred feet! Roll four!" There were several, staggered *whumps*; two from the fo'c'sle, and two just behind Garrett on the quarterdeck. Heavy kegs vaulted skyward, almost straight up it seemed. Shortly after, four more kegs rolled into the sea aft, from racks piercing the taffrail. It was at times like this—virtually the only times anymore—that Garrett wished his ship had engines. Certainly, he'd love to be able to flee from a mountain fish, but he wanted to get the hell away from the depth charges they'd just dropped even more. They could break *Donaghey*'s back if she wasn't far enough away. Fortunately, the wind was in her favor. He stared at the great fish. You could never predict how they'd react. The bombs usually scared them away, but cannon fire—especially if it hit—sometimes caused the monsters to go amok and attack whatever shot at them.

Oddly, the huge beast was just lying there, wallowing in the swells like a dead whale surrounded by a school of dolphins. He'd never seen that reaction before. The bombs from the Y guns splashed down about half the distance to the fish. Breathlessly, those around Garrett waited. The Y gun bombs would detonate at thirty feet—probably at about the same time the depth charges blew. *Tolson* had surely fired her Y guns as well, hopefully in a pattern complementing theirs. The timbers of the ship shuddered again, and the sea around the mountain fish and in *Donaghey*'s wake spalled like cooked flint. With a mighty convulsion of foam and smoke, the waves contorted into an inverted cataract of spume. Despite their fear, *Donaghey*'s crew gave an exultant cheer as water rained down on them—along with countless flashies, pieces of flashies, and a ten-foot-long gri-kakka flipper that nearly crushed a 'Cat gunner.

Garrett wiped the lenses of his binoculars with his shirtsleeve, then stared through them again. "Now I've seen everything," he said incredulously. Despite the cannon fire and depth charges, the mountain fish hadn't moved. It hadn't dived or swum away, or even attacked. It hadn't done anything. He looked at Saaran. "Say, you don't suppose it's *dead*?" He looked back at the fish. "You know, I think it's dead! Smitty!" he yelled. "Get up here, you ball-headed Kraut! Your willy-nilly broadside found a weak spot and killed the damn thing!"

Smitty arrived amid enthusiastic cheering, grinning ear to ear. "I just wish I knew which gun did the trick—and where it was aimed!" There was a roar of laughter and stamping feet.

"It might have been fire from *Tolson*," Saaran reminded him. "Or the combined fire of both ships. It is said, however, that the inestimable Dennis Silva once killed such a creature with a single shot from a four-inch-fifty."

"It was four shots!" Smitty denied. "I was there! One shot might'a killed it, but he shot that big empty forehead hump three times first!"

Garrett patted Smitty on the shoulder, then looked back at the gathered Grik ships, now off the starboard quarter. The broadside they'd fired into the gaggle had left it even more disarrayed. He raised his glasses. "Helm," he called. "Mr. Saaran, we'll come about and finish that mob. Prepare to wear ship!" The Grik were no longer flinging gobbets of meat over the side, and the swarm of feeding fish, those not killed by the depth charges, were beginning to abandon them for the mountain of bleeding meat floating nearby. Now, most of the Grik in view, furry, upright, vicious-looking crosses between an emu and a komodo, just stood there, staring sullenly. Their plan, clearly to break the blockade by destroying Garrett's entire squadron at one act, hadn't worked, and he was suddenly stunned that the Grik had been capable of conjuring such a scheme, not to mention implementing it. Grik always seemed ready to attack with everything they had, or flee with equal abandon. To design a plan that called on them—even Hij—to cold-bloodedly, calculatingly, sacrifice themselves for others of their kind was so utterly alien to anything they'd come to expect from their foe, it was still difficult to imagine. There was no doubt they'd deliberately lured the mountain fish, hoping it would destroy all of Garrett's ships. They had to know it would destroy them as well. *Damn.*

Donaghey had come about, steering to bring her port broadside to bear on the bows of the enemy where they were linked together. *Tolson* was preparing to pummel the north side of the confused raft of ships. At just over one hundred yards, Garrett opened his mouth to give the command to fire. He never had a chance. With a cataclysmic eruption of fire, shattered debris, and a massive, towering mushroom of dirty white smoke, all eight Grik ships simultaneously blew themselves up.

Greg Garrett opened his eyes to see Clancy's fuzzy, worried face hovering near. Greg was totally disoriented, and it took him several moments to figure out where he was. He decided he must be lying on his back somewhere on the quarterdeck, but looking up, he couldn't see the sails, yards, or the spiderweb of cordage that should have been overhead. That confused him even more. Clancy's mouth was moving, but at first Greg couldn't understand anything he said. There was only an all-encompassing, high-pitched buzz, with a kind of muffled warbling creeping in around the edges. He stared hard at Clancy and began to realize part of the warbling sound was the communications officer calling his name. He shook his head, trying to clear it, and propped himself up on his elbows.

His vision was clearing, and other sounds began penetrating the incessant noise inside his head. He commenced a rapid inventory of all the new aches and pains he felt, but decided nothing was broken. Looking at himself, he saw that he was spattered with blood, but except for a few small tears in his clothing, he thought he must be okay. Most of the blood had to be somebody else's. He suddenly realized the sky was empty because the mainmast had snapped off just below the top, taking the main yard and everything above over the side. Tangled stays and shrouds stretched taut across the deck, and the bulwarks on either side were smashed. Even as he watched, bloodied, disheveled Lemurian sailors hacked at cables, and each one parted with a sound like a rifle shot. The ship beneath him wallowed uncomfortably in the uneven swells, and there was a great grinding, pounding in the fibers of the deck from the shattered mast working alongside.

Glancing farther forward, he saw that the foremast was gone completely, snapped off at the deck of the forecastle, and its remains had already been cleared away. Looking around with increased urgency, he realized that only the bowsprit and mizzenmast still stood intact. A great many bodies lay scattered on deck, some moving, others not, and the pitiful cries of the wounded began to seep through the ringing buzz. The surgeon was on deck, along with Marine corpsmen and pharmacist's mates, moving from one prone figure to the next. Some they quickly inspected before moving on, and others they had carried below to the wardroom. What had been a taut, beautiful, well-run ship had suddenly become a scene of devastation and chaos.

"Mr. Garrett! Thank God!" he finally heard Clancy say. "I thought you were a goner when I first laid eyes on you."

"What happened?" Greg asked. It may not have been the most original phrase under the circumstances, but right then, it was the most appropriate.

"I'm not sure, sir. I was belowdecks in the wireless shack when I heard this god-awful, humongous boom—and something hammered the ship. I came up here"—Clancy gestured around—"and seen all this! Jesus! One fella I ran into told me those Grik ships, all eight of 'em, just blew the hell up! All at once! My God, the only way they could've done it like that, simultaneously, is electrically! Electrically!" he repeated. "No fuse would've worked. They'd have gone up like a fireworks show, not all at once. And they couldn't have done near as much damage that way. I swear." He shook his head.

"How about *Tolson*?" Greg asked, managing to stand with Clancy's help.

Clancy pointed. "Hell, sir, she looks worse than us. Lost every stick."

Garrett saw *Tolson*, completely dismasted, wallowing helplessly to leeward, surrounded by a sea of floating debris. *Revenge* was standing by her, apparently undamaged, trying to rig a towline. "Where's Saaran?" he asked.

"In the wardroom," Clancy said. "Looks like he's maybe got a concussion. Something conked him on the head. Caught some splinters too. You're lucky, Skipper. Smitty was with you when I came on deck, but the surgeon said you ought to come around soon, and Smitty took off to help with damage control. You were out about twenty minutes."

"Do we have communications?" Garrett demanded.

"Yes, sir. One of my strikers just reported. We can't get *Tolson*, or at least they can't respond, but we've got *Revenge*." Clancy shrugged. "Our wireless aerial's on the mizzen, and it's still mostly in one piece."

"Okay," said Garrett, shaking off Clancy's supporting hand. "Tell *Revenge* she'll have to try to tow us both. Then get a message off to HQ; tell them what happened . . . and they might want to kind of expect a call for assistance." He smirked. "Like there's anything they can do about it. As far as I know, there's not another Allied ship for five hundred miles!"

"Maybe they're doing another coast recon of the proposed LZs?" Clancy speculated.

"Maybe . . . and we wouldn't know it either. They won't make a peep in case the Japs have helped the Grik come up with a transmission direction finder of some sort," Greg fumed. "Let's just hope we won't need any assistance *Revenge* can't give us!" He paused. "Thanks, Clance. You get back to the radio shack and keep your ears open."

The new steam frigate passed a heavy cable to *Tolson* and eventually, carefully picking her way through the raft of floating chunks of eight entire ships, pulled Russ's derelict close to *Donaghey*. In the meantime, much to Greg's relief, Smitty and the 'Cat carpenter reported that his ship's leaks were under control. Most were caused by the pressure of the blast-opened seams, but some were made by pieces of Grik ships striking at high velocity. A bowsprit had speared *Donaghey* like a harpoon amidships. Garrett's ship would float, but she'd lost a lot of people. All the Marines in the tops, for example, had gone over the side. With so many predators in the sea, their deaths had probably been quicker than drowning—if even more horrifying. Almost a third of the crewfolk and Marines exposed on deck were dead or wounded.

Garrett saw Russ near *Tolson's* stern, a bloody rag around his head, directing a detail preparing to send or receive a cable. Greg already had a similar party waiting in his ship's fo'c'sle. He raised a speaking trumpet. "Are you okay, Mr. Chapelle?"

"I'm fine," Russ replied. "My ship ain't," he added bitterly. Bloody water gushed down *Tolson's* sides from the scuppers, her pumps working hard. "We're staying ahead of the flooding, though." He paused. "If you don't mind my saying, *Donaghey* looks like a porcupine." It was true. Greg had peered over the port side and was amazed by the number of timbers and splinters sticking in his ship. "I bet you could build another whole ship out of all that junk!"

"I promise not to throw any of it away, then," Greg countered. "You might need it."

"You said it," Russ shouted back ruefully.

They eventually passed a cable from *Donaghey* to *Tolson*, and when it was secure, *Revenge* took up the slack on both ships. Slowly, they began to move, gaining speed, and settling on a southwesterly course at about five knots. Garrett glanced back at the debris-strewn sea. The dead mountain fish still lay, a mile or more astern, huge and seemingly as invulnerable as an island, yet the sea around its wallowing corpse was stained red, and predators—gri-kakka, "super sharks," and flashies in their countless multitudes—churned along its flanks. He looked to the northeast, toward whatever port the eight Grik ships had put out from. He could still barely believe it. The enemy had executed a carefully, redundantly planned operation to break the blockade, and it had worked. Every time the allies thought they had the Grik down, the damn things pulled some crazy stunt that stood all their preconceptions on their heads. Granted, they were dealing with some "civilian" Grik now, but how much difference should that make? Something had changed; something fundamental. He sighed. *Well, that happens in war,* he supposed. He only wished he and *Donaghey* weren't always on the receiving end of these discoveries. He took some comfort from one fact, however. The allies had changed too. No Grik in the coming campaign against Ceylon and India could have any notion of the new Allied equipment and tactics. Hopefully, they'd be basing whatever preparations they were making on the capabilities they'd seen at the Battle of Baalkpan. They too would be surprised.

Massive sharks and a few gri-kakka shadowed the wounded train. It must have been the bloody water trailing behind that drew their attention. Slowly, as the trickle decreased and diluted, most veered away, back to where they knew an endless meal awaited—but a few continued dogging them. One massive creature, bigger than any shark had a right to be, with a fin as high as a killer whale's, cruised effortlessly past *Donaghey*, just under the surface. Its back was a mottled grayish blue-black, and while maybe a quarter *Donaghey*'s length, it looked nearly as broad. Garrett suppressed a shudder. In a moment, the fish was gone, outpacing them, apparently intent on examining the other ships forward. Saaran appeared on deck, a bulky wrap around his head, and glistening smears of the curative "polta paste" applied here and there across his chest and shoulder.

"What're you doing here?" Garrett asked. "You look like hell."

"Doc Miller told me not to sleep," he said. "If I work, I won't sleep."

Garrett grunted. "Okay. If you're determined to run around, see if you can put a detail together to sway up a new main-topmast and a few yards. Get some sail on her." The mizzen looked okay, but the remnant of the mainmast didn't have much support left. "We'll have to rerig the shrouds and stays as well. See if we can do anything to get a new foremast stepped." He looked around. "I don't know what we'll use.... Anyway, *Revenge*'ll have enough worries dragging just one ship behind her." Suddenly, *Donaghey* seemed to slow, and *Tolson* began to slew to starboard. "What the devil?" As Garrett watched, *Tolson* continued turning, until she was almost beam-on to the following *Donaghey*.

"Hard a'port!" Garrett cried, hoping they had enough steerageway to miss the other ship. At the moment, they were aimed directly at her, amidships.

"Hard a'port, ay!" replied the helmsman. Slowly, slowly, *Donaghey* wallowed left, edging more and more aft of her sister. It still looked as if they might hit her in the stern, and everyone tensed, expecting an impact. Somehow, they managed to clear the other ship, but only by a few feet. Garrett shouted across to Chapelle. "What's going on?"

"Beats me," came the wind-muffled reply. "*Revenge* just stopped all of a sudden! I don't know what's up! We had to turn to keep from hitting her, just as you did!"

Clancy ran up the companionway. "Skipper," he cried, "something hit *Revenge*! She's taking water aft!"

"*What?* What hit her?" Greg demanded.

"I don't know. I don't think they do yet. That's all I got so far."

"Well . . . get back down there and find out!"

"Aye, aye, sir!"

Garrett could see *Revenge* now, as *Donaghey* eased past *Tolson*. The steamer looked odd, dead in the water, and low by the stern. Before long, the tow cable grew taut, and *Donaghey* began to turn to starboard, pulled around by her attachment to *Tolson*. To Greg's amazement, he saw boats starting to slide down *Revenge*'s quarter davits into the sea. "What . . . ?"

Clancy ran back on deck. "Skipper!" he said, shock in his voice. "Cap'n Barry has broadcast a *distress* signal! He says something *ate* his ship's screw! With it all new and shiny, he thinks something hit it like a Heddon Zig Wag lure! His words. They didn't see what did it, but there's blood in the water aft. Anyway, her shaft is warped all to hell, and the packing and all the support timbers were shattered before they managed to secure! He—he says whatever happened, it couldn't have been much worse if they'd taken a Jap torpedo in the ass, and they can't stop the flooding!"

With a tight chest, Garrett suddenly remembered the huge shark he'd seen. He'd often wondered what some giant denizen might think of a ship's turning propeller—especially when it hadn't yet turned dingy and green. . . . "What can we do?" he asked.

"Well, Pruit—I mean Cap'n Barry—asks if we can stand by to take his crew aboard—us and *Tolson*."

"My God. We're going to lose *Revenge*? He's sure?"

"I'm afraid so, sir."

Greg thought fast, considering the wind and current. The tightness in his chest became a vise around his heart. "Tell *Revenge* we'll stand by and any boats we have in one piece'll be over as soon as we can send them." He paused. "Tell him also that we're going to need every musket and every last round of ammunition they have time to save. Make sure he understands that. Bring every single weapon he can grab! Make sure HQ knows what's going on."

"Aye, sir," replied Clancy, looking at him strangely.

Garrett pointed at the distant coast of Ceylon. "Don't you get it?" He laughed, the slightest hint of hysteria in his voice. "If we can't get enough sail on this wreck, this ship and *Tolson* both are going to wind up on the beach . . . *over there*! It looks like the invasion of Ceylon may start a little early." He turned to Saaran. "Of course, *our* invasion'll be like dropping a bug with no legs right in the middle of an ant mound!"

Not a soul was lost when *Revenge* finally went down. The semiwatertight, compartmentalized design kept her afloat longer than anyone had a right to expect, and not only was the entire crew saved and distributed between the other two ships, but all the small arms, ammunition, and a large percentage of her other supplies were salvaged as well. Captain Barry came aboard *Donaghey* with a little less than half his crew—*Tolson* needed the extra hands more—and he was horrified by the loss of his brand-new, beautiful ship. All he could do was stand by the quarterdeck rail, knuckles clenched white, and watch while *Revenge* slid under the sea by the stern.

"God!" he gasped when the waves closed over the stars and stripes still fluttering at the masthead, and he burst into tears.

"I'm awful sorry, Pruit," Garrett said, a little uncomfortably. He could imagine how the other man felt, but couldn't stand to see him bawling like that. "Come on, pull yourself together. We've got to sort out this mess and get your guys working with mine to bend as much canvas as we can. The current's running strong and the wind's picking up out of the southwest. We'll lose everything and everybody if we can't claw away from that shore." He pointed at the coast of Ceylon, growing noticeably closer. Barry wiped his face on his sleeve and nodded.

"You bet," he said roughly. "I'll do whatever I can. So will my guys."

"Thanks, Pruit. Let's see if we can get them helping out with the divisions they're accustomed to." He nodded toward *Tolson*, wallowing aft. "And not only do we have to save this ship, but we've got to save her too. She doesn't even have anything left to jury-rig."

Barry nodded, looking at the repairs already completed. So far, *Donaghey* had close to a full spread on her mizzen, a course on the main, and a pair of staysails rigged to the bowsprit. Alone, it wasn't enough to keep *Donaghey* off the beach. "Okay," he said. "My exec went to *Tolson*, but I've got my bosun and a lieutenant. How can we help?"

By nightfall, *Donaghey* had a new main-topmast, a topsail, and another staysail rigged. The repairs had been unbelievably perilous, with the ship pitching and wallowing in the mounting seas. There'd been injuries, but amazingly, no one was killed or lost over the side. Still, their last glimpse of Ceylon before it was swallowed by the gloom showed it disconcertingly close—less than ten miles away, according to Smitty's best guess. Garrett's long experience at estimating ranges as a gunnery officer put it at just over eight. The wind continued stiffening, and the sea grew more determined to break the battered ships. On *Tolson*, Chapelle was pushing his crew to the breaking point, rigging a pair of short masts out of spare topmasts, but the only canvas she had yet was a shortened course and a couple of staysails. It took a little strain off *Donaghey*, but the staysails on both ships, while necessary, were pushing them farther to leeward—ever closer to shore.

Together in the wardroom, beneath the light of a swaying lantern, Garrett and Saaran scrutinized the charts they'd worked so hard on, throughout their deployment. With sinking hearts, they realized that no matter how they calculated it, *Donaghey* couldn't clear the southern coast of Ceylon with *Tolson* in tow. Realistically, it was almost certainly too late for *Donaghey* to make it alone.

"So that's it," Garrett said as quietly as he could over the wind, the tumult of labor on deck, and the increasing noises of the working ship. He took a deep breath and looked at Saaran almost helplessly. "What now?"

Saaran scratched the fur on his forehead. "The sea is rising, and so is the tide. If we have no choice but to run ashore, perhaps we can choose where we do it."

"What difference will that make?"

"If we are not *forced* ashore among jagged rocks, but *drive* ashore at high tide, on a soft, sandy beach . . ."

"We let the wind and heavy sea carry us as far up on the beach as it can," Garrett interrupted with dawning hope.

"Yes," Saaran continued, "and the flashies will not be active in the nighttime shallows, particularly with the sea running high."

Greg nodded. "If the ships don't break, and we make it until low tide, we off-load the ship's guns, supplies . . . If we fort up, maybe make it to some better ground . . . we might have a chance."

"A slim chance," Saaran agreed, "if we can hold until rescued." He met Garrett's eyes and blinked determination. "And if we can't hold that long . . . at least we will die killing Grik." Saaran coughed a laugh. "We may be a bug with no legs falling in an ant mound, but we do still have our teeth!"

Greg blinked back in the Lemurian way. "Pass the word. We'll have to coordinate with Russ on *Tolson*; keep our ships as close together as we can, when we make our run in." He sighed. "I'd better get Clancy to inform HQ." He smiled and shook his head. "God help us."

CHAPTER 2

////// *Aboard USNRS (United States Naval Reserve Ship)*
Salissa (CV-1) First Fleet HQ, Andaman Island

Pete Alden, once a sergeant in doomed USS *Houston*'s Marine contingent on another earth, and now General of the Marines and All Allied Armies, looked at the message form in his hand with a sick, sinking feeling. It had been given him by an intensely staring, silver-shot, brownish red Lemurian, who sat perched on a decorative stool like a brooding bear, his long tail swishing in agitation behind him. The Lemurian was "Ahd-mi-raal" Keje-Fris-Ar, overall commander of First Fleet, and all Allied forces in the West, or CINCWEST. Keje had grown more (outwardly, at least) unflappable as the war went on, but he was clearly concerned about the contents of the message.

Alden spent several moments reading it, absorbing the implications. Keje's unease was well founded. "Goddamn," he said flatly. "*Tolson, Donaghey,* and *Revenge* all survive a giant Grik bomb, then *Revenge* gets sunk by a *fish!*" He shook his head. "I swear, every time we try to throw a normal war around here, and it looks like something might finally be going our way, it all drops in the pot."

Keje scratched his reddish brown furry ears, and nodded grimly. "So it seems. So it *always* seems. But bad as that is, the implication of Mr. Garrett's report is even more troubling than it first appears. Without coming right out and saying so, his evaluation of the current, tide, and prevailing winds, coupled with his position, suggests a real possibility *Donaghey* and *Tolson* might well be driven upon enemy shores! By the Heavens above! With the crew of *Revenge* aboard, there are more than a thousand souls on those ships! Somehow we must assist them!"

"Do you think they'll go ashore?" Alden asked.

Keje held out his hands. He'd taken on many human mannerisms, just as humans had reciprocated. "Much depends on the damage to *Donaghey*, and whether it can be repaired in time. Honestly, I'm not hopeful. By the description, *Tolson* is helpless, and I cannot imagine Mr. Garrett abandoning her even if he could."

Pete was shaking his head. "Greg won't deliberately sacrifice his ship and crew. He'll take as many off as he can and cut *Tolson* loose if he has to. He knows the stakes, and they all knew the risk of blockade duty in those seas. They volunteered."

Keje blinked. "I agree Mr. Garrett would not deliberately sacrifice his people, but I know the man's character as well as you, I think. He'll do everything in his power to save *Tolson*, and he might try too hard, too long. With much of the crew of *Revenge* aboard already, he'll be hard-pressed to get everyone off *Tolson*. If he takes any, he will feel compelled to take them all." Keje shook his head. "I fear they will go ashore. We must plan as if they will, regardless."

An insistent knocking in the passageway interrupted them. "Enter," Keje said distractedly. Marine Captain Risa-Sab-At, commander of *Salissa*'s Marine contingent, led General Lord Muln Rolak and General-Queen Protector Safir Maraan into the compartment.

"Is it true?" asked the old, scarred General Rolak. "We hear *Revenge* has sunk and the rest of Gaarrett's squadron is in distress!"

"Word sure travels fast," Pete observed.

"It does," confirmed Safir Maraan. As usual, she was resplendent in her silver-washed armor that contrasted so strikingly with her almost blue-black fur, but so complemented her flashing silver eyes. "Every ship in the fleet has a receiver after all, and besides, as large as *Salissa* Home is, she is not nearly large enough to frustrate anything so powerful as the 'scuttlebutt,' as Amer-i-caans say."

"I asked you here to tell you this news myself," Keje said, "but as usual, I suppose the scuttlebutt has its place—so long as it does not distort. I dislike keeping secrets from our people. I doubt the general nature of the information you received could have fully conveyed the implications of this tragedy, however."

"The blockade is broken," Rolak said, "and surely we must extend whatever assistance we can."

"Surely," Keje agreed, "but USS *Tassat* is already nearly back *here* from mapping potential points of attack. We have absolutely nothing close by to send."

"Dreadful news indeed," Queen Maraan said. "Is there nothing we can do?"

"We're obliged to think of something," Keje said. "Obviously, we *must* rescue them from the terrible end they face at the hands of the Grik, but also, honestly, they know too much to be taken. The language barrier might once have provided some protection for us and our plans—if not for our poor people the Grik might capture. But now we know many Grik 'Hij,' their 'elevated' class, at least read and write the 'scientific tongue'—and the Jaaps have told them we use it. There may even be Jaaps on Saa-lon and . . . well, we know they communicate with the enemy—and some speak 'Amer-i-caan.'"

"We *must* rescue them!" Rolak agreed.

"Yeah," Pete said, "but what Keje's getting at is that we can't just send a ship or two, since the Grik'll probably pull out all the stops to get our guys. A rescue will take a lot of resources; air recon to find the ships, or air strikes to keep the Grik off the survivors, for example. We'd hoped to keep those resources—particularly the planes—secret until we're ready for the big show."

"General Alden is right," Keje declared. "Certainly that is part of what I was getting at, but there's another element." He paused. "We planned to begin offensive operations against Saa-lon and Indi-aa within weeks, depending on the weather and the arrival of *Arracca*'s battle group. The weather is currently less than ideal for combat operations, but it should soon improve. If we don't wait for *Arracca*, however, *Salissa*'s battle group can sail by late day tomorrow. Geran-Eras affirms that her *Humfra-Dar* battle group can likewise be ready. *Arracca*'s group could arrive here, refuel, and join us at the objective within a week or two of our arrival there. My question to you generals is whether the ground forces can be embarked and prepared by then."

"By tomorrow afternoon? Now wait just a second, Admiral," Pete said. "Are you proposing we set out with the whole damn fleet on the biggest operation of the war, and invade, willy-nilly, wherever the hell our damaged ships wash up? That's nuts! We don't have any known strategic 'objective' right now for *Arracca* to join us *at*. All the planning and preparation we've spent months on would go up in smoke! Alan Letts just got here, after surviving the longest flight in the history of this world, most likely, in one of those new three-engine, up-size 'Nancy' kites Mallory dreamed up. They had to land and refuel I don't know how many times in some of the creepiest places imaginable. . . ."

"It was your idea to establish those fueling depots," Safir pointed out.

"So? We need 'em. But Letts is kind of . . . delicate—and he's a brand-new father. He's also the closest thing to a real logistics guy we have. He volunteered to leave a cushy berth and come out here to help us straighten out the kind of screwed-up mess we had at Rangoon. If that happens on Ceylon, we could lose everything! He needs time to do what he came here for, and damn it, we need him to do it! If we don't even know where we're going and what to do when we get there, it'll be a logistical nightmare, and even Letts won't be able to save us."

"But you have been working on 'logistics.' So have the executive officers of all the ships. Progress has been made. I've seen it," Rolak said.

"Sure, we've made progress on the basics, but it takes a guy like Letts to figure out all the angles nobody else ever thinks about—stuff we might need in any situation. Thanks to Rolak's pet Grik, we actually have a rough map of Ceylon. We know where their troop concentrations and population centers are, and we've been making our landing plans based on that. If we just go ashore at some arbitrary place, without a plan, it'll be a circus."

Keje looked at Alden for several moments, contemplating. Finally, he sighed. "There is no choice, General Alden. We must prepare as if the fleet will move tomorrow. You have already designed multiple plans for various landing sites. Perhaps we can modify one of those."

"But . . ." Alden began, but Keje held up his hand.

"You still think in terms of your old war," he said, "when all things happened so very quickly. You'll have sufficient time to form or revise a plan. Consider: Saa-lon is more than a thousand of your 'miles' from here. The fleet can move only as quickly as its slowest ship, and many of our transports rely entirely on sails, so we cannot count on more than an eight- or ten-knot average. The voyage will take five, perhaps six days. We should have communications with *Donaghey* at least until she is driven ashore—if she is—so we'll have a good estimate of her position." He paused again. "If the worst happens, it will likely occur late tonight or early tomorrow. That should leave you sufficient time to form a plan of battle while we are underway. You have done more with far less information before. So has Mr. Letts."

Pete nodded resignedly but shifted uncomfortably on his stool. "Okay, Admiral, you're the boss. But I guess you've figured that if the 'worst' does happen, those guys'll be on the beach, all alone, for those same five or six days, no matter what we do. You really think they can hold that long against the whole damn Grik army?"

Keje sighed. "I suppose not. They may not even survive the grounding. At this stage, all we can do is speculate and hope *Donaghey* makes enough sail to pull herself and *Tolson* clear. We should learn that soon. If Mr. Gaarrett and Mr. Chaa-pelle save their ships, we will happily stand down and resume awaiting *Arracca*'s arrival, and you may continue to plan a landing anywhere you desire." He frowned. "If that doesn't happen, we must pray our people can hold out long enough for us to arrive. Gaarrett, Chaa-pelle, and Mr. Baarry are some of our most resourceful officers, commanding veteran crews. If anyone can do it, they can. Perhaps we will arrive to find a 'beachhead' already established for us!" He looked at everyone present in turn. "We will issue an alert order and prepare to move the fleet. Consider it a drill. If we must rescue our people, however, we will do so with no half measures. If it is required that we deploy our new weapons, 'tip our hand' so to speak, it will not be in sprinkles here and there, like a late-day squall that briefly comes and goes, but as a Strakka storm that will not pass until the enemy is scoured away!" He glanced at Pete and knew the Marine's mind was already racing; examining, evaluating, and discarding tactical scenarios. "We will make all preparations for getting underway, but as soon as we get final word from *Donaghey*, we will have a meeting here, of all ship and field commanders." He paused. "That is all."

After the others departed to oversee the implementation of their orders, Keje and Pete strode upon what was left of *Salissa's* (or *Big Sal's*, as the Americans still called her) battlement. Once a broad structure at the base of her center wing tower, it was much abbreviated now, placed off-center to make room for her "flight deck"; the old "battlement" was increasingly referred to as the "bridgewings." Keje and Pete paused at the rail and gazed upon the broad deck below, cluttered with "Nancy" float-planes, their blue paint a dark gray-black in the gathering twilight. Indistinct shapes moved among them, checking lashings, making sure the craft were secure. Inevitably, the two leaders looked higher, to stare out across the broad anchorage they still called "Port Blair."

It was a heady sight. Never in all Lemurian history had the people amassed such combat power. The various ships had dissolved into mere outlines now, but they were well lit while their crews made all the various preparations. *Humfra-Dar* rode at anchor nearby, virtually identical to *Big Sal*, and similarly covered with aircraft. An even dozen powerful new steam frigates ringed the massive seagoing, sailing "Homes," turned steam-powered aircraft carriers. USS *Dowden,* USS *Scott,* USS *Nakja-Mur,* and USS *Kas-Ra-Ar* had been joined by USS *Haakar-Faask,* USS *Naga,* USS *Bowles,* USS *Felts,* USS *Saak-Fas,* USS *Clark,* USS *Davis,* and USS *Ramic-Sa-Ar.* All were considered "DDs" and, according to tradition in the "American Navy," were named for fallen heroes. Two dozen of the fast, razeed, Grik "Indiamen" they'd rebuilt as corvettes (now almost universally considered "DEs," or "Destroyer Escorts") also filled the harbor, along with forty unaltered Grik "prize" transports. Almost a hundred of the largest, swiftest feluccas in the Alliance constantly came and went, loaded with supplies as well. In all, First Fleet averaged seventy-odd ships present at any given time, and when *Arracca* arrived, she'd add herself, four more steam frigates, and six corvettes. Grik fleets were often bigger, but without the Japanese battle cruiser *Amagi*, they'd never possessed a fraction of the combat power anchored in Port Blair.

The shore facilities were nothing to sneeze at either. Big wooden cranes and booms had been rigged along the new docks situated in the calmest, most protected portion of the bay. Huge warehouses and other port facilities had been established, packed with sufficient supply reserves to last the fleet for many months, with more arriving all the time. Huge tank batteries were kept topped-off by regular visits of "Indiaman" oilers and tankers from Baalkpan and Talaud, and a floating dry dock was even under construction by skilled craftsmen who'd once built the monumental seagoing Homes. Nothing as big as *Big Sal* would ever fit in it, but it would handle just about anything else in the Alliance. Perry Brister had hit on the scheme when it occurred to him that all the master shipwrights who used to build Homes were now resentfully toiling at jobs anyone could do in the production-line-oriented Allied shipyards. With the sophisticated Lemurian pumps, building floating dry docks would be a good way to get the most out of the highly professional artisans. Besides, with the Allied fleets scattering across the known world, it would be easier to tow dry docks to them than tow damaged ships back to Baalkpan—and soon Maa-ni-la—where the only two real dry docks existed.

Beyond the warehouses, an honest-to-goodness airfield, complete with revetments, was being built, using crushed limestone and coral. Nothing would use it for some time, if ever, but it was always better to be prepared. Finally, the various facilities of Port Blair were surrounded on all sides by heavy batteries and defensive fortifications. The allies had come to Andaman to stay.

"It's a hell of a sight," Pete muttered after the silence between him and Keje had stretched too long.

"Yes," Keje agreed, clearing his throat. "I'm sorry we disagreed before."

Pete shrugged. "We didn't really disagree. I was just doing my job, pointing out problems. We've had a lot of them, you know, and problems on the battlefield cost lives. I never want to land on another Grik beach when all the stuff I need to accomplish my mission is still aboard ship, or already unloaded miles away. That's the sort of thing Letts can help with, but this offensive stuff is as new to him as it was to us at first. It'll take him time to get things sorted out. I'd have liked to let him practice up a little. You know, do a few training exercises." Pete shrugged. "Maybe he still can."

Keje looked at the Marine. "Well, in case he can't, shouldn't you call a staff meeting of your own? Begin preparations to embark troops?"

Pete shook his head. "I passed the word as soon as I heard the rumors, before I ever came to see you. That's one thing we *have* sorted out; everybody knows what ship to board, with what equipment. It's our job to make sure those ships off-load where we need them. As you said, I guess there'll be plenty of time to decide that once we know where we're going—if we're going." He paused. "No, I figured I'd hang around here until we get the word. Then, if I have to, I can hit the ground running. I'll have my staff meeting when—if—we call everyone aboard here. I already have a few ideas, but we'd better call Letts out now. Get him figuring the angles too, and wrapping his brain around what we might have to do. Let *him* get a running start."

"Agreed," Keje said. "We will fetch Mr. Letts, and we can all wait together. Hopefully, once we know the score, we can sleep tomorrow away. If not . . . perhaps it's more appropriate in a way. Once more we shall move to war in reaction to necessity, and those who die will do so to protect others. I confess, this cold-blooded planning for battles that we begin leaves me feeling . . . most odd." He snorted. "I think I have been away from the fight too long!"

"Maybe so," Pete agreed. "Your tune's a little different than it was right after Baalkpan." Keje looked at him sharply, but Alden continued without pause. "Remembering the way things used to be, I guess I can even understand your desire to 'react.' Most of your folks never used to fight anybody unless they were attacked—but you know this has gone way past that, and you've got to forget it. You've seen some action and've got plenty of guts—everybody knows! Your rush to rescue Garrett's task force proves it again. But one thing you have to get through your head is, bad as it was before, this war's going to get a whole lot worse. I saw it at Rangoon. Grik'll eat *each other* if they have to, to stay in the fight, and now we're taking the fight to their ground, it's liable to get meaner than we can imagine. Top all that off with the fact that, even if we had a bellyful and decided to quit chasing them, they'd just turn around and come after us again!" Pete shook his head. "You knew from the start, way before you took your admiral job, this is a fight to the finish and it's 'us or them.' I pick us."

He looked at Keje for a moment, then stared out at the bay. "You know what the scariest part of all is? The Grik are finally starting to wise up. This stunt they pulled against Garrett's task force is another example, and it stinks. I don't know if they were just trying to bust the blockade . . . or get us to come a-running."

"You think we play into their hands if we . . . react . . . as I've ordered?" Keje asked.

"No," Pete answered simply. "I don't think they have a clue what we're about to land on them with. I do think we have to start keeping our eyes peeled, though. They sucker-punched Garrett, and if we don't watch out, they might do it to us. Initiative's our best asset, and we lose a lot when we react. I'd much rather they react to what *we* do, than the other way around. Whoever has the initiative has the edge. Besides, there's nothing 'cold-blooded' about this war. The very idea of killin' Grik always heats *my* blood."

Keje looked at him. "General Lord Rolak told me you were beginning to 'enjoy' this war, but I did not credit it."

"He's one to talk," Pete retorted. "His people used to fight wars for sport!" He scratched his bearded chin. "Although I've heard him admit this isn't a 'fun' war a time or two." He sighed. "No, Admiral, I don't like this any more than you do, and I *really* don't like losing people. . . . Given a choice, I think I'd enjoy explorin' this world you got here instead of fightin' my way across it. That said, I do get a kick outta killin' Grik. The bastards need killin'. They're ugly, mean, and vicious, and if we don't kill them, they'll kill us; it's as simple as that." Pete shrugged. "With that in mind, rubbin' 'em out doesn't bug me at all. Sue me."

Commodore Jim Ellis from USS *Dowden* collected Alan Letts and came out to the massive ship, joining them in Keje's spacious "admiral's quarters," now substituting for *Big Sal*'s old "Great Hall." As the evening progressed, more commanders gathered of their own accord. Generals Rolak and Maraan returned, and Captain Jis-Tikkar (Tikker)—commander (COFO) of *Big Sal*'s 1st Air Wing—"drifted by." Geran-Eras and Al Vernon arrived from *Humfra-Dar*, and that set off a flood of other naval officers. Soon, Cablaas-Rag-Laan from USS *Scott*, Jarrik-Fas from USS *Nakja-Mur*, and Mescus-Ricum from *Kas-Ra-Ar* joined them, as did the captains of all the other DDs in port; *Haakar-Faask, Naga, Bowles, Felts, Saak-Fas, Clark, Davis*, and *Ramic-Sa-Ar*. All the warships in First Fleet except *Tassat*—and those in Task Force Garrett, of course—were now represented. Finally, realizing the "big meeting" was forming up regardless of how the *Donaghey* and *Tolson* situation turned out, Pete Alden went ahead and sent for the commanders of the various land forces as well. It was good to have everyone together; it was rare that such meetings took place. For the time, however, there was little for anyone to talk about, and there was an awkward air in the vast compartment.

Scrawny, redheaded "Colonel" Billy Flynn approached Pete through the crowd. His mustache and chin whiskers were going white, and he was twisting the ends of the mustache unconsciously, in the Imperial style. *At least he hasn't started braiding it,* Pete thought. This was only the second time he'd seen the fortyish former submariner since the man arrived with his "Amalgamated" regiment a few weeks before. Since then, the regiment, composed of volunteers from a wide variety of Homes and settlements not yet official members of the Grand Alliance, had been on training maneuvers in the hills.

"Evening, General," Flynn said, with only a trace of irony. He remembered when Pete was just a sergeant. Of course, Pete recalled when Flynn was just the chief of the boat on S-19.

"Billy," Pete greeted him. "How are your fellas shaping up?"

"Swell, although more than half aren't 'fellas.'" Flynn lowered his voice. "Female troops sure take getting used to!"

"Tell me," Pete agreed. "That's the way these 'Cats are. Most of them, anyway. You won't catch me complaining about how they fight, though. How about you? How are you doing since you traded your flippers for a bayonet?"

"You can have my flippers, and my dolphins too, in this kooky sea," Flynn replied. "I'll take a bayonet any day. I saw my share of shore fighting at Baalkpan as you'll recall, and that wasn't nearly as scary as swimming with fish that could eat my old boat." He shook his head. "You know, I was in the Army once. In the Great War, back home. I was seventeen. The only part of France I ever saw was covered with trenches, shell holes, and rotten body parts. Next thing you know, they snatched me up, put me in the British Army, and made me fight Bolsheviks in the snow and ice! I didn't really mind that so much, you know? Fightin' those Red devils was kind of like fighting Grik—they'd just come at you in swarms. The Brit commanders weren't much account; the only guys you could really rely on besides ours were these Canuk artillerymen. . . ." Billy shrugged. "Anyway, after that was over with, they cut us loose, and if a kid wanted to stay in the service and get fed regular, he had to be willing to do scary, unusual stuff." He grinned. "So I joined the Navy and went in subs."

"You probably could have had a ship, here," Pete said.

"Nah. I like what I'm doing. My 'Amalgamated' may not be Marines, but I'd stack them up against any Army regiment!"

"I bet Queen Maraan would argue that!"

Flynn chuckled. "Now, Pete, the Black and Silver Battalions of her 'Six Hundred' might as well *be* Marines! They train with 'em, after all."

"So? Everybody trains the same now. The Marines spend more time on landing ops and close quarters melee combat like they might run into on a ship, but that's about it." He paused. "And, of course, your 'Amalgamated' is 'elite' in the sense that they have the first rifles." Pete shook his head. "I still don't think that's fair!"

"I thought you were hot for 'smoothbores,' and 'buck and ball.' "

"I am . . . for these 'line up and blast away' tactics we have to use, but if everybody had rifles—especially the breechloaders Bernie Sandison's been promising—we could kill the bastards before they get close. What's the latest dope on that, anyway?"

"My regiment carries muzzle-loading rifle-muskets," Flynn confirmed, "but they're only fifty caliber instead of the standard sixty-two. Ordnance has settled on a fifty-eighty cartridge that I understand will kick like a mule but still uses the same bullet and rifling twist as the guns in my regiment. That way, when the time comes to convert 'em, all they have to do is install that trapdoorlike breechblock Silva came up with, ream a chamber, and alter the hammer. Simple. Your smoothbores'll have to be rebarreled, or have a rifled liner installed. In fact, it's my understanding the plan is to send out hammers and 'barreled actions' for replacement in the field to save the time and effort of shipping the guns back and forth. You'll get the new stuff and send back the old. They'll convert 'em and either build new guns around them, or send them out to another unit to do the same."

Pete was impressed. "Say, that makes sense!" He shook his head. "It still isn't fair. I've got one whole corps of veteran troops still armed with bows and spears, and you show up with rifles!"

"It helps to have friends in high places," Flynn said, "and to become operational right when a batch of rifles is ready to be sent out!"

"Well . . . just remember, your troops are *riflemen*! I know they've got bayonets, but I don't want them close enough to the enemy to use them unless it's absolutely necessary, got it?"

"Got it."

"Commodore" Jim Ellis brought Alan Letts, Lord General Rolak, and Safir Maraan to join Flynn and Alden. He was looking around the crowd. "You know, Keje's going to have to feed this bunch, or run them off."

"Hello, Jim. Rolak." Pete bowed to Queen Maraan. "Your Highness." He shook Alan's offered hand. "Mr. Letts." He gestured around. "When I suggested we bring you out here, I envisioned a . . . less crowded environment where we could put our heads together. It looks like you might've parachuted right into a swamp full of alligators. I wish you could've had more time to get your bearings."

Letts nodded. His fair skin had suffered during the long flight from Baalkpan and his face looked like a radish. In a few days, he'd start to peel. "It's liable to be a challenge," he agreed, "but this is exactly the sort of thing I pitched at Adar to get him to let me come. I guess we still haven't heard anything?"

Pete shook his head but looked around the compartment for Keje. He located him near the big, ornately carved table, talking with Geran-Eras from *Humfra-Dar*, Tikker, Al, Lieutenant Leedom, and other wing leaders. He noticed a few stewards had begun to circulate with trays and large pitchers.

"I fear we will have to cancel the game," Safir interjected, trying to lighten the conversation. Lemurians had recently taken to baseball like fiends, and upon learning it was traditional, nearly every ship in the "new" Navy had formed a team. Some of the Army and Marine regiments followed suit. Most weren't very good yet, and their grasp of the rules was still somewhat vague, but there'd been an ongoing tournament on Andaman, and Safir's Silver Battalion team had been slated to take on *Dowden's* the following evening.

"We may have to postpone it," Jim allowed. As its coach, he was justifiably proud of *Dowden's* team. The Dowdens and Silvers were the best in the "First Fleet League," and it had promised to be a great game. "Maybe we'll reschedule it to be the first ball game in the history of Ceylon."

"Hear, hear!" Rolak growled. The old warrior wasn't much interested in baseball. It struck him as a confusing waste of energy for adults to "play" what resembled a "youngling's game" when they could be training for battle, but he wasn't insensitive to the genuine entertainment it appeared to provide everyone. Safir called him a "grump" and implied he didn't like the game because he couldn't understand it. Maybe she was right, but he was utterly in favor of playing baseball on Ceylon, because that would mean they'd taken it.

The snack trays gave way to a full-meal spread, laid out buffet style, as the night progressed. There were consistent reports from *Donaghey*, carried by a short little orange-furred female 'Cat in the comm division. She was as anxious as everyone to hear the news, and she'd been on duty far longer than the roster prescribed; yet regardless of Garrett's reports, the issue remained in doubt. Everyone present in *Salissa's* admiral's quarters seemed to sense a growing fatalism in the periodic messages, however, and the atmosphere and conversations among the leaders of First Fleet began to resemble a deathbed vigil. Garrett's words remained hopeful, but his position estimates, plotted on the big map in the compartment for everyone to see, kept showing *Donaghey* and *Tolson* inexorably closer to the enemy shore.

Shortly after midnight, the orange furred "signalman" appeared once more, and Pete took the message form from her hand and gazed at the words. "Well," he said, in the suddenly quiet compartment, "they're going in." He looked around, and his gaze fastened on Keje. "Both of them." He strode to the map and pointed. "They can't make it around this point here, east of Matara. Garrett says the tide's running, and there's a sandy shore. . . . They're going in together—trying to stay close. He says they'll resume contact if they make it in one piece—and don't lose the transmitter." He rubbed his brow. "His best estimate is five degrees, fifty-six north, by eighty degrees, thirty-two east." Pete glanced at the orange 'Cat. "Run on now. Maybe we'll get something else." When she was gone, he faced the gathered officers. "I guess now we know where they'll be, one way or another. We have good charts of the coast now, and Rolak's pet has told us where things are." He paused. "I know some of you haven't met 'Hij Geerki' and probably wonder why we pay attention to him. . . . Well, I won't try to explain now, but suffice it to say, his advice makes sense. Now we can start making plans." He nodded at Keje and handed him the message form.

Keje also scanned the page in the lingering silence. Finally, he cleared his throat. "First Fleet will complete preparations for getting underway tomorrow. . . ." He paused and frowned. "Later today, as soon as is practicable. Haste is essential, but so are those preparations. You must spare no important arrangements. If you cannot in conscience sail with the fleet, make it known immediately. There will be no shame—this incident has taken us all by surprise. Mr. Letts will compile a list of any units not entirely ready for embarkation, and which ships, for mechanical or supply reasons, cannot sail today. These will be formed into a secondary squadron and provided with suitable protection to move as soon as possible." He paused and took a deep breath.

"My friends, we've worked and sacrificed for this moment a long, long time. True, the *exact* moment may have been forced upon us"—he flicked his large red-brown eyes at Alden—"but it is our moment, regardless." He paused. "As has recently been pointed out to me, I was not 'on the ground' at Raan-goon, though *Salissa*'s planes participated in that fight, and I understand the nature of our Ancient Enemy grows even darker and more abominable as we strike at their lands. Saa-lon and Indi-aa are long-established territories—perhaps even the jewels of their eastern empire. Wresting them away will not win the war, but it may strangle the enemy of vast resources, just as it undermines their sense of racial superiority—the Grik have never been on the defensive before! Raan-goon was an isolated outpost. They may not even know it's lost. There will be no way they can hide or ignore the loss of Saa-lon and Indi-aa, and we cannot foresee what effect that will have on their society as a whole." Keje sipped from a cup of seep a steward had handed him.

"I *can* foresee the advantages we will gain! No more will we be fighting on Mi-Anaaka—Lemurian—land, where our younglings and old ones suffer so gravely. No more will our land Homes be ruined by battles! As the Grik are pushed back, our own defenses grow deeper, more secure. We will gain the resources and even the 'in-dust-rees' the enemy has developed there, including much steel, and even something like this 'rubber' that our makers of things so crave! We must expect the Grik to 'adapt,' to make efforts to counter our straa-ti-gees, and it's essential we keep our eyes peeled for ever more imaginative traps such as that set for Task Force Garrett. Do not grow complacent; do not expect the Grik to continue always as before. We are invading his world now, and just as we made changes with the help of the first Amer-i-caan destroyermen, to defend our Homes, we have to expect the Grik to do the same—perhaps with the aid of their 'Jaaps,' their 'Cap-i-taan Kuro-kaawa.'" He took another sip, and held his cup high. "May the Heavens protect and guide us in this noble endeavor, just as they always so unfailingly direct us through all the perilous seas of life!"

There rose a determined cheer, and the enthusiastic stamping on the deck reverberated throughout the abbreviated superstructure of *Salissa* Home—USS *Salissa* (CV-1).

CHAPTER 3

////// *Off New Scotland, southeast of the New Britain Isles, in the "Eastern Sea"*

USS *Walker* (DD-163), the old "four-stacker" destroyer and possibly the sole survivor of the U.S. Asiatic Fleet on a lost, increasingly less relevant "earth," slashed through the brisk, breezy sea off the southwest coast of New Scotland. On that dimming world she'd been swept from—saved from, most likely—by an eerie, anomalous squall, New Scotland would have been several islands, including Maui, Molokai, Lanai, and Kahoolawe. Here, due to lower sea levels (there was now definitive evidence this "earth" was locked in an "ice age") and the random nature of volcanism, the clustered islands were one. The old destroyer had been healed of the recent damage she'd sustained, and she bounced through the swells on three boilers like a happy puppy racing to meet a massive, full-grown playmate she hadn't seen in ages.

At long last, Task Force "Oil Can," composed of the stupendous Lemurian seagoing Home, *Salaama-Na*, two more "Amer-i-caan" steam frigates, some sailing tenders and dedicated oilers, and the Imperial steamers *Ulysses* and *Icarus*, had arrived. *Salaama-Na* dominated the squadron with her huge sails, or "wings," and it was toward her, flagship of the task force, that *Walker* sped. Unlike some others of the great Homes, *Salaama-Na* hadn't been altered into an aircraft carrier, or more appropriately, a seaplane carrier/tender. Her beautiful, awesome lines hadn't been altered in any way. That was one reason it had taken her so long to arrive—she, like others of her kind, was very, very slow—but it didn't make her a less welcome sight.

Captain Matthew Reddy, "High Chief" of the ever-growing "Amer-i-caan" clan, CINCAAF, (Commander in Chief of All Allied Forces—by acclamation), and more specifically—currently—CINCEAST, was grinning broadly at the sight of the huge ship. His green eyes, often capable of icy remorselessness, sparkled with pleasure, and his mood was reflected by the mixed human/Lemurian—"American"—crew around him in *Walker*'s pilothouse, and indeed, throughout his veteran ship. Matt had been grinning a lot lately, despite the added pressure and responsibility of a "whole new war" here in what their allies considered an impossibly distant "far east." Nearly two years of constant war and the associated stress had taken their toll, but that was a kind of stress for which he'd always been well equipped. His long funk had suddenly been erased by almost-miraculous news of a very personal nature. Compared to the relief that gave him, even an added theater in an apparently endlessly growing war seemed barely able to touch him.

"That *Salaama-Na* is sure a sight for sore eyes," he said. "I'd rather she was one of the flat-tops, converted or new, but I don't think anything quite as impressive as one of those seagoing Homes has ever put to sea on this world *or* back home!"

"She's a welcome sight, and that's a fact," agreed Brad "Spanky" Mc-Farlane in his gruff but amiable way. Spanky was a little guy; short and skinny, but the power of his personality and supreme engineering authority always left people the impression he was bigger than he was. He'd been *Walker*'s engineering officer—a "mustang"—ever since she joined the old Asiatic Fleet, and he and Chief Bosun's Mate Fitzhugh Gray had been with the ship longer than anyone now alive. Spanky was Minister of Naval Engineering for the entire Alliance, but he'd also recently become *Walker*'s executive officer. There was no question which of the two he personally considered the more important job. "I think I'm happier to see the oilers she's got with her! This little jaunt to meet our friends is liable to leave our bunkers suckin' air!" he added.

Chief Gray grunted agreement. In contrast to Spanky, Gray was almost as tall as Captain Reddy and even more powerfully built—despite being "in the vicinity" of sixty. The flab he'd accumulated after years on the China Station had reverted to muscle since "the Squall," and, physically, he'd thrived on their adventures. He'd also become something far beyond a chief bosun's mate, although that "something" was still ill-defined. Carl Bashear had taken his old job aboard *Walker*, but even he considered Gray as something like a "super bosun." Most of the surviving original destroyermen from *Walker* and her lost sister *Mahan* had been promoted, many to a lofty status; so had the survivors of the old submarine S-19. Matt refused to appoint himself anything higher than captain, but he'd been acclaimed commander in chief, and there was only one "Captain Reddy." For Gray, it was even more complicated. He wore a lot of different hats now; he commanded the Captain's Guard detail, for example, but he'd been the highest-ranking NCO on *Walker*, and for his deeds and vast moral authority, he'd become the most exalted NCO in the Alliance. Few officers would've even considered actually giving him an order. He'd even refused orders issued by Adar, the High Chief and Sky Priest of Baalkpan, and Chairman of the Grand Alliance, because they'd interfered with his Navy oath! What kind of "promotion" could possibly have meaning for the man? Matt thought he finally had it and was toying with the establishment of "Chief Bosun of the Navy," which would basically confirm Gray's "super bosun" status.

It would be more than just a title. Matt knew chiefs had their own culture, almost like an exclusive fraternity one never really left even if they received commissions. With all the Lemurian "chiefs" entering the fold, it was probably time for that growing fraternity to have some form of "supreme authority" of its own before they made up too many new, wacky rules. The age-old, traditional strife between the deck (ape) divisions and the engineering (snipe) divisions served a purpose, but Matt could see things getting out of hand as time went by—as things became more dominated by the very literal-minded Lemurians. The last thing they needed was an equivalent to warring labor unions aboard Navy ships! Gray could lay down the law and establish firm traditions everyone would respect—while making sure the chiefs maintained that unifying brotherhood that made them so effective at not only controlling their divisions and getting along with one another, solving little problems aboard ship before they became big enough that officers had to "notice" them, and frankly, culling poor performers from their own ranks.

"Oil's a fine thing," Gray grumbled, "but I'm just as happy to see those new steam frigates, or 'DDs' I guess they're callin' 'em." He seemed unhappy with the term. "What are their names?"

Matt looked through his binoculars. "They're flying their numbers, so I guess the one to leeward of *Salaama-Na* is *Mertz*, named for our old mess attendant we lost at Baalkpan."

"A hell of a thing," Gray snorted. "Get killed servin' sammitches, and they name a destroyer after you!" He looked at the surprised expressions. "Not that I'm against it! Besides, it'll be a hoot to see how Lanier reacts! Mertz deserves a statue for puttin' up with that nasty, bloated bastard so long." Earl Lanier was *Walker's* unpopular cook, and Ray Mertz had been his long-suffering assistant. "What's the other one?"

"She's *Tindal*," Matt replied grimly. "They launched her in Maa-ni-la as *Lelaa*, but when they found out Captain Lelaa-Tal-Cleraan wasn't dead after all, they named her after Miami." "Miami" Tindal had been *Walker's* chief engineer during the recent action at Scapa Flow. Matt's face became an unreadable contrast of sadness and barely suppressed . . . glee. Their allies in the Fil-pin Lands had also discovered that Nurse Lieutenant and "Minister of Medicine" Sandra Tucker—the woman Matt loved—had also survived a terrible ordeal. Ironically, it was her abduction, along with that of others, that brought *Walker* and her crew so far from where Sandra was ultimately found—and embroiled the Grand Alliance in yet *another* war. Sandra, Princess Rebecca Anne McDonald, Sister Audry, Abel Cook, Midshipman Stuart Brassey, the "ex"-Tagranesi "Lawrence," and the . . . inimitable . . . Chief Gunner's Mate Dennis Silva had all been rescued by the remnants of "Task Force Laumer." Incredibly, the battered submarine that Lieutenant Irvin Laumer had been sent to salvage had endured grounding, a year on an island beach, and ultimately a colossal volcanic eruption and tidal wave, before finding the important castaways adrift in the Fil-pin Sea along with seventy-odd survivors of Lawrence's Grik-like people.

"*Tindal*'s a good name," Spanky said at last, breaking the awkward silence that ensued.

"Yes, it is," Matt agreed. "So's *Mertz*. Ray was a good kid, and making sandwiches in the middle of a fight probably takes more guts than shooting at the enemy."

Walker continued her sprint toward the approaching squadron. All the ships, except *Salaama-Na* and the two Imperials, *Ulysses* and *Icarus*, were flying the Stars and Stripes—the flag of the American Navy and everyone, Lemurians included, who'd joined that "clan." Matt directed *Walker*'s speed be reduced to one-third, and had the ship's whistle sounded in greeting. A gout of white steam gushed from the whistle, emitting a throbbing, bass shriek. The greeting was answered by similar tones from *Tindal* and *Mertz*, whose whistles were copies of *Walker*'s, and by higher-pitched toots from *Ulysses* and *Icarus*. The Imperial frigates also loosed an exuberant, thundering broadside in salute.

"I wish old Harvey Jenks was here to see this!" Gray said. Again, he noticed surprised stares. He and the Imperial commodore got along fine now, but there'd been a time when they hated each other. Jenks couldn't come today because he'd been across the island for several days, coordinating civil and naval preparations in Edinburgh for the upcoming campaign against the rebels and "Holy Dominion" forces on New Ireland. He was due back, and would likely be in Scapa Flow by the time the ships made port.

"I just meant, you know, that big 'Cat Home is a hell of a sight and . . . well, our fightin' ships are prettier than his!" he defended. Everyone in the pilothouse laughed.

At a much reduced speed, which left her skinny, round-bottomed hull wallowing sickeningly in the swells, *Walker* escorted the new arrivals into the Imperial Home Fleet port of Scapa Flow. Sufficient space for *Salaama-Na* had reluctantly been set aside by an incredulous harbormaster, who'd disbelieved her described dimensions. He'd been told by Matt *and* Jenks that the thousand-foot vessel simply wouldn't fit in the

otherwise-generous dock space allocated to "American" ships, not if
Walker, *Simms*, *Tindal*, and *Mertz* were to have a place. At least the huge
Home wouldn't need the space for long; only until she off-loaded her
cargo of replacements, prefabricated tank batteries, and the heavy machinery sent to support the Allied presence there. She'd then moor away
from the dock, as was customary with ships her size, until Sor-Lomaak
decided to leave.

All Scapa Flow turned out to see the arrival. Everyone loved to see
Walker underway, and this was the first time she'd moved other than to
"switch sides" at the dock to facilitate repairs since the battle that saved
the Empire from a quick Dominion victory. Still, today she was only part
of the attraction. By order of the Governor-Emperor, the massive harbor
forts bellowed a welcoming salute with their heavy guns. This was answered by each arriving ship; a few shots from the light guns on the oilers, creditable broadsides from the returning Imperial frigates, sharper,
fewer, louder, reports from the "American" frigates, and a massive, rolling, booming roar from *Salaama-Na*'s new fifty-pounders. All was
punctuated by a perfect four-gun salvo from the sleek gray destroyer.
Whistles shrieked and bells rang, and lizard birds and flocks of colorful
parrots swirled in the air over the harbor.

The American frigates were a hit with their clean lines unmarred by
paddle wheels and with the distinctive contrast of the white paint against
the dark hulls between their gunports. Like *Walker* and *Simms*, they
were oil burners, and they didn't produce the black, choking plumes of
sooty smoke as Imperial steamers did. Ultimately, however, even though
she wasn't technically a warship, *Salaama-Na* was the focus of attention.
In a way, she represented a primitive technology. She moved primarily
by sail alone. Only at times like this, when confined in restrictive waters,
did her hundred massive—but even more primitive—sweep oars come
out to propel and shift her closer to the dock. But she also represented a
native sophistication inherent among the Imperial's new Lemurian allies that predated human contact. Some of the old journals and logs of
the "Founders," the crews of the ancient "East Indiamen" that went
among the distant "ape folk" after the "Passage" to this world, hinted they
possessed "momentous vessels," but except for a few crude drawings, little more was mentioned. It was encouraging—and a little humbling—

that the Lemurians (*don't call them "ape folk!"*) were, and had been so advanced in terms of industrial and structural engineering. The sturdy American frigates—not to mention the flying machines!—demonstrated how seamlessly that ingenuity could be mated to a technology beyond even that of the Empire.

Eventually, amid continuous fanfare, *Ulysses* and *Icarus* were secured at the Navy dock where the survivors of the naval battle off Scapa Flow still underwent repairs. The Allied warships tied up as well, and the oilers and transports moored nearby. With agonizing care, *Salaama-Na* snugged up to what would ultimately become the Allied fueling pier, capable of handling several "normal size" ships at once. With the crowd, now largely composed of female dockworkers shouting at others to "stand clear," gathered alongside, the various commanders and their staffs came ashore and were escorted to where Governor-Emperor Gerald McDonald lounged on the seat of a carriage, his wounded legs still immobilized. With the awkward assistance of a muscular, one-armed, dark-skinned man named Sean (O'Casey) Bates and Gerald's pale, slender wife, Ruth, the Governor-Emperor managed to stand.

"Welcome!" he boomed with a broad grin. "Welcome to you all! Welcome, Sor-Lomaak, High Chief of the sovereign *Salaama-Na* Home, and all the beautiful Allied ships accompanying her! I'm more grateful than I can express for the safe return of *Ulysses* and *Icarus* as well! Please do excuse this informal greeting—an appropriate reception is being prepared—but my exuberance could not be contained!"

Looking at the man, Matt didn't doubt he was sincere, but his pale, sweaty face testified to his pain. It was a miracle he'd kept either leg, let alone both. *Walker*'s own surgeon, Selass, daughter of Keje-Fris-Ar, vaulted onto the carriage and whispered something to Ruth, who self-righteously repeated it in her husband's ear. With a dismissive wave, the Governor-Emperor allowed himself to be seated once more. "Tonight, then," he said, less vigorously, "please do join me at Government House where I can welcome you properly and we can discuss those things that need our most immediate attention!"

After a few more personal greetings, the carriage pulled away with Selass still aboard, and Matt looked at the newly arrived Allied officers. First, he stepped to Sor-Lomaak and saluted. As a head of state in his own right, Sor-Lomaak, while a member of the Alliance, wasn't under Matt's military authority unless he chose to be. He was a tall 'Cat, almost as tall as Adar—which still left him half a head shorter than Matt. As had most Home High Chiefs, he'd risen from the "Body of Home clan," and was built a lot like Keje; broad and strong, instead of slim, with the disproportionately powerful upper body of the "wing runners." His fur was a black-blotched brown.

"We haven't met, Your Excellency," Matt said. "Welcome to the Empire of the New Britain Isles." Sor-Lomaak seemed flustered, both by the salute and Matt's words. Realizing he'd unconsciously spoken English, Matt repeated his greeting in his improved, but still-clumsy Lemurian. Sor-Lomaak blinked appreciation.

"I am glad to have finally arrived upon this strange land—far beyond the point I thought it possible to even stand."

Matt winced. Lemurian religious dogma as taught by the Sky Priests had taken some serious hits of late, and he wished the revelations of such things as consistent, worldwide gravity had been allowed a more . . . comfortable absorption. "Glad to have you, sir. If you need any assistance unloading your cargo, I'll be glad to help coordinate it." He paused. "Things are a little strange here, as you've surely noticed. Human females do much of the labor, and though we're in the process of working that out, their status is somewhat unusual."

"So I gathered when we touched at Respite Island," Sor-Lomaak observed.

"Yes. Well, I expect this war's going to set a lot of Imperial institutions on their heads, and it'll probably be an easier transition if they recognize the necessity for themselves." He grinned. "We'll help guide that recognition, of course."

"Of course."

"In any event," Matt continued, "I think you'll find the Imperials will treat your . . . *our* people well. Besides the fact some of my Mi-Anaaka Marines practically saved their country for them, they seem genuinely fascinated by 'Cats. Almost too fascinated at times! Some of my guys get tired of being . . . well, petted."

Sor-Lomaak laughed heartily. "Better petted than feared—or reviled."

"There's a little of that too," Matt admitted, "but mostly by our enemies here." He shook his head. "I swear, the 'Holy Dominion' is human, but they're just as crazy as Grik, and smarter. They don't think anybody, humans or 'Cats, are 'people,' except for themselves." Matt paused and blew through his lips. Talking 'Cat always kind of . . . tickled. "The Imperials are scared of our Marines, though," he added with satisfaction. "It seemed weird to them that our guys didn't really try to take prisoners in the land fighting, for example." He shrugged. "You probably understand. In our war against the Grik, 'quarter' has never been a priority for either side," he said dryly. "They're used to different ways here, although that may change too. The Dominion, or 'Doms,' they call them, aren't much for surrendering."

Excusing himself from Sor-Lomaak, Matt returned the salutes and shook the hands of the captains and senior officers of *Mertz* and *Tindal*. All were Lemurians, as were the crews of both ships, even the engineers. Matt had to admit he felt strange about that, but also . . . proud. The feeling probably wasn't all that dissimilar to a sense that "junior was growing up." Not only had their Lemurian friends learned to grasp the technological leaps the humans brought them, but they embraced them, used them, *commanded* them, and in many ways, they'd begun to *improve* upon them. "Junior" *had* grown up, technologically, and—somewhat sadly—militarily. Matt was confident that for the most part, the Allied naval officers had learned many things *better* than their teachers could show them, and if Pete Alden might once have been uncomfortable bestowing the sacred title of "Marine" on what many had considered "catmonkeys," Matt knew Pete had no cause for discomfort in that regard anymore.

Looking at his Lemurian . . . colleagues, Matt smiled, and together they walked back toward the American dock, discussing equipment they'd brought from the Fil-pin Lands, logistical matters, and more of the oddities of life in the Empire.

The reception, held on the torch-lit, manicured grounds surrounding Government House, was a resounding success. Long tables draped with spotless cloths formed expanding semicircles around a large round table positioned near the broad, residential porch. There was no dancing, but strains of Vivaldi once more drifted in the light, warm breeze to the delight of the newly arrived Lemurians who'd never heard its like. They hadn't tasted many of the meats laid before them either; chicken, plump parrots steamed on beds of port-darkened rice, succulent pork prepared in a variety of ways. All were domestic descendants of "Passage" livestock, and the juicy, tender quality of the fare was much appreciated and graciously complimented. Exotic fruits and vegetables were enjoyed as well, but even Matt couldn't tell how many were native to this world and which might be the result of cross-pollenization. The port wine was sweeter than Lemurian seep, but it had subtle similarities. He'd cautioned against serving anything stronger. 'Cats had hard liquor, but theirs had unpredictable effects on humans. Only their excellent beer produced conventional and generally benign results. Imperial spirits might make the Lemurian guests ill, at the very least.

Besides the lack of dancing, there were other differences from the only other festivity Matt had attended here: the Pre-Passage Ball. That was when things began coming to a head. In retrospect, considering the extent of the treachery rampant at the time, the lack of security had been naïve to say the least. In contrast, the Governor-Emperor now sat with his back to the front entrance of the grand house, with all the most important guests seated at that central table. Flanking it were spotlessly attired Imperial and Lemurian Marines. The Imperials looked very decorative in their yellow-faced red coats, black dress shakos, and white knee breeches. The 'Cats were magnificent in their white leather and blue kilts, accented with polished bronze greaves and helmets. The bayonet-tipped muskets held in their distinctive "rest" positions were immaculate, highly polished—and loaded. No one knew how many traitors still roamed New Scotland, but they were taking no chances this night.

The music and jumbled roar of conversations between Allied and Imperial officers seated at the tables nearby was sufficiently muted by distance to allow those at the Governor-Emperor's table to communicate without shouting. The discussions during the meal were limited to pleasantries and cultural questions and observations. Matt had cautioned his officers not to harp on the "female question," since those discussions and negotiations were touchy. Though most assuredly underway, they also remained private. That something be "done" about the virtual enslavement of Imperial women had been a prerequisite to Imperial membership in the Grand Alliance, but it went to the very root of their culture. Most Imperial leaders at the table agreed that the institution was barbaric, and now, that the Company had been shattered, outdated, and even unsustainable. There was significant disagreement on how to proceed, however.

Sor-Lomaak was enjoying himself, with the newly arrived frigate captains translating the conversations. Chack-Sab-At, a major now, was at Matt's side. He said little, but glanced at his Marines on the porch between each bite he took. Courtney Bradford, the odd Australian engineer/naturalist, sat at Matt's other elbow, disinterested in the "normal" foods the 'Cats and human destroyermen ate so greedily, virtually dissecting the unfamiliar dishes he sampled. He was deeply involved in a discussion with Governor-Emperor McDonald about the Empire's lens-making industry. He was desperate for a "proper" microscope, beyond those the Empire already had.

Spanky had remained aboard *Walker*, but Chief Gray, ever protective, was there. He wasn't doing much protecting now, though, and was plainly bored. They'd caught the relayed message concerning TF Garrett's plight shortly before leaving the ship, and he hated doing nothing when friends were in peril. He scowled at the plate before him, picking disapprovingly at the rich food. Commodore Harvey Jenks, who'd arrived later than expected, leaned past his dutifully silent wife and whispered something in the Bosun's ear. Gray grunted, nodded, and seemed to take heart. Matt suspected the commodore had probably reminded him there'd be plenty to do soon enough.

Matt looked at Lieutenant (jg) Fred Reynolds, in charge of *Walker*'s meager air division. The kid was picking at his food too, but not from boredom. He still blamed himself for the life-threatening wounds Ensign Kari-Faask, his 'Cat spotter and friend, had suffered when he pressed his attack too closely on the Dom troop transports that had threatened Scapa Flow. She was improving, but that first taste of responsibility for the life of another, especially a friend, had rattled him. *Walker*'s gunnery officer, "Sonny" Campeti, was trying to chat him up, but occasionally, he cast a worried look at Matt.

"That gennel-maan yonder asks if you'd scoot the bottle on around, sur?" Matt looked up in response to the voice that sounded in his ear and saw Taarba-Kar, better known as "Tabasco." The rust-colored 'Cat was one of Lanier's mess attendants, filling in as his "personal steward" while Juan Marcos, the little Filipino, was test-driving his new wooden leg. Lanier had almost burst a vessel when Juan "stoled" Tabasco for the mythical "Skipper's Steward Division" and the 'Cat promptly deserted him to attend "classes" at the church/hospital that had become an amputee ward. Matt stayed out of it. Long ago, Juan had established a position of moral, if not official, power aboard his ship, and Juan's tragic but heroic wound had only strengthened it. He looked where Tabasco was pointing.

Across the table, beside Sean Bates—the one-armed, one-time "outlaw" they'd met as Sean O'Casey, now Gerald McDonald's prime factor and chief of staff—was Lord High Admiral McClain. Matt wasn't sure what he thought of him. By all accounts, the man was a mariner extraordinaire, and had the trust of Gerald and Harvey Jenks, but he was also a stalwart of the "old guard." He'd long resisted Jenks's drive to explore the world beyond Imperial frontiers, and he, almost alone among Gerald's staff, resisted the proposed reforms regarding the "female question." He resisted almost all change as a matter of course, in a devil's advocate fashion, and Matt wasn't sure if that reflected his honest position or if he was just testing their suggestions. Matt wondered how well he'd adapt to the strategies and tactics required by this "new" war. He nodded at the man and passed the bottle along.

Sean Bates suddenly stood and glanced at those surrounding him. "P'raps now's a good time ta adjourn ta the library, ta discuss the campaign that laies ahead," he suggested. "As ye know, the Gov'ner-Emp'rer remains easely tired, an' I s'pect many here could use a wee rest after yer long voyage."

"Nonsense, Sean, we needn't rush . . ." Gerald began, but Matt also stood.

"May as well. It's been a long day, and we should crack the book and get everybody on the same page. Besides," he added, "I'm anxious to get back to *Walker* and check on developments in the west."

"Of course," agreed Gerald, accepting the excuse. "By all means then, let us adjourn to the library." He gestured around at the other tables.

"They shan't miss us. It's good to see our . . . peoples . . . agreeing so well! We've much to accomplish together, and I'm glad we've had this opportunity to begin as friends!" He sobered, looking at the diners, Imperials and Lemurians, mixed together. "They *must* be friends," he added, nodding significantly at Chack, acknowledging the crucial role he and his Marines had played toward that end. "Soon they'll guard one another's lives."

The library was surprisingly quiet, considering the unabated noise outside. Matt had been in the room many times now, and the furnishings reflected their owner well. Gerald was like a cross between Jenks and Bradford, personalitywise. He had the bearing and reserve of his commodore and friend, combined with the eccentric curiosity and (suppressed) enthusiasm for science of the Australian. As plenipotentiary at large for the Alliance, Courtney had been in the room even more often than Matt, but he was immediately drawn to the bookshelves as the officers filed into the room. Matt had to tap his elbow and point to the great map dominating the room's south wall.

"You don't actually need me for this," Courtney complained. "These military machinations are quite beyond me. If you insist I pay attention . . . I may well ask a question!" he warned.

"As long as you're not asking where we all are a month from now when you suddenly notice we're gone," Matt countered.

Those who knew the Australian laughed. He was prone to a notable absentmindedness. That notwithstanding, he had a natural talent for analysis, and when he kept his thoughts on a single track long enough, he was very good at pointing out obvious flaws in plans that others had overlooked. Matt wanted him paying attention.

The officers and guests made themselves comfortable (a relative thing for Lemurians, since all the chairs were designed for people without tails) and Governor-Emperor McDonald allowed himself to be ushered to a divan, his legs propped up. Matt noticed with pleasure that Ruth McDonald didn't excuse herself but chose a chair near her husband.

"There's one . . . small thing we need to have understood before we begin," announced Lord High Admiral McClain, glancing at Ruth. He looked around the room with a closed expression. "Who's the authority here?"

"The Governor-Emperor, of course," Matt replied patiently.

"I mean, the *military* authority," McClain pressed.

"I am," Matt said simply, "as we've discussed before. I remain 'Commander in Chief of All Allied Forces, by acclamation.'"

"The Empire of the New Britain Isles did not 'acclaim' you, sir."

"James!" Gerald scolded, and Commodore Jenks stirred angrily.

"With respect, Your Majesty, I speak only truth," the admiral maintained.

"You speak out of place," Gerald said more forcefully. "Captain Reddy was acclaimed by the other Allied powers long before we became one. You *shall* not forget that even before our alliance was made—before they had any 'obligation' to help us—they willingly spilled their blood to defend us from the despicable Dominion! We've joined *them*, and heartily! They didn't join *us*." He paused, gulping an angry breath. "We may know this region of the world better than they, Lord High Admiral, but largely due to your influence, that knowledge is sorely limited. We know next to nothing of the extent of the enemy realm, for example, but that part that borders the vast Pacific. How deep does it go? What lies beyond?"

"My apologies, Your Maj—"

"Let me finish, damn you, sir!" Gerald practically roared. He stopped, forcefully composing himself. "We must not start like this!" he continued quietly. "The time for petty, egoistic squabbles is past. We face a wicked, determined enemy here *and* in the west! Our allies stand poised to deliver a heavy blow to the Grik, but we're still on the defensive here. The enemy holds a significant portion of our very homeland! We must throw him out! Captain Reddy and his strategies have been much more recently successful at that than any we can draw upon!"

"Thank you, Your Majesty," Matt said, partially to cover Chief Gray's muttered "puffed-up bugger" and the few ensuing chuckles. Admiral McClain reddened, and Jenks stood and moved toward Matt to add his support. "I'm glad you brought up those 'strategies,' because the first thing we need to get clear is, just like our war in the west, we can't have limits to our 'war aims' here. We're going to fight this war hard, ugly, and as fast as possible. There're no rules except victory, and there'll be no 'negotiated peace.'" His green eyes flashed. "They picked this fight, but we're going to finish it." He sighed. "Maybe we won't have to kill them all, as we'll probably have to do to win in the west, but to accept anything short of complete surrender'll only waste the blood already lost."

There were a few sharp cheers, and the 'Cats stamped their feet in approval. Admiral McClain didn't cheer, and even the Governor-Emperor seemed dubious.

"That will be . . . costly," he said.

Matt nodded. "Yes, it will, but believe me when I say it's the only way." He recalled his interview with the Dominion "Blood Cardinal," Don Hernan de Devina Dicha. "Those guys are absolutely *nuts*. Hell, you know that. We beat them now, knock 'em back on their heels, make 'peace'—it'll start all over again in a decade." He looked at Gray's grim face. "That's how it works," he said. "We *know*. The only way to end a war forever is if somebody wins and somebody loses . . . bad." He watched Ruth's face as she stared at her husband. She wouldn't speak, not yet, but she'd already considered the implications of another, future war. Matt helped Gerald come to the same conclusion. "If you don't get right with that, wrap it around you, and wade through the awful fact that for us to win, they have to *lose*, one of these days, maybe when your daughter, Rebecca, is in your place, there'll be another war; and honestly, they're liable to win that one because they have the depth, resources, and manpower. Right now, we have a technological edge, but in ten years? Twenty?" He shook his head.

"He's right, Your Majesty," Jenks said. "I've seen their war in the west, and it's the most savage thing you can imagine, but little more so than the fighting we saw here, at the Dueling Grounds!" He *was* exaggerating, but only slightly. The Dominion forces that attacked, without warning, had done so with massed artillery against *civilians*. "The Grik are . . . animals, but *men* would never behave as the Dominion forces did. They, their leadership, this . . . perverted church they worship, must be erased from the world."

"All right," Gerald said softly, glancing at his wife. He wouldn't leave this mess to be faced by the daughter they thought they'd lost. "How do we beat them *this* time . . . and forever?"

Matt nodded at Harvey Jenks, who stepped to the huge map, fingering his long, braided, sun-bleached mustaches. He paused and drew his sword; a most appropriate "pointer" under the circumstances. Matt had seen the blade many times, even faced it in "practice," but he'd never really appreciated its workmanship before. It was heavier than his own well-battered Academy sword, with a subtle curve toward the tip. Despite all the use it had seen, there were few nicks, and the bright, almost-purple steel was unmarred by rust and lovingly tended. Jenks raised the sword against an island west of New Scotland.

"First, we have New Ireland," he said. "The enemy has captured it entire, it would seem, with the aid of Company traitors there." He glanced at Matt. "Elsewhere, the Company is no more. It's broken, along with its monopoly on trade, by order of the Governor-Emperor, and distributed among loyal shareholders. Those same shareholders will now become chairmen of their various *new* companies, and for the duration of the current hostilities, their ships are engaged as auxiliaries to the Imperial Navy, under naval regulations." He looked back at the map. "The harbor defenses at New Dublin are not the heaviest in the Empire, not compared to those here and at New London and Portsmouth on New Britain, but they're probably the most formidable. A sustained bombardment of the forts there is difficult because they're on the windward side of the island and mount thirty-pound guns. We can match that and more with numbers, but with their elevation, not in range. Any ships attempting a bombardment will suffer heavily, and any disabled vessel will likely be driven ashore."

After this had been translated to him, Sor-Lomaak leaned forward. "My fifties will outrange their thirties," he said confidently, "and even if we are hit, with her sweeps, *Salaama-Na* will *not* go ashore!"

"I was hoping you'd say that," Matt said, grinning.

Jenks grinned too. "Thank you, Your Excellency. You've just finalized Major Chack-Sab-At's and Major Blair's plan." He looked smugly at Matt, and motioned the two Marines, one Lemurian-Amer-i-caan, and the other Imperial, to approach the map. They'd fought together splendidly at the Dueling Grounds and become fast friends. Blair still walked stiffly from a wound, but he was anxious to strike back at the Doms.

"Sirs," Chack began, blinking only slight self-consciousness, "Major Blair and I believe the enemy will expect us at New Dublin, or possibly Easky in the south. We will not disappoint him." There were murmurs, and McClain looked alarmed, but Chack continued. "A large naval force composed of the heaviest ships of the line and as many *former* Company ships as possible, will menace New Dublin. The Company ships will linger in sight but out of range, as though they carry troops—which they will, but not *all* of them by any means." He bowed to Sor-Lomaak. "This task force will be gathered around the powerful—and ominously large—*Salaama-Na*, which will open a steady bombardment of the harbor defenses, supported when possible by Imperial warships. This should, ah, collect the attention of the enemy." He grinned, showing sharp, white fangs. "The enemy may call troops from Easky or they may not, but it doesn't matter, because Mr. Blair will land at Cork, east of there, and fortify these mountains." He pointed at the Wiklow range that began at the northeast panhandle of New Ireland, then fishhooked back into the sea, east of Easky. "He'll hold there until any Easky troops, or possibly some from across this other range at New Dublin, try to push him off—at which point *my* force, landed in the extreme north at Bray, will march down the Valley Road and slam into their flank!"

"Lovely," muttered McClain, "and delightfully complicated. But what will it accomplish? The enemy will still hold New Dublin, and you cannot expect me to believe you'll scale those heights behind the city and take it from behind!"

Chack looked at him with his big, amber eyes. "Why else would I do as I propose?"

"You must be mad."

"But you believe that is my intent?"

"There can be no oth . . ." McClain's jaw clamped shut.

"Indeed," said Major Blair. "That will clearly be our intent and the enemy must prepare for it, regardless how imprudent it appears—and we *will* make the attack . . . !"

"What?" McClain was incredulous.

"In the dark of night, coordinated with an attack by boat from the sea, launched by the bombardment fleet—which the Doms will now consider a diversion!"

"By God!" Gerald barked approval.

"I told you those guys were clever," Matt said, prodding him.

"I knew it already, but this! It's better than chess!"

"Quite clever," McClain muttered under his breath.

"In any event," Jenks said, "hopefully, that'll solve the problem of New Ireland." He waited for the approving applause to wane, then returned to the map. He drew the point of his sword down along the coast of California, near where San Francisco ought to be. "But, even more important than New Ireland, our continental colonies are at risk," he said abruptly. "Before, or while we do anything else, they must be secured. The vast majority of our raw material comes from there and without them, we can't sustain this . . . front . . . in the wider war, on our own. It's that simple. If we lose those colonies, we'll represent nothing but a material drain on our new allies who have concerns of their own, and that just to keep us alive." His gaze fell heavily on Lord High Admiral McClain.

"Fast ships were dispatched, immediately after the attempted invasion, to warn the colonies of a Dom attack," McClain said in response. "We now know the attack here was premature, that it was originally planned to coincide with the Founders' Day festivities. The combination of the Christmas Feast, followed quickly by the New Year and Founders' Day observances, would have left us singularly unprepared." He paused. "We still don't know if the Temple of the Popes is aware of the current situation, or that hostilities have already begun, but we do know that after January fifth, things are 'automatically going to happen.'" There were murmurings at the now-infamous phrase that had been made public shortly before.

"Obviously," McClain continued, "one of those 'things' was to be the attack here. We must presume other operations were meant to coincide with it. In my view, the next most logical enemy objective is our garrison on the Enchanted Isles, not Saint Francis."

Courtney perked up. "The Galápagos Islands?" he interrupted insistently.

"Aye," McClain confirmed, looking at him oddly, "though only the enemy calls them that. The 'Insulae de los Galápagos.'"

"Good God!" Courtney exclaimed. "We mustn't allow those"—he searched for a suitable epithet—"buggerers of a . . . an otherwise-sensible faith to defile that place!"

Matt almost chuckled, but thoughts of the very dark . . .

perversion . . . of Catholicism practiced by the Dominion stopped him. "The islands aren't the same here, Courtney," he reminded.

"Of course not!" Bradford exclaimed. "But they're liable to be different in *very* fascinating ways!"

Matt sighed. "Go ahead and find a book, Courtney. We've got war stuff to talk about."

Muttering, Bradford stood and marched to the shelves.

Matt closed his eyes and shook his head. "Your Majesty?" he prompted.

"Yes. Well. Obviously, we mustn't let the Enchanted Isles fall, but they're well fortified. The enemy will likely bypass them and hope they wither on the vine. The colonies are the main, immediate concern."

"I beg to differ," McClain said.

"We have *perhaps* two weeks," Jenks said. He pointed at the map with his sword. "The Doms may even now have an army poised to strike from the south, but the land bordering the Sea of Bones is a terrible place; a sparse, rocky desert inhabited by unimaginable horrors. Oddly, the lands on either side are just as fertile as it is desolate, but therefore teeming with vast numbers of large, terrifying beasts." He shook his head. "Any force attempting such a march would likely lose half its number before the first shot was fired. I predict the assault will come from the sea, as it did here, and it's on the sea we must meet it."

"The fastest ships, the frigates, might get there in time," Gerald observed. "Ships of the line are too slow." He paused. "And they will evidently already be employed elsewhere. The questions are, do we have enough to send, and will they have the weight of metal required when they get there?"

"I mean to take *Walker*," Matt announced. "We might even beat the dispatch sloop you sent. With Commodore Jenks along to talk to the locals, sound the alarm, rouse the colonial defenses, we can at least have them ready for what's coming." He looked measuringly at Lord High Admiral McClain. "That'll leave you to command, or choose somebody to command, the biggest force of fast steamers you can wrangle together, including *my* ships here. They have to sail immediately, and for God's sake, don't forget my oilers!"

CHAPTER 4

Maa-ni-la
Fil-pin Lands

"For the last time, I'm tellin' you to take it back!" Dennis Silva practically roared. The raggedly clad, one-eyed, sun-bronzed giant loomed menacingly over a much shorter, but entirely unintimidated (brevet) Colonel Tamatsu Shinya. Shinya no longer wore his ruined Japanese Imperial Navy uniform, having traded it for the blue kilt, white leather armor, sandals, and bronze greaves of the Lemurian-Amer-i-caan Marines. The only real difference between his appearance and that of many others on the broad "parade ground" on what should have been the Bataan Peninsula, was that he still wore his old, Imperial Navy hat, and he had no fur—or tail. He also had the vertical red stripes of an officer on his kilt instead of horizontal NCO stripes around the bottom above the hem.

"And for the last time I'm telling *you*, Mr. Silva, that I *will not* . . . unless you force me to prefer charges of insubordination!"

"Then do it! I ain't never *seen* me this insubordinate before!" Silva ranted.

"What on earth is going on here?" demanded Sandra Tucker, arriving with a small escort including the Grik-like, "ex"-Tagranesi, Lawrence, Captain Lelaa-Tal-Cleraan, Lieutenant Irvin Laumer, and a small group of "graduated" Marines. Sandra had recovered considerably from her recent ordeal, as had the others, and her once-red, peeling skin was turning a dark tan. Her normally sandy brown hair still looked almost bleached blond, however. Irvin was much the same, but he'd cut his hair very short and shaved his beard. Lelaa and Lawrence looked the same as always, but they'd physically recovered from their adventure. All except Sandra (and Silva) used the brief pause in the argument to exchange salutes, even Lawrence. Trading salutes with the strange, furry/reptilian creature still seemed ridiculously odd.

Silva and Shinya were silenced by Sandra's appearance, and she took a moment to gaze at the adjacent parade ground portion of the Advanced Training Center (ATC) established here, away from the city, where troops could perform large-scale maneuvers, as well as small-arms, artillery, and mortar practice without disturbing or hazarding the Maa-ni-la inhabitants. It was actually quite a scenic spot. The Maara-vella mountains loomed over the closest thing to a coastal plain she'd seen since Aryaal and Baali. Herds of paalkas grazed the grassy, rolling foothills in the distance, inured to the thousands of troops and their noisy weapons. Maa-ni-la Bay stretched broad and peaceful to the south beneath a warm, clear sky. The island fortress of Corregidor was a fortress here as well, even more imposing due to the lower sea level. The small, almost-quaint town of "Maara-vella" was the only settlement on the peninsula, and it often shook with the thunder of live-fire exercises and mock battles, but the town had no cause for complaint. It had more or less evolved to support the training facility, as well as the harbor defenses. Sandra liked it. Baalkpan was too enclosed by the surrounding jungle; she preferred open spaces. She always felt lighter of heart when she visited there.

Belatedly, she noticed the staring Lemurian faces; Marine officers and Maa-ni-los in their black and gold kilts. "Silva," she said with a sigh, "what have you done now?"

"I ain't done *nothin'* this time—honest! It's what this damn, jumped-up Jap's tryin' to do to *me!*" he almost whined.

"Mr. Silva!" Shinya warned, his tone angry.

Somewhat shocked, Sandra realized she believed Dennis. He'd done many . . . questionable things during their acquaintance, but he'd never really lied about it. She honestly doubted he'd ever lie to *her*. After some of the stunts he'd pulled—and told her about—she couldn't imagine why he would. Few imagined atrocities could compare to his very real, common-knowledge deeds. She looked at Shinya. "What *have* you done to him?"

It was Shinya's turn to project a defensive expression. Sandra Tucker was a tiny thing, but her authority, moral and official, had few limits. Not only was she Minister of Medicine for the entire Alliance, and few veteran soldiers hadn't been treated or saved by her hands, or those she taught at one time or another, but she enjoyed the profound friendship of Saan-Kakja, High Chief of all the Fil-pin Lands. In addition, she had—and deserved—the daughterlike worship of Princess Rebecca Anne McDonald; only heir to the Empire of the New Britain Isles. She was also, incidentally and famously, the fiancée of Captain Matthew Reddy.

"Against my better judgment," Shinya explained, sourly, "I informed this ridiculous oaf he's out of uniform—still—and someone about to be decorated and promoted should set an example."

"See?" Silva demanded. "He said it again! 'Promoted'!"

"What's the matter with that?" Lelaa asked, blinking confusion.

"*What's the matter with that?*" Silva mocked. "He's tryin' to make me a *officer*! A—a *loo-tenant!*" He smoldered. "I *can't* be a *officer*! Hell, I might as well drown myself."

Lieutenant Laumer's face reddened. "And what's wrong with being an officer?" he asked darkly. He was also to be promoted to full lieutenant from a jg, a move he much appreciated. In his defense, he really didn't know Silva well at all.

"Well . . . nothin'—for a officer," Dennis tried to explain. "They squirt up the ladder all the time. They start out officers—born to it, you might say, with no offense meant—and that's what they do. But I *ain't* a officer; never have been, and never wanna be. I don't know *how*! I swear, I'll screw it up so fast, it'll make your heads spin smooth off!"

Sandra nodded. "I think I get it," she said. "Mr. Silva, you must apologize to Colonel Shinya this instant! I don't believe he's the one who . . . inflicted this honor upon you; the confirmation came from Acting Chief of Staff Steve Riggs. I guess he thought your recent . . . accomplishments deserved recognition and reward. I doubt he expected you to react so negatively, though. Spanky's a 'mustang,' after all. So is Mr. Chapelle now, as well as Campeti. It's not as if you'd be a freak."

"Yeah, but . . . Spanky's a different sort!" Dennis insisted. "An' he 'jumped up' before the war. Ask the Bosun how *he'd* feel to get bars pinned on! You think he'd consider it a promotion?" He shook his head. "With gobs of respect, I'm good at killin' things and blowin' stuff up. If I was a officer, they'd wind up puttin' me in charge of somethin' I got no more business bein' in charge of than a fried chicken's ass!" He blinked. "Um, 'scuse me, ma'am . . . but it's a fact!" Silva's expression changed; it became dark—and something else. He looked hard at Sandra. "Miss . . . Minister, Lieutenant . . . whatever you want me to call you, *you know me*. You know what . . . I've done . . . an' what I'd do again in the same situations. Give me a squad of Marines; a handful o' mugs with guns, and that's fine. Make me chief over a division; I can handle that." He paused, then continued quietly. "But don't ever put me in charge of more fellas than I can ever get to know before I wind up gettin' 'em killed."

It hit Sandra then. The mighty, monolithic, irrepressible—arguably psychotic and inarguably depraved—Dennis Silva was *afraid*. He feared no man or beast on this entire messed-up world, but he did fear himself and his own shortcomings. He'd become an incredibly valuable and resourceful man, but not because he was necessarily "good." A number of times in fact, as he'd alluded, he'd done some *very bad* things no "proper" officer could have condoned, much less done, but they'd been the *right* thing to do, regardless. More than once, he'd saved Sandra's life, and Rebecca's and Lelaa's, and no telling how many others—maybe the whole Alliance—by naturally and ruthlessly doing what *had* to be done without hesitating to consider the morality. In Sandra's opinion, that made him a dangerous but indispensable asset. He was right, she suddenly realized. He had no business being an officer, and regardless of his excuses, it wasn't because he couldn't lead—Sandra knew he could. He might be sincere about his fear of being responsible for more than a handful of men or 'Cats, but in reality, he simply *couldn't* be an officer, and all that implied—morally and behaviorally—and still be Dennis Silva.

Sandra looked at Shinya. "You know, let's give him this one for now." She lowered her voice. "For a number of reasons." She spoke up again. "Captain Reddy's considering creating a 'bosun of the Navy' post for Chief Gray. Maybe we need something similar, within that hierarchy, for gunner's mates who reach Silva's lofty status. Bernie Sandison gushes about Silva's work in the Ordnance shops back home, and the Lord knows we need gunnery instructors, here and in Baalkpan!"

"That's somethin' else!" Silva interjected. "I got orders back to Baalkpan to slave away, cookin' up shi . . . stuff in Bernie's shops! Hell, I can't do that!"

"Mr. Silva!" said Shinya. "I've heard quite enough of what you will or won't, can or can't do! You'll follow orders for a change, beginning with your apology to me, and all those present here!"

"Well, I'm *sorry*, Colonel, damn it, but I can't keep Riggs, way off in Baalkpan, from givin' boneheaded orders! The Skipper's in the *east*, and *Walker's* in the *east*." He nodded at Sandra. "Miss Minister Tucker and the Munchkin princess is goin' east to the Empire. My standin' orders from the Skipper himself are to watch out for 'em, and that's what I'm gonna do. You don't think, after all this time pertectin' 'em from Imperial traitors, rampagin' sea monsters, and natural catastrophes, the Skipper'd want me to just quit, do ya? 'So long, ladies. Run along back into the mercy-less unknown! My pertectin' days are done!'" He put his hands on his hips and shook his head. "No, sir. You may be a colonel now, an' Riggs may think he's somethin', but *Captain Reddy* is my boss!"

Sandra and Lelaa both chuckled, and Laumer shared a look of consternation with Shinya. The two had become friends, and he sympathized with the former Japanese officer.

"Now *I'm* sorry, Colonel Shinya!" Sandra apologized, "But the lug's right. At least he used to be." She gestured at her companions. "In fact, one reason we came out here was to find Mr. Silva and relieve him of his responsibility to the princess—and thank him again for saving all our lives." She looked at Dennis. "I'm sorry Mr. Silva, but your new orders stand, confirmed by your 'boss,' Captain Reddy. Princess Rebecca—

and I—will have more than sufficient protection on our voyage to the Empire of the New Britain Isles, and they really do need you in Baalkpan. You're to continue your excellent work in the experimental ordnance division with Bernie Sandison and await further orders. I'm sure it won't be long before you have another combat assignment, probably with First Fleet."

Silva's jaw dropped, leaving him wearing an uncharacteristically stunned expression. "But . . ."

Sandra smiled sympathetically. "You should know that the princess objected to this order. For some misguided reason, the child's quite taken with you. That may have something to do with your having saved her so many times. Frankly, believe it or not, I'm not in complete agreement with it either, but we'll be perfectly safe aboard the new, purpose-built carrier, *Maaka-Kakja*, and there won't be anything she or her battle group can't handle that you'd have to protect us from. You'd be bored out of your mind."

"Thank you, Minister Tucker," Shinya said, bowing rather stiffly and casting a triumphant glare at Silva. "Certainly your new escort will behave more . . . responsibly."

"I'm sure," said Sandra, dryly. She turned back to Silva. "Now, I may be other things too, but I'm still a naval officer, and *I'm* giving you an order you'd better obey!" She wrinkled her nose. "While your attire may strike you as fashionable, you're no longer on 'convalescent leave,' and it's time for you to rejoin the Navy! You'll march directly from this place, down to the Navy Yard supply depot—without passing the compound housing the female immigrants from Respite Island! Nurse Pam Cross does *not* need to hear about shenanigans of that sort. She's angry enough you've been gone so long, pretending to be dead."

"She don't own me," Silva said sulkily. "Besides, even if she did, what's the harm in lookin'? There's been few enough female critters—ladies—to oogle. . . ."

"You'll draw an entire new duffel," Sandra continued steadfastly. "Hopefully, they can fit you. I don't know if the Maa-ni-los have ever tried to outfit anyone of your proportions before."

"Yes'm," Silva said, apparently conquered at last. His woeful expression was already beginning to fade, however. In its place, his customary, lopsided, somewhat unnerving grin began to reappear. He scratched his faded, crusty eye patch. "You reckon they can replace this thing?"

"I'm sure they will, once they see it, if they have to make one on the spot!" Sandra said, growing a little concerned about the grin, and Silva's sudden surrender. "Now go!"

Silva saluted sharply, and when all present returned the gesture, he did an about-face, and began striding toward the ferry that would take him across the bay.

"What a horrible man," Lelaa said fondly, watching him go. "I've heard . . . rumors, that Nurse Paam Cross is not the only female who awaits him back home."

Sandra snorted. "You mean Chack's sister, Risa-Sab-At?" She shook her head. "There's no question she and Silva—and Pam!—are great friends. Beyond that, I refuse to speculate. Besides, Risa's with First Fleet, and too busy to pine away over anyone, I suspect. And she's not the 'pining' sort." She turned back to Shinya. "Again, Colonel, I'm sorry. Sorry for my rudeness, and sorry you had to deal with Silva. He heard about the 'promotion' after the morning wireless traffic—I don't know how. Scuttlebutt, I suppose. Anyway, he just . . . panicked, I guess. Somehow, he got the idea you recommended him."

"Well . . ." Shinya hesitated. "I suppose I did. Mr. Silva and I have rarely seen eye to eye in the past, but he's a magnificent warrior. I thought, particularly after his recent exploits on your behalf, that we need such warriors in leadership positions." He gestured at the parade ground. The officers had long since stopped gawking, and the NCOs had never allowed the enlisted troops to start. "We have new weapons, new tactics, and new troops who've not been tested." He shrugged. "I'd hoped to persuade him to take a company of Marines."

"You do him great honor, Colonel Shinya," Sandra said seriously, "and though I suppose he deserves it, take my word; Dennis Silva should *never* become an officer. It would ruin him." She took a long breath. "It might ruin all of us, in the end." She paused, staring back over the throng of troops, ignoring Shinya's curious expression. "With that issue settled, I'll turn to the other thing I came to see you about. You have orders as well—of a sort. Captain Reddy specifically asked me to deliver them, and get your honest appraisal."

"Of course."

"As you know, we have a whole new war on our hands. We can't let up on the Grik, but we must help Captain Reddy and our new Imperial allies. I'll be departing aboard *Maaka-Kakja*, and there'll be plenty of green sailors aboard." She smiled at Lelaa. "For example, Lelaa will command, and she's never even conned a steamship! Her aircrews have only just learned to fly, and she'll be working up her wing en route. My question to you is, in your honest opinion, how many troops can we send with her, and are you free to lead them?"

Shinya concentrated. "Most of my best troops are still involved in search and rescue activities, in response to the effects of the tsunami. Even if I could send them now, 'best' is a relative term." He waved at a regiment of Maa-ni-los rapidly moving from a column into line. "Their drill is good, their execution almost flawless, but only a very few of the NCOs have ever seen action; some were volunteers at Baalkpan, you'll recall. You asked my honest appraisal, and I must say I hesitate to send *any* of these troops to Captain Reddy. He's grown accustomed to leading veteran soldiers." He paused. "Regardless. He wants Marines, I understand, but their amphibious training is not yet complete. Perhaps two of the Fil-pin regiments might be up to the task. Of course," he added wistfully, "much as I'd like to, I can't lead them." He hesitated. "Honestly, I'd prefer that we had time to draw some force from General Alden, then plug these regiments into his larger force as originally planned."

"Colonel Shinya, Matt currently has less than *thirty* effective Marines. More may still recover from wounds, but he needs troops—*our troops*—rather badly right now. He said the Imperial Marines fight well, but our tactics are superior—the tactics you're teaching here. For Chack, or even Matt to have a real say regarding Imperial land tactics, he must have a credible force. Even if the Imperials are inclined to listen to Chack—and Matt thinks they are—he needs more than thirty instructors!" She paused. "Tell me, Colonel: are these troops more or less as well trained as those who met and defeated the Grik at Baalkpan?"

"More. Much more—with one glaring exception."

"Yes. Combat experience. But how many had that at Baalkpan? A quarter? A third at most?" She shook her head. "How much combat experience did *you* have the first time you went into combat? Look, I get it.

These are your troops, and for all practical purposes, this is your army. You formed it, trained it like a child, and you love it, don't you?" Shinya didn't respond, but Sandra knew she was right. "You've done a good job. You've set the wheels in motion and established a sound regimen here." She gestured back at the parade ground. "These 'Cats, these Lemurians, don't really much need us anymore, you know. Sure, we showed them the way, but as far as the basics are concerned, there's not much left to teach them. They're building and flying airplanes, operating steamships, building muskets, and sending Morse! Now that the various industries are starting to hit their stride, they're even improving on designs we've given them." She took a breath. "They're also fighting their own battles now." Her voice softened. "Colonel . . . Tamatsu . . . most of these troops will soon be going west, to First Fleet and General Alden. He'll take good care of them—and they don't need you anymore. Training will continue here just as well without you. You've said yourself that things around here pretty much run themselves. Captain Reddy—Matt—*does* need you, and so will the troops you need to lead east to his assistance!"

Shinya suddenly brightened. "Perhaps you're right," he allowed. "You *are* right! It would seem I've been wrong about everything today!" He shook his head. "It's this constant training," he said. "Each day is the same for me, while far away, my friends continue the struggle. I've been away too long, and it's almost ruined me!" His expression became concerned. "It might have ruined these fine troops if I'd continued to delay their deployment." He looked at Sandra. "Thank you. Forgive me, but . . . how did a nurse ever become so wise in the ways of war . . . and men?"

"You mean how does a *girl* know these things?" Lelaa asked before Sandra could answer. "That's easy. All girls know. 'Cat girls or Hu-maan. Males are all the same." She glared at Irvin Laumer. "We girls fight because we have to. Males too, maybe, but girls get sick, wounded, have younglings; they go home and forget the war until they maybe have to fight again. You take males out of the war and it eats them from the inside out, like a nugli woodworm, as long as others still fight! Back before the Grik came, before we had this war, I knew males were silly. Now I know they're all a buncha' dopes!" She laughed, and Sandra—and even Laumer—joined her.

Lawrence sniffed. "I a 'ale, and no 'nuglis' eat Lawrence!"

"Nonsense!" Irvin said, still chuckling. "Look at you! You're in uniform now!"

It was true. Lawrence had been "with" the Alliance for quite a while, primarily as Princess Rebecca's friend and protector. He'd even gained respect and notoriety despite his resemblance to the Grik "Ancient Enemy." It was becoming increasingly recognized that not all "Grik-like" creatures on the world—far more widespread than previously known—*were* Grik, and many races that resembled them had wildly different societies. Lawrence's own people, from an island they called Tagran, had some rather bizarre cultural practices concerning their young—by human or Lemurian standards—and the matriarchal system they practiced was rather extreme as well. In fact, the recent tidal wave caused by the catastrophic explosion of the volcanic Talaud island had so devastated Tagran that the matriarch had banished all but a handful of the island's population so a few might survive the starving times to come. Of the hundreds set adrift to find another home or die, only seventy-odd survived the later waves that overwhelmed the southern Fil-pin Lands. They'd been rescued with Sandra, Silva, and the others by the remnants of Task Force Laumer and the battered S-19.

High Chief Saan-Kakja gifted the "ex"-Tagranesi with the virtually uninhabited Fil-pin island of Samaar to possess as a Fil-pin territory—as Fil-pin subjects. There'd be no independent matriarchy of such a despotic sort as to condemn so many of its own people neighboring *her* Home! This was a complete departure from any previous Lemurian customs, except for a few now-extinct cultures that had inhabited Jaava. Before, all "daughter" colonies, like their seagoing Home counterparts, were independent. The Tagranesi—"Sa'aarans" now—could have the land if they could conquer it, but Saan-Kakja was their sovereign. Sandra wondered if Saan-Kakja, with the Imperial example, was taking a step toward empire herself, but she rather doubted it. More likely, she merely intended to keep a closer eye on *this* daughter colony than others in the past, simply due to the nature of its inhabitants. That was understandable.

Ancient Chinakru, leader of the Sa'aarans, and governor of the new colony, wasn't offended. Saan-Kakja had become a surrogate matriarch in the eyes of his people to an almost-worshipful degree. He'd immediately proclaimed all his people subject to her military service and command. Saan-Kakja knew the Sa'aarans couldn't fight a war and build a colony at the same time, but agreed to accept four, including Lawrence, as a token force. They had no military training, but like Lawrence, they were innately, possibly instinctively skilled at fieldcraft. They'd become army scouts, and their "uniform," like Lawrence's, was a modified version of that worn by the Fil-pin regiments, altered to fit their different shapes. The leather armor was dyed in a camouflage pattern, and gray kilts had been tightly twisted and redyed in green. The result was near invisibility for the otherwise brown-and-orange-striped Sa'aarans when they melted into the woods. The three other Sa'araan warriors were preparing to leave for Baalkpan, in fact, to participate in an "expedition of discovery" led by Abel Cook and an old Lemurian hunter called "Moe." Cook was a protégé of Courtney Bradford's, and the mission was a long-delayed effort to find—and hopefully peacefully contact—some feral Grik-like creatures known to roam the dense jungles of north Borno.

"I in uni'orn," Lawrence agreed. (He could understand Lemurian or "American" quite well, but there were some sounds he simply couldn't form.) "I go where I sent, I kill who I told, 'ut no nuglis eat I when I here, where 'riends are!"

"Well said!" complimented Lelaa. "There's plenty of war to go around, for all of us. There's no point in longing for it when it is far away."

"True," Sandra agreed, "but even I'm a little anxious to get underway—the better to *keep* the war as far from here as possible."

"I know why you're anxious," Lelaa proclaimed, "and it has nothing to do with war! Tell me, now there are human females, 'women,' coming here from the east, are you going to finally mate . . . 'marry' with Captain Reddy and stop torturing each other, yourselves, and everyone around you?"

Sandra blushed visibly, even through her tan. "That, Captain Lelaa, is privileged, 'secret' information. While I may allow that you have a 'need to know,' for various reasons"—she straightened and stuck out her chin—"this gossipy, tale-bearing pack of pubescent males surrounding us, does not."

Irvin chuckled, and even Shinya smiled. Lawrence glowered as best he could. Of them all, he truly was a—rapidly and visibly maturing—"teenager," and he took the jest a little more personally than the others.

"As we speak, USS *Maaka-Kakja* is being loaded and provisioned for her voyage," Lelaa said. "Her sea trials were necessarily brief"—she blinked embarrassment at Laumer—"but the very . . . awkwardness of those trials should have revealed any major flaws." It was Irvin's turn to blush. No decision had yet been taken as to what to do with the old S-boat he'd raised from the dead. She might be broken up for her priceless steel and other components; her diesels, electric motors; the list was endless. He was against it and hoped she might eventually be returned to duty as a submarine—despite the added hazards lurking in this world's seas. For the time being, she'd be stabilized and towed to Baalkpan before any decision was made, and that released Irvin Laumer to serve as Lelaa's exec, or "salig-maastir" since he did understand the fundamentals of maneuvering a ship—albeit a much smaller one—under power. Lelaa would continue to teach him the consummate seamanship she'd learned from a lifetime on the waves, while he taught her how to operate a ship without sails. Saan-Kakja admired them both and thought they'd make a good team.

Lelaa's reference to their handling of the massive vessel was not exaggeration, however, and while Irvin blushed and Lelaa blinked, both readily admitted they had a lot to learn. Neither had a clue about flight ops, for example. A few instructors from the Army and Navy Air Corps Academy in Baalkpan had been arriving periodically to teach Fil-pin cadets to fly the "Nancys" being built in Maa-ni-la, and each improvement made in the standardized model was forwarded immediately with detailed explanations. Ultimately, a few improvements cooked up in Maa-ni-la started going back to Baalkpan. Some of the most important training information was constantly being updated as well, and Captain Jis-Tikar, or "Tikker," COFO (Commander of Flight Operations) aboard *Big Sal*, and ultimately First Fleet, forwarded every new, real-world combat technique his fliers learned—sometimes the hard way. Although Tikker's and Mallory's tables of organization had been established, there was no COFO for Second Fleet yet, and if they couldn't swipe one of the Baalkpan instructors, Lelaa and Irvin didn't know where they'd get one.

"In any event," Lelaa continued, "*Maaka-Kakj*a must sail within the week. She'll be accompanied by *Pu-cot* and *Pecos*, the two new, 'fast fleet oilers.'"

"What of warships and transports?" Shinya asked.

"They should be unnecessary. *Maaka-Kakja* carries fifty of the new fifty-pounder smoothbores for serious pounding at close range, and she has four of *Amagi*'s five-point-five-inch secondaries, tied into one of the functional fire control computers that were located above the waterline when *Amagi* sank."

Shinya nodded. "You're right. She should have little to fear. But what of the troops? How many can we take and where will they be put?"

"*Maaka-Kakja* has sufficient space for three full regiments, all their field artillery, pack train, and supplies," Lelaa said proudly. "It will be crowded, of course, with thirty assembled aircraft and another thirty stowed, but you forget; the ship was built for this, not merely converted from a Home. Her hull dimensions are much the same, as you can see"— she pointed at the distant shipyard, and the monstrosity dominating the fueling pier—"but inside, she's laid out much differently and needs only a crew of about a thousand, including flight crews and support elements."

"We can also carry another full regiment, split between the oilers," Sandra prompted.

"I should think so," Shinya said thoughtfully, gazing at the troops on the parade ground. "Roughly four thousand Fil-pin soldiers and Marines," he mused, "would initially outnumber the existing Imperial troop levels, if Captain Reddy's assessment is accurate. What are Saan-Kakja's thoughts regarding sending such a large percentage of her army to this 'other' war?"

"She doesn't like it," Sandra admitted, "but backed by Matt's and Princess Rebecca's arguments, she recognizes the necessity. The Empire and the Holy Dominion are very far away—impossibly far, Meksnaak, her Sky Priest, still says—but there's nothing but the hostile sea between them and the Fil-pin Lands, and now they know we're here. She'd much rather have a friendly Empire of the New Britain Isles as a beholden, distant neighbor, than this . . . perverted, expansionist, 'Holy Dominion.'"

"I see," Shinya said. "In that case, four regiments it shall be." He turned from the group and raised his voice. "Orderly! Pass the word to all commanders; I don't care if they're here or on maneuvers in the mountains! Mandatory officer's call at my HQ tent at"—he glanced at his watch—"nineteen hundred hours—that's fifteen hand-spans from now! I'll be choosing 'volunteers' for a mission, and if they aren't here, they'll definitely miss the show!" He looked at Lelaa and grinned. "Now, tell me truly; not even a 'girl' could ignore such an attractively phrased invitation!"

Suddenly, they were all alarmed by the distant, insistent gonging of a harbor alarm bell, coming from the direction of Fort Maara-vella. It was quickly echoed by others, and the wind-muffled *thud* of one of the great guns in the fort, firing a warning. Shinya ordered another orderly to assemble all officers immediately; then he, Sandra, Lelaa, Irvin, and Lawrence quickly followed the roughly mile-long path Silva had taken earlier down to the ferry pier. They arrived, breathing hard, to find Silva and a group of assorted prospective passengers still waiting for the wide-beamed steam ferry only now approaching from across the bay.

"I bet you're wonderin' what all the fuss is about," Silva grumped as a greeting. He pointed at the mouth of the bay, beyond Corregidor. No one but the humans had ever seen anything like it. Creeping along, black smoke wheezing into the sky, was a medium-size freighter, a Japanese "maru" by the look of her, beneath the easily defined white flag with a red circle in the center, streaming from her foremast. She was low by the bow and seemed somewhat the worse for wear. "Goddamn Japs is invadin' the Philippines," Silva growled. "Again!"

Shinya rapidly collected an armed party of about forty Fil-pin troops and commandeered the ferry to take them out to the wounded ship. Silva went, of course, even though he didn't have his trusty BAR, or even his giant "Doom Whomper" musket, made from a 25-mm Japanese antiaircraft gun. He did have his M-1911 .45, '03 Springfield bayonet and the pattern of 1917 Navy cutlass he always carried. For him, those weapons should be sufficient for nearly anything. Lawrence, Irvin, and Shinya all accepted Maa-ni-la Arsenal "Springfield" muskets, and black leather cartridge boxes of ammunition. Shinya was annoyed to see Sandra and Lelaa take muskets for themselves, naturally intending to accompany him to investigate the intruder. He fumed. If those on the strange ship were hostile, a single machine gun . . . He had to put it out of his mind. It wasn't as though he could order them to stay behind. Lemurian females and the few American women could be so . . . infuriatingly uncooperative! The women beginning to arrive from the Empire behaved more as he was accustomed to, but then he was as horrified as anyone by their formerly "indentured" status. He wondered what that said about him.

"Take in all lines," Silva roared, effectively taking command of the ferry's small deck crew.

Shinya stepped into the cramped, offset, pilothouse directly in front of the single, smoldering funnel. Inside, the small vessel's equally small captain stood alone. The little guy was blinking nervously. "Steer to intercept that ship," Shinya said. In the background, he heard Silva's loud command, "Shove off!"

"But . . . maybe we let Navy ships, closer in, deal with it!" He gestured at one of the speaking tubes beside the wheel. "My signalman already report!"

"Good. Then tell him to send that we're investigating the visitor *before* it has a chance to study our harbor defenses!" The defenses he referred to were already manned, their heavy guns trained on the apparent Japanese ship. Except for the warning shot, none had fired, however. Their crews were under standing orders not to fire on any "anomalous" vessels that might appear without direct orders—unless they were fired on first. "You might also recall that this ferry is a naval auxiliary and you hold a reserve Navy commission." Shinya waved at another voice tube. "If that connects you to the engine room, do tell your engineers to 'step on it'!"

With the loud, monotonous, *whackety-whack, whackety-whack* of the early-model compound engine belowdeck, the relatively new, but already hopelessly outdated little ferry turned toward the strange intruder that seemed to be slowing in response to their approach. "Lay us as close alongside as you can," Shinya instructed, and taking the 'Cat's speaking trumpet, he moved back outside.

"What do you make of her?" Silva asked.

"Probably the same as you," Shinya replied. "She's a Japanese freighter from our 'old' world. Most likely, she arrived here the same way we did. *When* is the first question that strikes me. When and where she 'came through,' as well as how much trouble those aboard her will cause for us."

Silva looked at the dilapidated, heavily damaged ship, and grunted. "She don't look in any shape to cause much trouble, unless she sinks in the main channel and we have to steer around her from now on. Look at all them bullet holes!" Dennis couldn't hide the glee the sight of a shot-up Japanese ship gave him. "I bet she got strafed by planes!" he chortled.

"You may be right," Shinya agreed as they drew closer. Many of the holes did appear to have been caused by heavy machine-gun fire. He let Silva's attitude wash over him with as little notice as a clam gives the marching waves. He knew it wasn't personal, not anymore. He'd long since become almost as "American" as the Lemurian recruits who joined the Navy. He hadn't taken the oath they took, the same oath every human destroyerman had once taken, but he was still "one of them," sworn to the same cause they fought for on this world. If Silva had been given to considering his words before they flew out of his mouth, even he might have been more careful of his tone. The others joined them.

"It's a Jap ship, all right," Silva announced. "A 'ma-roo.' You can kind of tell, even without that damn meatball she's flyin'. Jap-built ships always have a sorta funny look to 'em, like you're lookin' at regular ships through the bottom of a beer bottle. Not ugly, like Dutch ships," he hastened to add, glancing at Shinya, "just . . . weird." His expression changed. "Say, I never got a chance to ask . . . anybody who'd know. How come Jap freighters an' such always hang 'Ma-roo' on the end of their names? Seems like it'd be confusin'."

A little startled by Dennis's unusual chattiness, particularly with him, Shinya tried to explain. "There's a . . . spiritual root I've never closely studied, since I've not been particularly spiritual. I suppose the simplest translation of 'maru' to a sailor might be something like 'beloved home,' but the term also implies an invocation of spiritual protection."

"Didn't work," Silva observed, poking a yellowish wad of Lemurian "tobacco" leaves in his cheek. The local stuff was even worse than the Aryaalan substitute he'd used before, but if there might be a fight, he wanted a chew. "Looks like she's been through a shredder."

"Who knows?" Shinya replied absently, as the damage to the ship became more apparent. "Maybe it did."

Dennis looked at him. "I thought you just said you didn't believe in all that. You gettin' religion, after all?"

Shinya managed a chuckle. "I said, 'I've not been' spiritual, and that's true. I didn't say I *am* not." He shifted uncomfortably, just as unaccustomed to sharing his inner thoughts with the big man, or anyone—with the occasional exception of Pete Alden, Adar, Captain Reddy, and maybe Lieutenant Laumer—as he was to hearing them. "When I consider all we've been through and accomplished, in the face of such a clear distinction between our cause and the evil we resist . . . I find it . . . difficult to imagine there has not been some . . . divine force at work," he admitted.

"Me too," Silva proclaimed with pious conviction, and sent a yellowish stream arcing over the rail. "Say, I see folks movin' around on her now." He squinted his good eye. "None of 'em seems to be pointin' anything noisy at us."

"It may be a 'Jaap' ship," Lelaa said, squinting her far better eyes, "but those 'folks' on her are People—'Cats, like me." She paused. "At least most are. Some are hu-maans."

The battered ship slowed thankfully to a stop just as the ferry came alongside. From the raised letters on her old, straight-up-and-down bow, she was the *Mizuki Maru*, and the battle damage, rust streaks, and cracked, pustulent paint gave the lie to her name, as Shinya translated it. Her appearance wasn't the only thing that made a mockery of "Beautiful Moon," but those on the ferry couldn't know that yet. To their surprise, an oddly familiar face appeared at the rail, peering down at them. The face was all that was familiar about the man, however. He wore leather armor, similar to that used by the Alliance, but the style was more reminiscent of a traditional samurai.

"Commander Sato Okada!" Shinya cried incredulously.

"Yes, I am Okada, although 'Commander' is no longer appropriate." The man shook his head. "That does not signify at present. I am here regarding a matter of utmost urgency, and I must speak to the highest-ranking representative of your Alliance immediately. I presume, in this place, that would still be High Chief Saan-Kakja?"

"That's correct," Shinya answered, "although you must be satisfied with Minister Tucker and myself before you enter the inner harbor. Forgive me, but you made it quite clear you have no allegiance to the Alliance, and your personal animosity toward me and other prominent members gives sufficient reason to question your arrival here, even under such"—Shinya gestured at the ship—"extraordinary circumstances. I must insist this party be allowed aboard before you proceed."

Okada grimaced, but nodded. "Very well. I understand your caution, perhaps more than you will believe." He looked away. "These are indeed dreadful times." He stared back at Shinya. "You were right," he said woodenly, "long ago, when you warned that my honor might yet make heavy demands upon me. . . ." He stopped, nodding at a group of Lemurians who'd gathered to lower a cargo net. "Please do hurry aboard," Okada snapped, "so you can quickly establish my benign intent. In addition to the urgency of my errand and information, you may have noticed this ship has a leak."

Saan-Kakja's Great Hall

"The world we left has gone so terribly wrong," Sato Okada almost whispered, "I have begun to wonder whether our coming here might have been a merciful escape for us all."

Okada was the only one standing in Saan-Kakja's Great Hall. He refused to sit, didn't seem able, and paced almost continuously during the interview. There was a small audience for this . . . momentous event, despite the furor at the dock when *Mizuki Maru* tied up and the boarding party marched tensely ashore with Okada, his officers—and three bedraggled, almost-emaciated human passengers. Sandra's and Laumer's faces had been stormy as they helped the two weakest men down the gangplank. Silva's one eye glittered murderously as he watched from the ship. He'd stay aboard and supervise the placement of more pumps and hoses, but he wouldn't go down in the holds again. He might claw through the steel with his fingernails and sink the hideous abomination he stood upon.

This initial gathering was only for senior personnel so they could absorb what Okada had to say and take measure of his tale before deciding if it had any bearing on current priorities. The story, or part of it, would emerge, of course; Saan-Kakja kept few secrets from her people. But sometimes a thing had to be examined before it was allowed to run loose. Her Sky Priest, Meksnaak, disapproved of this "naïve" policy and sat on a cushion to her left, brooding. Saan-Kakja-s new "best friend," Princess Rebecca Anne McDonald, heir to the Empire of the New Britain Isles, was poised on a comfortable chair to her right, her skin restored with curative lotions and her blond curls carefully coiffed. An expression of concerned distaste distorted her elfin face. Shinya and Lelaa were the senior military representatives present, although Irvin Laumer, "Tex" Sheider, Colonel Ansik-Talaa, and Colonel Busaa of the Coastal Artillery had been allowed. Okada's officers, two Japanese "rescued" from the Grik at Sing-aa-pore, and one Lemurian, all dressed like Okada, remained silently seated. Two of the three "passengers" remained seated as well, attended by Sandra and a corpsman. They wore soft robes in place of tattered remains of what had once been uniforms. One of the men had been too weak to attend.

Saan-Kakja watched Okada now, with her mesmerizing, ebony-striated, golden eyes. Her silky, gray-black fur lay as smooth and perfect as skin. Her ears twitched with compassion for the man. "Perhaps it was an escape for you, but your arrival also saved us from the Grik," she said in her small, satin, but determined tone.

"Not *my* arrival," Okada denied bitterly. "I *aided* the Grik, as first officer of *Amagi!*"

"And ultimately, it was you who warned Baalkpan that she and the 'invincible swarm' of Grik were on their way," Shinya reminded patiently, but with a strange new brittleness, "and thereby saved the city."

"At the cost of my ship—and how many Japanese lives?" Okada retorted. It was the old argument again, the burden that had tortured Okada since his initial "capture" after that terrible battle. Shinya was concerned for a moment that he might retreat into his armored lair of self-pity and remorse, and for the first time, he almost didn't care. But Okada suddenly straightened, and his face bore a new determination.

"As I said, the world we left has gone insane, and that madness continues to spill into this one." He practically seared the Americans present with his stare. "It appears . . . the war we were taken from, that showed such promise for my people, my Empire . . . all of East Asia . . .

has turned against us. The Americans managed a few surprising, costly victories, and now their industrial might has begun to tip the scales." He paused. "In response, it seems some of my countrymen have begun to behave . . . dishonorably."

One of the gaunt "passengers" struggled to rise, his pale face beginning to flush, but Sandra held him back.

Shinya saw this and stood. "Dishonorably?" he demanded, incredulous. "Please spare us the nationalistic rhetoric of another world," he said harshly. He'd seen the ship too; he'd entered that stinking, hellish hold, and the same smells he'd endured in the lower decks of captured *Grik* ships almost drove him to his knees. From that moment, all his doubts and uncertainties about the path he'd chosen melted away. His people "back home" *had* run mad. They'd become Grik in human form, much like Captain Reddy described the Dominion. He'd caught himself praying to whatever force he'd begun to suspect existed that his people's madness might be cured by defeat.

"Start at the beginning and tell us everything!" he demanded. His attempts to assuage Okada's conscience were over, and he was building a towering rage. "Do not dishonor *yourself* with further 'patriotic' excuses, or I'll counsel Her Excellency"—he nodded at Saan-Kakja—"to have you and that . . . diseased vessel expelled without delay!"

Somewhat chastened, but with a resentful expression, Okada began. "When I first came to Maa-ni-la prior to 'repatriation' to my beloved, but sparsely inhabited 'Ja-paan,' the city teemed with Lemurian 'runaways' from other Homes. With the addition of the Fil-pin Lands to the Alliance, those malcontents had few places left to go other than the Great South Island that, so far, hadn't joined the cause. I interviewed thousands. Some were merely cowards, but others had honor, and simply wanted to be left alone. I took the hundred or so with warrior skills— some even disillusioned veterans of the Grik war—who were attracted to the traditional, militantly isolationist Japanese lifestyle I described to them. Together, we established a bakufu—a shogunate—near what would have been Yokohama."

"A shogunate!" Shinya interrupted Okada's narrative. "You *are* ambitious! And I presume you are the Seii Taishogun?"

Okada didn't flinch or apologize. "Someone had to be, and I rule no settlements that do not desire the protection of my Lemurian samurai! We are *not* an imperial government! As I said, I based the system on ancient precedence modified by hindsight, to glean the more benevolent aspects of that culture. I teach Bushido and Kendo—you will not find better swordsmen than my samurai—but I stress the obligation to serve not only myself, but their fellow beings. Also, my samurai are not nobles, but commoners with noble ideals, perhaps more like a militia, dedicated to defending their people from the terrible predators that lurk upon our land—and invaders, of course. They train for these duties diligently, but they hunt and kill the great fish for their oil and flesh. They are not the aristocratic, bureaucratic leeches they once became on our world!"

"So you say . . . for now," Shinya muttered. "Tell me, do you have *female* samurai?"

"Yes," Okada said simply, and Shinya blinked. "As you know, female Lemurians can be formidable warriors. With their size and agility, few males can match them in 'the way of the sword.'"

"Please continue your tale, of the pertinent events," Saan-Kakja directed.

"At first, things went well. Most of the preexisting settlements around the Okada Shogunate willingly fell under its umbrella and enjoyed a new security and prosperity. According to their wishes, many of the Japanese sailors rescued from the Grik at Singapore were sent to us, and our society began to thrive. Then, in a single day, war found our new Ja-paan, and everything changed."

"What happened?" Princess Rebecca asked, her gaze intent.

"A short distance up the coast from our tiny new Yokohama, we saw dense smoke rising from Ani-aaki, a 'protected' settlement," Okada reported somberly. "A me-naak rider brought news of a most bizarre invasion. Iron ships had appeared off the coast, and humans came ashore. At first they seemed friendly, only afraid and confused. They spoke Japanese, a tongue many of my people have begun to learn, but did not know where they were. The people of Ani-aaki tried to explain what might have happened to them, based on our experience, but they didn't want to hear. They didn't believe it at first. Then they *did* believe, and officers came ashore to talk some more. The boat went back to the ships, and dozens returned, bringing many, many humans." He gestured at the two weak men. "Back and forth the boats went, until the beach before the village was packed." His face darkened. "Then things went very bad. Troops with rifles, *Japanese* troops, began taking food, supplies, anything they could find. Some of the local samurai tried to resist. . . ." He paused. "They were shot. A panic ensued, and many people fled into the forest." Again he gestured at the two men. "So did a number of the people brought ashore." He shook his head, his face contorted with grief, rage, and shame. "The troops began shooting everyone! They killed the young, old, males and females, all while still looting the village. Even the humans they brought ashore tried to help the People, but they were weak and easily killed." He looked around the chamber at the horrified faces and agitated blinking.

"Two other boats came ashore with what must have been heavy machine guns . . . and killed *everyone* they saw! Many more tried to flee into the forest, but most were shot down. Finally, when nothing and no one remained, they set fire to the village and left." He took a deep breath. "They transported the crew from *Mizuki Maru* to other ships and simply abandoned her there." He shrugged. "She was badly damaged, as you've seen, and slowing the other ships down."

"What other ships?" Sandra demanded with an edge.

Okada looked at her grimly. "A quite-modern Japanese Imperial Navy destroyer, I'm afraid, and one of the tankers she was sent to escort—to Yokohama. The destroyer is the *Hidoiame*, and she's less than a year old." His face wore a strange expression. "She is the newest thing in anti-submarine warfare, I'm told."

"Who told you?" Sandra and Laumer both demanded at once.

"One of *Mizuki Maru*'s crewmen who elected to remain behind, and also fled into the woods," he said matter-of-factly.

"Well . . . who's he, and why would he do that?"

"He was the ship's cook," Okada said simply. "And he is likely the reason they killed all the people they brought ashore." He looked at the uncomprehending faces. "You see," he added bitterly, "when asked if he could, if it came down to it . . . he refused to *cook* them!"

There was a collective, horrified gasp in the chamber, but Okada continued remorselessly on. "His act probably kept the officers from slipping entirely over the edge, and they decided to just kill all the 'useless' mouths instead."

"Defenseless prisoners, you mean!" grated the tall, skinny man at Sandra's side. He looked much older than he probably was; his hair prematurely white and his eyes and cheeks sunken in. He'd given up trying to stand, but there were tears on his face and he clearly intended to talk. "All those men were prisoners of war, not as if you could tell it by the way they treated us. More than five hundred men, slaughtered!" He glared at Okada. "And that's not the half of it!" He paused to collect himself. "I'm Second Lieutenant Jack Mackey, forty-one-C, from Big Spring, Texas. I was in the Thirty-fourth Squadron of the Twenty-fourth Pursuit Group." He nodded at his companion. "This is Second Lieutenant Orrin Reddy of the Third Pursuit Squadron, out of San Diego. He's also forty-one-C—we were 'newies' together." He looked apologetically at Sandra as the tears began to pool at his feet. "The Thirty-fourth was almost all Texans," he said. "There were other Southern boys too, but only one Yankee, out of Illinois . . . I don't know what happened to him."

"There were fellas from everywhere in the Third," whispered the man beside him, but that was all he managed to say. He couldn't seem to take his eyes off Saan-Kakja, however.

Mackey nodded. "Look," he said, "I don't know much about what's going on here. Sometimes I think I'm still in hell and this is just a dream. I hope somebody besides him"—he jerked his head at Okada—"can fill us in, but I guess something weird happened to us, and some of you too." He shook his head. "Tin cans, submarines, PBYs—all that stuff you said after you met us with the ferry—seems as if this joint's a regular dumping ground for folks and stuff that disappear where we're from. . . ."

"*When* are you from, Tex?" Sheider asked anxiously. "I mean, sure, you were in the Philippines when the Japs came, but when did you get, you know, *here*?"

Taken aback, Mackey looked at the submariner. "Well, we figured, once we saw Japan was all goofed up, it must've had something to do with a screwy storm we went through a week or so before. What? Did the same thing happen to you?"

"Yeah. Well, the destroyermen saw it; we were underwater," Laumer supplied. "Said it was a big, scary green squall of some kind."

Mackey shook his head. "We didn't see it. We were all belowdecks on that damn, nasty tub. We felt it, though. Queer."

"We 'came through' around March first, 'forty-two. You've got almost two years on us. What happened to you . . . and how's the war going?"

Mackey blinked and looked disoriented. "Gosh, I don't know where to start! I'll tell what happened to us; then maybe I can bring you up to speed on the war later." He looked at Okada. "The Jap's right, though. We didn't get a lot of news; I was in a camp outside of"—he shrugged—"well, I guess not far from here," he said oddly. "But sometimes, Filipinos on the outside who had radios stashed snuck in the big headlines to us when they could, to keep our morale up." He glared at Okada again. Apparently, the man's earlier comments still rankled. "The Jap's goose is cooked, and we've got 'em on the run. That was why they started shipping us prisoners out of the Philippines to Japan where they could keep working us to death. We got on that damn maru—you should've seen the sign they posted! Everything you can imagine, basically breathing at the wrong time, would get you shot and thrown over the side! Anyway, we were some of the first ones sent. More than a thousand got on another ship, just a few hundred on the one that brought us here—it was just stopping through. Had a bunch of Brits, Aussies, Dutch, and Javanese slaves already in her. Neither ship was marked to show there were prisoners aboard, and the other ship got torpedoed and sunk by a sub. We got strafed by planes and took an aerial torpedo, but the fish just poked a hole in the bow and didn't go off. Drowned a bunch of guys down in the forward hold—hell, the Japs on deck shot fellas trying to get out! It was unbelievable!"

Okada stood still at last, staring straight ahead, his face granite. Shinya looked almost ill.

"They kept us down in the holds like animals, cattle—worse! Hell, nobody would ship *animals* like that! I don't know how many died every day; starved, sick, thirsty, covered in filth. . . ." For a moment, he couldn't go on. "Finally," he said at last, "we got to Japan—only it wasn't there! We didn't know what was up, but the Japs on deck got all screwy and yelled a lot. A couple of our guys were China Marines, out of the Fourth, and had some of the lingo. They said the Japs kept jabbering that 'the world was gone,' or something. Anyway, there was nothing we could do but wait in the dark until things sort of settled down."

One of Saan-Kakja's attendants brought refreshments, and Mackey took a mug, staring at the 'Cat the whole time. Like most Lemurians, she wasn't wearing a top, and because he was seated, her breasts were prominent and right at Mackey's eye level. Sandra understood his reaction; it had been universal among *Walker*'s crew when they first met the "People." Mackey had seen Lemurians before now, among Okada's folk, but he couldn't be used to it yet. She nodded, and he took a tentative sip from the mug.

"Uh, thank you, ma'am," he said to the 'Cat, a little self-consciously.

"What then?" Sandra pressed gently.

"After that, things went pretty much like Okada said. They herded us ashore and just started shooting." Mackey looked at his companion. "Orrin and I and a bunch of other fellas lit out as best we could." The tears started again. "Most were too weak or too far gone to even try, and of those that did, just a few made it."

"How many?"

"All told, maybe sixty out of five hundred," he said, taking a long gulp from the cup and holding it tight in both hands. "Mostly Americans and Filipinos, I guess, but a few Brits and Aussies too. And some of those poor Javanese." He shook his head. "I think those poor devils had it worse than any of us. They *were* animals, far as the Japs were concerned, and were practically dead when we first saw 'em."

"Didn't they chase you?" Laumer asked.

Mackey shook his head. "What for?" He sighed. "I don't know. They couldn't feed us, they'd decided not to . . . eat us, and they damn sure didn't *want* us. Maybe they figured killing us was a mercy."

"So, sixty-odd survivors," Sandra said hopefully.

"No, ma'am. Not now. Some were wounded, and others just . . . died. Too far gone, I guess. I'll give Okada's people that. They did their best to save us. Took pretty good care of us, as a matter of fact." He passed Okada an almost-apologetic glance. "I was mainly mad about that 'happy East Asia' bunk he was spouting earlier. . . ." He considered. "I guess there're maybe forty-five of us left, or there were. He brought Orrin and me along to prove his story, and because we were some of the fittest officers for travel. Sergeant Cecil Dixon—he's the other man—saved us too many times to count. We insisted he come too. There're other guys in better shape than us; some Filipino Scouts, some Army footsloggers"— he shook his head—"and those China Marines. Weird ducks, but talk about survivors! We left them in charge."

"No other officers?"

"There are; even a captain and a major, but most are in pretty rough shape. Everything from dysentery to malaria. Some of them are probably goners too, unless you have quinine."

Sandra shook her head. "No quinine, I'm afraid, but we have other things that may help. We'll do everything we can." A bolt of terror suddenly slashed through her. "Commander Okada! Malaria!"

Okada was already nodding grimly. So far, the mosquitoes of this world, at least in the areas they'd touched, didn't carry or transmit anything they'd noticed. Animals and 'Cats did get sick with evident viruses, but nothing seemed to pass to humans, or vice versa, and mosquitoes left nothing but large, itchy welts that sometimes got topically infected. Some of *Walker*'s crew had suffered from malaria before, but there'd been no recurrences. Sandra theorized mosquitoes here had evolved a means of "decontaminating" the blood they took. After all, passing diseases among one's food supply seemed a rather illogical evolutionary adaptation. Or maybe it wasn't that at all. Maybe something in the diet here, perhaps even the various inebriating or curative products derived from the amazing polta fruit once again played a role? Regardless . . .

"Those with diseases of that sort are kept inside at all times, smeared with protective lotions, and surrounded by a cordon of smoky fires." Okada said. "It is all we can do."

Sandra noticed he didn't blame the sick men for this new threat to "his" people. Furthermore, he'd already considered the risk, and he took it anyway. That spoke well for him.

Throughout this exchange, Saan-Kakja had remained silent, absorbing all. Like her friend Rebecca, she was a mere youngling, even by her people's standards; yet she'd displayed a level of maturity, wisdom, and determination far beyond her years in many respects. She continued to do so now by cutting to the heart of the matter.

"You have made your report . . . Mr. Okaa-daa. Forgive me if I'm not yet familiar with this new title you claim. I will try to learn how to speak it. You have my gratitude, and that of the Alliance as a whole, I'm sure. Not only have you rendered assistance to friends of our friends, but you bring warning of this . . . rogue force that wanders waters the Alliance considers its own. As I said before, we must decide how this news affects our priorities—and what we can do for you in return for this service."

"With respect, Your Excellency, I might make a few recommendations—and a request."

Saan-Kakja glanced briefly at her advisors and bowed her head.

"First, beyond a perhaps-increased patrol, equipped with the wireless gear you possess, we were not challenged short of your harbor defenses ourselves," he inserted pointedly, "you should not significantly alter your plans. I understand you suffered sorely from the tsunami that also lightly affected my land, and in addition to the Grik menace, you also confront a new enemy in the east."

"That is true," Saan-Kakja conceded, "and with the demands of war and disaster, few resources have been spared for patrolling waters we considered secure. That must change. But surely, with this 'Hido-i-aame' full of murderers on the loose, we cannot ignore it!"

"You must not," Okada agreed, "but it is alone and isolated for now. I trust you have monitored no transmissions of unknown origin?"

Shinya's face reflected some doubt, but he shook his head. "There's always . . . noise that sounds tantalizingly like communications, but nothing definitive from any but expected sources. If *Hidoiame* or her consort transmitted, they'd be heard."

"I'm sure they *can* transmit," Okada said, "Even *Mizuki Maru* has serviceable, if antiquated communications gear." He blinked. "I'm frankly astonished they didn't take it with them, or destroy it. Possibly, they were still somewhat overwhelmed. Regardless, you can be sure they've been monitoring *your* transmissions. Most likely, your code is secure, but they will recognize it as an *American* code. They will be cautious. They have no idea what they face, and no real understanding of their situation beyond what the people of Ani-aaki tried to tell them."

His face clouded. "They will search for a place to stop, refit, consider their circumstances—much as we . . . or the American destroyers did when they arrived. Though powerful, I doubt they will seek heavily populated areas, at least with the same aggression they displayed at my Home. That said, even with the tanker, one of their most pressing concerns will be fuel, and that narrows the regional choices their commanders might make. The American defenses at Tarakan Island should be strengthened, for example. It was well-known in our world to be rich in petroleum. If they arrive here, or at other well-defended Allied ports, they could stand off beyond the range of your heavy guns and do much damage to your forts, but not enough to survive a forced passage, I suspect. *Hidoiame* is no *Amagi*. Consider her a more modern, more capable version of *Walker*. Even she couldn't enter Maa-ni-la if you didn't want her to. If *Hidoiame* does come seeking assistance, enters within range of your guns, you will know her. You can pound her to scrap or force her surrender, and capture the murderers aboard. In any event, as long as she does not slip so far away as to join your"—he paused, and his jaw muscles worked—"*our* enemies, there are only so many places she can hide without our learning her whereabouts."

Saan-Kakja blinked. "And should we learn her whereabouts, what do you propose we do?"

"I have a request, several actually, but they all serve the same end. First, I beg membership in the Grand Alliance on behalf of my people. I understand there are elements who desire to create a more formal—even permanent—union of the member states, and I—we—do not wish to be considered part of that faction at present, but I will guarantee loyal service for the duration of the current hostilities, however long they last. To facilitate that service, I beg that a medical mission be sent to Yokohama to tend those injured in the recent invasion, and to transport the former prisoners back here where they may be more properly tended, and perhaps employed by the cause. Finally, I ask that *Mizuki Maru* be immediately moved into your new dry dock so she might be properly repaired and sufficiently modified with increased bunker capacity, armor, or protective structures for her machinery, and as much of *Amagi*'s salvaged secondary armament as can quickly be dispatched here from Baalkpan. These modifications will be undertaken with an eye to retaining *Mizuki Maru*'s original, helpless appearance."

Saan-Kakja hesitated only a moment. "O-kay," she said, and the colloquialism sounded strange from her lips. "The work you speak of will require considerable time and resources, but I will grant them if you tell me . . . why I should?"

Okada took a breath and his eyes flashed. "I'm sure you already suspect the answer, Your Excellency. *Hidoiame* is a threat to the Alliance. Moreover, her officers at least are responsible for the murder of helpless prisoners and more than a hundred People of Ani-aaki who were under *my* protection. I desire that my first assignment as a member of the Grand Alliance be to hunt down and take or kill *Hidoiame* and the tanker accompanying her, as well as everyone aboard them."

"Very well, Mr. Okaa-daa. I accept your offer, your counsel, and your request." Meksnaak stirred himself to protest, but Saan-Kakja silenced him with a glare. "It will be done," she said. "I will request the arms you ask in my next dispatch to Chairman Adar. I don't know what remains to be spared, but there should be something. A new frigate is currently being coppered in the dry dock, but the task will be complete in a few days. Your . . . *Maa-ru* will be the next ship to go in." She looked at Shinya and Lelaa. "Second Fleet will depart as scheduled, but remain extra vigilant for this Jaap destroyer."

"Thank you," Captain Lelaa said. "Maybe we'll find her. With our planes and long-range guns from *Amagi*, I hope we do! She can be no match for the mighty *Maaka-Kakja*," she boasted.

"You're probably right," Okada said, but added ominously; "unless she has torpedoes!"

That thought sent a chill through everyone. It had been so long since *Walker* had any torpedoes, they'd almost forgotten about the weapons. There were few enemy targets worthy of the complicated machines. Bernie Sandison had a program dedicated to creating more, but it had received a low priority. Saan-Kakja determined to recommend he "get on the stick."

"Colonel Shinya," she continued, "I'm glad you've decided to go east yourself. Please inform the quartermaster which regiments you will take, and what their requirements are." She gazed at him fondly. "I'll miss you." She looked at Rebecca, Sandra, and Laumer. "I'll miss you all. But Captain Reddy needs you, and we will be fine here."

The meeting began to dissolve. Okada looked at Shinya, gave him a brisk nod, and turned toward the chamber entrance, followed by his officers. Sandra, Laumer, and the corpsman helped the two former prisoners to their feet, and Shinya started to join them. Apparently, he thought better of it, and moved to speak further with Saan-Kakja.

"You're both fliers, correct?" Sandra asked the men.

"Yeah," Orrin answered, speaking directly to her for the first time. "Used to be. Probably not much use for us in the fight you've got here—although when there weren't any more planes, Mack and I both fought with the Forty-fifth Philippine Scouts. We were in an antiaircraft crew on Corregidor when Wainwright threw in the towel too."

"You might be surprised." Laumer grinned.

"About what?"

"We *have* planes, homebuilt mostly, and pretty good ones. But also a few you might recognize." Now Orrin remembered the one called "Captain Lelaa" referring to "planes," and his ears perked up.

"No kidding?" Mackey demanded. He took on an almost-dreamy look. "Boy, it'd be swell to fly again." Irvin Laumer looked significantly at Sandra. "Air Minister" Colonel (after his latest escapade) Benjamin Mallory was about to get yet another present.

"No kidding," Irvin confirmed. "As a matter of fact, one of our new long-range jobs'll be here tomorrow on its semiweekly run. It's a goofy-looking beast; kind of like a PBY with three engines."

The Baalkpan and Maa-ni-la "Internal Combustion Engine factories," or "ICEhouses" as they'd come to be known, had virtually perfected the manufacture of a ridiculously simple, and even further simplified, Wright-Gypsy-type engine. The Alliance relied on them for everything from aircraft power plants, to "portable" generators and boat motors. So many were being produced that they had enough to send out spares—and experiment with multiengine aircraft. The little engines performed well and were extremely reliable since there was so little to go wrong with them. Mallory took them so much for granted now that he'd started bellyaching for bigger, lighter, air-cooled versions, and had begun to experiment with radials. "Officially, they're PB-2s," Irvin continued, "but everybody calls 'em 'Buzzards.' You'll see why. Anyway, they carry ten passengers, or about two thousand pounds of freight. If you guys are up to it, we can get you and your buddy on its return flight to Baalkpan. That's where the real 'air stuff' is going on."

"That'd be swell," Mackey repeated, "as long as I know everybody we left behind'll be taken care of."

"Of course they will be," Sandra assured him. Suddenly, she remembered something she'd meant to ask earlier. "Excuse me, Lieutenant Reddy—Orrin. You said you're from San Diego?"

"Not originally," the young man replied. "I was born in Texas, like Mack, but my folks picked up and ran for California when the dust bowl hit."

"I don't suppose . . ." She shook her head. How common was the Reddy name?

"What?"

"Well, you wouldn't happen to be related to a Matthew Patrick Reddy, of the Navy?"

Orrin looked at her, astonished. "Sure. Tall guy? Brown hair, green eyes?"

Sandra nodded.

"He's my first cousin! Six, seven years older than me. Used to take me hunting and fishing on his dad's place. A *good* guy, but always bossing me around. I guess I needed it, though. . . . Say, you don't mean . . . ?" Sandra was still nodding, a grin spreading across her face. "I swear. The last letter I got from home, Mom wrote that he and his whole ship were MIA." The sudden excitement seemed to tire the young man, and he slumped. "Of course, *I've* been MIA since shortly after that. Where is he?"

Sandra sobered. "Right now, he's halfway around the world." She managed a grin. "I'll be going to join him with our new aircraft carrier within the week."

"You his girl?"

Sandra hesitated, but only for a moment. Old habits die hard. "Yes," she said. "I am."

Orrin shook his head in admiration. "I figured you must be, soon as I realized what you were talking about. You're the best-looking dame around, and Cousin Matt always could pick 'em!"

Sandra's face heated, but the grin stayed. "There aren't many 'dames' to choose from, but that's starting to change. There are almost none where you're going yet, but some will be along once they've been processed. There are plenty where Matt is now."

"Maybe *that*'s where we should go?" Mackey suggested hopefully.

Sandra laughed. "Maybe one of you, if you're fit, but not all. Captain Lelaa might need someone with combat experience to advise her on air operations, even if our carrier aircraft are seaplanes." She looked at the two pilots appraisingly. "And neither of you fly until you've got some meat back on your bones. That's a medical order. Beyond that, if one of you feels up to the job, take it up with Captain Lelaa. The rest of you belong to Colonel Mallory!"

Orrin still seemed tired, but more engaged—far more so than during the conference. "Well of course I should go!" he said. "Matt Reddy's family, after all."

Mackey seemed philosophical. "Okay," he said, "but there has to be a trade-off, if I go to this 'Baalkpan' place."

"Sure," said Sandra. "Good people, a relatively secure rear area to rest up, and a *lot* hotter aircraft!" She looked at Orrin. "And I hate to tell you, but Matt's still going to be bossing you around!"

The next morning, the PB-2 flew over Maa-ni-la Bay when the purple-gray sky was marred only by an orange-pink slash. It rumbled over the water as if searching for a roost amid the haphazard cluster of masts and ships moored close in. Immense, seagoing Homes rested at anchor with their "wings" stowed diagonally across their decks like massive, snowy ridgelines, and Lemurians went about their morning chores aboard them. The two steam oilers that would accompany USS *Maaka-Kakja* east were jockeying for position at the fueling pier the carrier had abandoned during the night. They looked a lot like Allied frigates, but they weren't as heavily armed and had broader beams.

Like the "Buzzard" she did resemble, with her fixed wingfloats that gave her a droop-winged appearance, the PB-2 lumbered slowly in, banked, and settled for a landing on the water short of the new pier dedicated to her visits. Line handlers awaited her approach as the pilot killed all but the center engine and maneuvered her expertly to a stop.

Sandra, Lawrence, and Irvin Laumer watched all this from the pier.

Irvin was there to greet the tired passengers that crawled from the cramped waist of the plane. Most were "newies" from the Baalkpan Army-Navy Air Corps Training Center, and he'd take them to *Maaka-Kakja*. He didn't have to be there, but the ship didn't have a COFO yet. Besides, he liked to come down and look at the old S-19, moored nearby. She'd been his first command. There was just a skeleton crew aboard now, including Danny Porter and Sandy Whitcomb. Both had other jobs during the day, but they still slept on the boat. They'd accompany her to Baalkpan. Irvin knew the sub was a wreck, and her problems were almost insurmountable. Still, he couldn't help thinking they'd need her someday.

Sandra was there to meet the PB-2's copilot, or still more appropriately, her spotter/wireless operator who'd sent that he had a letter for her from Karen Letts, and after the traffic they'd begun picking up late the previous day, she felt compelled to get it herself. Lawrence came along simply because at some point, however briefly, Sandra might be by herself. She refused a protective detail, but he and a number of others had determined that nobody "important" ever be alone again. There was no mad "Company" warden in Maa-ni-la, but there were dissatisfied elements.

Tremendous activity was already underway at the waterfront. Troops had been crossing from Bataan all night and marching through the bustling shipyard district to bivouac on the plain beyond the city to prepare for embarkation. The predawn departure of the Maa-ni-la fishing fleet had caused some disorganization, but everything seemed back under control now. *Mizuki Maru* was still there, floating much higher in the water with the aid of shore-based pumps.

"Okay, dammit!" came a surly cry from within the passenger compartment of the plane. "I'm *gettin'* out! Quit pokin' me!" A last, unexpected passenger crept carefully through the tiny hatch, and Sandra was surprised to recognize Gilbert Yeager, one of the bizarrely eccentric, original "Mice," from *Walker's* firerooms. He was a chief now, but at heart, he'd always be a boilerman who loved nothing more than the music of steam and forced-draft fires. Despite his exalted status, he still looked like a rodent, sniffing the air and squinting his eyes. "Joint's changed since I was here last," he declared disapprovingly.

"Mr. Yeager!" Sandra exclaimed. "I never dreamed they'd pry you away from your . . . colleague, Mr. Rueben, once you'd been reunited!"

Gilbert snatched the new, somehow already grimy "Dixie cup" from his head and clutched it in his hands. "Beggin' yer pardon, Miz Tucker," he said, "but it was my damn turn, I s'pose. Isak went off last time, an' he's busy helpin' to overhaul them jug-jumpers on *Santa Catalina*. He'll prob'ly go back to First Fleet after that. They figgered there oughta be *somebody* in this new flat-top, might could light a fire in her guts an' make her go."

"I guess that means you belong to me," Irvin said with a neutral expression. He was ecstatic to have Gilbert for his experience, but . . . along with that experience, there was Gilbert to consider. He didn't know the man well, but his reputation was widespread. Oh well, at least he wasn't as weird as Isak. . . .

"You say so, sir," Gilbert replied forlornly. With the weary fliers and the unexpected addition in hand, Irvin took his leave of Sandra and Lawrence.

The 'Cat aircrew scrambled ashore, their new goggles pushed up between their ears, resembling another pair of darker eyes. They saluted Sandra. "Min'ster Tukker," one said, "this for you." He handed over a folded, rumpled sheet, sealed with a blob of wax. "We got more mail too!" he added. The other 'Cat, probably the pilot, saluted again and went to oversee the refueling of his plane. When he was satisfied it was in good hands, the aircrew would snatch a few hours of sleep before taking off again.

"More?"

"Yes! We bring new mail, person-aal!" The Lemurian seemed more excited that people could send personal letters so quickly than he was about wireless. "Whole big saack. I bring aa-shore, now I know somebody offish-aal here to see it get here!" He blinked seriously in the growing light. "I s'posed to waatch mail till then with one eye. No foolin!"

It wasn't really a very big sack, and Lawrence took it. Sandra unfolded the letter from Karen as they walked away from the pier. They were finally making real paper in Baalkpan. She smiled at the hurriedly written note from her friend, describing the antics of her new daughter,

Allison Verdia, but frowned when she noted Karen's complaint about her husband, Alan, going "off to the war" when he didn't have to. She felt a surge of irritation. Ultimately, it could be argued none of the "old" destroyermen, the humans, *had* to fight this war. When Lemurians took the same oath to join the same Navy the humans served, it wasn't *really* the same, and everybody knew it. The United States of America didn't even exist here. Though Matt considered the oath very real and essential, any 'Cat would tell you that ultimately, their oath was to Captain Reddy; the High Chief of the Amer-i-caan Naa-vee clan. Maybe Matt really didn't see a difference. Sandra knew the meaning of *his* oath hadn't changed—although it had been expanded considerably to encompass his new people. Still, if any of his "old hands" wanted to "retire" and go off in the jungle and live in a hut somewhere, Matt would probably let them.

She quickly forgave her friend. Karen had come a long way from the sobbing wreck she'd been when they first "got here." If she was feeling put upon because her husband ran off to the sound of the guns, leaving her with a new baby and all her responsibilities as Deputy Minister of Medicine—doing Sandra's job in her absence—it was understandable.

Sandra's attention snapped back to the moment at the sound of a horrified shriek.

In their path stood a dark-haired, dusky-skinned woman in the loose-fitting, somewhat immodest working garb of the recently arrived immigrants from Respite Island. Sandra knew that, as they were "processed," the women—virtual slaves within the Empire—were encouraged to wander the city at their own pace to grow accustomed to their freedom and this new culture. The processing consisted of little more than a checkup, a few short lectures about the laws and customs of Maa-ni-la, Baalkpan, and the seagoing Homes, and the assurance they could stay in their arrival compound where food and shelter were provided for a "reasonable" period while they decided whether they wanted to find a life in Maa-ni-la (there was plenty of work in the factories and ship-yards), go on to Baalkpan (this was encouraged), or even join the Navy. (As far as Sandra knew, this last option hadn't been seriously discussed with Matt; it was simply assumed. Female Lemurians joined the Navy, after all.)

The woman gave only the one cry, but stood ready to bolt, staring at Lawrence, her dark, pretty face contorted by an expression of terror.

"Don't run, scared lady," Lawrence said as softly as he could. "I not eat you!"

"Yes, please!" Sandra said. "He's a friend! Perfectly ah . . . tame." Sandra immediately regretted the inappropriate term. Lawrence wasn't an animal. She hoped he wasn't offended. "Do you understand?"

The woman assumed a doubtful expression, but some of the tension left her. "Course I do. Yer speakin' ainglish, ain't ye?"

Sandra was taken aback by the weird, almost-Cockney accent coming from what looked like a Polynesian princess. "Why, yes I am."

"An' he ain't a dee-min, then? Looks loik a dee-min, er divil!"

"He's neither, I assure you. He's my good friend, and a friend of Princess Rebecca McDonald, daughter of the Governor-Emperor. His name's Lawrence, and mine's Sandra Tucker. What's yours?"

The woman began to relax, but seemed to realize how brusquely she'd spoken to someone she shouldn't even have addressed where she came from. She almost fled again, but maybe the lectures had gotten through, and she went to one knee and bowed her head instead. "Diania," she whispered.

A burst of anger jolted Sandra. She hadn't had a chance to visit the immigrant women, and now she knew she should've made time. The now-dead "Honorable New Britain Company" had long fostered a system of virtually perpetual indenture of women in the Empire to such a degree that even "free" women had little status. Matt had sent reports that seethed with his own disgust regarding the situation, and inflamed Sandra's indignation, but this was her first real encounter with what he'd been talking about. "Stand up, Diania, and face me!" she demanded.

"Aye'm," said the woman, and hastily stood, but kept her head bowed. She might have been slightly taller than Sandra if she stood straight, but Sandra wouldn't press or berate her—yet.

"Remember," she said more gently, "it's different here than where you're from. Soon, it'll be different there," she swore. "You may always bow your head as a sign of respect, if you choose, but never kneel to anyone!" She gestured ahead. "Lawrence and I were just heading back to

Navy headquarters—to deliver the mail." She smiled. "Would you care to walk with us?"

"Ah . . ." Diania said, teetering, but nodded. "Aye'm, if ye wouldnae mind. P'raps ye may halp me wi' me thoughts."

"Of course," Sandra said, encouraged. Together, the trio resumed walking. "Maybe you'd like some advice about what to do next?" she guessed.

"Aye'm," Diania mumbled. "I labored in tha Comp'ny repair yard on Respite. I'm a carpentress by trainin'." She held out her small hands, proudly displaying the calluses. "I kin go ta the Manilly shipyard fer work, but I know naught aboot Baalkpan." She seemed amazed she had a *choice* to go there.

"It's much the same," Sandra said. "Not quite as large, and surrounded by thicker forests. Hotter too. But there's more innovation, more experimentation. It's becoming more iron and steel oriented, however. I suspect the machine shops are the finest in the world and the foundries are probably beginning to rival anything in the Empire." There was still much steel being salvaged from sunken *Amagi* in the bay, but Commander Brister had Baalkpan's first Bessemer process foundries turning out real steel now as well. He had both open hearth and electric arc blast furnaces to play with.

Diania looked dubious. She knew little about metals, except some made better tools than others.

Sandra suddenly smiled inwardly. "Of course, you *could* join the Navy. They're always looking for good carpenter's mates," she said in a casual tone.

That afternoon, many gathered at the "Buzzard's Roost" to witness the departure of the PB-2. Lieutenant Mackey and Sergeant Cecil Dixon would be making the trip to Baalkpan, leaving Orrin Reddy to go east with Sandra and Task Force *Maaka-Kakja*. Sister Audry, the Dominican nun who'd endured the same captivity, travails, and terrors as those abducted by the criminal Billingsley, was going back to Baalkpan too, along with Sa'aaran "scouts" and Abel Cook. Now that it was time to go, Abel was reluctant to leave despite the exciting mission that awaited him. He had a fair-size, long-standing crush on Princess Rebecca, and there was no telling when he'd see her again. Sandra, Rebecca, and Captain Lelaa hugged Audry, and Tex, Laumer, Lawrence, and Midshipman Brassey gave her respectful salutes. Audry smiled wistfully, then made her way carefully into the cramped fuselage. The ground crew scampered out on the broad wing and spun the dorsal engine until it coughed to life.

"Now all that remains is that ridiculous Dennis Silva," Rebecca said. Her tone belied the words. She was sorry to see Abel go, and wasn't at all happy Dennis was leaving. Drooped across her shoulders was a small, strange, brightly colored, feathery reptile named Petey, who'd adopted the princess on Shikarrak Island. He had membranous wings of a sort, and though he couldn't fly, he could glide considerable distances. He also had a very foul mouth since he could imitate speech like a parrot— and some of the first words he'd heard were spoken by Dennis Silva. His vocabulary had improved somewhat, as had his possible understanding of the significance of a word or two. The only word he was known to understand entirely was "eat."

"Rid-culus Silva!" the creature chirped, acting suspiciously as if looking for the man.

"Here I am, you little creep!" boomed a voice.

"Creep!" Petey screeched. "Goddamn!"

"Shush now, dear," Rebecca said, stroking the little lizardy head. Her tone became more severe when she saw Silva bowling through the crowd. "Here you are at last! Everyone is waiting for you!" She paused, almost speechless. "What on earth have you been doing?" she finally managed. Silva was literally covered from head to foot with thick, dark grease.

"Uh . . . well, I was over at the bearing works, helpin' some 'Cats play machinist, see? Somethin' happened, an' . . . we had us a calammitus grease-packin' dee-zaster. Well, I realized the time, an' figgered I better light along here before I was listed AWOL an' hanged." He held up a tiny rag. "I'll wipe this goop off on the way. It'll give me somethin' to do."

"Silva . . . you're . . . indescribable." Sandra giggled.

"Aw shucks. Thanks," he said with his lopsided, signature grin, which always made Sandra a bit nervous. "Seems ever'body's always either wantin' me hanged, or heapin' me with praise!"

"Or grease," Laumer inserted.

Silva opened his arms wide and advanced toward Rebecca. "Gimme a hug, li'l sis!"

The princess backed away. "I will *not*! Go away this instant, you filthy beast!"

Dennis shrugged, then turned to Sandra and the others and snapped a sharp, greasy salute. "So long," he said. "Don't never say I didn't warn ya, when vicious sea monsters is pullin' yer ships down to doom, the beer's too warm, and ever'thing's goin' awry 'cause ol' Silva ain't there to save the day!" He darted for the plane, and just before he vanished through the tiny hatch, he tossed something at the water, but it took a wrong bounce on the dock and rolled to a stop on the wooden planks.

Its last passenger aboard, the ground crew spun the outboard props and scurried back to the pier. With the newly started engines at idle, the strange seaplane wallowed away and made for a clearing in the harbor traffic.

"He *is* a spiteful, senseless beast," Rebecca said sternly, tears streaking her face.

"Yes, he is," Sandra agreed with a small smile. Brassey had gone to retrieve whatever it was Silva tossed. He brought it to them, carefully unwadding a sheet of paper. "It would seem Mr. Silva got some mail as well," Sandra observed, taking the page. "I probably shouldn't read it." She did.

Lughead:

    Now you're not dead anymore, Mr. Riggs say's you're coming home.

    I know you won't want to, probably because something needs doing, but I miss you so bad. Risa's gone, you're gone, and I'm stuck here all alone. Our whole little family has fallen apart. You're MINE, you big goon, and if you skip out on me, I swear I'll marry that stump Laney, just to spite you.

               Love and lots of kisses,
               Pam

She wished she hadn't. The reference to Risa still didn't prove or disprove any of the theories regarding that part of the . . . relationship, but Pam's feelings were clear, and Sandra's heart went out to the nurse from Brooklyn. She also had the strangest feeling Pam Cross probably shouldn't have claimed ownership of Dennis Silva. She looked at the curious faces around her and quickly wadded the note back into a ball, then tossed it into the sea.

CHAPTER 5

////// *Grik Madagascar*

"General of the Sea," Hisashi Kurokawa, once ruler of *Amagi*, the magnificent Japanese Imperial battle cruiser, and now "High Councilor" to the Celestial Mother of all the Grik, peered intently through the crude iron bars at the drama unfolding in the cell. Inside, a female Grik of the lowest class, a "broodmare" for those Hij responsible for overseeing field labor (there were no female Hij outside the royal household), lay curled in a corner, smeared with her own blood and filth. She was larger than almost any male he'd seen; fatter, and with less formidable personal "weaponry." She wasn't half as massive as the Celestial Mother, of course, but she probably weighed four hundred pounds. She hadn't moved for quite some time, but he knew she was alive because of the whimpering. Despite his attempt at complete, clinical objectivity, he couldn't suppress the primordial thrill the pitiful sound stirred within him. *Good,* he thought. *At least I haven't gone mad.*

He wasn't there to enjoy the creature's torment, however, but to observe the results of an experiment he'd arranged with the cooperation of the "Chooser," an ominous, ghastly Grik he loathed, but whose assistance was necessary for the validation of Kurokawa's new theory. The Chooser was the ultimate arbiter of life and death, short of his sovereign, in all the Grik Empire. There were other "choosers"; many more. There were a few in each province of every regency. But as the chooser for the Celestial Palace, in the very household of the Giver of Life, this one was known only as *the* Chooser. Though reluctant at first, now he understood that Kurokawa's grand scheme didn't threaten his position or status, the Chooser had become the former Japanese officer's greatest patron at court, beyond even Regent Tsalka and General Esshk. Kurokawa was pleased by that, though the malignant monster's growing familiarity—and even overtures of friendship!—appalled him. But a happy Chooser was a powerful ally indeed in the great, twisted game Hisashi Kurokawa played. A year ago, he'd faced a hideous death. Now he had the ear of the most powerful being alive. He munched a cracker and stared through the bars. So far, the test was going well.

The "broodmare" (it actually helped Kurokawa to think of her thus, to keep his...enjoyment to a minimum), moaned, and haltingly reached out to caress one of the hatchlings that slid from its protective stance on her flank. It hissed at her, but as had been demanded, she tentatively tried again. This time, the small, downy bundle of needlelike teeth and claws allowed the gentle touch, but immediately hopped back to its place on her flank—disdainful of its claws—and resumed its militant pose. There were five other hatchlings just like it there. Across the cell, as far as they could get from the female and "her" young, three more hatchlings raced back and forth, clacking and skittering on the stone floor with their claws. Occasionally, one squeaked a petulant snarl at its nest-mates that seemed determined to deny them a meal. On the floor between the warring gangs lay the savaged carcasses of eight young: two "defenders" and six "attackers." Kurokawa had duly noted the statistics. "Fascinating," he muttered.

Behind him in the dank passageway, he heard unreproduceable Grik voices and advancing feet. He *recognized* the voices now, and he understood what they said, but speaking the vile tongue was beyond his desire or capability.

"I thought we'd find you here," General Esshk growled, and Kurokawa looked at the powerful Grik. All the hatchlings in the cell immediately forgot their antagonism toward one another and frizzed at Esshk's approach, uttering a low, warning moan.

"You have interrupted my experiment," Kurokawa complained. "I may have to begin all over!" Esshk couldn't speak the English the Japanese officer used any better than Kurokawa spoke Grik, but he also understood the words.

"You are a most sadistic creature," Esshk stated, a little wonderingly. "You realize what you put that one through," he motioned through the bars, "is tantamount to the 'Traitor's Death,' the most severe punishment the Giver of Life ever inflicts? To be slowly consumed by hatchlings . . ." The hardened warrior practically shuddered.

"There is a difference," Kurokawa insisted. "*This* one has not been bound, her claws and teeth pulled out . . . and her reward will be great."

"*If* she survives, and does not go mad. And no doubt you've threatened her with the complete 'treatment' if she does not cooperate."

Kurokawa didn't answer. The other voices in the passageway neared, and he identified them as those of Tsalka and the Chooser. They were attended, as always, by a significant guard. Also among them were three Japanese sailors. The sailors said nothing and wore nervous expressions. Suddenly, Kurokawa missed "General" Niwa, the closest thing he had to a friend. Niwa wasn't *really* a friend, of course, but he alone of all the men of *Amagi* had been truly loyal, he thought, and he'd become a confidant of sorts in a world where Kurokawa had no others. Niwa had gone to Ceylon with General Halik to observe enemy strengths and tactics when the inevitable invasion of that province began. The Grik had scant hope of holding the place, but Regent Tsalka insisted that *some* effort be made after all. At least they might bleed the "prey"—the very real "enemy" that former "prey" had become—the first true enemy the Grik had ever faced throughout their long history.

"Your ship awaits to take you to inspect the 'projects' underway on the continent," Tsalka hissed. "The Celestial Mother is anxious for a report, and so am I. I would still preserve my regency from the enemy, if possible!"

"All the projects proceed according to plan," Kurokawa assured him. "You would not . . . rush me again, would you?"

"Not at all," Tsalka denied quickly, remembering what happened the last time they struck before Kurokawa said they were ready: The loss of *Amagi* and most of the "Invincible" Swarm. "I am . . . anxious, that is all. Word from General Halik hints at some confidence."

Kurokawa had heard that too, but the confidence involved a scheme to break the Allied blockade so Grik ships, loaded with steel and other war material produced on Ceylon, might escape Colombo—not that Halik thought Ceylon could be saved. Kurokawa sighed and stood from his stool. "Fleet construction and some of the new ordnance principles have struck minor snags, largely due to incompetent labor, but the deadlines will be met. I go there to ensure that they are, and to add certain modifications that have recently struck my fancy. The 'Army' plan proceeds even better than expected, as General Esshk can attest." He gestured at the cell. "These tests confirm yet another of my fancies, that should result in an even greater efficiency among the 'new' Army troops and Navy crews. I'm quite excited."

"What of the aircraft you promised?" Esshk demanded. Kurokawa smoldered. Esshk wouldn't leave that alone.

"The . . . 'aircraft' I've undertaken to design and build are almost ready, in fact," he stated.

"But they are nothing like the aircraft you promised! They do not resemble your damaged 'floatplane' in any way, or the P-B-Y of the Americans that was destroyed," he said, failing to pronounce the letters P-B-Y properly, although his meaning came across. "I doubt the enemy has been idle. Most likely, they have replaced it by now."

"They can't," Kurokawa assured him, "not with anything nearly as capable, at any rate. Trust me, the aircraft I've designed will be more than adequate for the task. Besides, as I've said"—he closed his eyes and took a breath—"more often than I can count, Grik are *physiologically incapable* of operating aircraft forms even remotely similar to our needlessly damaged, and sadly no longer flight-worthy, type ninety-five."

"If your plane is so badly damaged, why exert so much effort maintaining it?" Esshk asked suspiciously.

"Because it's a priceless asset, a model for innovation and experimentation," Kurokawa snapped. "*You* forced me to *ruin* it, but gazing upon it, I still get ideas!"

Esshk seemed mollified. "Possibly, that is reasonable. But the craft your Hij construct!" Esshk almost threw up his hands. "How can such things fly?"

"Very well," Kurokawa assured. "And while they may be more labor intensive, and expensive in materials"—he shrugged—"we have plenty of both for that project, and they're significantly less complicated. Before long, we'll have them in their hundreds, and your doubts will be drowned by awe."

"They had better be," Esshk darkly warned, but Kurokawa ignored him. He was still terrified of Esshk, but he was safe from his ire—for now.

"And what of the . . . issue . . . in the south and west?" the Chooser suddenly asked, defusing the current tension. "That still remains, and lurks ever larger."

"Yes, how will we counter that as well?" Tsalka asked. "The creatures there have long been known to be hunters, but we haven't pushed them. The extent of their realm is limited and known—nothing lies beyond it. The Celestial Mother was 'saving' them for a pleasant diversion once the original Grand Swarm eliminated the Ancient Prey once and for all. With the destruction of that, the Invincible Swarm, and the current drain on our resources, we may be vulnerable to even such as they!"

"The drain is only temporary, and our losses will soon be replaced manyfold, with the implementation of the 'new protocols' devised by the Chooser, General Esshk, and myself. As for the beings in the south? Her Majesty has asked *me* to go to them," Kurokawa said smugly. "She believes since the 'southern hunter's' form is similar to mine, they may be more likely to accept the Offer from me." He shook his head. "I cannot go *myself*, of course. I have too much to occupy me here. I *will* send suitable representatives—who understand the price of failure."

"The Offer!" Tsalka moaned. "That is scandalous enough! To make the Offer based on what might be instead of what has been, has never happened before!"

"Enough," Esshk hissed at him. "*She* has decided. Precedence constrains you and I, not the Celestial Mother. Do you doubt she may do as she pleases?"

Tsalka lowered his head and blew a gust of air through jagged teeth. "Of course not."

"So," Esshk continued, addressing the General of the Sea, "we have brought the Jaaph Hij you requested."

"Hmm." Kurokawa lowered his gaze to encompass the three humans accompanying Tsalka's entourage. He motioned one forward. "Lieutenant Toru Miyata, I believe you are acquainted with the distinguished First General?"

Toru, who looked like a slighter, younger version of Niwa, controlled an impulse to gulp. "Yes, Captain—I mean, General of the Sea Kurokawa!"

"As a junior navigation officer, you're not essential to the projects underway. . . ."

I'm expendable, Miyata concluded with a sick feeling.

"And I therefore proudly accept your enthusiastic offer to lead this important, glorious mission! Given that you *are* a navigation officer, I trust you of all people to succeed for our Emperor, our . . . allies, and for me." Kurokawa's face clouded. "Others may have failed the Emperor, but the navigation division never did, when it came to getting us where we needed to go. For that reason, I hold you almost utterly blameless for the loss of my ship!"

"Wha . . ." Miyata jerked a bow. "Thank you, sir. May—may I ask the General of the Sea . . . what I've volunteered to do?"

"That's the spirit!" Kurokawa beamed genuinely. "General Esshk?"

Esshk produced a crude map from the folds of his cloak. "As you may have understood earlier, there's a group of hunters in the south that we had been 'saving' for some time now. They inhabit lands we care nothing for, and cannot escape. They're completely surrounded by a most hostile sea." He paused. "But priorities . . . change." He pointed. "Here. Their lands surround this place you call 'Cape Town' in a rough semicircle extending perhaps three or four hundreds of miles. Quite small, as I said, but they *are* fierce warriors. Good hunters. The Celestial Mother, in her benevolence, has decided to extend to them 'the Offer' to join the hunt. Do you understand what this means?"

Miyata nodded, and, clearing his throat, added a little shakily, "I do."

"Very well. It will be a difficult journey. We cannot take you all the way by ship. Even if the hunters there did not destroy it, no ship can swim around this 'Cape of Storms.' It is hideously cold, and the currents and seas are most intense." He coughed a Grik laugh. "To my view, the climate there is sufficient reason to leave them with it, but we would fight *with* them rather than *against* them just now."

"In that case, where will I go ashore?" Miyata asked.

"Here." Esshk pointed. Miyata vaguely recognized the area around the Moamba of his old world, about a hundred and fifty miles east of where Johannesburg should be. "From there, it is a trek of some three hundreds of miles across some of the worst country known. Open rocky plains, much of it, plagued by high winds. And it is cold, cold. There are also large, dangerous beasts"—he jerked his head in a shrug—"but they would never frighten you." He raised his gaze to Miyata. "Cross that plain and make contact with these . . . beings. You look like them, so perhaps they will not kill you on sight as they have done our previous . . . emissaries."

"What language do they speak? I understand your spoken language and I know a little English, but that's all. What if I can't communicate? They may not even be . . . true people."

"If you cannot speak to them, you will be killed," Esshk replied reasonably. "But make 'the Offer' if you can, and secure their assistance. Do that and you will be handsomely rewarded!"

"And . . . what do I tell them if they refuse?" Miyata asked.

"They will be exterminated," Esshk answered simply. "We are preoccupied, true, but not so preoccupied that we cannot swarm them under even as things now stand. This is their one chance."

"When do we leave . . . ah, First General?"

"Preparations are already underway. All should be in readiness within days at most. You know better what your species requires for survival in frigid lands, so prepare accordingly. Requisition what you need under my authority."

Miyata looked at Kurokawa, now ignoring him. "Yes, sir. Thank you, sir."

"Consider yourselves dismissed, to begin preparations." The three men bowed and were escorted away. Esshk glanced back at Kurokawa and gestured at the cell. "Have you observed the results you hoped to see?" he asked grudgingly, doing his best to conceal his revulsion. The "Traitor's Death" was rarely used, and even this . . . approximation, particularly when undeserved, awakened a primal horror. Tsalka couldn't bring himself to look inside the cell, and even the Chooser appeared uncomfortable. Only the "Jaaph" seemed unmoved. Esshk had long considered Kurokawa a barbarian, and at times an annoying pest, but he was valuable enough to overlook those things. This exhibition of utter, wanton, ruthlessness—even toward lesser beings—displayed a dispassionate side of the "man" Esshk hadn't seen. Oddly, Kurokawa was demonstrating the exact sort of disassociation most prized by the Hij: the ability to completely separate one's self from the consequences of one's acts or orders, to remain beyond the call of earthly urges even in the heat of battle. Esshk often struggled with that, in particular. The capacity for that was viewed as a Hij ideal, but Esshk had never seen anyone fully capable of achieving it—until now. Or was it only that Kurokawa viewed the poor creature in the cell as nothing more significant than an insect, and he didn't fully appreciate the trauma the female was enduring?

"Yes. The defensive hatchlings, the ones the Chooser once culled and you . . . ate as snacks, that we now groom for defensive combat, appear susceptible to nurturing contact, even at this early stage. They become . . . protective of the female that treats them gently, and defend it most vigorously from their 'normal' nest-mates that threaten her." He shrugged. "If we can inculcate this sense of *loyalty* to a 'mother figure' at this stage of their development, imagine the fanatical loyalty they will carry later, for the greatest 'Mother' of all." Kurokawa paused. "Loyalty is the most elusive quality a commander can desire of his followers," he said broodingly.

Outside, in the clear air, Miyata coughed to expel the stench of the Grik "dungeon." He looked at his companions. Both were young and from divisions not considered "essential" to current projects.

"Well," he said at last, "what did you two do to deserve this?"

"You . . . think this mission is a punishment, sir?" one asked nervously.

Miyata considered. In his mind's eye he saw the macabre East Africa "shipyard" he'd been recalled from; the seething mass of workers, the hot, swirling dust and perpetual stench of death and rot and feces, carried by the fitful, fickle wind. To him, even while the Grik constructed their new fleet, the scene more closely resembled a sea of maggots working among skeletal corpses. The stench did much to reinforce that impression. He blinked and found himself back with his companions on the steps of the "administrative" portion of the Celestial Palace. Below the slope it dominated, down in the harbor, scores of Grik "Indiamen" rode at anchor and multitudes of Grik trotted about like furry, reptilian ants, on errands or bearing burdens. He scowled. The smell out here wasn't much better than in the dungeon below—or in the shipyards.

"It's a suicide mission," he stated at last, "but not a punishment. Anything that gets me away from here is a reward."

Colombo, Grik Ceylon

"Your scheme seems to have been successful, General Halik," "General" Orochi Niwa said, entering the gloomy chamber through an ivy-lined entrance. The chamber was the throne room of the Imperial Regent Consort of Ceylon and all India, but with Tsalka away at court, Viceroy N'galsh had grudgingly turned it over to the "visiting generals" to plan the defense and hopefully, salvation of his lands. Normally, sunlight flooded the chamber and reflected down upon the throne at its center, but the sky was overcast and lamps were needed to view the maps on the table that had been brought into the room. Halik and N'galsh looked up from the maps as the Japanese officer joined them, awaiting the rest of his report. "The ship sent to observe has returned, and though it never drew close enough to sight the enemy, its Hij captain saw a massive explosion at sea. According to your plan, those newly elevated aboard the 'bait' ships were not to destroy themselves unless they were confident of destroying at least one enemy ship. If we act quickly, the cargo vessels stuck here might escape at last."

"I will see to it," N'galsh said, tinkling a small chime. An official entered the chamber. "Send word for the vessels in the harbor to make sail at once. At least one enemy is almost certainly destroyed, perhaps more. Others may be damaged, or occupied with salvage and rescue." He snorted irony at that. "Most should make it past them."

"Of course, Vice Regent, it shall be done," the official replied.

General Halik observed the exchange with pleasure. He was glad Niwa had finally established dominance over N'galsh. Not only had he grown to . . . enjoy Niwa's company, but if anything happened to Halik, Niwa must be obeyed. N'galsh had been reluctant to take direction from either of them at first, even Halik, since as a former Uul "entertainment warrior," he'd been "elevated" from the ranks and not the nest. Hatched a mere warrior, he ultimately gained notice in the staged combats the Giver of Life so enjoyed by continuing to prevail despite his advanced years. He'd been twenty seasons old; ancient for an Uul, when he was "chosen." Even before that, he'd begun to notice things, to "think," and in this war, the Celestial Mother had determined they needed more like him. So here he was on Ceylon, sent to "defend" it as best he could with the assistance of the former Special Naval Landing Force officer, Orochi Niwa. He was also to observe and recruit as many "like himself" as he could find before the place was likely lost. Evidently, he'd lost a double handful of those recruits that day, but the result should be worth the cost. He summoned the official back before he could depart.

"I want watchers to observe the beaches here," he said, drawing a claw along the southwest coast of the island. "Have First of Ten Hundreds Agrawer choose them with care. They must not attack if they sight any enemies, but bring the news back here." He looked at Niwa. "With the weather growing foul, a damaged enemy vessel may wash ashore. If so, and if any survive, we may learn their intentions—if local Uul do not savage them." Halik hissed a sigh. "They will not have learned, nor would they appreciate this concept of 'taking prisoners' you've mentioned. They will just kill them and eat them. It strikes me that this might be an excellent opportunity to attempt the procedure."

"Very good," Niwa said. "Perhaps I should go myself? If you're right, someone should be near with a grasp of the priorities."

Halik shook his head. "I am likely wrong and need you here to discuss the potential of these new 'recruits.' But I learned long ago to never ignore a potential advantage offered by an opponent: a weak sword arm, a tendency to lower his shield on the attack. These things can be exploited later, but only if you notice them. A few 'prisoners' might help with that. They can always be eaten later."

Niwa said nothing, but Halik caught the . . . different . . . expression. He gurgled understanding. "I know it is not your way to feed on the bodies of your enemies. To you they are not 'prey' in the manner they are to us. You fight them, subjugate them, but do not eat them. To me, that is as incomprehensible as what we do is to you. I foresee no meeting of minds on this issue. Even were I inclined to bow to your sensibilities regarding those we defeat, particularly those of your species, I could not."

Niwa seemed to shrug it off. "It's not the way of my people to surrender in the first place. If any of the enemy do, I wouldn't see them eaten, but they deserve no respect."

Halik looked at him a long moment. "Even so, my friend, if the time comes, I might save some few as 'pets' or 'advisors,' but that is the most I could do. In that event, choose carefully."

"My choice was made by General of the Sea Hisashi Kurokawa," Niwa said simply. "On this world, he stands in my emperor's stead and I obey his orders. It is fortunate for me that those orders paired me with you." He glanced at N'galsh. "Even with our perfect understanding, I feel compelled to go. I'd hate to learn survivors were slain by . . . overeager Hij on the scene."

"That will not happen," Halik warned the official. "See to it."

"I shall."

"Excellent. You are dismissed." The official bowed and backed from the chamber. Halik again looked at Niwa. "You seem to have settled in well," he ventured.

"Well enough," Niwa confirmed. "Under the circumstances. My orders are rarely questioned anymore."

"They should not be questioned at all! You bear a commission from the First General himself."

"There have apparently been few generals other than Grik for quite some time," Niwa observed dryly. "Perhaps they must grow . . . accustomed."

Halik nodded thoughtfully. He'd learned that, through the ages, "other hunters" were sometimes considered worthy enough to join the "Great Hunt" as partners to the Grik. To these, "the Offer" was made, just as it had been to Kurokawa—after conquest of his people and their mighty ship proved too costly. He sometimes wondered what had become of those earlier, "other hunters."

"Indeed," he said, looking at N'galsh, who'd remained uncharacteristically silent. "Excuse me, General Niwa. You have questions, Vice Regent?"

"I do." N'galsh took a breath. "My lords, you have now visited all the island. You have not seen India proper, but I have to ask: what now are your views? Can this land be saved?"

"That depends on a great many things," Halik replied. "That 'view' hasn't changed in the least." He dipped his head in a Grik shrug. "There are more, older Uul here, ready for the 'change' than I expected to find. Perhaps that is the way of things on the frontier. Nearer the Sacred Lands, the choosers would have taken most for the cook pots by now, or younger warriors would have slain and eaten them as they weakened . . . as I did. That guiding principle has now changed, of course, as have many others, and we have gathered in as many as we could. But the effort to identify the 'special ones' must not cease."

"No, Lord General. But beyond that, what are your thoughts?"

Halik looked at Niwa, and the Japanese officer began to answer for him.

"As General Halik said, it depends. Yes, we've seen the land, and some parts are defensible—with warriors *trained* in defense. Most Grik can't even comprehend the *concept*, and we're not authorized to waste many we find that can. We'll use some, but as we've discussed, most must be saved for 'proper' elevation, to become generals, officers, or under officers themselves. The bulk of our defensive strategy must rely on spoiling attacks, things the warriors here understand. We'll bleed the enemy as much as possible, but they'll expect it. That's the only way 'we've' ever fought. We might surprise them from time to time. In fact we've seen some good places to do that *if* they land where we think they will, and *if* they advance as we hope. Remember, we likely know less about them than they know about us, and they may have new technological miracles to throw against us."

"But what of *our* 'miracles'?" N'galsh insisted. "I know they exist! General of the Sea Kurokawa promised them, and they must be nearing completion by now. Why else break the blockade? Why else send all the materials—ship after shipload of them!—away just now if they weren't essential to the weapons he makes? I've seen some; those strange tubes a few of your guards carry, but there must be more!"

"There are," Halik assured him, "but they may not be finished yet. They will come when they are ready, if they are ready in time. They cannot be just dribbled in; they must arrive in sufficient numbers to be decisive. The Sacred Lands must be provided for first, but if we hold, we will get what we need. Help may even come in forms we cannot imagine. You speak of our guards and the guns they carry, the 'matchlocks' such as General Niwa's people once used. We will employ them, if only to test their effectiveness."

Halik's pupils suddenly thinned and he spoke with a new, bitter intensity. "But most of the troops here could no more learn to use them than flap their arms and fly. For ages, the most complicated arm Grik warriors learned was the crossbow—and only the smartest Uul use *them*! Perhaps our very society is to blame; intelligence among Uul has never been prized. But it has been 'the Way' for countless generations, and it has worked . . . until now."

He looked hard at N'galsh. "Report my words if you like, but things will change; they have already begun to. Compared to the eons before now, change is coming impossibly fast and it cannot be stopped. I was a sport fighter. Look at me now; listen to my words! Do I *sound* like a senseless Uul, destined by age for the cook pots so short a time ago?" He pondered his own words. "Maybe this change will be good. More such as I will become more than they are—more than they have ever been *allowed* to become. But what of you, N'galsh? How will you like *that*? We may save Ceylon for you and Regent Tsalka, but we have to become something completely different to succeed. I have no real notion what that 'something' will be, but it will most assuredly be other than what it now is, and it's possible *none* of us will like it very much."

CHAPTER 6

////// *Task Force Garrett—Ceylon*

USS *Donaghey* was hard aground on the mushy, sandy beach of south Ceylon. She'd driven in under all the canvas she could spread and the tide and swells co-operated nicely to deposit her as high on the beach as anyone had a right to expect. Mighty waves pounded her stern, bashing in the windows and slowly heaving her around until she was almost beam-on to the marching surf, but she was in no immediate danger of breaking up. *Tolson* hadn't been so lucky. She'd struck and stuck almost a quarter mile out and almost immediately turned beam-on to the wind and sea. She was a stout ship and it would take time for her to break, but unless the sea settled down, she certainly would eventually. Right now, she was in even more danger of rolling, and the first priority was getting her people ashore with everything they could bring with them.

Greg Garrett paced the enemy beach, looking out to sea. He hadn't yet fully absorbed the emotional impact of "losing" his entire squadron;

he was too good an officer to dwell on that in the midst of the emergency. He was heartsick to see *Donaghey* and *Tolson* as they lay, still just shadowy shapes shrouded in night, but his most immediate concern was saving what he could and preparing for the inevitable storm to come—from the Grik. Despite everything, their landfall had apparently been almost perfect. They'd grounded on what amounted to a little isthmus of sorts, protected on one side by the sea, and on the other by a swampy river mouth. It wasn't much, but it could have been a lot worse. Smitty remained by his side as he continued marching through the sand, examining the ground through the blowing grains and atomized spray, seeing what he could of the peninsula in the dark.

Marines had been the first ashore, and he encountered them from time to time, lone figures, watching for signs of life or distant lights that might indicate habitation. So far, there was nothing. Maybe their arrival had gone unnoticed and they'd have time to prepare. Smitty hadn't said a word during their inspection. He was waiting for Garrett to get the "big picture" in his mind. He was good at that. He didn't have long to wait.

"This is a good, defensible position," Garrett shouted at last, over the wind and crashing sea, "provided we can get enough provisions and fresh water ashore. There's no apparent source for either. That river'll be too salty. We'll leave *Donaghey*'s guns aboard her for now. She should hold together, and if she stays put, she'll make a fine flanking battery against any force coming along the peninsula at us, not to mention protecting us from a sea approach. We've got to get *Tolson*'s guns out of her, though, before she flips." He paused. "The bad thing is, there's nothing here to use as breastworks, nothing to fort up behind. No big rocks, no trees to knock down, nothing."

"*Tolson*'ll break up eventually," Smitty said. "We can use her timbers as they wash ashore."

"Maybe. That might take a while, though, and what if she doesn't? What if this storm plays out before then?" He shook his head. "After we get what we can out of her, if she's still holding together, we'll have to break her ourselves; then build trenches and reinforce them with her planks and beams."

"Cap'n Chapelle's gonna hate that."

"So do I. It's one thing to use what the sea takes off her; it's another to kill her ourselves." He shook his head. "Nothing for it." They'd returned to that portion of the beach being used to stack supplies and equipment taken from the ships. Hundreds of 'Cats scurried around, carrying barrels and crates from the few boats and dozens of makeshift rafts that labored ashore. Getting back out to the ships was the hard part. They had to pull themselves along heavy cables anchored to the land. Marine Lieutenant Bekiaa-Sab-At and Shipfitter Stanley "Dobbin" Dobson, both from *Tolson*, hurried up and hastily saluted. They were soaking wet.

"Respects from Cap'n Chaa-pelle," Bekiaa said. "Almost half *Tolson's* people are ashore . . . there have been a few accidents . . . and we're getting the supplies out that are in the most danger from the flooding. Skipper wants to know how you want to get the guns ashore." Garrett was glad Chapelle's priorities mirrored his. Surviving the night would be an accomplishment, but it would mean nothing without the guns to defend them.

"Float them in if you can," Garrett said. "If that can't be managed, we'll have to drag them."

"*Drag* them!" Dobbin sputtered. "Drag them two-ton monsters a quarter mile through the sand and surf?"

"Yeah," Garrett replied. "Secure them to cables and throw them off their carriages. *Donaghey* can pull them most of the way with her capstan. We've got almost a thousand men and 'Cats, probably three hundred already ashore. We'll drag them ourselves if we have to. The carriages too. They'll sink, but they're mostly wood. They won't weigh nearly as much in the water."

"Oh," Dobbin said thoughtfully. "I guess fellas *do* become officers for a reason."

Garrett chuckled at Dobson's unconscious, backhanded compliment. "Lieutenant," he said, addressing Bekiaa, "stay here on the beach. Any more Marines that come ashore, send them to Lieutenant Graana-Fas; he's with the supplies. I expect he'll send any Marines with dry muskets or bows to bolster our pickets. If any arrive with wet weapons or none, he'll probably give them something dry or put them to work here." He glanced at his watch. Fortunately, the precious device hadn't gotten wet. 'This night may be all the time we have; our only grace period. We'd better be prepared for a Grik probe, at least, by dawn. Maybe it'll come then, maybe it won't, but we have to be ready if it does. *When* it does, we can expect exponentially stronger Grik attacks very soon thereafter. If we're not dug in tighter than a tick, with heavy guns ready and waiting, we *will* die here."

"Ay, ay, sur!"

First Fleet

Like a massive herd of brontasarries, interspersed with the smaller, swifter, horned beasts they cooperated with in the wild, First Fleet raised its anchors and began to steam or sail forth from Andaman harbor. *Salissa*'s battle group was the first to leave, shaking out into its underway formation with the first rays of the sun. She was screened by the steam frigates, or "DDs" *Scott, Dowden, Nakja-Mur,* and *Kas-Ra-Ar,* which made up "Des-Div 1." The fleet oilers and transports followed, screened by the steam frigates of Des-Div 3; *Tassat, Haakar-Faask, Naga,* and *Bowles,* along with the swift, razeed corvettes, or "DEs." By the time *Humfra-Dar*'s battle group, consisting of the carrier, *Felts, Saak-Fas, Davis,* and *Ramic-Sa-Ar* of Des-Div 2, cleared the harbor entrance, everyone knew it would be dawn on Ceylon, and the risk of discovery to TF Garrett increased with every hour.

At least they knew most aboard the two stranded ships had survived the night. Everyone had been surprised when the transmissions never ceased. Chief Signalman ("radioman" just didn't seem appropriate anymore) Clancy, aboard *Donaghey,* had apparently managed to preserve his equipment and there'd been a blow-by-blow account of the grounding and the following, feverish effort to establish a defensive position. So far, the defenses sounded awfully thin, but ingenious attempts were underway to bolster them. Given enough time, the castaways might just manage to hold until help arrived. Occasionally, "Nancys" from Andaman's patrol wing (PatWing) 2 buzzed the ships on their predetermined scouting missions to ensure no Grik ships lurked nearby to observe the departure of the fleet. Once they were out of range of the island-based planes, Tikker and *Humfra-Dar*'s COFO would coordinate an almost-continuous CAP, or "Combat Air Patrol" to cover the fleet's advance. They might have to launch the long-awaited invasion of Ceylon at a time and place not of their choosing, but the enemy didn't have to know that. Chances were, even after TF Garrett was discovered, it would never dawn on the Grik that that was where the invasion would come.

There was a brisk wind, more out of the south now, when Alan Letts stepped to *Salissa*'s starboard bridgewing rail. He'd come to find Keje, but the "Ahd-mi-raal" wasn't on the bridge. Drawn by the panorama of the mighty fleet they'd built, he forgot his errand and couldn't help but stand and stare.

"It's a . . . stunning spectacle, is it not?" came a voice beside him. Letts turned to see Captain Risa-Sab-At, Chack's sister, standing beside him. Once a "wing runner" like her brother, a member of the "forewing clan" on this very ship, she commanded "*Big Sal*'s" Marine contingent these days.

"It is," he said, almost wonderingly. "I've seen these things built"—he gestured around at the frigates—"or turned into flat-tops like *Big Sal*, but the only time I've ever seen them *move* is when I'd shove wooden boats around on a map in Baalkpan. My God, I needed this! I love my job, my wife, my daughter; shoot, I love my life in Baalkpan, working for Chairman Adar. But finally seeing all this, being part of it . . . makes me realize how important everything I've been doing back home is."

"You are both glad you came, yet wish you were home?" Risa asked with a rumbling chuckle.

"Yeah . . ." Alan said thoughtfully. He shrugged. "But I had to come; somebody needed to sort out the logistical mess, and I've made a start. Besides, maybe desk weenies like me need to see the sharp end once in a while to keep a grip on what they do best"—he grinned—"just like crazed killing machines like you ought to push wooden boats around a map every now and then."

Risa coughed and swished her tail. "No thank you! I'm a Marine now, but being attached to the ship keeps me out of the fighting enough as it is. This war has changed a lot. Marines don't fight on the ships so much anymore."

Below them, on the flight deck, a PB-1B "Nancy" floatplane brought its engine up, and the noise stifled their conversation for a moment. With a signal to one of the 'Cats to the side, the plane plunged forward amid a kind of vapor of hydraulic oil and soared away over the purple-blue sea. A crew of Lemurians retrieved the cradle trolley from the end of the flight deck and hauled it back into position where the crane would place another plane upon it.

"Ingenious," Alan remarked.

"But slow," Keje said, joining them at the rail. "*Humfra-Dar* has *two* catapults," he added enviously, "that don't spray oil all over the deck. We don't have to use them when the wind is fair, such as now, but the pilots need the practice. I'm told the experience is quite exhilarating . . . much like being fired from a cannon, no doubt." He looked at Alan. "You were looking for me?"

Suddenly at a loss, Letts had to concentrate to remember why. "Oh yeah. Actually, I was looking for you, Pete, Lord Rolak . . . and Rolak's pet Grik. I was going over all the jillion things an operation like this involves when I had a weird thought. . . ."

Gathered in Keje's sprawling quarters, joined not only by those Alan requested, but by Risa, Nurse Lieutenant Kathy McCoy, General Queen Safir Maraan, and several other ground force commanders including even Billy Flynn, Letts seemed a little self-conscious. "Gee, guys," he said defensively. "I just got struck by a cockeyed notion. I didn't expect a staff meeting over it."

"This ain't a staff meeting," Pete said, "but a lot of the stuff you dream up is worth paying attention to."

"Are we still in contact with *Donaghey*?" Alan hastened to ask.

"Yeah," Pete confirmed. "They're digging in, hand over fist. Haven't seen so much as a sand crab so far, but I doubt that'll last."

"Maybe it will," Letts hoped. "Maybe the spot they went aground is secluded enough, the lizards won't notice."

"Maybe," said Pete doubtfully.

"You've been getting too much sun again, Mr. Letts," Kathy suddenly clucked in a motherly way. "What would Karen say if she saw you all red and peeling like that?"

Taken aback by this unexpected chastisement, Alan felt even more self-conscious. The sun did terrible things to his fair skin. "Why, I guess she'd be sore. . . ." He shook his head. "Look, all I wanted to do is ask the lizard a few questions." He looked at Hij Geerki, standing attentively behind Rolak's stool. The old Grik cocked his head. He came from a class of Hij required to do sums and inventories, and Letts intended to learn as much as he could from the creature about *Grik* logistics—among other things. Geerki understood written English and was beginning to pick up spoken words. He carried a writing tablet and a piece of chalk to answer questions.

"Do step forward, Hij Geerki," Rolak commanded. "You will answer this man's questions to the best of your ability."

"Aye, Lord," Geerki replied. He could say that much. He stepped closer to Keje's ornate table, careful not to touch it. This was the first time Letts had gotten a really good look at Rolak's "pet." Its feathery crest was long and graying and the once dun-colored, striated "pelt" of downy fur was shot with white, but still . . . Though it was ravaged by age, most of its teeth broken, lost, or worn to nubs, its claws clipped and rounded, it was still a fearsome sight. Even if its skin hung loose over atrophied muscle, it was bigger than Lawrence, and while Rebecca's friend had become "one of the guys," and wasn't really a Grik at all, this thing still had a profound aura of savage . . . otherness . . . about it. Alan had been in the fighting for Baalkpan—briefly—and the only live Grik he'd ever seen this close had been trying to kill him.

"Well, ah, listen, Geerki. I'd like to know more about those Grik horns—how they work, what the different sounds mean, things like that." He looked around. "Do you think he understands me?"

"Ol' Geeky understands," Pete confirmed. "And evidently, he'll even tell you the truth, if he knows it. Sometimes he doesn't, and he's been known to make up stuff he thought Rolak wanted to hear, but that's over now . . . ain't it, Geeky?"

"O'er," Geerki agreed solemnly. Quickly he wrote on the tablet: "No more make up. Not know, say so. New masters not like old. Want honest only. Better honest not know than lie, make masters glad."

"Huh." Alan looked at Rolak. "You trust him?"

Rolak blinked affirmative. "I suppose I do," he said. "As best we can tell, he either tells us the truth or—now—tells us he doesn't know. He's given us a good picture of Grik population and industrial centers, as well as warrior concentrations—as they were when last he was on Saa-lon."

"Why?" Alan wondered aloud.

Pete shrugged. "He's figured out we're not 'prey'; can't be, since we kicked hell out of the warriors he 'belonged to.' That makes us 'hunters' like any other that might've done the same thing. Turns out the devils fight one another all the time when there's not somebody like us to pick on. Anyway, the 'civvies,' like him, belong to whoever wins, and at Rangoon, that was us." He shrugged again. "Weird."

"And perhaps useful . . . or problematic," Keje said.

"In any event, if he knows the answer to what you ask about the horns, he will tell you," Rolak assured him.

Hij Geerki knew quite a lot about Grik horns, as it turned out. Like many other things, he'd been responsible for their procurement. Through a series of questions, alternately written and spoken, Geerki described how they were made, used, and what the three tones they were capable of making meant. It had long been a mystery how the sounds were made. Grik were even less suited to blowing horns than Lemurians were; yet as the Allied armies had discovered, sound commands on the battlefield were essential. The allies had resorted to drums and simple whistles even 'Cats could blow. Various tattoos or sequences of whistle blasts meant different things. The same was true for the Grik, but they'd contrived instruments blown by a bellowslike device to create the blood-curdling, rumbling roars they used. The horn itself had two holes in it, and a different sound resulted from the simple expedient of depressing the bellows with a wooden plug stuck in either or none of the holes. One sound was a warning. Another was blown to assemble all warriors within earshot. The last was a signal to attack.

"I'll be damned," Pete confessed. "Hell, we've captured some of the gizmos. Didn't know what they were."

"Are any aboard here?" Alan asked.

"I don't know. Could be. I'll find out. If we kept any, they might be back on Andaman."

"We're still close enough for a plane to bring one out, as long as it refuels for the return," Keje suggested. He looked at Alan. "Why?"

"Well, think about it. I'm no infantryman, but just imagine the confusion we could cause if we had some of those horns to toot on at the right time."

"Wow," Pete said. "That's a swell idea." He paused. "And one that doesn't leave this compartment," he warned. "We might make use of it at some point, but it'll take more than a couple of horns to pull it off. It'll probably only work once on a large scale, and that's the only way it makes sense to use it." He looked at Letts and scratched his beard. "You know, we need to keep this in our back pocket, but maybe start up a 'dirty tricks division'—start getting some guys to work making more 'Grik horns,' and cooking up other angles on stuff the Grik do that we can use against them." He grinned. "This is the sort of stunt you plan a battle around, and I want more of 'em to choose from!"

"Ha!" barked Rolak. "A 'dirty tricks division'! That is just what we need to put some 'fun' in this dreadful war, and maybe it will help us win it!" He looked around. "Obviously, Mr. Letts should be in charge. . . ."

"As if I didn't have enough stuff to do already," Alan interrupted, but he was grinning too.

"Indeed," Rolak agreed. "I suspect you and Hij Geerki will be spending a *great* deal of time together!"

CHAPTER 7

////// *Adar's Great Hall*
Baalkpan
December 25, 1943

dar, High Chief and Sky Priest of Baalkpan and Chairman of the Grand Alliance (COTGA), sat stiffly on a heap of cushions in the "War Room" section of the Great Hall. Ironically, it was one of the few places he could find "peace" anymore, since only those invited, or had a "need to know" what was discussed inside, were ever allowed. He took refuge there more and more often during the days when office seekers, deputations from other Allied powers, and representatives of the Home and Allied Councils sought him out to berate or cajole him concerning what he saw as trivial matters. Some were trivial and others weren't, but Adar wasn't a High Chief by temperament, at least in the jovial fashion of his predecessor, the Great Nakja-Mur. Once a simple Sky Priest, a celestial observer who'd charted *Salissa* Home's nautical wanderings by plotting her position on the Sacred Scrolls of the prophet Siska-Ta, he'd become a "War Leader"; a position, even a concept, unimaginable to most Lemurians just a few years before. He hated it.

He longed to be just a simple warrior; to personally fight the hated Grik, but he had neither the training for, nor the "luxury" of engaging in such a personal craving. Perhaps because he was a Sky Priest, able to grasp the evidently progressively more flawed, but still pertinent "big picture" of life, he was possibly uniquely qualified to lead the Grand Alliance through the ever-expanding panorama of an increasingly global war. Right now, he wasn't leading anything, even the conversation flowing around him. He merely sat listening intently, his silver eyes fastening on each speaker in turn.

"Some of Ben's toys are washouts, if you'll pardon the term," said *Walker*'s former comm officer, and Adar's acting chief of staff, Steve Riggs. He was also "Minister of Communications and Electrical Contrivances." "But we might save some of the radios. There were even a few spare sets aboard *Santa Catalina*. Might help Pete with his mashed-up comm. They're short-range sets, of course, but still plenty useful, tactically. We can have the operators speak 'Cat in case the Japs still have, or have developed, a new means of listening in."

"Good idea," said Rolando "Ronson" Rodriguez, the former EM who'd taken over most of Steve's day-to-day responsibilities, particularly where it came to electrical power and comm development. "I'll pry what I can from Colonel Mallory. We'll be able to *build* similar sets soon, now that we're blowing glass and we've got a vacuum chamber to assemble tubes in." He shrugged. "It's just a little thing now, 'proof of concept,' but it works, and we've made some rectifier tubes already." He grinned. "They're pretty big and look like a squash, but at the rate we're going, we'd have voice comm with *Walker* in a month—if she were closer."

"How will we get the sets to General Alden?" Karen Theimer-Letts, Acting Minister of Medicine, asked. She'd quickly fastened onto the radios as something else they could send to First Fleet—anything to assist the mission her husband Alan was on.

"We can send one of the 'Buzzards,'" said the dark-haired Commander Perry Brister. He'd been *Mahan*'s engineering officer and was now Minister of Defensive and Industrial Works.

"Have to ask Ben," Riggs said. "We've got only four of the things, and we're working their asses off. One's a dedicated trainer."

"We should have built more," Karen murmured.

"Ben argued, and I agree, that they're underpowered," said Riggs. He held out his hands. "We need bigger engines—or bigger planes to handle four of the ones we have. We're working on both. We've taken the basic 'Nancy' design about as far as it can go. We might build more 'Buzzards' as light bombers—Ben really wants bombers!—but what we really need is a bigger, more powerful plane to carry more bombs, freight, or passengers." He looked at Sister Audry, seated next to Adar. "Speaking of passengers . . ."

"I told you all I am able," the nun said tartly. "I gave my word. I personally owe the man a great deal, as do we all, and all I'm currently at liberty to say is that he got on the plane as ordered, but 'left' somewhere between Maa-ni-la and here. We made four stops, for fuel and sleep. Search where you like."

Adar grumbled a chuckle, unable to restrain himself. He enjoyed the idea that the young and apparently attractive—by human standards—but almost annoyingly principled holy woman, could feel so obligated to such a depraved creature.

"Those Air Corps guys saw what happened," Riggs said darkly. "I'll get it out of them."

"I bet Bernie gets it first," said Ronson. "They went down to the field to report to Ben Mallory and Mr. Sandison's there." He shook his head. "Is he ever gonna be hot!"

Karen looked almost accusingly at the nun. "What will you tell Nurse Cross? I don't want to be the one. Her little heart will break!"

"I'll speak to her, and Lieutenant Cross will understand," Audry said. A strange expression crossed her face. "I don't expect any of you to believe it, knowing the man, and I'm sure he would disagree, but somehow . . . I'm convinced God has a purpose for Dennis Silva." She was confronted by astonished stares. "I didn't expect you to understand. He's a beast, true, but God created the beasts as well. In this case, I have come to suspect His influence over Mr. Silva's behavior, since by pure coincidence, through no possible connection to the man's senseless . . . notions, he always seems to be where he's needed most." She shrugged, at a loss.

"Perhaps you would have to see it," she ventured. "I grant he is profane, sacrilegious in the extreme, and routinely engages in every deadly sin. He may have even invented more, yet . . ." She shrugged again. "If something has prompted him to disobey *your* orders, I suspect he has a reason, vague though it may be, and I cannot discount the possibility he is unconsciously moved by a higher power." She actually blushed. "I know I must sound mad . . . Silva, of all people . . ." She touched the cross at her breast.

"O . . . kay," Riggs said, eyes still wide. "Well, the sister's right—we do owe him." He shook his head. "We'll write it off that he's shell-shocked—moonstruck—whatever. 'Temporarily and unwittingly employed as God's attack dog' might go to his head. No charges I guess, so long as he turns up soon."

"He'll be trying to join *Maaka-Kakja* and go east," Ronson predicted, "but she's already sailed. "No way he could've gotten back to Maa-ni-la from wherever he wound up before she left. He'll show in a few days."

"About that," Adar interrupted. "I dislike that Saan-Kakja's most formidable battle group will be leaving the vicinity of the Fil-pin Lands with these unknown Jaaps on the loose. We have already dispatched four of the precious five-point-five-inch guns to go to Okaa-daa's *Mizuki Maa-ru*, but do you think he will find them?"

"He's got the best chance," Riggs said, "and looking like just another Jap freighter that 'came across,' he might get close enough to take or sink them. Anything we've got never would, except maybe *Walker*, and she's already pulled her hook for the American West Coast!" He paused. "Man, this war just gets bigger all the time!"

"Can we trust Okaa-daa?" Adar asked pointedly.

"I think so. Saan-Kakja, Minister Tucker, and Shinya do too. After what happened to his 'shogunate,' they all believe he's *extremely* sincere. As for the Fil-pin Lands, I think they're safe. Tarakan might be another matter. The same ship carrying Okada's guns will stop there with more troops, and another five and a half to add to the one already there. If these rogue Japs try the place, their 'can will take a beating, and even if they knock out the long-range guns, there are enough troops and big, short-range guns to make a landing impossible."

Adar sighed and stood. "Very well, my friends. I must return to my peculiar duties, and you all have much to do. There is so much going on;

Task Force Garrett has ground ashore and First Fleet will attack Saa-lon within days. Our new Imperial 'allies' will attempt to retake their 'New Ireland.' Even now, Captain Reddy steams into the void toward I know not what. . . ." He blinked anxiety. "It seems, once again, our fates are beyond our control, and all is in motion toward multiple, inevitable crises to come over the next week or so that will again determine whether we are winning, losing, or still just holding on. The tension fairly tears my insides."

"That about sums it up, Mr. Chairman," Riggs said. "It's a war." He looked at Karen. "I'll try to get those radios out to Pete before the balloon goes up."

ArmyNavy Air Corps Training Center
Kaufman Field
Baalkpan

Colonel Benjamin Mallory was stripped to the waist and sweating in the steamy, humid air beneath the glaring sun. A squall had pounded the airstrip in the broad clearing northeast of the city that bordered the Saanga River. All the tarps they'd rigged to shade the laborers and shield the sensitive machines had gulped as much water as they could before collapsing. A few "hangars" were already up, protecting several of Ben's precious machines, already partially assembled, but they needed more every day. There were many "hangars" down at the broad river mouth, more like boathouses really, where the trainers and PB-1Bs of PatWing 1 were guarded from the weather and hoisted from the water.

Ben was exhausted, like everyone else, but the longer they waited to open what remained of his fifty-six roughly forty-by-ten-by-six-foot "Christmas boxes," the more likely were the contents to suffer irreparable harm. Each mighty crate, arranged along a crushed and packed limestone "taxiway" near a massive warehouse structure weighed about eight thousand pounds, and contained either the fuselage or wing assembly of a Curtiss P-40E fighter. Many crates had been damaged by time, the elements, or flooding down in the hold of the *Santa Catalina*. The salvage effort to rescue the ship and her priceless cargo from its swampy grave near distant Tjilatjap (Chill-Chaap) had been monumental, and cost more than a few lives. Ben figured he owed it to the dead to put as many of the planes in service as he possibly could, and besides, he *wanted* them.

Six were definite write-offs. That was how many fuselage and wing boxes—twelve total—were almost entirely submerged in the flooded ship. Even now, dozens of 'Cats, supervised by the former torpedo officer and Minister of Ordnance Bernie Sandison, were cannibalizing the corroded carcasses of anything potentially useful as spares for other planes, or parts for other projects. The aluminum was badly oxidized after its long immersion and sudden exposure to the sultry, salty air. It was being sent to the smelter where the salvaged remains of the dead PBY had already gone, to be turned into ingots more precious than gold.

That left twenty-two planes that *might* be made to fly. Ben grimly accepted that the realistic number might be closer to eighteen or twenty, but that was still a heady, and quite reasonable figure. *Santa Catalina* had been transporting the planes to Java, far too late as it turned out, but for probably the first time in the annals of military history, the shipment included everything needed to immediately pitch the planes into action, except fuel. There were spare engines, tires, radiators, hoses, propeller blades, instruments . . . everything. There were crated .50-caliber Brownings, drums of Prestone and hydraulic fluid, cans of grease, bundles of priceless, specialized tools, and despite the manifest, closer to *three* million rounds of ammunition. The men who'd been on the ship, the crew, pilots, and ground crews that went with the planes, had evidently scrounged more ammo at the last minute. Sadly, when they found *Santa Catalina* a year after her grounding, there were no men aboard. There was evidence they'd left—well armed—and all hope for them wasn't lost, but the wildly dangerous, primordial jungle of South "Jaava" was full of appalling and often utterly unexpected terrors.

Once the prizes were safely in Baalkpan, getting the heavy crates here from the dry dock where *Santa Catalina* lay had been almost anticlimactic. First, they were hoisted out and set on barges that brought them within a mile of the airstrip Adar and Brister had been preparing since the planes were discovered. The most nerve-racking job had been getting them ashore and brought near the warehouse where they could be opened and the planes assembled. Ben was still at a loss to describe the sight of using balky teams of "brontasarries" to drag crates containing modern, high-performance aircraft, on rollers, to their present location. Now, all that remained for Ben and his highly motivated but technically unprepared Air Corps cadets, consisting of the 4th and 7th Bomb Squadrons—reassigned to PatWing 1—and the 3rd, 4th, and 5th Pursuit, detached from the 2nd Air Wing for "extra training," was to put the things together.

In that respect, the Curtiss-Wright Company came to their assistance across the chasm between worlds. They'd foreseen the need to assemble the planes in primitive conditions and done everything they could to ease the process. The engine was already installed on the fuselage assembly, and the landing gear was likewise mounted in the wing. Each crate also contained a hefty volume of assembly instructions. The problem was getting the two bulky, heavy objects suspended, properly oriented, and bolted together. After that, it was a supposedly simple matter of installing the tail surfaces, propeller, and attaching all the hydraulic, electrical, and cable connections—supposedly. Without a proper building to work in, most of the heavy stuff was being done in the open air with a pair of mighty timber hoists Ben designed on wheels of their own, that could be moved from one crate to the next. In this manner, a crate was cracked, the top and sides removed, and the contents inspected. If found satisfactory, one of the hoists was manhandled into position by dozens of 'Cats, either pushing or pulling until it stood ready to lift the assembly from the iron brace cradling it. With several chain hoists, lifting the heavy wing or fuselage wasn't that hard. Moving the two together and positioning them just so was an unmitigated bitch.

"Easy there, you pack of fuzzy runts!" Ben roared. "Stop! Belay! Quit lowering the damn thing!" He was heaving on a tagline, trying to torque the tail ever so slightly to the left as a fuselage descended toward a wing. What seemed a gallon of sweat had just burst through his eyebrows and gushed into his eyes. "Just hold on a second, wilya?" he said less forcefully. "Here, take this a minute," he growled to a swarthy, 3rd Pursuit Squadron Lemurian beside him, handing over the rope. "Keep the same tension," he warned, then trotted over to a bench where his grimy T-shirt was wadded into a ball, retrieved it, and sopped up the sweat on his face. Walking around the port wing, he studied how the fuselage looked as it neared the leading edge. "Okay," he said grudgingly, "that's not so bad. Start her down again, but take it easy!"

He was trying something new on this one. Instead of attempting to bolt two free-swinging structures together, they'd blocked up the wing with the landing gear already down and locked. This way, the procedure wasn't quite the . . . kaleidoscope of motion the first attempts had been, but now all the adjustments had to be applied to the fuselage as it came down.

"Easy does it!" he crooned, watching the gap narrow. "Hey, you back at the tail, a little more left!"

"My left, you left?" cried the 'Cat he'd given the rope.

"You lef . . . *Your* left, you nitwit!" He studied the correction. "Okay, keep her coming . . . down . . . down . . ." There was the slightest gasp of painted aluminum coming together, then a creaking groan as the wing began bearing weight. "Stop!" he shouted. He sighed heavily and wiped his face again. "There! See if you can wiggle the front bolts in; then we'll let her down some more for the rest."

Two 'Cats scampered under the big, flared cowl. "Ow!" one cried.

"Yeah," Ben said. "Watch where you put your hands; that skin's hot! You other fellas, soon as that's secure, get some shade and water!" He turned back to the bench.

"You Colonel Mallory?" asked a tall, thin man he'd never seen.

"Yeah . . . Say! You must be Jack Mackey! Adar told me to expect you."

The man saluted. "Second Lieutenant Jack Mackey, reporting as ordered, sir!"

Ben returned the salute, then waved it aside, grinning. "You can forget that stuff unless there's Navy types around. You like Jack or Mack?"

"Mack."

"Mine's Ben," Mallory said, sticking out his hand. They shook. "Where's your pal?" he asked. "They said there'd be two of you."

Mack tilted his head. "He's over there, with the 'Navy type'—Mr. Sandison. He told me to come see you. Sergeant Dixon'll be along. He's the best crew chief in the business. Stayed over there to make some suggestions, I think." He shook his head. "He really needs to take it easy, sir."

"The way I heard it, the Japs gave you a rough time," Ben said grimly.

Mack forced a brittle smile. "The way I heard it, things haven't been too rosy around here either."

Ben nodded. "I guess neither one of us knows the half of it, do we?"

"No, sir."

"C'mon, let's go collect Sergeant Dixon and Mr. Sandison and find some shade." He raised his voice. "Hey, you 'Cats, take five . . . or ten. Catch some shade, but don't run off! We still have work to do, and then more ground school!" Several Lemurians, mostly cadets, had gathered around the two humans, their large eyes going back and forth between the speakers. Ben suddenly noticed a few of them blinking . . . well, not *hostility*, but something close.

"Hey, what's with you guys?" he asked, surprised. He focused on one, a "Navy" jg whose name had somehow become "Soupy." He was already a pilot with PatWing 1. "What gives?"

"With respect, Col-nol, that's what we want to know."

"Huh?"

Soupy looked at the fighter they'd been working on, his ears slightly back. "We hear scuttlebutt. These guys may be just the first of more 'old world' Amer-i-caans show up here. That's swell, but I went to Chill-Chaap, bust my ass, fight swamp lizards, puke on crummy ship. I keep bust my ass, build Pee-Forties." Soupy's tail swished. "I don't volunteer for all that to watch some skinny guy, just show up, fly *my* plane!"

For a moment, Ben was speechless. Sure, he'd been ecstatic to learn there were other pursuit pilots in the world, real ones, with combat experience. The resource they represented was priceless. He didn't know how many there were yet; *one* more was twice as many as they'd had . . . but Soupy had a valid point.

"That's not *your* plane, Lieutenant," he finally said, "it's *mine*! Look up there on the nose and you'll see where I chalked an M when we first opened the crate back at Chill-Chap. M means 'Mine.' It means 'Mallory.' As a matter of fact, you open up any of those crates and you might as well imagine an invisible M scratched on every one, because they're *all* mine! You want to chalk an S, or paint a naked picture of your girl on one"—there were chitters of amusement—"you're going to by God earn it in the air!" He shook his head. "I *guarantee* you've earned a shot—all of you have—but so have Lieutenant Mackey and any other experienced pilots who show up here, because right now, they know more than you." He looked at Mack. "That's going to change. If you or anyone else wants to fly these ships we've worked so hard to save, you're first going to help me teach these 'Cats every single thing you know about them. After that, it's up for grabs, and don't expect it to be a shoo-in. 'Cats are natural born acrobats, and I've seen them translate that into flying." He looked at Soupy and the others gathered round. "That's the deal."

Soupy was nodding. "Okay, Skipper. Just so long as it fair. Good to meecha, Lieuten-aant Maa-kee."

"Uh . . . thanks," Mack said, watching the "deputation" depart.

"Oh boy," said Ben, chuckling. "Let's hit the shade," he shouted, so Bernie could hear. Once under a grove of trees with palmated leaves beyond the line of crates, Ben offered Mack a rough-looking, but comfortable lounge chair and poured him a mug of cool water from a carafe nestled in a damp cloth. He saw Sandison approaching, walking slowly and accompanying another thin man.

"You really going to give those . . . Lemur . . . 'Cats a shot at those ships?" Mack asked. Ben looked at him. "I meant every word."

"You think they can handle it?"

"What do you think? Who flew that ungainly goose that brought you here from the Philippines?"

"It's not the same."

"Why not?" Ben took a breath and scratched his nose. "Look. I know you're new here, but here's *the Word* on Lemurians: it doesn't matter what they look like, what color they are, or whether they're guys or gals; they're people just like you and me, and you'll treat them that way."

"I already got *that* word from Lieutenant Tucker—not that I needed it. It's pretty obvious how things stand. Hell, there're *Japs* on our side! That's weirder than . . . anything else I've seen."

Ben nodded sincere understanding, even though he still had only a vague idea what Mack and the other survivors of that hellish ship had been through. "Good. Just make sure you spread *the word* if more of your guys get here. This isn't the States, with 'colored' drinking fountains, or India, China, or even the Philippines. 'Cats generally have a good sense of humor. You can razz 'em for being short, stripey, furry, or having tails, and they'll throw it right back at you for being freakishly tall, 'naked,' ugly . . . or *not* having a tail, but it's all in fun. *Always.* We've been through too much together as real, honest to God friends for any of that other crap to even much *occur* to anybody, them or us, and that's the way it stays, clear?"

"Clear, Colonel."

"Good." Ben shrugged. "Besides, we still have the Grik, and plenty of 'bad' Japs to hate."

Bernie Sandison and a winded Sergeant Dixon arrived. "I think the sergeant here will be a big help assembling these machines," Bernie said distractedly. "He's done it before, and knows a lot of the mistakes they made in the Philippines when the E models showed up." He shook his head. "What a nightmare. No wonder the Air Corps got plastered! Even if they got on a Jap's tail, the guns wouldn't fire! The assembly instructions with the planes tell you how to put them together, but they don't say squat about really making them work."

"Then I'm *very* glad to see you, Sergeant Dixon," Ben said, but he noticed Sandison was still bothered by something.

"Thank you, sir," Dixon replied. "Glad to be here."

Ben cocked his head. "What's the matter, Bernie?" he asked.

"Well . . . it's that damn Silva! He was supposed to be on the 'Buzzard' with these guys. I *need* him here! He's the one who came up with the idea for the breechloaders we're working on. He's just going to waste out there. . . ."

"What happened to him? Comm said he got on the plane. . . ."

"Silva?" Mack asked. "Big guy? Eye patch?"

Ben looked at him. "Yeah."

Mack shook his head. "It was the damnedest thing. The guy's nuts. We talked about it with this Dutch nun, and she just said, 'He's always doing stuff like that.' Say, you know? She acted horrified when he did it. Called him all sorts of things! But later, she seemed to think it was funny!"

"What did he *do*?" Ben asked, rolling his eyes.

Mack started to answer, but Bernie interrupted him. Sergeant Dixon had already told him. "He got on the plane through the port hatch, covered in grease, visited for a few minutes, then squirted out the starboard hatch right into the water!"

"In the *water*? On purpose?"

"Yeah," Mack confirmed. "What's the deal with the water?"

"Don't get in it," Ben murmured thoughtfully. "Especially in the shallows—like anywhere in the Malay Barrier . . . Grease? What did he say?"

"He said a lot of things that didn't make any sense to us," Dixon admitted, "mostly to the nun. But he did say the grease was an 'experiment' some old, ah, Lemurian named Moe suggested. Said it was time he 'give it a shot, since he had too many orders to follow at the same time.' Does that make any sense?"

"I hope that grease saved Silva's miserable hide," Bernie said darkly, "so I can kill that maniac myself!"

"Now hold on, Bernie," Ben said. "Maybe he had a reason." Ben caught himself. He didn't really know Silva very well. He was an odd duck, that was certain, but why was he defending him? He shook his head. "Hang him when he gets home. In the meantime, don't worry about it. You'll bust a seam. Besides, from what I've heard, he's more aggravation than he's worth."

Mack gestured at the hangars. "How many planes are ready to fly?"

"None," Ben confessed. "That's another reason I'm glad you guys are here. We've been bolting them together and getting them in the dry, but all the technical stuff has had to wait." He looked at Dixon. "You know how to hook all that up?"

"Sure."

"Good. Figure out what you need, labor and toolwise, and have at it." He looked at the man. "But take it easy, wilya?"

"Yes, sir." Dixon paused. "What about the guns? Where are they, and do you want them in?"

"They're in that big warehouse, and hell yes, I want them in. Just two per plane for starters, though. We've got more guns than we can use, but 'they're' thinking about sticking a gun in the nose of some of the 'Nancys'— our single engine jobs—so we need to save back as many as we can. There might be a Jap plane out there somewhere, and right now all we've got to throw at it are spitballs. That's another chore for you; familiarize yourself with the 'Nancys.' Figure out if they can handle a gun without shaking themselves apart, and if they can, cook up a way to mount one."

"Yes, sir. Uh, Colonel Mallory? How come you call them 'Nancys'?"

Ben's expression became pained. "*I* don't usually call them that, but I guess it's stuck. Don't worry about it; it's a long story."

CHAPTER 8

////// *Mid Pacific*

"I say," said Courtney Bradford, stunned, as if he'd just made some momentous discovery. "It's Christmas Day!" He glared around the darkened bridge of USS *Walker*, casting a suddenly scandalized look at the new first lieutenant, Norman Kutas. Norm had been chief quartermaster's mate, and still kept the log. Norm looked back, his scarred face crumpled in a frown, made even more gruesome by the poor light. He had the morning watch, 0400 to 0800, and was the only other human on the bridge.

"Yes, sir, Mr. Bradford, I know," he said, "but it ain't like there's a Christmas tree, presents, and kiddos chompin' at the bit."

"There should be," Courtney said with conviction. "We've let too many of our traditional observances fall by the wayside. It's scandalous, sir! Scandalous! And here I was, left alone to discover it. . . . It shall not stand!"

"I was going to mention it to the Skipper when the watch changes," Kutas defended.

"But you didn't 'mention' it to *me*! No 'Merry Christmas, Mr. Bradford' did I hear!"

"Well, with the rest of the bridge watch being 'Cats, who wouldn't know Christmas from Armistice Day, I guess it slipped my mind. You've never been up this early, that I recall, and besides . . . I sort of figured with your 'Darwin this,' and 'evolution that,' you weren't such a Holy Joe."

"That's the *second* time someone has questioned my faith on such an assumption!" Courtney declared. "And what would the captain do?" he demanded, righteous indignation beginning to swell. "Last Christmas came and went without so much as a notice. . . ." He paused, reflecting. "Perhaps understandable, under the circumstances, but not twice in a row! I recall Captain Reddy took note of the unremarkable date of your misguided separation from the British Empire, but again Christmas is upon us without fanfare!"

"The Imperials had a few decorations up," Kutas offered, a little lamely, "for their 'Christmas Feast.'"

"Unacceptable! And of no use to you as an excuse. What's the time?"

Kutas was increasingly flustered. Bradford's stream of consciousness mode of communication was well-known, but it always caught his victims off guard. The Lemurians on the bridge were amused by the discussion, but, as Kutas had predicted, had little idea what it was about. The chronometer on the forward bulkhead was long deceased, and Kutas looked at his watch. "Uh, oh four forty-three," he said.

"Close enough," Bradford proclaimed, and passing a suddenly horrified Min-Saakir, or "Minnie" the female bridge talker, Courtney Bradford sounded the general alarm. Amid the raucous cries of a duck being burnt alive, he twisted the switch for the shipwide comm and spoke into the bulkhead microphone. "Merry Christmas, everyone," he said in a kindly tone, reproduced as a snarling shout. "Yes indeed, it's Christmas Day! Joy to you all!" He released the switch with a satisfied expression.

"God . . . dern it!" Kutas moaned. "Seventeen minutes early for morning GQ! The Skipper's going to skin me for your stunt!"

"Piffle!" Bradford said, suddenly a little hesitant. "What is seventeen minutes?"

"It's a *quarter hour* for tired destroyermen, Mr. Bradford!"

The ship quickly came to life on the black sea, under the purple-smeared sky. Fire controlmen scampered up the steel rungs to the platform above, and drowsy lookouts joined those on the bridgewings, who'd remain at their posts until the sun was fully up. They were no longer cramped by the torpedo directors that hadn't pointlessly made the trip. Dark shapes shuffled quickly to their posts on the fo'c'sle below, on the number one gun, and Earl Lanier's distinctive bellow came from the galley just aft, demanding that the men and 'Cats "line up, straight and smart, and wait your goddamn turn! No, it ain't ready yet; you got a date?" A few minutes later, taking longer than usual, Captain Reddy trotted up the metal stairs behind them, looking at his watch.

"Caap'n on the bridge!" Staas-Fin (Finny) cried loudly.

"As you were," Matt said. "Report, Mr. Kutas."

"Fire control, engineering, an' lookout stations manned an' ready, Mr. Kutaas," shouted Minnie, her voice high-pitched and soft as usual, but touched with a note of anxiety.

"Uh, calm seas, northwesterly winds, no casualties or contacts, Captain," Kutas said.

"All guns manned and ready," Minnie squeaked.

Matt looked around, nodding at Courtney where he stood somewhat defiantly near the captain's chair. "Merry Christmas, all," he said amiably, then glanced at his watch again. "Thing seems a little off today."

"I ah, doubt it, Skipper," Norm said with another gruesome grimace. Chief Gray and Commodore Harvey Jenks appeared on the bridge together, followed quickly by Carl Bashear and Sonny Campeti, both comparing watches.

"All stations report 'manned and ready,'" Minnie said, looking at the captain. He'd obviously figured out what happened and turned his gaze to Courtney.

"Mr. Bradford, you've been with us long enough to know I'll tolerate no interference in the normal operation of this ship. If you ever pull a stunt like that again, you'll lose all bridge privileges indefinitely. Is that understood?"

"I only wanted—"

"Is that understood?" Matt demanded. Courtney finally nodded, and Matt strode to his chair. "Very well. Pass the word for Juan . . ." He paused, remembering his indomitable Filipino "steward" was still recovering on New Scotland. "For 'Tabasco,'" he amended. "Coffee."

"Aye, aye, Skipper," Norm said, clearly relieved.

"What is 'Kis-mus'?" Lieutenant Tab-At, or "Tabby," asked Spanky McFarlane when the skinny exec cycled through the air lock into the forward fireroom. Just as Spanky had been elevated from his beloved engineering spaces, the gray-furred 'Cat—a full member of the "elite" and bizarre fraternity of "Mice" created by the "originals," Isak Rueben and Gilbert Yeager—had been raised to take his place as engineering officer. The terrible steam burns she'd once suffered were healing nicely, and fur was even creeping back across the ugly, gray-pink scars.

Spanky handed her an akka egg sandwich, and perched on a battered metal stool, nodding benignly at the other 'Cats in the fireroom. There was only one boiler in there now, number two, the rest of the space devoted to a massive fuel bunker. Number two was their current "problem child," though, and his arrival with an egg sandwich—Tabby's favorite— had become a morning ritual wherever he suspected she'd be applying her greatest attention. It was his way of "keeping in touch" with engineering in general, something he considered necessary despite Tabby's professionalism, while at the same time proving to her and himself that they could still be "friends." Spanky loved Tabby like a daughter, niece, or *something*, but it was no secret the onetime 'Cat version of a pinup in a fur suit was crazy about him in a more . . . uncomplicated way.

"It's a religious day where I come from, 'mongst lots of folks," he said, munching his own sandwich. "Celebrates the birth of Jesus Christ. Folks would give each other presents and try to be nice for a day."

Tabby looked at her sandwich. "I heard of that 'Jeezus' fella, from Sister Audry. She said he washed away all the bad stuff people do with blood." She brightened. "Kinda like we been doin' 'gainst these damn 'Doms' lately!"

Spanky shifted on his stool. "It ain't exactly the same. . . ." Spanky was a nominal Catholic, and no matter how "backslid" he considered himself, the utterly twisted and perverted version of Catholicism the Dominion was trying to cram down everyone's throat in a "convert or die" manner hit him very personally. He knew the new "Bosun of the Navy," Chief Gray, felt the same. "Jesus died for our sins, washed 'em away with his own blood," he said.

Tabby was silent a while, as were the other 'Cats. The only sounds in the fireroom emanating from the blower, the rush of water past creaking plates, and the trembling roar of hellfire in the boiler. "Well . . . we ain't gonna do that," she said decisively. "We gonna drown their sins in *their* blood . . . or the goddamn sea!" She finished her sandwich and looked at Spanky with suddenly liquid eyes, her ears to the side in a submissive . . . seductive way. "Thanks for the 'Kis-mus' saammich, Spanky," she said softly. "You gave me a present. I be nice to you all day!"

His face reddening, Spanky stood. "Well," he said casually, "I guess I'll check the other spaces before I see the Skipper. I'm OOD for the forenoon watch." He paused. "Carry on," he added, before cycling through to the aft fireroom.

Courtney's hideous breech of protocol had been largely forgotten by the time the sun gushed over the horizon and bathed the limitless, purple sea with an achingly clear and sharp radiance. Not a single cloud marred the sky, and visibility seemed infinite. A cool breeze circulated through the pilothouse, and the group that gathered there earlier mostly remained. Courtney had eagerly broached the subject of what they might encounter—besides the enemy—as they neared the Americas, a subject that until now, only he had seemed interested in. Now, with that coast less than a week away, everyone seemed curious, and Jenks did his best to answer their questions. As an explorer and something of a naturalist himself, he was able to make some interesting observations.

"But that still doesn't explain why they seem so . . . single-minded," Matt said, referring to a virtual procession of "mountain fish" they'd spotted—and duly avoided—the day before. The ridiculously huge beasts were notoriously territorial, and none of the "Americans," human or Lemurian, had ever seen two in close proximity, certainly not the apparent dozens they'd seen, dotting the horizon like a distant island chain.

"I can't explain it," Jenks replied. "Particularly since it's not an annual event that might be explained by migratory habits. It seems continuous. All I know is that, year round, occasional groups of the devils are observed, traveling through these comparatively barren seas, always on an easterly course. There are collisions, usually in the dark, but they seem disinclined to attack vessels as they sometimes do in the west." He shook his head. "As I mentioned before, the shallow bay between what you call the Baja peninsula and the mainland is referred to by the Doms as 'el Mar de Huesos,' or the Sea of Bones. That may provide some explanation, given study, but I've never ventured there. The Doms claim it, and even in less . . . hostile times, I've never been allowed entry."

"You reckon they go there to die? The old ones, maybe?" Gray ventured gruffly. Matt looked at him carefully. At sixty-something, the Bosun was still a pillar of strength, but he'd begun to make comments now and then, as if starting to feel his age.

Jenks shrugged. "That would seem a sound assumption, but not all the migrants are of the largest size. Perhaps some grow bigger than others, but based on size alone, one would infer specimens of all ages make the trip."

"Fascinating!" Courtney gushed. "Tell us more about these flying creatures, these 'dragons'!" he demanded.

"They can be a menace," Jenks confessed. "They look much like the 'lizard birds,' as you call them, or the small 'dragon fowl' we hunt at home, with fowling pieces, but they're much larger. Bigger even than the ones Mr. Bradford compared in size to an albatross." He paused, looking at Courtney. "Speaking of those midsize creatures, did you know, though seen throughout the isles of the Empire, and even as far as the continental colonies, they're known to nest only on a small atoll in the Normandy Isles, far to the west of New Wales?"

"Oh my," said Bradford.

"About these 'dragons,'" Matt persisted. "You say they're a menace? I guess they fly, but they don't . . . spit fire or anything?"

"Heavens no." Jenks chuckled. "But they're large enough to snatch seamen from ships, and they're quite clever, I'm afraid. They carry their prey to great heights and dash it against land or sea to kill it or render it senseless before they eat it. They've been known to bombard ships with rocks in excess of a hundred pounds."

"Shit!" the Bosun exclaimed.

Bradford eyed him. "Please. It *is* Christmas!"

"I was about to beg pardon," Gray defended himself.

Spanky clomped up the stairs aft. "Mornin', Skipper," he said. "Everybody."

"And a Merry Christmas to *you!*" Courtney said sourly.

"Yeah. Hey, what's this about 'dragon bombers'?" he asked. Matt filled him in. "Wow. Better get busy training the 'Cat gunners to hit flying targets!"

"Hey, you're right," said Campeti. "I'll get with Stites and see how we can do that without wasting a bunch of ammo. Maybe those Jap pompoms we mounted where the numbers three and four torpedo mounts used to be'll come in handy for something."

"Do it," said Matt. He looked at Jenks. "What other . . . surprises can we expect?"

"Probably not much you haven't already seen, at least at sea. The grikakka, you call them, are considerably larger off the coast, and something like your 'flashies'—perhaps the same species—are just as thick in the shallows as you're accustomed to within the barrier. Sharks too, like the one that disabled *Revenge* and caused all that trouble for Task Force Garrett."

"Say," said Campeti, "I wonder how that's going?"

Matt shook his head. "No way to know. The comm post we set up on that mountain on New Britain can probably still hear us; our transmitter is a lot more powerful. But Palmer said everything from there finally faded out last night. We're cut off, comm-wise." He brightened. "At least we know Admiral McClain, the fleet, and our oilers are on the way—a day late." He shook his head. "Nothing for it, I guess."

"Skipper, you know no big fleet ever sailed on time, with such short notice," Spanky consoled.

"Keje and First Fleet did," Matt replied. "And so did Task Force *Maaka-Kakja.*" He rubbed his face. "I hope that was the right thing to do. With that murderous Jap 'can running around . . ."

"I told you to expect such things," Bradford reminded him. "My theory regarding how objects and people arrive on this world is still all ahoo, but I'm convinced that metal and magnetism, or electrical conductivity is somehow involved. With a global war underway back home, brimming with magnetic or conductive weapons scattered prolifically about, we're likely to have more visits here as time goes by."

"I'm not so sure," Matt said slowly. "I mean, I agree with your theory for the most part, but I'm not convinced that nothing from 'here' ever wound up 'there.'"

Courtney stared at him blankly.

"Jenks's 'dragons,'" he explained. "The 'sea monsters.' If a few things from here got snatched the other way over time, that could explain a lot of human mythology."

"Don't forget the 'mer-lizards' of Chill-Chaap!" the Bosun snorted through clenched teeth, trying not to laugh.

Courtney's eyebrows furrowed. "Blast!" he said suddenly. "My beautiful theory is assailed! Now I shall lie awake at night, trying to reconcile this new variable, deprived of sleep!"

"Don't sweat it." Matt laughed. "When you get it all sorted out, I'm sure it'll make perfect sense. Remember, we came with the ship, and we're not magnetic!"

"But . . ." Courtney clamped his mouth shut. The 'Cats on the bridge were just beginning to "believe" in the invisible force of gravity. He didn't want to distract them with even more "invisible" powers just now. Maybe some of the 'Cat EMs would understand, and he was sure Matt did, despite what he'd just said. Spanky and Palmer probably did as well. . . . Suddenly, he realized he'd inflicted consideration of the greatest "invisible" power of all upon *Walker*'s crew just that morning. He shook his head. "I am the most incredibly inconsistent creature alive," he admitted.

"Yeah, but at least you're consistently inconsistent," Gray jabbed.

"Lookout reports a sail, off the starboard bow!" Minnie interrupted.

"Range?" Matt asked, raising his binoculars.

"Lookout say 'on horizon.' It so clear, an' with no range-finder. . . ."

Matt thought for a moment. The sea was calm, the sky cloudless . . . and the kid needed to get back on the horse. "Call the air division to action stations and have them stand by for flight operations," he ordered.

* * *

Lieutenant Fred Reynolds heard the call he'd both dreaded and craved. He yearned to get back in the air, but he hated that somebody had to ride the "Nancy" with him—somebody who might wind up dead because of him. Kari Faask, his friend and former spotter/wireless operator/ bombardier and copilot, had remained aboard despite Selass-Fris-Ar's misgivings, but she was still recovering from serious wounds. Fred spent almost all his off-duty time with her, escorting her around the ship, gently helping with her therapy—and generally treating her like a china doll. It helped salve his conscience. His first real taste of responsibility as an officer had resulted in a lost plane, a wounded friend, and a severely shaken self-confidence that hadn't had much to rebuild on. He'd manage, he was a good flier, but without Kari in the backseat . . . He wondered who Mr. Palmer would replace her with.

The deck crew chief, Jeek, met him as he emerged from beneath the amidships deckhouse and handed him his leather helmet, goggles, and scarf—pretty much the only "special" equipment he required to fly. After his previous flights in the open-air cockpit, he'd taken to wearing a peacoat, which he already had on. It seemed hot as hell right now, but he'd welcome the coat's warmth when he got in the air. Jeek escorted him to the "new" plane they'd assembled from parts stowed in the torpedo workshop, aft. Jeek, or somebody, had painted the word "No" on *both* sides of the forward fuselage this time. Jeek had painted it on Fred's first plane after he returned from the action against "Company" warships sent to intercept them, and Reynolds somehow contrived to shoot his own plane in the nose with a .45. Despite his resistance, the tradition stuck, but now it seemed appropriate. He viewed the warning as a reminder not to pull *any* stupid stunts.

"The engine is still warm," Jeek assured him, uncharacteristically serious. He worried about his pilot and the funk he'd settled into. "We ran it up for morning GQ." Implicit also was Jeek's reminder that Fred should have been there for that. Reynolds looked at the plane and did a quick walkaround. It looked just like his old one, a PB-1B with its broad, high wing and single four-cylinder engine. If not for that and the reversed position of the prop, the thing looked much like the old PBY Catalina that inspired its form.

"That's fine, Jeek," Fred said. "Thanks." He clambered up the ladder to the cockpit and settled himself in the wicker seat, strapping himself in. The rest of the air division scampered about, preparing the plane for launch. They hadn't done the "real thing" for a while, but they drilled for it every day. Fred was impressed by how efficient they'd become since that first awkward time. He felt the plane settle slightly aft as his new spotter clumsily joined him. He didn't look back to see who it was, not yet; a 'Cat was hooking the forward lifting points to the crude davit arrangement that would hoist them up and lower them into the sea, and he always liked to make sure that was carefully done. "Cast off the tie-downs," he shouted, noticing way coming off the ship by the diminishing wake alongside. "Take her up!"

The mostly wood and fabric plane creaked as the davit took its weight, and taglines, attached to the pin-release lifting points, controlled the plane's orientation as it swung out over the water. He motioned for the 'Cats on the davit to let him down. With a shuddering *splap!* the "Nancy" was in the sea and Fred lost no time. "Contact!" he shouted aft.

"Contact," confirmed a familiar—wrong—voice. He turned.

"Kari!" he shouted back, incredulous. "What the devil are you doing here? Doc' Selass'll skin you!"

"She not here. Beside, she release me for light duty," Kari said. "Sit in airplane while somebody else fly not hard. She no say I not fly!"

"That's because it never occurred to her you'd be so stupid!" Fred roared. Somehow, Kari managed to stand and grasp the prop.

"You been actin' too goofy to fly with anybody not say how goofy you are. You think I let you fly with some dope not know you?" She paused, waiting for a response. "You say 'contact,' right?"

Fred turned back to stare straight ahead. "Contact," he confirmed in a subdued voice. Propping the motor was bound to hurt the wound in his friend's side, and Kari-Faask didn't even *like* to fly.

The takeoff was uneventful, and soon, amid the contented drone of her plucky motor, the "Nancy" was winging her way toward the distant contact while *Walker* resumed her twenty-knot gallop to close.

"Just one ship, it looks like," Fred instructed Kari to report, through the speaking tube. From about two thousand feet, he could see the horizon beyond the stranger, and nothing else was in view. "White sails," he added with mixed relief. Dominion warships wore a red suit—but that didn't mean the contact was friendly. "I won't get any nearer than necessary to make an identification," he assured his companion self-consciously.

"You go close as you have to," Kari scolded. "You go in mast high, an' I drop my little bombs if Cap-i-taan Reddy says. You fly close enough to shoot them with you *pistol* again, you have to. Hear?"

His face hot, Fred could only nod. Evidently, they were seen before too much longer, and the ship suddenly hove to, its sails flapping in helpless disarray. A few white puffs from small-arms fire, at ridiculously long range, blossomed on the deck. They were more a reaction of panic at the sight of such a strange contraption as the plane, Fred thought, than any type of disciplined response. Still, conscious of what happened last time, he maintained his altitude and settled into a banking orbit about a thousand yards out.

"Is 'Comp'ny' ship," Kari declared, identifying the red-and-white-striped flag through an Imperial telescope. Her precious Bausch & Lomb binoculars had been lost in the last crash.

"They can't know the situation in New Britain yet," Fred said. "Send it."

"What we do?"

"We keep circling until *Walker* gets here. Company ships have cannons, and they might shoot them at us, if we get low enough. I bet they won't shoot at *Walker*!"

Reynolds was right. The old destroyer raced to within five thousand yards, put an intimidating and unanswerable shot into the sea just forward of the Company ship, and continued to advance while the target hove-to more creditably and "officially," yanking her flag to the quarterdeck. Fred and Kari watched *Walker* churn to a halt off the sailing ship's bow, guns trained out to port.

"Signal at halyard," Kari said. "Says 'well done, return to ship, recover on starboard side.'"

"Sounds good to me," Fred said, feeling better about their first jaunt together since that last, traumatic flight. "Let's go home."

Six Imperial Marines were on *Walker*, under Jenks's personal command. All the 'Cat Marines had remained on New Scotland either recuperating from wounds or preparing for the campaign against New Ireland. Jenks, the Bosun, the Marines—and Chief Gunner's Mate Paul Stites and his BAR—crossed to the "prize" in the rebuilt motor whaleboat. The Bosun was coxswain. Shortly after they went aboard the vessel—her lines similar to most employed by the Company for longdistance cargo transport, and little different from the Indiamen that inspired her—the whaleboat returned with Jenks, the Bosun, and two other men. Matt was waiting with a security detail when they climbed the metal rungs on the hull just aft of the amidships deckhouse.

A portly, dark-haired man sporting an "Imperial" mustache was first aboard, eagerly saluting *Walker*'s flag and everyone he saw. Matt suppressed a chuckle, imagining the warning Jenks or Gray must have given. The man goggled at the Lemurians and was clearly astonished to see the aircraft that had frightened him so being lifted to the deck, aft of the searchlight tower. Another, younger officer followed him, with similar behavior, and Jenks brought up the rear. The Bosun exchanged places with "Boats" Bashear, a 'Cat signalman, and the short-tailed Gunner's Mate Faal-Pel (Stumpy), who hopped down in the boat with a Thompson before Bashear advanced the throttle and steered the boat back toward the "prize."

"I'm Captain Halowell," gushed the portly man. "Honorable New Britain Company Ship, *Pompey*. I know Commodore Jenks by reputation, and he told me to expect a Captain Reddy. Are you he?"

"I am," Matt replied.

Halowell was practically wringing his hands. "Honestly, Captain, you gave us quite a fright. I still don't know whether to be distressed or relieved by his detention!"

Matt wondered what it was about the situation that would cause relief, but he forged ahead with the first—agreed—protocol regarding just this possibility. "I'm sorry to distress you further, but I believe Commodore Jenks has a formality to attend to."

Jenks nodded and stepped forward, removing a folded page from a pocket of his weskit. "Captain Halowell, I'm pleased to inform you that the Company you served has been disbanded for its role in a murderous, treasonous plot against the Empire. You and your officers will face an inquiry, at which your logs will be opened and examined to ensure you played no part." He glanced at the list. "The ship *Pompey* is now the property of a consortium of loyal stockholders who've formed the 'New Wales Freight and Transportation Company,' but she has also been commissioned for an indefinite period as an auxiliary to the Imperial Navy."

The man was nodding in what seemed a wholly agreeable fashion. "Splendid," he said. "Damn the Company and good riddance, say I. There's a warden aboard *Pompey*, sirs, a most disagreeable scoundrel! Do hang him, I beg, or drag him through the sea for the monsters to sample!"

"If he deserves it, he'll surely be hanged," Jenks assured. He paused, glancing at Matt. "Judging by your . . . cargo, you've recently come from the Dominion. What's the situation there? I should inform you that a state of war now exists between us."

"'Cargo'?" interrupted Matt. He looked at the Bosun, just reaching the deck.

"Broads, Skipper," Gray confirmed. "Like we figured. Swarms o' dark-skinned dolls packed in like Norway minnows."

"War?" declared Halowell, insensitive to the exchange. "Thank God! Then you know?"

"Know what?"

"Why, the cause for my relief!" Halowell paused, seeing their expressions. "I see . . . or rather I don't. I know not what sparked the war at home, but I assure you war has commenced already upon those dark, eastern shores!" He shuddered. "We were down the coast from Acapoolco at the usual place. . . ." He looked about curiously, again taken aback by the gathering 'Cats, then specifically addressed Jenks. "As *you* know, Commodore, the 'trade' has been officially illicit for some time as far as the Doms were concerned. They'd rather cut the bleeding hearts from the poor wenches than sell them to us now! But commerce as usual hasn't been much discouraged beyond the provincial capital. A veritable harbor city has arisen at Puerto Marco, where women bring us their own daughters to spare them the stone knives of that twisted faith. Stone knives, for the love of God!" The man paused, his horror obvious. "In the event, we were anchored with several other Company vessels, our cargo already shipped, awaiting only the tide. During the night, Doms—thousands of 'em!—attacked every other ship and slaughtered all aboard. Only the whim of chance had *Pompey* moored the farthest out. Perhaps the fiends assigned to us became disoriented in the gloom and attacked another ship. . . ." He began blinking rapidly. "It was horrific, sirs, the screams. . . . You could tell by those that they even murdered the 'cargo.'" He shook his head. "There was nothing we could do. We cut our cables and bore away as quickly as we could. Some galleys gave chase, but we caught a favorable wind that proved our salvation."

"Can you imagine why they'd do such a thing?" Jenks asked. Dominion atrocities didn't surprise him, not anymore, but there had to be a reason.

"Indeed, sir. From the time we entered Puerto Marco, we heard rumors of mighty fleets and large armies. There were no warships in port, save the galleys, but you can't keep a secret like that. Our suppliers hinted, the victuallers warned, even the 'cargo' had heard things . . . and there was a distinct shortage of labor, particularly young men, to be had. We knew something was stirring, the other captains and I. That was why we had already determined to depart before our holds were quite full and travel in company. Alas, too late."

"Lucky," grunted the Bosun.

"For us," Halowell granted.

"Did you gain any notion where these fleets were bound?" Jenks asked.

"The rumors were of the normal sort; nothing definitive. But enough agreed on a few destinations: the Enchanted Isles garrison is perhaps the most probable, since it lies the closest and the Doms have always claimed the islands. Considering the treachery at home you spoke of, I now give greater credibility to the very heart of the Empire as a possibility. Certainly the colonies on the northern continent are at risk. Those three were mentioned most and strike me as most likely, particularly having heard your news."

"We expect an attempt on the colonies," Jenks confirmed. "That's why we hurry there."

Halowell looked around. "This one ship? Granted, she's a wondrous thing, with amazing speed, but . . ."

"This one ship, if she's all we have," Matt said. He looked around at the staring faces of his crew, his people, furry or not. "By the way, Captain Halowell, this 'cargo' you speak of, these women. I expect they're 'indentured' to the Company, as usual?"

"Aye," answered Halowell, sensing something in Matt's tone.

"Then I must inform you that 'trade' of that sort has been stopped, by Imperial decree, and any such 'cargos' now in transit are considered contraband and subject to seizure. Pending a final ruling by His Majesty, the Governor-Emperor of the New Britain Isles, regarding the legal status of the *people* constituting said cargoes, the indentures of every human being aboard *Pompey* now belong to USS *Walker* and the United States Navy. How many do you have?"

"Ah . . . just under two hundred, sir." Halowell groaned, suddenly realizing the personal loss this meeting involved, namely his percentage.

"From this point until you reach the Allied, United States Navy docks in Scapa Flow, those people are no longer 'cargo,' but passengers. They'll be afforded every courtesy and fed and watered in proportion to anyone else on your ship to the extent of the crew going on half rations themselves, if necessary. Do I make myself clear?"

Halowell looked at Jenks and saw an equally severe expression. He gulped. "Aye, Captain Reddy. Most clear."

"Good. Now, I believe we've all hung around here as long as we should. Commodore?"

Jenks smiled. "Captain Halowell, I have the honor of issuing you a temporary commission in His Majesty's Navy, incidentally placing you under the jurisdiction of the Articles of War. Congratulations. I presume the commission will be upheld following your inquiry provided you make no effort to 'lose' or alter your logs. The judges understand the position Company masters have been in, and they've been surprisingly lenient in most matters. Besides, the Navy needs the ships and experienced captains. Now, considering the possibility you're *behind* a major enemy fleet, I suggest you make as much sail as you consider safe, sail southwest for several days, then attempt a record passage." He started to turn, dismissing the two former Company officers, but stopped. "You might arrest your 'warden' and anyone else you suspect of being a Company informer, but don't hang them yourself. Let the court sort it out."

Later, back on *Walker*'s bridge with *Pompey* rapidly diminishing astern, Jenks chuckled. "I don't remember your discussing the disposition of 'contraband' with His Majesty."

Matt shrugged. "I like Gerald, but I doubt your courts're much different from ours back home. The ultimate disposition of those people could take months if Gerald doesn't jump in, and I don't know if he can yet. In the meantime, we took 'em; they're ours. They'll have the same choice we gave the women we 'bought' on Respite. They can do what they want. We've got other things to worry about right now. Do you think the Doms could put together *three* big fleets?"

"I honestly don't know. It's possible."

Matt sighed. "Well, we can chase only one. Your people on the 'Enchanted Isles' and everyone in the Empire are on their own. All we can do is stick to the plan and try to protect the colonies."

Jenks looked aft at the distant sail, beginning to blend with the afternoon haze that had consumed the knife-edge horizon of the morning. "I hope they appreciate the 'Christmas gift' you've given them," he muttered.

"Who? Oh, the women on that ship?" Matt shook his head. "Where I come from, freedom isn't something a man can give; it comes from God. You're born with it. Sometimes men have to fight to keep others from taking it away, and all too often good men give their lives so that God-given freedom can endure. That's the gift; blood for freedom. What I did today cost me nothing. It was just right."

"I wasn't talking about those women. Their situation is improved regardless—admittedly more so since your arrival in the Isles. No, I mean my own people . . . and the freedom you gift them with the blood of yours, human and Lemurian."

CHAPTER 9

////// *Ceylon*

"Boy, this is one hell of a cruddy Christmas!" Greg Garrett grumbled to himself.

"What?" shouted Pruit Barry, about ten feet away, trying to make himself heard over the roar of heavy guns, the crash of a brisk surf, and the warbling shriek of maybe two thousand charging Grik.

"I said, I think it's Christmas!" Garrett yelled back.

"Oh. Wow."

Flocks of crossbow bolts sheeted over the breastworks and an occasional roundshot geysered damp sand high in the air. Ravaged *Donaghey*, though working hard against the beach under the assault of a heavy sea running at high tide, pounded the attackers racing down the narrow peninsula, scything great swaths in the tightly packed mob. Lieutenant Bekiaa-Sab-At, her white leather armor dingy with mud and stained black with blood, stood. "Muskets, archers, present!" she roared.

Slightly fewer than seven hundred sailors and Marines prepared. Most of the Marine muskets had gone to sailors, since they were easier to learn than the powerful longbows, and the Marines already knew how to use those. "Mark your targets!" Bekiaa warned. This wouldn't be a massed volley; those relied as much on psychological impact as anything else, and here, in previous assaults, they hadn't been getting their money's worth for the first time. They were starting to run dangerously low on ammunition, particularly musket balls, and it was better to make each one count. Their arrows were holding out rather better. Details raced out between assaults, braving the frighteningly improved enemy artillery, and retrieved as many arrows from sand and corpse as they could. At least the "Grik fire" bombs hadn't been an issue. They couldn't maneuver the heavy, catapult-like weapons within their shorter range—not that they didn't try at first. Smaller, shorter-ranged versions of the things, carried by packs of troops, made tempting targets and were never allowed close enough to deploy and launch.

"Commence firing!" Bekiaa screeched.

A hundred and fifty-odd Baalkpan Armory "Springfields" rattled independently, the dull *slapp* of heavy balls striking flesh distinct and gratifying. Arrows *thwanged* and *whooshed* over the breastworks, the impacts less dramatic, but the resultant wails of agony just as real. Six of *Tolson*'s eighteen-pounders, so laboriously retrieved and emplaced, shook the earth and vomited fire, choking smoke, and almost two thousand three-quarter-inch copper balls. The big guns were the primary killers. Firing into the dense, narrow press, they could not possibly miss, and each ball not absorbed by the sand often accounted for multiple Grik. A great, collective moan reached the defenders through the smoke, but only about five hundred of the enemy did.

"Shields!" Bekiaa cried.

Shields came up, many hastily built from *Tolson*'s now-shattered corpse, and the remaining Grik slammed into them with unabated ferocity. Though outnumbered now, they still might have broken the line if they'd had the sense to concentrate their blow against a single point. As it was, they simply charged straight at whatever opposed them in whatever direction they were pointed when visibility returned. Bayonets and polished barrels flashed under the relentless sun, and spearmen advanced behind the shields and the grisly, personal slaughter began.

Greg and Pruit stayed out of it. Both held .45s in their hands, and Barry had an '03 Springfield slung on his shoulder. Somewhere on the left, where the sandy spit bordered the river mouth, Russ was supposed to be doing the same; commanding his "section" of the line, but leaving the fighting to his sailors—bolstered by Marines with the proper training for it. Bekiaa had the center, seconded by Graana-Fas, and Greg determined to have a word with her regarding her "proper" place as well. Slowly, the killing subsided, and another hoarse, thirsty cheer began to build, punctuated by the squeals of the last Grik to be slain.

"Stay here, won't you, Pruit? I need to have a word with our intrepid young Marine commander," Greg said.

"Sure," said Barry. "Somebody better, or we won't have her much longer." The Grik artillery resumed, a shot skating through the sand nearby. "Keep your head down! Their guns aren't very big, and we drive 'em off every time they try to deploy in front of us, but they've got a lot of 'em, and they're getting better with 'em too."

"You bet," Garrett replied, crouching lower in the trench behind the works and cinching his helmet tighter. He took off at a trot, his right arm extended so he could pat each defender as he passed, saying, "Good job! Good job! We'll lick 'em yet!" Most glanced back, blinking thanks or encouragement of their own, but he came across far too many who couldn't hear him anymore.

Short of Bekiaa's position he found Jamie Miller, *Walker*'s young pharmacist's mate on another world, and now an able surgeon in his own right. He was working on a Lemurian sailor, one of *Tolson*'s, by the name stitched on the Dixie cup lying nearby in the watery bottom of the trench. Two of Miller's assistants held the 'Cat down while the kid tried to stop the bleeding from a bad neck wound. Greg could tell it was hopeless.

"When are we going to get some *help* here?" Miller seethed when the bleeding stopped on its own.

Greg squatted beside him. "I wish I knew, Jamie. The fleet's coming as fast as it can. The last position we got would still put them about two days out." He paused. "You know Clancy's dead, right?"

Jamie nodded. The night before, three Grik ships approached under cover of darkness and attacked *Donaghey* from the sea. It shouldn't have, but it came as a complete surprise. Only the enemy's crummy gunnery saved the stranded ship, and her seaward guns, once alerted, cut them apart. One Grik ship sank, another beached a couple miles to the east, and the third drifted ashore, afire from stem to stern. Even now, her blackened bones were breaking up in the surf. But *Donaghey* was badly mauled herself. One early, lucky shot, crashed through her comm shack and killed the young radioman while he was sending the evening report. Another of their dwindling "original" destroyermen was lost.

"Yeah, well, he ain't the only one," Jamie snapped. "Counting 'walking wounded' still fighting, our casualties are past twenty percent. Not as many from that last attack," he allowed, "since our protection's improved, but sooner or later the Grik are going to get their act together."

Greg nodded. He had plenty of "combat" experience now, but this was only his second "shore action." Already he could tell it was a lot different from his last. These Grik were better fed and far more motivated. Even so, he got the distinct impression they were just "locals," thrown at them because they were closest—militia, basically. If anything, the first "attacks," while violent and costly, had been even more disorganized and, well, *amateurish*, than anything he'd heard of before. If they'd thrown better troops at him then, it would probably be all over by now. In the meantime, the Allied defenses had been strengthened considerably.

Notwithstanding the naval attack, however, the quality of Grik field artillery had improved disproportionately with their infantry, even though Greg's heavy guns kept it at arm's length on the "mainland" beyond the broader area where the peninsula touched. He reasoned that artillery was probably beyond the grasp of your everyday Grik, and there must have been a "regular" battery stationed nearby. It had probably taken a day or two for the "Grik brass" to figure out what was going on down here, and he expected better troops, with possibly different tactics at any time.

"We'll be fine," Garrett said. "You're *doing* fine. Keep up the good work. I need to talk to Lieutenant Bekiaa." With an encouraging smile, he hurried on.

Bekiaa-Sab-At was drinking water from a bottle offered by Marine Lieutenant Graana-Fas. Graana (nobody dared call him "Granny" to his face) was one of Greg's own Marines from *Donaghey*, and he'd somehow managed to participate in nearly every Allied action against the Grik. He was second to Bekiaa here out of choice, and Greg wasn't sure why. Bekiaa had seen some sharp fighting with the creepy—and ultimately strangely benign—"toad lizards" north of Tjilatjap, but until now, that was about it. Maybe Graana saw something in her, as Greg admittedly did. She was certainly fearless.

"Cap-i-taan Garrett!" she said, handing the bottle back and saluting.

"Quit that!" Greg said with a smile. "You want some Grik gunner to see, and knock my head off with a cannon ball?"

Bekiaa chuckled. "No, Cap-i-taan."

"Good. And while we're on that subject, you need to stop hopping around on top of the breastworks and wearing a target for every Grik crossbowman that says, 'Shoot me, I'm important!' Is that perfectly clear?"

"But . . ."

"I have tried to tell her," Graana confided. "I asked if she thinks I would have lasted this long, making such a spectacle of myself."

"But you *do*!" Bekiaa accused.

"I do not. I lead in a press, in a charge, but never single myself out for the enemy's sole attention!"

"Well . . . but perhaps if I do that, I distract him from another? Maybe many others."

"Ah, but who will *lead* them if you are slain?"

"You."

"Yes," Graana said, accepting the compliment, "but what of tomorrow? Next week? Next year? If we spend our good commanders a battle at a time, who will lead those future Marines, not yet even under arms, in future battles?"

"Others will rise."

"Yes, but they'll start at the beginning, all over again, without the benefit of what you might teach. They'll be doomed to make the same mistakes you and I already recognize as such!" Bekiaa had no response to that.

"Listen to him," Greg said. "That's an order. If you're going to lead the center, you're going to take care of yourself. We can't spare you; either of you."

"Ay, ay, Cap-i-taan Garrett," Bekiaa agreed. Suddenly a runner, one of *Revenge*'s machinist's mates, rushed to join them.

"Cap-i-taan Garrett!" he gasped, "Cap-i-taan Chaa-pelle's compliments, an' would you peese joining him on de lef? The Griks is up to some-ting dere!"

Greg nodded and followed the runner through the zigzag of ditches, finally reaching the extreme left where Chapelle peered over some of his lost ship's timbers at the broad mouth of the river and the land beyond.

"Hi, Greg," he said, gesturing over the embedded planks. "What do you make of that?"

Garrett raised his binoculars. The morning haze, thick with lingering gun smoke, lay heavy on the calm water in the lee of the peninsula, making it difficult to penetrate to the dense foliage on the other side, maybe half a mile. It looked like large numbers of low, dark shapes were assembling along the distant shore, however.

"Huh. Looks like they may try to cross. Those must be barges." He rubbed his nose; the dust and grit got into everything, and he felt a sneeze coming on. He shook his head. "Doesn't make sense. They have to know we see them. Why let us do that? If they've got the sense to try a flank attack, you'd think they'd have the sense to hide it."

"Maybe they meant it to come last night or early this morning, and just didn't get enough grease on the wheel."

"Maybe. We'll see." Garrett looked to his new left, where the network of trenches extended farther, parallel with this calmer beach. Four of *Tolson*'s guns were spaced along it, for just such a possibility. "Be ready to secure this flank. Send somebody good to the other end, but stay here yourself. *This* might become the center when they try again." He glanced back up the spit of land to the east, then back across the river. "I wonder what they're up to," he muttered to himself.

"I wonder what they'll do now," General Niwa pondered aloud.

"Indeed," agreed General Halik. He hissed disgust. "Your instincts were right. You should have come down days ago. Your authority could have prevented this disaster. Never have I seen so many destroyed by so few."

"We didn't know," Niwa interjected.

"We should have. The possibility was there, and you saw it more clearly than I," Halik snorted. "Still I remain but a sport fighter, a 'tactical warrior.' That must change."

"If you'll forgive me, you already grasp more than General Esshk ever did."

"No doubt General Esshk would agree, but when thought replaces— what is that word? Valor! When thought becomes more important than the valor of the hunter, I fear few of my kind are fully prepared for the consequences."

"That's what we're here to change," Niwa reminded. They'd both arrived the previous day, prodded by reports of contact and battle that grew steadily more reliable and frankly, appalling. Lost was any opportunity to capture prisoners, due to the unexpected number of the enemy, and the futile, unordered attacks by local warriors that encouraged the enemy to construct ever-stronger fortifications. Halik had ordered the naval attack upon hearing one of the enemy ships was still in the fight, but it didn't have the weight to succeed—he saw that now—and he'd revised his plan accordingly. The flank attack was Niwa's idea, but Halik quickly grasped the advantage. Unfortunately, few others had, nor had they understood the necessity that it be coordinated with the last frontal attack. Now the enemy doubtless saw the barges and knew what was coming. Another coordinated attempt might be made because the enemy had to shield the riverfront approach now. The flank attack, combined with another frontal assault bolstered by Niwa's guards and better troops, might find a weakened defense, but it would be costly.

"Perhaps after dark, tonight," Niwa ventured.

Halik shook his head. "We'll never keep the troops focused that long. Few yet understand the idea of defense—that remains one reason attacks upon defensive works are so costly. No, when our new troops join the ravaged remnants to their front, we must strike immediately and carry as many of these locals along as possible when our own make their thrust. They should punch through somewhere."

"They should, but such an attack in broad daylight, without even the river fog as a shield?"

"Many will die," Halik agreed, "but that can no longer be helped.

Perhaps this 'practice' will ensure better performance when we meet the enemy's main attack, wherever it falls."

"If we have anything left to meet it," Niwa grumbled.

Halik gargled a laugh. "Whatever we lose will be but a tithe against our reserves . . . and those who survive may learn a lesson. You estimate the enemy numbers at six or seven hundreds, not counting those aboard the ship. I agree. The next attack will go forward with nearly ten times that number, from three directions. They may counter each thrust; in fact, I hope they do, because it will weaken them, not us. They cannot be strong everywhere. But the timing is critical. Losses will be extreme," Halik acknowledged, "but sometimes, knowledge must be gained with blood. Once gained, perhaps it won't be forgotten!"

"I hope not," Niwa said. "You say we spend but a tithe, but that 'tithe' is likely to be shattered. Are a few thoughtful survivors worth that cost?"

"Yes."

Niwa shrugged. "Then go ahead. If you've no objection, I'll watch the waterborne assault. I'm curious how effective it will be."

"Very well, but observe only. Do not get swept along. We must not lose you, and I might find myself craving your counsel."

Niwa saluted in the Japanese way and with a bow went to join a column of Grik squirming through the coastal jungle, toward the barges.

Only *Donaghey*'s mizzen remained standing, its top crowded with lookouts. A series of signals from there informed Garrett of a number of disconcerting things at once; three more Grik ships were in the offing, a major concentration of Grik was massing just beyond his view to the east, and the barges they'd been told to watch had begun streaming across the river mouth.

"Well. It looks like they've finally got all their shit in the sock at once, this time," he said grimly, using one of General Alden's favorite terms. It was early afternoon, and he'd just returned to Bekiaa's position in the center. "Runner!" he shouted. "Get over here! Listen," he continued when he had the young Lemurian's attention. "Go to Captain Chapelle. Tell him it's about to get messy. He's to send what he can to support the guns on the north coast, but only as much as he thinks he has to, got it? The gunners'll have to chew those barges up. I think that's mostly a distraction from a really heavy hit on our front! We got ships coming in again too. They're hitting us everywhere at once. Got all that?"

"Ay, ay, Cap-i-taan Gaar-rett! Ships, barges, an' swarms o' Griks! Support North baa-tery, but only as needed."

"You got it. Now scram!"

The Grik artillery had been desultory since morning, just a few rounds an hour to harass them. Suddenly, it opened up with a renewed frenzy and frequency that outpaced anything they'd experienced yet. More guns must have arrived, and some were big ones. The distant jungle fairly erupted with smoke, and incoming roundshot competed against the surf with its similar, more insistent sound.

"Take cover!" Garrett yelled, and dropped to the bottom of the trench, pulling his helmet tight. The damp sand convulsed and shuddered, and the air was full of descending clouds of grit. "All guns but those positioned directly to the front, commence counter battery fire!" he yelled, hearing the command passed along. "Those to the front, load case shot and hold!"

Even in the trench, he felt the crack of one of *Tolson*'s long guns, and heard the squeal of the truck as the gun recoiled back on the wooden deck they'd built in the sand. Moments after the *shoosh* of the shot was lost in the distance amid the increasing tempo of thunder, he thought he heard the distant *clap* of the exploding shell raining fragments on the enemy gunners. He crawled to the top of the trench, squeezing past a pair of sailors with muskets, and peered over the breastworks. White puffs nearly a thousand yards away sprayed blackened shards, some large enough to see from here, through the trembling treetops overhanging the unseen enemy guns. The six cannon on this line were joined by *Donaghey*'s, even as she prepared to defend against the approaching Grik ships on her opposite beam. At some point, they'd lose her support. She didn't have enough crew to serve both sides at once. A staccato booming came from the far left, as the guns guarding the river approach opened on the barges full of Grik.

"I wish we'd gotten more guns out of *Tolson*," he murmured. They were lucky to have the nine they had. The frigate had held out as long as she could, but finally rolled onto her beam ends, submerging more than half her armament. Several 'Cats were killed when that happened. All that remained was to begin the task of breaking her up and floating timbers ashore. Once begun, the sea accelerated their task, and a constant stream of debris, more than enough for their needs, washed onto the beach. Of the noble *Tolson*, all that remained in view was a shattered skeleton in the surf.

"They're coming, Skipper," said Saaran-Gaani, squeezing in beside him, his dark amber eyes wide with excitement. Greg's exec from *Donaghey* had found him. Smitty was directing the guns on the stranded ship and Saaran no longer had a purpose aboard. He'd asked permission to join the fight ashore. Greg looked east and saw a malignant mass of Grik forming in the distance across the dazzling white sand and the sea of dark corpses.

"Do you have a weapon, Saaran?" The brown and white 'Cat blinked affirmative, and patted his sword. Garrett sighed. "No!" He looked around. "Lieutenant Bekiaa!"

"Sir?"

"Any muskets lying around, from the wounded and dead?"

"No, sir. Sailors buy it, Marines take 'em back."

"The 'Sailing Master' needs a spear, then. Like you, I'd rather he didn't get within arm's length of those bastards!"

"Can you *use* a musket, sir?" Bekiaa asked Saaran Gaani. He nodded. Like everyone, he'd familiarized himself with the new weapons and fired a few shots. They didn't use longbows on the Great South Island, and he'd be useless with one. "Will you kill Grik?"

"Until they kill me," he replied matter-of-factly. Bekiaa blinked approval.

"Take mine," she said, and tossed it to him, followed by her cartridge box.

"But . . . what will you use?"

"Cap-i-taan Garrett has instructed me to stay back from the fighting. If I need another, one will be available." She grinned, her tail swaying almost flirtatiously. "I hope *that* one will not return to me until *after* the fight!"

"Dern it, Bekiaa," Greg said, flustered, "I told you to quit risking yourself worse than a private soldier, and now you're making a pass at a recruit!"

"He's an officer! There is nothing improper."

"Nothing improper . . . !" Greg closed his eyes in the face of the on-rushing horde. He should probably get back to the right and rejoin Pruit; it was just a hundred yards or so, but Captain Barry would do fine. He was closest to the covering fire of the ship, and the Grik had been veering north of there as they neared the line. He might as well ride it out here. "You just concentrate on killing Grik," he told Saaran, taking his own advice and sliding back from the breastworks. "Don't get all aflutter."

Saaran glanced back. "A most . . . fascinating female," he remarked.

"Sure." Greg moved to join Bekiaa. The enemy artillery began to lift, even while *Tolson's* old guns redoubled their fire. Explosive case shot would soon become canister again. "It's *very* improper to leave poor defenseless male—sailors!—thinking about weird, predatory Marine broads right in the middle of a battle," he said formally.

"All I said . . ."

"It's never what gals *say* that gets a guy killed. It's what they *think* she said . . . or did." He looked appealingly at Lieutenant Graana-Fas. "Is she like this all the time?"

"I don't know, sir. We're from different ships." He lowered his voice. "Perhaps she . . . offsets . . . or compensates? Replaces one risky behavior with another? Don't ask me; I was a carpenter at Baalkpan. Before this war, there were no 'Marines' here. How is it where you are from?"

"Well . . . since there aren't any female *line officers* of any kind, battlefield romance is sort of rare."

The banter was a tonic, helping them keep their minds off what was coming. Judging by what little Greg could see from his perspective, it was going to be bad; by far the strongest push yet. As the hissing roar and weapon-on-shield rumble of the charging wave of Grik built to overwhelm the guns, Garrett took a sip from his "grogged" canteen and passed it to Graana-Fas and Bekiaa. He fiddled nervously with the pattern of 1917 cutlass hanging from his belt, expecting for the first time that he might have to actually use the damn thing. He'd practiced some, with the Marines. Everyone had to. But he'd never pulled it in combat before except to wave it around. Unlike a few of the weapons (most notably Silva's and the Bosun's) that had reached this world in an unopened crate aboard *Walker*, Garrett's cutlass looked brand-new.

The oiled wooden grip had a few little dings from carrying it around, but the black oxide finish on the guard and blade was practically unmarred. His fingers almost seemed to heat, touching the thing, and after he retrieved his canteen, he opened the flap of his holster and drew the 1911 Colt.

He looked south, at *Donaghey*'s standing mizzen, trying to read the signal flags. Only the lookouts there would have a real idea of what they faced. His blood ran chill when he saw the message that essentially said, "Enemy too many to count." *So. This is it*, he thought. The mast trembled and a gout of smoke billowed from *Donaghey*'s seaward side while a few guns tried to keep firing at the mass descending like an avalanche on the breastworks. No one spoke now; the banter was over. Nervous 'Cats tugged at their armor and a few veterans windmilled their arms to ensure their range of motion. Muskets were already loaded and held at the ready, and Marine archer/spearmen cast nervous glances at their NCOs waiting for their own order to prepare. More spearmen arrived from the right to bolster the line, and Greg realized Barry must have seen that the center was going to take a pounding.

He hefted the Colt. Unlike the cutlass, the pistol fit his hand like a glove. Its black-blue oxide finish had evolved into a general bright gray appearance but there was no rust. The checkered walnut grips were warm with memories of other walnut things he'd known from another world, and he wondered if there were any walnut trees here. His eyes and thoughts lingered on the UNITED STATES PROPERTY stamped under the slide on the left side of the frame, and he reeled with a sense of unreality such as he hadn't felt in a long, long time. *I'm a kid from Tennessee who's about to die on the other side of a different world!* Suddenly, he realized how Captain Reddy must have felt at the Battle of Aryaal, with all the Grik in the world swarming down on him. Greg had seen it from the ship. He'd *known* the captain was dead . . . but he wasn't. He didn't give up and he didn't die.

With growing determination, Greg pulled the slide back on the Colt and released it, letting it chamber a round. Calmly, he pushed the magazine release button and caught the two-tone device. Fishing in his pocket, he thumbed a copper-nosed cartridge in on top of the others, then shoved the magazine back into the well until it latched.

"About two hundred yards, Skipper," Saaran-Gaani shouted, barely audibly.

"Very well," Garrett replied. "Let's go to canister," he recommended. "Lieutenant Bekiaa, commence firing at your discretion."

General Halik had never seen anything like it. He was accustomed to small-scale combat, one-on-one, in the sport-fighting arena. Even before, when he'd been part of larger actions against other Grik, "his" battles had been narrowly viewed from his own perspective without thought for the larger issue. Now he watched from a distance, not so different from those who once viewed his fights so many times in the past, but he'd designed this attack, he and Niwa, based on fundamental principles he'd learned in the arena. Feint, slash, parry; the unexpected blow from the side, the demonstration to gain an opponent's attention while preparing a blow from a neglected quarter—all were appropriate here, writ large, and yet . . .

"The enemy fights well," he admitted grudgingly. "They react much quicker, I think, than we would in similar circumstances." The "amphibious" attack across the river mouth was disintegrating, each barge full of Grik savaged in turn, with no opportunity to reply, by typhoons of small projectiles—"canister and grape," fired by those three heavy guns. The heavier thrust at the center had been decimated as well, by canister, arrows, and musket fire, but at least it could respond, and it hit the enemy defenses with an awesome crash clearly audible over the other thunders of battle. He saw nothing of the attack from the sea, but the back mast on the stranded ship had fallen.

"They're *all* 'Hij,' General Halik," said Niwa. He'd rejoined the Grik leader after watching the waterborne assault depart. The confusion and chaos he'd witnessed, even among their "better" troops, appalled him. "That's something even First General Esshk has difficulty comprehending. The lowliest warrior in their ranks can recognize the ebbs and flows of battle, or call attention to perceived threats. *Of course* they react more quickly." He paused. "The barges are a waste of Uul. If that attack had begun in darkness, it would have fared better."

"Probably, but it still serves a purpose. It is the blunted jab that holds a portion of the opponent's attention. When he is forced to forget it by the battering sword, it might yet become the fatal thrust." He snorted apologetically. "I am new at this. I have never even faced this enemy before." He hissed a sigh. "I do not expect the 'prisoners' we'd hoped for, but I *am* learning from them."

"Remember, these are castaways, stranded warriors with no support," Niwa warned. "The larger force will be more difficult."

"I understand, but still I learn how the enemy thinks and fights. I see for myself the value of prepared defenses, these 'breastworks'! Once our armies learn to use such things, at need, do you believe they could be dislodged?"

"No," Niwa said.

The tumult of battle reached a crescendo, and the enemy line began to falter in the center.

"Look! Oh, look, General Niwa!" Halik cried. "We have broken through!" He looked at Niwa. "Let us send a company of our 'special troops' to join this exercise!"

Greg Garrett inserted his last magazine and racked the slide. Grik were *in* the trench behind the breastworks! The line had been holding well enough and with his limited view, he'd begun to feel a sense of optimism. Then, with a suddenness that left his thoughts reeling, the shield wall at the barricade simply disintegrated under the unexpected weight of a solid block of Grik reinforcements. He saw Graana-Fas thrust upward with a spear from the bottom of the trench, impaling a squalling Grik, and sling it among the wavering troops behind him. While he was thus occupied, more enemies leaped down upon him, and he fell beneath their hacking swords and gnashing teeth and claws. Greg fired at them, but one shot was spoiled when Bekiaa, covered in blood, dragged him out of the trench to the rear, where another shield wall was trying to form.

"Where's Saaran?" he yelled, but Bekiaa didn't respond. Grik were milling in the trench below, their wickedly barbed crossbow bolts flying past in thrumming sheets. Garrett fired down into the momentarily stalled Grik, joining a volley of muskets and arrows that piled them deep in the damp sand. His slide locked back.

"Here!" Bekiaa screeched, handing him a musket, a bloody, blackened bayonet fastened to the muzzle. "Find ammunition!" Bekiaa had a musket now as well. Greg scooped a black cartridge box out of the sand and glanced inside. Empty. He saw another and opened the flap, discovering three paperlike cartridges, each containing a .60-caliber ball and a trio of "buckshot" atop a load of powder. He had some caps in his shirt pocket already—just in case. Loading as he'd been trained, he joined the fusillade firing into the trench, yelling as savagely and incoherently as any of the 'Cats forming alongside him. Shields protected him now, placed there by Lemurians joining them from other parts of the line. A bolt grazed his inner forearm as he rammed down his final charge, and he looked up for a moment. Uncountable Grik had assembled beyond the trench, pausing for an instant across what had become a river of corpses they could almost walk across.

"Form square!" Bekiaa thundered.

Square? But that must mean . . . They were surrounded. Somehow, the line at the breastworks had fallen apart across a broad front. Only a few of the great guns spoke now, those facing the river, and maybe a couple on the extreme right, near the ship. *Donaghey's* guns still thundered furiously, but none was directed at the Grik infantry anymore, and Greg smelled wood smoke in the air.

He'd seen Lemurian Marines form a square only once before, and that had also been at the Battle of Aryaal—when everything fell apart. They'd saved themselves, managing to retreat in good order while embracing troops from other broken regiments. They did the same now, creating a temporary shield-studded barricade that sailors and other Marines could join, but this time, they had nowhere to go. The Grik were streaming across the trench now, and he poked at them with his bayonet as they came snarling toward him, battering at the shields with their sickle-shaped swords and their own bodies, slashing and gnawing with their teeth.

"I need ammunition!" he cried.

"There is no more," Jamie Miller shouted. Somehow, the young surgeon had joined him in the press, a spear in his hands. The kid looked wounded, wearing so much blood, but didn't act like it.

"We have to make it to the ship," Greg roared. "Bekiaa? Can we move the square to the ship?"

"What good will that do?"

Greg wasn't sure. He assumed Pruit still had something there, and if they could get more people aboard her, they might still ply *Donaghey*'s landward guns. But he couldn't see the ship anymore, over the mass of furry-feathery, reptilian shapes, and the wood smoke was growing thicker. Bekiaa probably thought *Donaghey* was afire. If she was . . . But trying to fight their way to Chapelle was impossible. It was twice as far, and there wasn't even the chance of more ammunition in that direction. "Just do it, damn it! It's our only choice!"

Slowly, the square moved like a vast turtle festooned with thousands of crossbow bolts jutting from shields like porcupine quills. The Grik seemed to divine their intent, and fought even more furiously to hold them in place and finish them. Wounded 'Cats fell and were left for the enemy to shred. Grik waved body parts, arms and legs, and even battered at the shields with the macabre clubs.

"Don't stop!" Bekiaa shrilled, her voice beginning to go. Greg had always been amazed by the volume Lemurians could achieve, but Bekiaa's voice was nearly finished.

"Don't stop!" he repeated, over and over. "We can't help the wounded. Stay on your feet, whatever you do. If you fall, you're dead!"

As if his words had summoned the bolt, Jamie Miller fell to the sand, black fletching on a dark shaft protruding from his side, his boyish face already pale and slack.

"No!"

"Leave me!" gurgled the former pharmacist's mate, blood erupting from his mouth to pour down his beardless chin. Greg didn't even stop to consider the hypocrisy. He grabbed the boy's arm and tried to drag him, but Jamie pitched forward, face in the sand, and became a deadweight.

"No!"

"You must leave him," Bekiaa croaked, moving beside him now. "He's dead," she pronounced gently. With tears welling in his sweat- and grime-crusted eyes, Garrett released the boy's arm, feeling the lifeless fingers pass through his. Someone else had taken up his cry in Lemurian: "Don't stop! Don't stop!"

The shields were falling apart under the constant drumming of bolts, and more and more sailors and Marines fell in the painfully bright sand, staining it dark and red. Through it all, they continued to kill, and the enemy losses were disproportionately high, but Garrett had concluded that didn't matter; the Grik reserves seemed infinite, and the square was all he knew anymore. He lost the musket, wrenched from his hands, and with none of the reservations he'd felt before, the cutlass came from its scabbard. Soon it was notched and black with blood.

He heard the surf, and thirst and exhaustion threatened to overwhelm him. The sun was high overhead, the sweltering heat a torment as harsh as death. He knew he couldn't drink seawater, but he thought if they reached the ocean, he might take a moment to sip from his canteen. His personal war became one of reaching water, if only for the momentary relief it might bring. Smoke dried his throat even worse. It had reached a point where it stung his eyes and made it nearly impossible to breathe. *Donaghey must* be burning . . . yet her guns still fired. In his muddled mind, he couldn't reconcile that.

Through the gasping, panting, trilling, and screaming of his comrades, he heard a different sound; shouts of encouragement, congratulation, relief. Still the chant "Don't stop!" continued, but in a stronger, persuasive tone. A nearby crash of an eighteen-pounder stunned him, but it brought him out of the metronomic, cutlass-swinging zone he'd entered, and he glanced to his right, through the pink smear of sweat and blood clouding his vision.

At the water's edge, a new, hasty breastworks had been added to the old, and two guns barked again, geysering sand into the air and sweeping down a mass of Grik rushing to get between Bekiaa's square and the haven the works represented. The avenue momentarily clear, the square shattered and raced for the trench.

"Hurry, hurry!" came the shouts now. "Get your tails clear!" Almost before the last survivors staggered over the barricade, a stunning volley of arrows and "buck and ball" slammed the pursuing Grik to a juddering halt.

"Lay it on!" came Pruit Barry's voice. "Hammer 'em! Fire at will!" For a few moments, the faster-firing arrows took up the slack, but soon the first muskets began crackling again. Greg stumbled toward Barry.

"My God, Greg," Pruit said, "you look awful!"

"I feel awful," Greg croaked, opening his canteen at last and taking a long gulp. He looked at *Donaghey* a short distance away, surrounded by swirling foam. She looked worse than he felt, but there were no flames. "I thought she was burning," he said. "Where's all the smoke coming from?"

Pruit shook his head. "Of the three sailing frigates we built, she's always been charmed. Faster, tougher, prettier . . . She's destroyed *six* gun-armed Grik ships while *beached*, for cryin' out loud! All the smoke's from one of the last three, half-sunk, aground, and burning a couple hundred yards to seaward. The other two were dismasted coming in. I bet they wind up near the one from last night."

"Not charmed," Garrett said. "Just damn good gunnery. Smitty deserves a medal when we finally get around to making some. So do you."

To punctuate the statement, one of *Donaghey*'s landward guns sent a roundshot churning through the momentarily checked Grik horde, spewing weapons and body parts in all directions. The Grik reacted little, beyond waving their weapons and hissing louder.

"I guess she's out of canister," Greg observed. "Roundshot's okay with them bunched up like that, but canister would be better." He pointed at Pruit's magazine pouches, and Barry handed over a couple.

"I wonder why they stopped?" Bekiaa asked, referring to the Grik as she joined them. Her once-white leather armor no longer showed any white at all. She gasped her thanks when Pruit handed her his canteen.

"I don't know. Orders, I guess. Imagine that. We stopped 'em, sure, but normally they'd've come on again by now." He gestured around. "And we'll stop 'em again. After that? I bet we're down to three hundred effectives. God knows if Chapelle's even alive." He snorted. "Eventually, they can just walk across us and stomp us to death."

"Cap-i-taan!" someone shouted. "Something happens!" Barry and Garrett both trotted to the breastworks. Resentful-looking Grik were making a lane for something coming through their ranks.

"What the hell?"

Oddly attired—uniformed—Grik trotted through the gap and formed two ranks facing the barricade. For a moment, the shooting stopped while the allies, amazed, watched this very un-Grik-like behavior.

"What are they carrying?" Bekiaa asked. They look like . . ." She hefted her weapon. "Kind of like muskets!"

"God almighty! I think they are!" Garrett said, recognizing the shape, if not the function. They were long, fish-tail-looking things, with levers underneath instead of trigger guards, and an odd arrangement on the side held what looked like a piece of smoldering match. "Shoot them!" he commanded.

'What's the matter with you, you bunch of fuzzy goofs?" Barry yelled. "Fire!"

Immediately, muskets resumed crackling and arrows swooshed. The uniformed Grik began to fall, and those behind them recoiled a bit from the renewed fusillade, bellowing their rage and frustration. But the front ranks of the Grik, even while taking casualties and blocking the replying bolts of those behind them, stood impassive, enduring the beating without apparent notice. One of the strange Grik horns brayed in the distance—a new note—and the enemy raised awkward-looking guns with all the appearance of taking deliberate aim.

"I'll be da . . ." Pruit began, but the Grik volley silenced him forever. A ball—it had to be a ball—struck him above the left eye and the side of his head erupted pink, flinging him backward into the trench. He wasn't alone, and there were cries of confusion and pain.

"Kill them!" Garrett roared, and the 'Cats around him roared as well, in anguish and anger. The horn squawked again, joined by many more, making a dreadful, familiar sound. The rest of the Grik charged.

"Now, at last I see what we face," Halik remarked grimly, watching the final, remorseless assault. There'd be no stopping it this time; the numbers were too overwhelming for the pitifully few enemy survivors to resist. "That . . . formation . . . the enemy assumed, to join those others by the sea . . . masterful! How can they achieve such a thing, even in the face of certain defeat?"

Niwa recognized what could only be admiration in the Grik general's voice. "It is called courage, General Halik," he said, oddly sick at heart. "Grik Uul are capable of fantastic discipline; they fling themselves forward with no regard for themselves—usually—but they're driven by instinct, urges they don't understand. Much of that 'instinct' is conditioned, but it serves the same purpose. The vast difference is that they obey commands to do what they're conditioned and instinctively inclined to do. Our enemies, the human Americans and Lemurians, 'tree folk,' each recognize the danger and challenge as well as any Hij, as I said. They stand and fight with their hearts and minds while retaining the ability to think and plan, even until the very end." He gestured toward the distant ship and the rapidly shrinking semicircle around it in the surf. "They *know* they're doomed, General, but still most do not 'fall prey.'"

"Our 'special troops' performed well in their initial trial," Halik pointed out.

Niwa nodded. "Yes. I saw none flee. The survivors will make excellent trainers and 'firsts of twenty' or more, but was it courage that made them stand, or merely more intense conditioning? That's the key question. How can we build true courage among 'our' warriors?"

Halik was at a loss. "I honestly do not know. How exactly is this 'courage' formed?"

"Think. You managed it on your own. It must be built atop a foundation few Uul survive to lay: character . . . and a cause."

Halik's crest suddenly rose. Distant from the fighting, he'd been holding his helmet under his arm. "What is that annoying sound?"

Niwa heard nothing over the climactic roar that heralded the final moments of the battle. Soon it would be over, and all the defenders slain. "I don't know," he said, surprisingly glum, but then he *did*.

Suddenly, six very peculiar-looking craft—*air*craft!—lumbered over the trailing mass of Grik warriors, jostling to get in the fight. They were clearly seaplanes, strangely reminiscent of the American PBY Niwa had seen. American insignias were distinct on their blue-and-white wings and forward fuselage. Over the horde, barrels detached and plummeted down, cracking open and spilling their contents in the sand. A few warriors were crushed, but Niwa was too stunned to suspect what was to come. The first flight pulled up and away, banking east over the water, their motors audible now over the hush that had fallen over the horde. Another flight came in, a little higher. Small objects fell, apparently thrown or dropped by someone in the back part of each plane. Realization dawned and despite their distance, Niwa pulled Halik to the ground as the beach erupted in a long, orange fireball that roiled with greasy black smoke.

Both Greg's pistols were empty; his own, and the one he'd taken from Captain Barry. He didn't know where the dead man's '03 Springfield wound up. Still conscientious, he'd thrust the Colts in his belt, and his pockets clacked with empty magazines even though he doubted he'd ever refill them. His cutlass was now scarred and stained, and he had a wide, bloody cut on his forehead from a blow that left him dazed and more than half-blinded with blood. Bekiaa had dragged him into the water where, hopefully, someone would hoist him onto his ship. It was probably appropriate that he should die on *Donaghey,* but there were still others fighting here, knee-deep in the surf, and he couldn't leave them. Bekiaa had vanished.

He heard the planes, but the sound didn't register. A Grik warrior lunged at him, off balance in the surf, and Greg hacked down across its neck, driving it into the pinkish foam. He hacked it again for good measure. There were more Grik, though, many more, and he raised the cutlass again. An unnatural, all-consuming *goosh!* interspersed with a staccato of small detonations heated his face, and an eerie brightness glowed through the bloody film in his eyes. It was followed by the most unearthly shriek of agony and terror he'd ever heard before.

Donaghey's guns, silent for some time as she conserved her final shots, barked almost over his head, and the concussion sent him reeling forward. Deafened, he almost fell. Exhausted as he was, he might have drowned in the knee-deep water. Bekiaa suddenly had him again, dragging him forward, *toward* the enemy! Her helmet was gone, and several crossbow bolts dangled from her leather armor like ornaments. He had no idea if any had found her flesh, but she didn't care if they had. She was blinking with joy, and her ears were flattened against her skull in feral satisfaction. He almost fell again as they reached the sand, but she continued urging him forward. Others joined them, their harsh voices cracking with thirst and savage delight. Ahead, he finally saw the flames and caught the distinctive smell of burning gasoline, combined with the equally singular stench of cooking flesh and burning leather.

Wild shapes convulsed and capered in the flames, amid the continuous anguished squeals. Grik warriors on this side of the inferno fought with frantic abandon, slaying one another to escape the maniacal rush of survivors and the hellish fire behind. Steadily, they were pushed back, past the breastworks they'd so recently overrun. Some broke and ran through the flames, mostly dying in the attempt. A pair of the uniformed Grik still stood, mechanically loading their weird guns, seemingly oblivious, until they were cut down. Garrett remained confused, his head throbbed, and he couldn't focus. All he knew was that something astonishing must have occurred. He *should* be dead already.

Another flight of planes, "CV-1" boldly stenciled on their tails, rumbled past, bombs tumbling amid the enemy beyond the fire, and suddenly Greg Garrett *knew*. First Fleet had arrived at last. He spun and wiped his eyes with his salty wet sleeve. His vision remained blurry, but he stared hard out to sea. Far to the south, near the hazy horizon, he could just distinguish the range-distorted shapes of ships and smoke, stretching as far as he could see in either direction.

"It's *Big Sal* and *Humfra-Dar*!" he croaked, dropping to his knees in the sand. "God bless Ben Mallory and his 'Nancys'!"

Bekiaa collapsed beside him. "I am going to be very nice to the Air Corps, in the future," she gasped.

General Halik was hissing words Niwa didn't understand. He assumed they were profane.

"We must withdraw," Niwa said. More planes were bombing the artillery positions. A bright flash amid a thunderclap of sound and a cloud of white smoke testified to the almost-certain eradication of a battery nearby.

"This army is largely intact! We can still finish the enemy on the beach!" Halik insisted.

"Spoken just like Regent Tsalka or General Esshk at Baalkpan," Niwa sneered. "Think! With those things"—he pointed at a passing plane—"pounding your Uul at will, most will turn prey and be of no use even if they're successful! Call them back, General, withdraw and re-form. Then we can consider what to do next!"

"Will they land here? It makes no sense," Halik replied after a moment, taking Niwa's advice and beginning to think critically again. "We are far from any industrial centers."

"I don't know," Niwa confessed, "but there's a good harbor nearby. Regardless, with their planes and likely big guns, we can't stop them on the beach, in the open." He sighed. "We must let them land, wherever they choose, and see what develops. Attack them in the jungles perhaps, where their planes will help them little. However we proceed, for now this army must withdraw with its will and experience intact. Remember, we weren't sent to *save* Ceylon, as much as to learn what we can of the enemy and how to counter him."

Halik nodded. "You are right, my friend. I fear my blood began to boil with the passion of the arena. We will pull back what we can. As you know, sometimes that is not easy. We have other armies at our disposal, but this one has faced the enemy. It might be easier to teach what we desire." He paused. "We will let the enemy land and see how he deploys. Try to discover his intent, then devise a strategy based on that." He raised a clawed hand. "I remember our instructions, but I am not ready to concede Ceylon just yet."

By nightfall, the beach around *Donaghey* was packed with Marines, as well as both the Silver and Black Battalions of Safir Maraan's "Six Hundred." The bulk of the fleet had moved up the coast a short distance to a more protected anchorage where it launched the first "official" invasion of Grik Ceylon. There was little resistance. For the most part, it seemed as if the army that nearly exterminated the survivors of *Revenge, Tolson,* and *Donaghey* had simply vanished. Of those survivors, fewer than four hundred still lived, mostly wounded, and Kathy McCoy came ashore with a large medical contingent to triage and stabilize the injured before sending them out to *Dowden,* which stood offshore to defend against more Grik naval attacks. Ultimately, the wounded would be moved to *Salissa* or *Humfra-Dar.*

"It must have been a great battle," Safir Maraan said softly, gazing at the sea of enemy dead. The stench of their cooked flesh was still strong, despite the wind that drove it inland.

"It wasn't so great," Greg quipped, sitting on a crate in the sand while Kathy herself stitched his scalp. Russ Chapelle was patiently waiting his turn under the nurse's needle. He had several long claw gashes on his chest, but he'd survived, as had a fair percentage of those near the river. It was almost as if they'd been forgotten for a time, once the main line collapsed.

"It looked pretty 'great' to me," Russ said, "Especially the way you pulled everybody into a square to save what you could. Then, of course, the planes' cooking the Grik was swell!"

"I didn't do the square," Greg admitted. "Lieutenant Bekiaa did that. She did nearly everything that kept us alive. Her and Smitty."

"That's 'Cap-i-taan' Bekiaa now, according to General Aalden," Safir said.

"Any sign of my exec? Lieutenant Saaran-Gaani?" Garrett asked.

"He's okay," Russ told him. "A little worse for wear, like all of us, but he made it to us on the left when things fell apart." He pointed at the sea. "Already out on *Dowden*."

Garrett sighed with relief. "Good. We lost so many. . . . I saw Barry buy it. One of those goofy Grik muskets."

"They're matchlocks," Russ said. "I bet that was a nasty surprise. We sent some to Alden. The good thing is, they won't be worth a damn in the rain. We might use that."

"What about Jamie?" Kathy asked, finishing her sewing.

"Dead," Garrett said simply. "I . . . saw that too."

"Well," said Russ after a silent moment, "I guess us Navy types are out of it for a while. They're gonna try to patch *Donaghey* up and pull her off, but it's Pete's, Rolak's, and Her Highness's fight now." He nodded at the "Orphan Queen."

"Not if I can help it," Garrett swore. "*Donaghey*'ll be out of the war for months. Pete had better find me an infantry assignment or, by God, I'll scratch up a regiment out of the guys we had here!"

Russ brightened. "Hey! That's not a bad idea! You rig it; I'll join it. Maybe they'll give us that spitfire Bekiaa. Hell, we'll win the war all by ourselves!"

CHAPTER 10

////// *TF Maaka-Kakja*

*D*iania crept down the dark companionway, deep in the bowels of USS *Maaka-Kakja*. Even this far from the engineering spaces, muted machinery noises were audible, and the very wooden fibers of the enormous ship trembled with life. She touched a bulkhead to steady herself on the stairs and felt the throbbing pulse of the twin triple-expansion monsters so far aft, beating like a mighty heart. There was only ambient light from the deck above so close to the forward magazine, and she felt small and vulnerable in the gloom. She had difficulty suppressing a sense of superstitious dread, summoned from distant memories of the admonitions of Dominion priests. She still believed in demons, but they weren't the animalistic beasts of her childhood—or maybe they were. To her, the most fearsome demons of all were the priests themselves.

She'd become a devout follower of the English faith since her childhood indenture, and even after her freedom was purchased by the "Americans" on the skinny iron steamer, she clung to it still. The Americans, of both species, seemed to care little what she believed as long as it wasn't harmful to them or their cause. She kept her faith and found, through conversation, that it wasn't much different from that of the Lady Sandra. If it had been, *that* might have caused her to convert, since she was utterly convinced that Sandra Tucker hung the moon.

Diania was in the Navy now; she, along with a number of other Respitan women, had taken the oath to defend the Constitution of the United States—whatever that was. She didn't really care what the "Constitution" was; she'd have sworn an oath to a rope if Lady Sandra said she should. There'd been some commotion over her enlistment, mostly among the human men, she'd noticed, but she supposed that was to be expected. Women served as Naval Auxiliaries in the Empire, but none were allowed *in* the Navy itself. Lady Sandra clearly held more power than any woman she'd ever heard of; yet she wielded it with an ease and confidence Diania had rarely seen in men. It was all so strange, but exciting too. The Lemurian females took her induction as a matter of course, and she'd made a lot of friends. Even Sandra wouldn't let her run around without a shirt, though, as female 'Cats sometimes did, and she wondered what to make of that. Still, she was in the Navy, with all the "rank and privileges" due any "seaman recruit"! She'd been told she could "strike" for any position she desired, and though she'd been a carpentress, she didn't know if that was what she wanted to do. The great engines fascinated her, but so did the frail-looking "airplanes." She yearned to learn more about *Maaka-Kakja*'s many weapons. For now, however, she was more than content to be Lady Sandra's "steward" while she learned the ropes and figured out what she *did* want to do.

She descended below the magazine compartments and the muted voices beyond locked doors, down into the very bottom of the ship. She knew the sea rose high around her outside the mighty hull, and down here she could even hear its booming, disconcerting rumble. Sometimes, she still grasped distant, nightmarish memories of her childhood voyage in the hold of a Company ship. The smell of rot and mildew brought them most readily to mind, but here, the new timbers still smelled sweet and the bilge had not yet soured. She took a lantern from its hook and advanced toward a raised deck where the officer's stores were kept. She planned to cook something special tonight; as special as she knew how, for Lady Sandra and her friends. She needed some of the purple-brown sugar the "People" used for the glazed topping she wanted to make.

Something stirred in the darkness beyond her feeble light, startling her. All the thoughts of demons must have left her on edge. "Innyone there?" she called quietly. She heard another noise, a slight rustling. "Ach! You! Gi'out! Thisiz off'ser's stores! I'll report ye!" she said, as menacing as she was able. Clutching the lantern and ready to swing it, she advanced. "Gi'out, I say! Show yersef!"

There was a loud *clunk!* and suddenly a gray-white form lunged from the darkness and fluttered in front of her face, accompanied by a thundering "Booby, booby-boo!"

Diania sprawled backward over one of the massive diagonal braces and dropped the lantern in the shallow water of the bilge. It hissed and died, plunging the compartment into darkness. With a cry, she scrambled to her feet and raced for the feeble light of the companionway she'd just descended, launching up the stairs like a rocket. Behind her, the deep, demonic voice continued chanting, "Booby-boo! Booby-boo!"

The demon didn't pursue her. She made it through the darkened forward magazine spaces where the various types of ordnance were stored, levering past a growing number of staring 'Cat sailors and working her way aft. She'd chosen to traverse that deck instead of the one above because of the quicker association with non-demonic creatures, but now she was anxious to get into the light. Gasping, she raced up the companionway forward of the number one fireroom and found herself on the broad but cluttered hangar deck. Spinning, looking for someone she knew, she attracted even more stares before scrambling to starboard through the jumble of "Nancys" and the surprised crews working on them. There was only one place left to go; she'd find Lady Sandra on the bridge. She might not believe her—Diania didn't know Sandra's position on demons—but she'd seen *something* in the hold, and people had to know . . . before whatever it was ate a hole in the ship!

It was windy topside, and Sandra's increasingly customary ponytail had been undone by the stiff, westerly gale. She faced into the wind alongside Colonel Shinya and Captain Lelaa, her still sun-streaked and tow-highlighted hair streaming to leeward. It was too long, she thought, longer than she'd ever allowed, and it was difficult to control and much too difficult to style. Matt had once hinted that he liked it long, however, and she meant to surprise him. *Who knows how long it'll grow before I see him now*, she thought moodily. She didn't know exactly what she expected would happen when they reunited in "the Isles," but she was sure what she *hoped* for. With the end of the "dame famine," their own situation had finally changed, and she supposed she harbored inner fantasies of a dramatic, romantic, Imperial wedding. But *Walker* wasn't there. She'd steamed into the vast Eastern Sea to protect their new allies' important colonies from a threatened Dom attack.

It was necessary she knew, and only the old destroyer had the speed to get there in time, but she was beginning to wonder if hers and Matt's stars weren't doomed to be crossed forever. She sighed. *We've all been through so much, and I've become . . . such a sight; nearly* thirty *now too. . . .* She couldn't always suppress an almost-instinctual concern that he might not even *want* her anymore. She honestly doubted that. She didn't think she'd have fallen for him if he was *that* sort. But she was a woman, and despite her outward confidence and professionalism, she possessed normal apprehensions and insecurities common to the species, she supposed. She sighed again.

Lelaa-Tal-Cleraan felt the almost-imperceptible working of the ship and watched the oilers pitch dramatically alongside. The whitecapped sea had become a sparkling metallic gray beneath a humid, gray-blue sky. She heard her friend's sighs and suspected what was on the human female's mind. She found it vaguely amusing that the "iron woman" could worry so about nothing. She didn't personally know Captain Reddy well, but his and Sandra's unrequited love had reached almost-mythical, if imponderable dimensions within the Alliance. Of course, based on the extremely limited examples, human mating customs in general were imponderable to Lemurians. The People were straightforward about such things, and either a male or female, usually of higher perceived status, might "propose" to a prospective mate. Sometimes, among sea folk, this even involved mating outside one's "clan," or specialty, but that was rare. Those within the same clan, or among land folk in general (Aryaal and B'mbaado aside) who were considered "equal," often gravitated toward "matrimony" in an apparently more "human" way, through a style of courtship in which prospective partners became intimately acquainted. All this was more tradition than rule, but it was fairly universal—at least before the war. Now, many of the old clans— wing runners, Body of Home, etc.—were becoming increasingly diverse and fragmented into something like "clans" representing the various naval divisions. There were attempts to found ordnance clans, engineer-ing clans, deck clans, all under the greater umbrella of "snipe" and "ape" clans, within the overall "Amer-i-caan Na-vee" clan, but this sort of reg-imentation was frowned on and even discouraged by the senior officers. It was all very confusing, and the "sub" clan system itself was probably doomed. Regardless, considering how long Matt and Sandra had "courted," and how well they had to know each other by now, Lelaa thought it appropriate to worry about the man's *safety*; he was a warrior on a dangerous mission. She considered it silly to worry about his feel-ings.

Tamatsu Shinya was thinking about other things. The effort to "lib-erate" New Ireland was scheduled to begin almost immediately. He un-derstood the political necessity but thought the attempt precipitous. Chack and Blair's plan seemed sound, and he had confidence in it. Be-sides, even if it failed, or came apart in some unforeseen way, TF *Maaka-Kakja* should arrive in plenty of time to prevent a disaster. Still, he worried. He didn't know these "Doms" and had no "feel" for them. All he knew came from Chack's and Captain Reddy's reports. The new enemy appeared almost as insensitive to losses as the Grik, but they were human and *had* to be more tactically flexible. Didn't they? Even though it failed, the plan to seize the Empire had been bold and cunning, and strategically, came far too close to success. He felt he needed to be work-ing on a plan of his own, but the only "maps" they had of New Ireland were rough sketches Jenks had left. Surely better ones would be available when they stopped at Respite Island? He brooded.

Sandra, Captain Lelaa, and Colonel Shinya were all jarred from their respective thoughts when Diania suddenly burst upon the bridgewing, gasping for air. The dark-skinned woman sketched a hasty imitation of salutes she'd seen, and, eyes wide, breathlessly proclaimed, "Beggin' yer pardons, but there's a daemon in the for'ard hold!"

Rendered speechless by the sudden, distracting news, Sandra noticed a disturbance down on the flight deck and saw a group of 'Cats assembling around a tall, blond-headed figure with a shiny new eye patch. The man bowed occasionally to those around him as he strode toward the offset conn tower, or patted them on their heads. He was looking up at Sandra with that weird, distinctive grin.

Sandra's eyes narrowed. They'd learned that Silva had somehow escaped the "Buzzard," but no one had any idea where he was. "I believe you, Diania," she said angrily, "but the 'demon' is on the loose now."

"I ain't AWOL," Silva denied, "I been here all along—not 'absent' a'tall!" He was standing in Captain Lelaa's "great cabin," surrounded by a collection of humans and 'Cats. He'd never get a more sympathetic hearing since nearly everyone present owed him their lives, but this was a serious matter. Despite his plea, he was inarguably absent without leave, and in direct violation of orders. In contrast to the last time they'd seen him, covered with grease, he was actually fairly presentable. Some, such as Lawrence and Princess Rebecca—and, Petey, her weird little pet—were openly gleeful to see him, as was Midshipman Brassey. Irvin and Shinya appeared less pleased.

Sandra couldn't tell what Lelaa or the other Lemurian officers thought, and she groaned. When it came to rationalization, Dennis Silva was an artist, and judging by his opening shot, this was liable to be a masterpiece. What was more, she knew Lemurians were susceptible to the type of "performance art" Dennis excelled at. Ultimately, Silva's punishment would be decided by Captain Lelaa, but Sandra felt compelled to play the role of the "reporting officer."

"Mr. Silva, as I'm sure you're aware, 'here' isn't where you're supposed to be!" Sandra said severely. "And you're 'AWOL' from where you were ordered to go!"

Dennis affected an expression of concentration. "An' I've given that a lot of thought since Mr. Riggs passed them silly orders," he admitted. "Has anybody ever seen fit to in-vestigate whether he's a Jap . . . or even a *Grik* spy?"

"My God, Silva!" Laumer burst out. "Are you insane?"

Brassey and Princess Rebecca stifled chuckles, and most of the 'Cats' tails twitched with amusement.

"It's possible," Silva confessed, "but you know, that scamp never liked me much ever since . . ." He paused. "Well, it ain't pertinent, an' I won't refloat bygones if he won't. But think about it; my original orders, spoke right at me by the Skipper himself, was to guard the Munchkin Princess to the death. After our recent . . . situation with the Comp'ny, I'm pretty sure them orders oozed over onto you, Lieutenant Tucker. You need me. Maybe Bernie thinks he does, back in Baalkpan, but I can wire any screwball schemes I come up with back to him from here, but I can't protect you ladies nor help the Skipper from *there*. That's what got me wonderin' about Mr. Riggs; such a blatant misallocation o' resources—me—in time o' war, can only benefit the enemies o' freedom, baseball, an' beer."

The 'Cats roared and stomped their feet. Even Captain Lelaa grinned. Irvin covered his eyes with his hand and even Shinya stared hard at something else in the compartment. Sandra glared at Lelaa. As the senior naval officer, she should've at least tried to keep a straight face. Sandra realized she should have let Laumer do the grilling, but while now a genuine hero, the submariner and current exec of *Maaka-Kakja*, was still a little in awe of Silva—and most of the "original" human members of the Alliance. He had a tendency to overcompensate for that, and Sandra hadn't known if he'd be too harsh or too lenient on Dennis. When the tumult died away, she persisted.

"Mr. Riggs is not a Jap—or Grik—spy! He's acting chief of staff to the most powerful figure in the Alliance. You can't pick and choose which of his orders to obey!"

"I can when they come over the wireless! Shoot, they might've been fake! Captain Reddy's orders came face-to-face, an' his orders trump Riggs any day. Always follow the last, highest-up orders you get; that's my motto!"

"But . . . Captain Reddy *confirmed* the orders!" Sandra said adamantly. Silva was already shaking his head.

"Over wireless. Which he's too busy to go over every little housekeepin' chore in the Alliance, an' old 'Gap Sparks' Palmer probably gapped it up." He shrugged. "Wire the Skipper again, get him to personally exvoke his standin' orders to me, an' I'll go to Baalkpan, meek as a sheep."

"You know, he's probably right about the confirmation," Shinya said, surprising everyone. "A ream of routine requests was sent to *Walker*, once the relay was in place and communications were reestablished. All were granted."

Sandra looked at Shinya, as startled as the others. She rounded back on Silva. "How long did it take you to figure all this out?" she demanded. "If you'd pulled this before the 'Buzzard' left Manila, you might've gotten away with it." She paused. "Come to that, how did you get back to Manila in time to sail with us? We all saw you get on the plane!"

"Dee-vine providence!" Silva exclaimed piously, casting his one eye to the overhead. "You personally ordered me on the plane, an' I got on. Wouldn't *never* disobey a direct, face-to-face order. Beyond that?" He shrugged and his twisted grin spread. "I've always been mortally fearful o' flyin'. I guess, combined with that an' all the other things I had to say, I must'a been miracled aboard!"

"Only to be discovered once it's too late to fly you back to Maa-ni-la, and *Walker* has steamed beyond wireless reach yet again," Shinya observed dryly.

"Is that so?" Silva asked innocently. He glanced at Diania, standing away from Lelaa's "wardroom table," ready to refill Sandra's water cup if asked. The small woman was staring at him with barely restrained fury. "I do apologize for startlin' your girl there, by the way," he said. "I was whoopin' some empty grain sacks off me when all of a sudden, there she was! Scared me half to death!"

There were chuckles, and Diania's dark face darkened further.

Lelaa cleared her throat. "Regardless of *Walker*'s position, this task force is currently steaming under blacked? Blanketed . . . communications to prevent discovery by the mysterious Jaap destroyer, the whereabouts of which is still unknown . . . but perhaps you considered that as well?" she pondered aloud, contemplating the big man looming before her. She shook her head, blinking. "Until Captain Reddy can be consulted, to resolve this matter, Mr. Silva will cease berthing in the forward hold, and will be entered as a chief gunner's mate in the ship's rolls." She looked hard at Dennis. "Work with the gun's crews; they're all 'green,' I think you say? *Behave* yourself, or you'll be returned to the hold—in irons!"

"Aye, aye, Cap'n Lelaa!" Silva said. "Gunnery'll be up to snuff directly!"

Lelaa paced the offset bridge, surveying her domain. "Tex" Sheider had the watch, and she was free to simply enjoy her ship, and honestly, her position. It hadn't been that long since the biggest thing she'd commanded was a medium-size fishing felucca. It had been her Home, her life. When the war came, she'd been given a razeed Grik prize, a Navy "corvette," or "DE." She'd loved USS *Simms*, but when she was destroyed by Billingsley, and Lelaa herself joined Sandra and the others in captivity, she'd never expected to command anything again, even if she survived. She certainly hadn't expected to command something like *Maaka-Kakja*, the largest, most powerful, and advanced vessel likely ever built on this entire world. She loved it.

On the bridge, she was surrounded by an assortment of devices she'd once have considered miraculous or magical, and was amazed that she'd almost begun to take them for granted. What was more, she *understood* them, and People, *Mi-Anaaka*, operated them with growing precision and practiced ease despite their inexperience compared to other "carrier" crews. Much of that was due to *Maaka-Kakja*'s veteran teachers. The still-weak Orrin Reddy was doing his best to help organize the air wing, and though he wasn't very communicative, Gilbert Yeager taught engineering by example extremely well. *Now I have Dennis Silva,* Lelaa thought somewhat smugly, *to shape my gun's crews.* Things couldn't be much better from her perspective.

As the sun faded aft, quickly plunging the sea into darkness, she blinked her trust at Tex and stepped out on the starboard bridgewing. The oilers were out there, churning doggedly alongside through the calming sea as the wind continued to lay. They were venturing more canvas now, to ease the burden on their engines and bunkers, and the sails flashed from purple-gold to gray. Soon, darkened as they were, the ships would be invisible to all but Lemurian eyes, and she welcomed the cover of night. Danger lurked in the darkness; even her people's vision had its limits. Sleeping, wallowing mountain fish, with their blue-black bodies, could become virtually invisible against the black sea and sky. But oddly, the massive beasts appeared to actually avoid *Maaka-Kakja*—a courtesy they didn't always extend even to her huge sailing cousins. Tex proposed that *Maaka-Kakja*'s size, combined with her massive pounding screw and—to the sound-sensitive behemoths—thunderous, machinery noises, might actually *frighten* them. Lelaa didn't know, but the oilers had orders to stay as close to her as they dared. So far, it was well.

What concerned her more, and made her prefer the uncertain night, was the rogue Japanese destroyer and its reputedly incredibly malevolent "Long Lance" torpedoes. She'd never seen torpedoes before, even though she knew *Walker* and *Mahan* had carried the things. One still existed in Baalkpan, a damaged "condemned" specimen from the other world, but she hadn't been to see it. Someone had said there should be a few aboard *Amagi*'s dwindling corpse, but she didn't know if they'd been recovered. Bernie Sandison made no secret of his efforts to make some and Captain Reddy would love to have them, but in truth, they terrified Lelaa. She hated the very idea of torpedoes. She'd been wholly convinced by the Jaap Okada, that mighty as *Maaka-Kakja* was, she had no defense against them. She suspected the rogue destroyer was far away, but if by chance it wasn't, Lelaa-Tal-Cleraan embraced the darkness that might protect her ship—her new Home—from the puny vision of any bad hu-maans lurking nearby . . . and their torpedoes.

Strange music reached her ears from two decks below, from the vestigial "battlement" where *Maaka-Kakja*'s 5.5-inch guns were situated around her "island." The battlement provided a high, unobstructed gun platform, and plenty of space for defenders too. It sometimes served as a social gathering place for off-duty crew away from the hot engineering spaces and hazards of the flight and hangar decks. The amusements there could sometimes distract those on duty, but over time, that concern ebbed away. Those on watch were allowed to listen, but woe was he or she caught watching. Few ever were. This was their Home too, and just as wing runners or watchers remained vigilant during amusements on the sailing Homes, they did the same on *Maaka-Kakja*. Lelaa wasn't officially on duty now, so she listened—and watched.

The instruments she heard were familiar; bows with tight strings and resonance chambers. "Laaukas," mostly. Many Mi-Anaaka knew how to play them, and they were compact and portable. The tune was unfamiliar, though . . . if it could be called a tune. It had the jaunty, repetitive air reminiscent of "Amer-i-caan" songs she'd heard, but the players were obviously learning it as they went, while a familiar voice hummed the melody. Suddenly, the voice broke into song.

"Ooooh! Cat-monkeys got long tails on Zambo-anga!

"'Cause Zamboanga ain't Zamboanga anymorrr!"

Lelaa recognized Silva's deep voice, but realized Orrin Reddy was singing along, squinting at a piece of paper in his hand. The Imperial midshipman, Stewart Brassey, was trying to play a laauka.

"An' the whales didn't get 'em, 'cause the whales would be chikkin,

To face things I have seen here, that's for sure!"

It was nonsense, but Lelaa chuckled in her throaty way. She'd tried to be strict with Silva that day, but didn't think she'd succeeded. She couldn't help it. She hated the big ridiculous brute . . . and adored him. He'd saved her life and avenged *Simms*, and done so many other things, but as Sandra said, he *was* depraved. Whatever else he'd done to get aboard *Maaka-Kakja*, he'd abandoned Paam Cross, a female who was devoted to him, for some reason. And even Lelaa occasionally speculated what exactly there was between him and Risa-Sab-At. . . . But the song amused her. She didn't know what a "chikkin" was, but "whales" were something like mountain fish . . . she thought.

Oh, we won't go back to Subic anymore,

Oh, we won't go back to Subic anymore!

Oh, we won't go back to Subic, we drink seep instead of tubic!

Oh, we won't go back to Subic anymore!

Orrin had harmonized quite nicely with Silva on that verse. Lelaa liked songs with harmony. She could see the growing musical throng much better than Orrin could see his page, and noticed Gilbert Yeager standing off to the side. He'd attempted some of those last words, and she was stunned to see tears streaking his face. She didn't understand. The song sounded like others she'd heard hu-maans sing with mirth.

Oooh! The birdies ain't real birdies in Maa-ni-la!

Instead of feathers—they have teeth and fur!

Some are green and blue, and they eat each other too!

. . . an' I can't make up nothin' that rhymes with furrr!

Those in the crowd laughed and stamped their feet, but Gilbert was gone.

Oooh, we lived ten thousand years in old Chefoo,

The Japs got it, and then Caveetee too!

I wouldn't give a fart for a piece of either part,

But I'll make 'em rot in hell before I'm throooo!

Lelaa realized Colonel Shinya was beside her in the dark. "You are a 'Jaap,' as they say, yes?"

"Yes."

"You had a war, on your world. Do Amer-i-caans really hate you that much?" She paused. "Does Silva?"

Shinya hesitated. "Some do, even here. Even now. There was . . . unpleasantness. I never witnessed anything like what Commander Okada saw, perpetrated by either side, but 'my' war with the Americans was different . . . earlier. I cannot say how things would have gone had the war continued as it was when I . . . left it, but it was ugly enough already. And there were rumors of things happening in China. If the tide truly has turned as Okada says, it's possible things have become as ugly as they are here." He sighed. "But I don't think Silva hates me, not anymore." Unconsciously, he blinked irony in the Lemurian way. "We're on the same side now, are we not?"

"His song might leave some doubt, and he sings it to my People." Lelaa shook her head. "I am 'Amer-i-caan' now, in the Na-vee clan, but I don't hate Jaaps. I hope my people don't come to."

"American songs are almost meaningless," he assured her. "This one more than most."

Lelaa looked at Shinya. "Okada *must* stop the rogue destroyer, or you may end up mistaken."

CHAPTER 11

////// *Southeast Coast of Africa*

t was blustery, wet, and very cold. Lieutenant Toryu Miyata stood forlornly on the soggy sand with his two companions, Aguri and Umito. Wrapped in damp fur coats, they were watching the Grik longboat struggle back through the heavy breakers they'd just barely—in Toryu's view—survived. He'd longed to escape the Grik, and the mission he'd embarked upon had seemed a good opportunity at the time, but the journey so far had been a hellish experience. And it had only begun.

The "Cape of Storms" on this world had apparently earned its name for the same reason as the one "back home." Not only was it so designated on the ancient, stolen charts, but the storms were even more intense and constant. The Grik didn't believe any ship could round the cape, or even steer too close, and the world beyond was unknown to them. Toryu supposed that was one good thing. The only charts they'd captured intact from the long-dead British Indiamen showed only the coast of Africa and Madagascar. The Grik had been forced to earn their knowledge of other places.

Because of that, the transport that brought his little expedition had set them ashore far short of their destination. They'd have to trek overland across unknown and probably hostile country long before they could deliver General of the Sea Kurokawa's note to the strangers of this land. The Grik had a few frontier outposts to the north, and the "others" apparently maintained their own to the southwest. Toryu would have to cross the "no-man's-land" between them—and he hadn't even escaped the Grik. There were six Uul warriors along, and a low-level Hij— probably a lieutenant or something—named Bashg. He was to command them, interpret General Esshk's orders, and generally "lead" the expedition.

Ordinarily, Toryu believed he'd have killed Bashg and as many Uul as he could as soon as they arrived. He and his friends had discussed that very thing: kill their captors and flee to the mercy of the "others." Toryu and Aguri each had a precious Arisaka rifle and fifty rounds of ammunition. Umito had a Grik crossbow that had been fitted to him. The problem was, Bashg and his troops weren't "ordinary" Grik. They were some kind of "elite" Grik trained by Niwa and Halik before they left for Ceylon. Bashg was imperious and rude and probably not much of an "officer" to have been given this assignment, but his troops displayed an alarming level of awareness compared to other Uul Toryu had seen. They also carried guns.

The guns weren't really that threatening, particularly under the circumstances. They were essentially simple Japanese matchlocks formed to fit Grik physiques. Easy to produce, they were the most foolproof firearms Kurokawa and the surviving Japanese engineers could—or would?—give the Grik. They weren't terrible weapons, but they were useless in wet air. Toryu doubted they were even loaded. Their matches certainly weren't lit.

No, the guns weren't the issue. These Grik also carried swords, of course, and truly were superior warriors. Two Arisakas and a crossbow might not be fast enough. They also had a long way to go, through dangerous country. They'd need the Grik to defend them and carry their supplies—at least for a while.

"I can't believe they made it back through the breakers," Aguri said, referring to the longboat. Toryu couldn't see it anymore, but Aguri was taller.

"A shame," managed Umito, but he paid for his words with a racking cough that sounded deep and wrenching. Toryu looked at him with concern. The cough had begun during the wet voyage south, then west. They couldn't stand being belowdecks on the Grik ship—the stench was simply too great—and they'd slept exposed on the cold, damp deck.

"Come," snarled Bashg in his own tongue. The three of them had been chosen for the mission partly because of their ability to understand some Grik and speak some English, which Bashg could sometimes grasp. "Get things. We go!" Bashg wrapped his own fur coat more tightly around himself. "Sooner we go, sooner we done! Get back to warm!"

Toryu and Aguri slung their rifles and headed for their packs. Another coughing fit from Umito made them look back. He straightened, shaking, still staring out to sea. The Grik ship that brought them was piling on sail, beginning to slant away to the north, northeast. Leaving them behind.

"You get you sick man moving!" Bashg warned. "He make slow, we eat him!"

Toryu rounded on Bashg. "I'll kill any of you who tries! The rest of you might kill us, but then where will you be? Who'll deliver the message to the 'others'? Your mission will fail and Esshk will give you the 'Traitor's Death'!"

Bashg stared hard at Toryu, then at Aguri who'd stepped forward as well, but his hand never neared his sword. "All well," he said at last. "We no eat. He make slow, we carry. We only eat if he die."

Umito joined them, walking slow, taking quick shallow breaths. "Thanks, Toryu," he whispered raggedly. "I'll be fine once we get out of here."

Toryu nodded, trying not to show how much he was shaking with fury and terror. He feared Umito *wouldn't* be fine, but even then there was no way he'd stand by and see him eaten. He suspected that would be when, one way or the other, he'd part company with the Grik.

Colombo, Grik Ceylon

General Halik lounged on Tsalka's old throne in the regency palace, staring at a map of the island. He was exhausted, and if he noticed N'galsh's indignation over his usurpation of what the vice regent considered *his* "chair" in Tsalka's absence, he made no sign, and N'galsh didn't speak it aloud. General Orochi Niwa stood by the map, doubtless just as tired, but unwilling to sit as he pointed out various places along the southern coast.

"The enemy has landed here, here, and here," he said, "in impressive force. I imagine, combined, they have even greater numbers than we faced at Baalkpan, and their discipline and disposition are proportionately superior as well." He paused. "And, of course, they're better equipped." His tone carried what Halik had come to recognize as genuine admiration. "They've built a *real* army, with uniform armor, accoutrements, and apparently, large numbers of standardized muskets," he enthused. "Not to mention their many steam-powered warships!"

"Or their flying machines," Halik added darkly.

Niwa nodded, becoming more solemn. "Indeed. Honestly, I suspected they might have created some aircraft, but the numbers, sophistication, and frankly, skill with which they were employed, came as a complete surprise." He shook his head. "That, and their ability to transport them here in the first place. I *never* expected aircraft carriers!" His admiration returned, but his expression was thoughtful. "We must consider the enemy airpower in every plan we make. Consolidation will be difficult, and we must use the terrain and jungle to best advantage. We'll have to move carefully and employ misdirection whenever possible, because whatever we do might be observed. We must also find some way to combat these aircraft—shoot them down!"

"How?"

"I don't know," Niwa replied honestly. "Perhaps if we lure them low enough, into a specific, pretargeted place, we might have some success with even field artillery, loaded with canister—they *are* rather slow." He shook his head, still considering. "Perhaps something else . . ." He looked at Halik. "We must pass word of these developments to General of the Sea Kurokawa—and General Esshk at once! The enemy will certainly move to blockade us again, in greater force than ever before!"

"That has already been ordered. All remaining ships in Colombo except our own 'escape squadron' will dash out this very night under cover of darkness. Perhaps some will get through." Halik studied the map again. "The enemy concentrations are slightly isolated from one another. How will they proceed, and can we use that?"

"It will be difficult," Niwa confessed. "We didn't expect landings where they occurred, and it will take us time to deploy in response." He shook his head. "I doubt *they* intended to land where they did, but it's turned out fortuitous for them, in the short term. They'll likely consolidate as they advance, and we'll have to watch for opportunities. There's nothing we can do against their beachheads—oh, if we had planes of our own!—so their strength will build behind them. But they have far to go, and we should seize numerous chances to bleed them as they move." He rubbed sore muscles in his neck. "We must have a care, however. They may retain reserves, make further landings. They can watch what we do and take advantage."

Halik blinked. "But what if we use this 'misdirection' you mentioned to lure them into committing those reserves, or some force, where they only *think* we are weak?" He drummed his claws on the arm of the throne, sitting up. "They have already shown an aversion to losses, a desire to rescue those who are doomed. If we strike a mighty blow somewhere they do not expect, might it not delay their advance? Cause confusion? Doubt?"

"That . . . is possible. They do cherish the lives of their warriors more than we," Niwa said with irony.

Halik let it pass. He already knew Niwa disliked the wanton waste of Uul. So did Halik, for that matter; he'd been one. There still existed a difference between them regarding the definition of "wanton," however. "We fight for time," he declared. "Time is our ally, possibly more than theirs. With time, we might match their marvels and even their warriors. Kurokawa and General Esshk would surely rather employ our own new wonders here than on sacred ground if we can hold this place long enough for them to do so decisively."

Actually, Niwa believed Kurokawa wouldn't, but he couldn't stall Esshk—or more particularly Tsalka—if Ceylon held out, especially if Halik won a few victories. N'galsh would doubtless have stressed that proposition in the dispatches he sent with the blockade runners. "A stunning victory might give us the time you seek," he conceded at last.

"Good," said Halik. "Instead of attempting to oppose the enemy everywhere, we will concentrate all our thoughts on devising a strategy to crush a portion of his force so unexpectedly and thoroughly as to give him *pause* everywhere . . . and then we shall see."

South Ceylon Coast

"Lizard Beach 2" was a dozen miles east of the "Sand Spit" where Task Force Garrett ceased to exist. In wounded and dead, the once-formidable squadron had ultimately exceeded eighty percent, and a portion of the new assembly area had been designated for the rest and reorganization of the bedraggled remnants under Greg Garrett's command. Garrett and Chapelle had temporarily remained behind to oversee the effort to refloat *Donaghey*. The grisly battlefield was now secure, and an Army company, chosen by lot, remained to recover and try to identify the dead. Many Lemurians would fly to the Heavens in the smoke of pyres, but the lost humans, and a surprising number of 'Cats, based on their stated preference, would be temporarily buried in a less exposed area, until they could be disinterred and taken back to the growing Allied cemetery at Baalkpan.

Meanwhile, four companies of the 1st Marines and both battalions of General/Queen Protector Safir-Maraan's personal guard were sweeping inland to link Lizard Beach 2 with Lizard Beach 3 (west of the "Sand Spit"), as troops from those points advanced inland to join them. So far, there'd been little opposition besides the occasional cluster of disorganized Grik, likely separated from their army, that the planes of *Salissa* and *Humfra-Dar* had harried into the jungle. Allied troops were also encountering Grik "civilians" for the first time since Hij Geerki "surrendered." These were apparently some kind of local "overseers" who managed Uul workers in fishing and agricultural activities. Even they tried to fight, but not very well. All were "mopped up" with relative ease with the exception of gangs of feral Grik "younglings" that roamed the jungles, turned out of holding pens at some of the rough, adobelike structures that served the Hij "overseers" like plantation houses. The feral younglings appeared willing to attack anything, and they added another dimension to the fight since, unlike their adult counterparts, they used the trees to hide and even to travel to some extent. There was a strange reluctance to kill them at first; Lemurians doted on younglings. But these creatures were wild, vicious animals even worse than the undisciplined, uncultivated Sa'aran young of the "ex"-Tagranesi. At least those were somewhat "tame." It wasn't long before Grik younglings were shot on sight.

In Garrett's and Chapelle's absence, Saraan-Gaani was in charge of the survivors at the "rest and reorganization" area. He sat on a stool beneath an awning, a "corps-'Cat" finally tending the many small wounds he'd received in the fighting. None was serious, but with his large percentage of white fur, he'd looked a lot worse than he was. Lieutenant Bekiaa was with him there, her own amazingly few wounds already attended, and she'd been teasing him over his discomfort at the hands of the medics. Saaran-Gaani wasn't sure if she was still flirting with him, or if she ever had been. He liked her, but she was more . . . forward than females he'd known in the south, and he wondered if she actually was compensating a little for the horrors she'd endured. It didn't matter. It was no time to contemplate such things. The spectacle before him on the broad, protected beach was sufficient to hold his attention.

Dozens of ships of various shapes and sizes were moored offshore; transports close in, with shoals of broad-beamed boats plying to and fro, depositing troops and supplies. Farther out were the "DDs" and "DEs," guarding the helpless flock, and even more distant lay *Salissa* with her own screen of warships. "Nancys" flew back and forth between the carrier and points inland, scouting, or throwing a few bombs at any enemy concentrations they saw. Now and then, one landed among the anchored ships, leaving a passenger to come ashore. A floating pier was already under construction to service the planes from the beach. The activity ashore looked chaotic to Saaran-Gaani, with some troops running around and others just milling about. Different regimental colors were mixed, but those of Baalkpan and Aryaal/B'mbaado prevailed. It looked like most of those in a hurry wore the blue and white of Marines, although the black and gold of Maa-ni-la was represented and seemed purposeful, for the most part.

He wondered at that. The Marines were all veterans, as were the majority of the Baalkpan and Aryaalan/B'mbaadan troops. But many of the Maa-ni-los were "green." Maybe it was just that the less organized, such as his own people, simply hadn't been given anything to do yet. The "rest and reorganization" area could boast little organization at all. Makeshift shelters had been rigged here and there, and the survivors of TF Garrett lounged on the beach in the morning shade, close enough to the shelters to escape the inevitable squalls of the day when they manifested themselves. Saaran-Gaani was a little chagrined to see that Bekiaa's remaining Marines had at least bivouacked in a creditable way, while the crews of *Donaghey*, *Tolson*, and *Revenge* were mixed and scattered. He sighed. All the survivors had *fought* like Marines or they wouldn't be here, but with no ship beneath them and no immediate task, the sailors had reverted to a complete "off-duty" state that contrasted strikingly with the more regimented Marines.

"I must come up with something for them to do," he said, nodding at a group of sailors playing one of the many universal Lemurian "hand" games.

"They still need rest," Bekiaa said. "Only two days have passed since their ordeal."

Saaran-Gaani didn't mention that it had been his and Bekiaa's ordeal as well. "Yes, but once relief becomes lethargy, and perhaps fear, it will be harder to return them to their duty." The medic finished applying the curative polta paste to his now-clean wounds and left them then. Saaran-Gaani sighed with relief and continued. "I must get them back on ships, I suppose—although many might resent being separated after all they've been through together. I wish Cap-i-taan Gaar-rett were here to sort this out, but he sent word last night that progress is slow on *Donaghey*." He considered. "She *must* be saved if possible. She's my ship, my Home, but she's also the last of her kind . . . and her role at Baalkpan must be considered. Perhaps the only more significant remaining name in our Navy is *Walker*. Her loss would be hard on the people of Baalkpan, and the Alliance in general."

"As will *Tolson*'s be," Bekiaa agreed. "That's bad enough." She looked at him and blinked irony. "How very astute for a 'South Islander'!"

Saaran's tail twitched irritably. "I'm as Amer-i-caan as you, now."

"Aa-ten-shin!" someone cried, and there was a general stir outside the shelter. Saaran and Bekiaa stood, although they couldn't see who was approaching. The sailors who'd come to their feet parted, revealing General Alden, Admiral Keje-Fris-Ar, Colonel Flynn, and Lord General Muln Rolak, accompanied by a number of staff officers.

"Good morning, Lieutenants!" Keje boomed, and the officers with him returned the salutes they received.

"Good morning, Ahd-mi-raal, Gener-aals, Colonel," Saraan-Gaani replied.

"How do you feel?" Alden asked them.

"Fine," Saaran and Bekiaa chorused.

Keje grunted. "One of the reasons we came ashore . . ." He glanced around. "Where has Mr. Letts run off to?"

"He has gone to begin the chore of organizing this ridiculous mess," Rolak muttered. "*Another* of the reasons we are here," he explained. "Thank the Heavens we did not face an opposed landing!"

"Yes. Well, one reason was to congratulate you two and your companions"—Keje gestured around—"for your survival and perseverance during the recent . . . situation." His gruff voice grew soft. "We came as fast as we could."

"We could not have asked for more, Ahd-mi-raal," Bekiaa said, "and as it turned out, you were just in time."

"Perhaps for some," Keje hedged.

"That's enough of that crap," Alden said tiredly, clearly continuing an argument between the two. "Nobody can do anything faster than 'as fast as they can'!"

"Just so," Rolak agreed, taking Alden's side.

Keje straightened. "Just so," he repeated. "In any event, we must see to the disposition of your people here, Commander Saaran-Gaani, Cap-i-taan Bekiaa-Sab-At."

Saaran and Bekiaa both gulped at the unexpected promotions.

"You have almost two hundred sailors and Marines fit for duty," Keje continued. "I feel the most appropriate thing would be to transport them to An-da-maan to await the arrival and refit of *Donaghey*. Captain Garrett has . . . virtually demanded that he be allowed to remain here, in the fight, while *Donaghey* is repaired"—he shook his head—"but that is impossible. With his experience at sea, he is far too valuable to further risk on land. The same goes for Mr. Chapelle. Both may resent my decision, but there it is." His tail swished and he grinned. "I am reliably informed that ahd-mi-raals may do as they please." He paused. "That said, the notion they proposed has merit. I see several options for your people here. You may all go to An-da-maan as a single crew, and assist in *Donaghey*'s refit. More ships are on their way, but it would be unfair to replace their crews as soon as they arrive. You may all go back to Baalkpan and be assigned one of the new steam frigates they're now building. It would likely take more time than refitting *Donaghey*, but you've certainly earned the rest and a more capable ship. Or, some of your people might choose to join the fleet and be absorbed into one of the ship's companies here."

Bekiaa hesitated but managed to speak. "Is there an option that might allow my Marines and me, at least, to remain here and do as Cap-i-taans Garrett and Chapelle desired? If you please, we do have a score to settle."

"This isn't baseball, damn it; it's war," Alden growled. "There's no such thing as an 'even score.' We fight to win, and your Marines are a ship contingent. The sailors aren't infantry at all."

"I propose that most of the sailors who fought at the Sand Spit are infantry *now*," Bekiaa said. "And were you not once also part of a 'ship contingent' as well, Gen-er-aal? Did that make you less of a Marine?"

"Bekiaa!" Saraan hissed, but Alden scratched his beard and chuckled.

"Good point, Captain." He groaned and looked at Colonel Flynn. "Make your pitch, Billy," he said.

The former submariner with the strange red mustache and chin whiskers grinned. "Well, it just so happens that the 'First Amalgamated Regiment' is a company short, and if I don't put one together, General Alden has threatened to snatch away the allocated rifled muskets and dole 'em out to a bunch of other fellas. That'll dilute their effectiveness, since the Lord knows where they'll wind up."

"Rifled muskets?" Bekiaa asked, confused.

"I know of these!" Saraan interjected. "They load like the muskets the Marines already have, but they are far more accurate. They spin the bullets like the"—he looked apologetically at Keje—"'Holy' '03 Springfields and Kraags the first Amer-i-caans brought!"

Keje grinned. "Do not be concerned. I will not denounce you as a heretic," he said. "I wouldn't, anyway; our Alliance is full of them now. And besides, Gen-er-aal Aal-den has convinced me that those first Springfields and Kraags could at least commune with the Maker, since their bullets must be divinely guided!"

"Oh-threes *are* holy . . . to me," Pete grumped, fingering the sling of the one he always carried. The weapon was somewhat battered now, but no one doubted it was clean—and capable of miracles in his hands.

"How many for a company?" Saraan asked, almost greedily.

"At least a hundred," Flynn said, glancing at Keje, "But maybe you fall in the same category as those other distinguished naval officers?"

Keje grunted. "Certainly. Commander Saraan-Gaani is a valuable naval resource . . . but he's also known and trusted by these people here." He glanced around at the curious faces that had gathered around them. "He has proven himself, according to Cap-i-taan Cha-pelle, and if he desires it, he may command this 'Dee' company you wish to form."

"Of course I desire it!" Saraan said. "Particularly if Cap-i-taan Bekiaa should second me!"

"It's settled then," Alden said, with the air of someone who'd solved a nagging problem. "If you can rake up the volunteers," he added, noticing the crowd around them growing even more as word began to spread. There'd be some who'd had enough, he knew, but Saraan would likely have more trouble keeping the number down than raking it up. He looked at Bekiaa. "The First Amalgamated isn't a Marine regiment," he said, "but you and yours'll still be Marines regardless, if you want in."

"I do," she replied, with a glance at Saraan, "as long as I'm still a Marine, and I keep my uniform."

Flynn laughed. "The Amalgamated wears many 'uniforms.'" He looked at Alden. "I personally prefer the name 'Flynn's Rangers,' as a matter of fact, but that doesn't matter either. All that does is that you can shoot!" He paused. "And sing. Sometimes we sing."

Pete rolled his eyes. "Get your volunteers," he told Saraan, "and report to Colonel Flynn by evening. Things are poppin', and we don't have time to screw around. I'm sure Flynn'll be happy to instruct you on the new weapons. Those you can't take will still have the choice of joining the fleet here or going back to Andaman with Mr. Garrett."

USS **Donaghey**

All her guns had been removed, and there were occasional moments of semibuoyancy as *Donaghey* waited for the tide to reach its peak. Her upper hull was a shambles after the beating she'd taken, but her bottom was still remarkably tight despite working on the beach for the better part of a week. Further testimony to the skill, ingenuity, and planning that built her in the first place. There was no doubt she'd float if they got her off, but they'd likely get only one chance. The "stormy" time of year kept a different schedule in the Western Ocean, and it was doubtful she'd survive until the next time the tide ran this high.

"Commodore" Jim Ellis was aboard to coordinate the effort and discuss the signals they'd make. He'd also delivered some unwelcome news.

"Damn," Garrett said. "I wanted to stay."

"I know," said Jim, "and I understand how you feel. The trouble is, frankly, you're too good at what you do. You and Russ both. Face it; you're heroes back home, *naval* heroes. You're the best frigate skippers we have." He grinned. "'*DD*' skippers. And you had to learn the hard way, without power. Honestly, if I had it my way, I'd send you both to Baalkpan to *teach*, so consider yourselves lucky." He looked at Garrett, leaning on the shattered capstan. There was a lot going on around the capstan on the deck below, where the heavy hawser was being secured. Offshore, *Dowden* and *Tassat* would try to bring *Donaghey*'s bow around and pull her off by the nose. The rudder had been unshipped to prevent damage to it or the sternpost. There, on the upper deck, however, the crew knew a "stay away" meeting when they saw it, and they had relative privacy.

"Okay." Garrett sighed. "At least I'll keep *Donaghey*—if we get her loose." He didn't want to jinx them. "But what about Russ?"

"Yeah, what about me? I can fight. Why can't I stay? There's no extra ships just lying around for me, that's for sure."

"There would be if it was up to me," Jim said cryptically. "There're a few out here I'd like to send to the school I wish you could teach." He sighed. "Politics," he spat. "I guess it was inevitable with the Alliance growing so, but I kind of miss the way it was around here at first."

"What, with us in charge of everything?" Greg chuckled.

"Well . . . yeah. Some of these skippers took the Navy oath and all, but I guarantee they got commands because Adar leaned on Keje because he needed to keep important people happy."

"Adar knows the stakes as well as anyone," Russ said, considering. "He wouldn't make Keje take anybody who was flat unfit—or has he?"

Jim shook his head. "No. They're decent seamen . . . sea-'Cats. Just kind of puffed up about not much. You remember the type."

"Sure."

"So what *about* me?" Russ asked.

"As of right now, you're going back to Baalkpan, but to complete and work up a new frigate and get your butt back in the war as fast as you can."

"Where? Here, or in the east?"

"I can't tell you that. Wherever you're needed most when the time comes, I guess."

Chapelle mulled that over. "Huh. Weird." He shook his head. "I'd love to go east and help the Skipper against those screwy Spics. . . ." His face brightened. "And there's the *women*, of course! Given my choice, though, I guess I'd rather keep killin' Grik."

Jim Ellis shrugged. "It doesn't much matter. Wherever we go, whatever we do in this goofed-up world, somebody or something always needs killing. In that sense, I guess it's not so different from the world we came from. Courtney Bradford would probably come up with something profound, but I guess what it all boils down to is the white hats and black hats in the Westerns." He tugged on the brim of his battered tan cover. "This one may not be white, but our guys' Dixie cups are, and you know? Maybe that's all they need to think about."

"That *is* profound," Garrett said. He still wore his white cover; his other was lost, but the white one had turned a blotchy tan. First, it had been stained with coffee—the result of a nutty order at a nutty time. Time itself had done the rest. "I wonder if some genius figured out, a long time ago, that officers and chiefs—maybe particularly chiefs—need to remember that sometimes things aren't all black or white."

"Tell it to Captain Reddy. He knows it like nobody I ever saw, but he's also figured out there's no way to sort out all the different shades anymore, even if there really ever was, which I doubt." Jim shook his head.

"It was easy against the Japs. They sneaked up and bombed Pearl Harbor; then they came after us. Easy. They were the bad guys and we were the good guys. Same here. The Grik want to eat all of us. In my humble opinion, that's bad. Folks can stay out of the fight, but if they do, they'd better stay the hell out of the way." He looked at Russ. "I don't blame you for wanting to stay out here. Sure, there's broads starting to make it to Baalkpan, but the situation in the east is a mess. Lots of different colors to worry about and the Skipper hates that." He paused. "I guess you did catch that a new Jap 'can came through, before Clancy bought it and you lost your comm?"

There were nods.

"I guess if it's any consolation, it looks like we're winning the war back home. We bombed Tokyo, smashed a bunch of their carriers at Midway, retook some place called Guadalcanal. Stopped their butts cold and started rolling them up. The guys that told us didn't know much more, but that's swell. It's a hell of a lot better than it was when we left. But here? In the east?" He removed his hat and scratched his greasy scalp. "We've got Japs chasing Japs, we're helping Brits fight Brits, and"—he looked at Chapelle—"some kind of goofy Spaniard Indians. Hell, there's even a tribe of Grik on our side! No, I don't blame you for wanting to stay out here at all."

The ship juddered beneath his feet, and Garrett held his watch to the lantern light. "I guess we'd better get started, Commodore," he said. "We've got about two hours. Just let us know when you're about to hit the gas." He glanced out at the lanterns on *Dowden* and *Tassat*. Other ships were beyond them, he knew, darkened in case the enemy chose to interrupt them. "We'll hold on for the first jolt, but I may have to have the guys run back and forth to rock her."

"I'll let you know," Jim promised. "We *will* get her off."

"Don't say that!" Garrett grinned. "Just go out there and break both your legs, blow the main steam line, and run aground yourself!"

"My, you're getting superstitious!" Jim laughed.

"Can't help it," Greg said.

CHAPTER **12**

////// *USS* **Walker**
December 30, 1943

*T*he sky was almost black in the west, and the clouds above were dark, high, and huge. In the east, the horizon around the rising sun was clear and golden. Long, choppy swells rolled in from the northwest, hitting the old destroyer on the port bow. The downdraft of the storm's leading edge sent cold, shattered spray against the windows of the pilothouse and the port side of the chart house. *Walker* was pitching and rolling in a corkscrew motion guaranteed to achieve vomit from all but her most seasoned crew. The cold, damp wind added to the misery. Few Lemurians other than "far rangers" or those from the Great South Island had ever experienced temperatures much below the seventies at night, and now, with the wind and humidity, along with a weak but genuine cold front, it felt like the fifties. 'Cats all over the ship were wearing Lemurian-made copies of "peacoats" that few had ever expected to need, and even the humans, so accustomed to the constant heat, were wearing peacoats and jackets off-loaded before the Battle of Baalkpan. The old wool smelled musty, and even Matt's leather jacket had him sneezing occasionally at the mildew.

Courtney was happy as a clam, standing on the starboard bridgewing with Jenks, bouncing up and down to keep his binoculars steady as he cheerfully described a flight of perhaps a dozen giant lizard birds, or "dragons" stooping and whirling on something far to the east. Jenks was fascinated too, but mainly because the beasts had never been seen this far north, and so far out at sea. Obviously, they were dogging something in or on the water; perhaps some wandering school of fish?

"They must be out of Guadalupe Island," Harvey Jenks speculated. "Dragons are somewhat migratory and often cooperate with one another, as you see," he said.

"Maybe," said Matt. Guadalupe was their "waypoint." They meant to turn north after sighting it on the chance the suspected Dom fleet would use it for the same purpose as it worked north along the coast. Jenks said the island might provide a decent anchorage, depending on the wind, and if the Doms were waiting anywhere for things to "automatically happen," it was as good a place as any. Putting a dogleg in their trip with their fuel so limited had been a difficult decision, but they needed to know what they were facing. They had six days until the cryptic date of January 5, plenty of time to reach their destination, with a few days to spare, but it was imperative they have something concrete to present to the authorities at the colonial port of Saint Francis—better remembered by the human destroyermen as San Francisco.

That's going to be a . . . weird landfall, Matt reflected. Jenks's description of the place didn't sound very familiar, and that made sense with the lower sea level. They certainly wouldn't pass under the Golden Gate Bridge. Still, it would be their first contact with what should have been their continental home, their own country. It would probably be even more painful than their arrival in the "New Britain Isles." Besides, it *was* cold. Sure, it was winter here, but the weather was more like Seattle. Jenks said the "North Coast" was under ice for much of the year, and pack ice could be a problem as far south as where Matt showed him Astoria to be on their own charts. A genuine ice sheet wasn't possible because of the tumultuous sea, but it wasn't right at all.

"I wish we could throw Reynolds and his plane over the side to fly over there and have a look; see if that's Guadalupe and if there're any Dom ships there," Matt said, looking at the sea. "Too dangerous. The trouble is, if we get too close and the enemy *is* there, they might see us before we see them, with their higher masts and lookouts."

"Not necessarily, Skipper," said the Bosun, who'd been watching the darkness in the west. He gestured toward it. "We'll have that as a backdrop, liable to blend right in. And we have better lookouts than they do."

"Hmm." Matt strode aft, starboard of the chart house, and stared up at the funnels. "Minnie," he said, addressing the diminutive talker, "get Tabby on the horn and tell her number three is making too much smoke." He looked around the pilothouse. "Might as well have a look."

Very shortly afterward, the lookout sighted land to the east, what looked like a peak rising from the sea. The threatening storm had dissipated somewhat, becoming more benign as one front surrendered to another, but the entire sky was gray. *Walker* approached the landfall at fifteen knots, and soon the peak of what had to be Mount Augusta, maybe five thousand feet high, sprawled out on the horizon into a rugged island about fifteen miles long, north to south. Careful scrutiny revealed no Dominion ships along its western coast, and Jenks suggested they pass to the north and see what might lie in what he called the "northeast anchorage."

The dragons Courtney watched earlier had disappeared, but similar shapes fluttered around the highest volcanic peak. Another peak brooded to the south, not quite as high, but shrouded by steamy clouds. It was probably active, Matt surmised. By early afternoon, they'd passed the sharp, northeast point and had an unobstructed view of the anchorage beyond. Almost at the same instant the lookout reported—his view as obscured by the point as theirs until now—those on the bridge caught their first sight of a forest of masts.

"My God, there they are!" Matt muttered. *So much for sneaking in for a look.* The first Dom ship, clearly distinguished by the red flag with the gold cross whipping at her stern, was only five thousand yards away. Beyond it lay more ships than they'd seen gathered since the Battle of Baalkpan; maybe a hundred. Most, particularly those anchored closest to the scant shoreline at the base of the high cliffs, were probably transports.

Through his Bausch & Lomb's, thousands of white dots—tents—were scattered in orderly clumps across the exposed slopes of the mountain. Apparently, they'd been here a while. The vessels encompassing the inner transports had to be warships, however, and all those would have guns. "Sound general quarters! Stand by for surface action, starboard!" he said loudly. The laryngitic duck of the general alarm squalled, and there was a short bustle in the pilothouse as men and 'Cats exchanged their hats for helmets.

"What will we do?" Courtney asked.

"You're going to assume your battle station in the wardroom," Matt said. "Without Selass here, all we have is a pharmacist's mate. You're our surgeon now, remember?"

"W-why, yes," Bradford stammered unenthusiastically, "and I shall do my duty . . . but what are we going to *do*?"

"We're going to stay out of range and hit 'em as hard as we can. They're at anchor, and we'll never have a better opportunity. See all those tents ashore? Those represent who knows how many troops. We sink their transports, and the invasion of the colonies is off."

"Attack . . . without warning?" Courtney gasped.

"Damn straight," the Bosun growled. "What do you think *they're* here to do?"

"Still . . ."

"Go below, Courtney," Matt said with an edge. Bradford vanished in a huff, but when he was gone, Jenks leaned toward Matt and whispered, "Actually, though I hate to say it, he has a point."

Matt goggled at him. "What?"

"We're at war with the Dominion, no question, but those people over there, aboard those ships, don't know it yet."

"What the hell are you talking about?" Gray demanded, equally shocked. "You want to run up a white flag, steam over there and *tell* 'em we're at war? They'll thrash us! Our only advantage is speed and range. We've got 'em served up on a platter, and you want to give that up? Did you forget how they started this war? They murdered women and children! Civilians!"

"I haven't forgotten," Jenks said bitterly, "but are we to start a war with them the same way?"

"It's already started!" Matt almost shouted in frustration.

Jenks pointed at the ships, still serene at anchor in the island's lee. Surely they'd seen them by now, but as yet, there was no visible reaction. "Not for them!"

Matt removed his hat and raked his hair back. "Talker," he snapped. "What does the lookout see?"

"Ahh, confusion aboard enemy ships," Minnie reported, and Matt slapped his leg with his hat.

"Mr. Kutas, come right thirty degrees. Slow to one-third. Stand by for flank. Pack Rat? Hoist the battle flag, if you please."

"Right thirty, aye," Kutas replied, and repeated the order to the helmsman. Staas-Fin (Finny) confirmed he'd rung the engine room and was ready to signal the increase. "Tabasco" scrambled up the ladder aft with Matt's pistol and sword belt. He snatched the battered hat from his captain and handed over a helmet. Matt put it on but gestured for his steward to keep the belt for now.

"Cap-i-taan," said Minnie, "all stations manned an' ready. Mr. Spaanky has auxiliary conn an' asks what the hell we doing."

"Tell him that, to suit the sensibilities of our allies, we're going to give the enemy a chance to shoot first. Tell Campeti not to return fire immediately but to wait for the command!"

"Ay, ay, Cap-i-taan," Minnie replied nervously.

"This is nuts," Gray said, glaring at Jenks.

"Cap-i-taan," Minnie cried, "lookout say rockets—flares—burst over enemy ships!"

Matt looked through the window to starboard as *Walker* steered to run parallel to the anchorage. He saw the dwindling sparkles in the sky. "I guess they're passing the word," he said, with a glance of his own at Jenks. Most of the Dominion ships were stern-on to the old destroyer as she steamed south, angling to cross down the line of anchored vessels, at a range of roughly fifteen hundred yards; close enough to entice a shot, but not close enough to make it easy. A few were starting to get their act together, cutting their cables and beginning to move backward, blossoming headsails pulling them around. Finally, one ship, its broadside clear, vanished behind a rolling cloud of smoke.

"All ahead flank!" Matt yelled. "Left full rudder!"

The helmsman spun the wheel and with a deep, vibrating groan, *Walker*'s screws clawed at the sea. A wide cluster of waterspouts erupted in her wake, and one shot struck the ship with a hollow boom.

"Damage report!" Matt demanded. "Rudder amidships."

Minnie shook her head. "Mr. Spaanky say a big ball whacked the stern at starboard propeller guard. It falling when it hit, an' splash in sea. Maybe just a dent."

"My rudder amidships," announced the 'Cat at the wheel.

"Very well. Hold your course. Damage control to the steering engine room!"

Another ship fired an erratic broadside, but *Walker* was picking up speed. At this range, few balls would skate off the wavetops, and all the geysers erupted aft. They waited a few minutes. Evidently, the enemy believed they'd chased the strange ship away, because there was no more firing. Nearing four thousand yards again, they had no chance of hitting, anyway.

"Helm, come to course one, six, zero!" Matt said. He looked at Finny. "Slow to two-thirds before we suck the bunkers dry. Minnie, tell Campeti we're about to settle down and when we do, I want him to *punish* those bastards!" Finally, he looked at Jenks. "Satisfied, Commodore?" He waited for a nod, then resumed. "Harvey, I consider you a friend, amazingly enough. Particularly considering the foot we started on. But there's only so much you can ask of this ship and her crew, especially with what's at stake—here and elsewhere. We all need *Walker*, and she needs her crew. I'll risk them both; I have many times, but what we just did was plain stupid. In case you haven't noticed, there aren't any rules in this damn war. You can say fighting like the enemy makes us like them, but that's not true. We didn't start it, and we can't hold ourselves to an artificial standard they don't even recognize." He straightened and took a breath. "So I went ahead and proved it to you again. But here's the deal: friends or not, that was the last time. Expecting more stunts like that one, to prove a point, to show we're better than they are, is pushing too far. We *are* better than they are, and I don't feel like proving it again!"

"Caam-pee-tee has a solution, Skipper," Minnie said.

"Very well. Commence firing."

The salvo buzzer rang, and the foredeck lit up under the overcast sky as the number one gun bucked and spit flame and white smoke. They had no tracers for the new ammunition yet, but the rhino-pig lard they lubed the projectiles with to keep the fouling soft left a spiraling smoke trail. It didn't matter. Matt had no doubt that the shells from numbers one, three, and four would converge either short or long of the target. The EMs had replaced all the ships old, corroded, electrical fire control systems and connections, and they'd finally compensated for the different velocity of the 4.7-inch dual-purpose Japanese gun that had replaced number four. They also had sharp eyes to watch for the fall of shot. A moment later came the cry from the fire control platform above to adjust "Down fifty! Match pointers! Fire!" This time the three exploding shells, two with black powder bursting charges and one with high explosive, demolished the first target, a Dom heavy of some sort, the first one that fired at them. Campeti immediately shifted to the next. In moments, perhaps a dozen enemy ships were burning or destroyed, and still the pounding continued. *Walker* ceased firing at the southern end of the anchorage and reversed course, to continue flailing at the enemy. The dark cliffs of the distant island glowed with the flames of burning ships.

"Damn," breathed Kutas with satisfaction. "It's almost like 'Makassar Strait' all over again," he said, referencing their only real success in their "old" war against the Japanese.

Some of the enemy was making sail at last, trying to escape the growing inferno, but none could succeed as long as *Walker* had ammunition. Matt knew he couldn't destroy them all—they simply didn't have enough shells—but they could break the force destined for Saint Francis and leave it too weak to accomplish its mission. As soon as enough of the warships were dealt with, he meant to move in closer and shatter as many transports as he could. For a while, he watched the slaughter with his jaw grimly set, oblivious to all but the destruction he wrought.

"Captain Reddy!" He finally heard his name over the booming guns and diminishing *swoosh* of shells. It was Jenks.

"What?"

"Your 'talker'!"

Matt spun. "What is it?"

"Cap-i-taan," Minnie repeated, "the lookout says those giant lizard birds are back. Dozens of 'em, an' they flying this way!"

Matt, Jenks, and the Bosun ran out on the starboard bridgewing and focused their binoculars. High above, and ignoring the enemy ships, came a ragged formation of the oversize creatures.

"My God," Jenks muttered. "I've never seen so many together!"

"Will they attack?" Matt asked.

"It appears that's their intent. Look, some have large stones in their claws!"

"Why ain't they dumpin' 'em on those Doms?" Gray demanded.

"I've no idea." Jenks paused nervously. "Captain Reddy, those dragons *really* shouldn't tolerate the Doms on 'their' island while they inhabit it!"

"Then what the hell?"

"I can't answer. I've never seen anything like it."

Matt tore his eyes from the binoculars. "Air action starboard!" he roared. "All hands not on gun's crews will take small arms and prepare to repel boarders, but try to stay undercover!"

It was incredible. There were forty or fifty of the things winging toward them. In most respects they looked like their smaller cousins the destroyermen had grown accustomed to, pacing the ship and shitting on the decks whenever they ventured near land. These "lizard birds" were bigger than Grik, however, and had a lot in common with the Ancient Enemy except for their wings and the bright colors of their furry plumage. The closer they came, the more terrifying they appeared.

Behind him, Matt heard the muffled thumping of feet on metal rungs as 'Cats raced up the ladder to the fire control platform, draped with belts of .30-cal for the machine guns mounted there. Others brought extra ammo to the .50s on the amidships deckhouse; beyond that, the Japanese pom-poms where the aft torpedo tubes used to be were made ready as well. Sailors scrambled to the rails with Springfields and muskets, passed out by Lanier, Chief Gunner's Mate Paul Stites, and Stumpy. The "dragon birds" were getting closer.

"Cap-i-taan!" Minnie cried. "Mr. Spaanky requests permission for the number four gun to engage the flying lizards!" Matt was surprised. He hadn't known they had time-fused shells for the dual-purpose gun. He'd never considered asking since the idea of shooting at airborne targets hadn't occurred to him before. If they had the shells, it was time to use them. "Absolutely," he said. Almost immediately, the aft gun boomed and an instant later, a black puff appeared in front of the advancing flock. The creatures nearest the detonation veered past it and kept coming. The rounds pumped out, in rapid fire, throwing a blanket of steel in their path. One puff shredded a monster's wing and killed another outright with slashing fragments. The dead one folded and dropped, and the wounded one spiraled downward, shrieking. There were short-lived cheers, but the creatures were close enough for the machine guns now.

All the while, numbers one and two continued firing at the enemy ships, but seeing the oncoming creatures, Matt couldn't leave the gun's crews out in the open.

"Cease firing and secure main battery, all but number four!" he ordered. "Helm, come to course zero, two, zero, all ahead full! Secondary battery and small arms will commence firing at targets of opportunity!" He gestured at Tabasco to hand him his belt.

"No, no, you idiot!" yelled Chief Gunner's Mate Paul Stites around a wad of yellowish Lemurian tobacco. "You gotta *lead* 'em! Shoot where they're *gonna* be, not where they *are*! You're just wastin' bullets!"

"How I know where they *gonna* be?" yelled the 'Cat striker behind the 'fifty, beside the "pom-pom pit." "I not see future!"

The "dragon birds" were splitting up, trying to encircle the ship, it seemed. But *Walker*'s speed must have come as a big surprise, and they appeared to be having trouble adjusting their approach as the old destroyer sped up. All the machine guns were stuttering now; the wind-muffled, crackling prattle of the .30s on the fire control platform, the throatier, deafening bursts of the .50s amidships. Reynolds directed his "Special Air Detail" on the pom-poms protecting his plane, and the numbing *bam-bam-bam*ming of the things was starting to really hurt. Stites was directing the fifties just aft of the pom-poms, under the overhang of the aft deckhouse where the 4.7-inch dual-purpose was banging away, and the position was . . . detrimental to normal conversation.

Most of the "secondary battery" was giving a good account of itself. Tracers rose and converged on their targets, staggering the beasts in midair. The things were fast, but they weren't Japanese planes. Some plummeted into the sea with roaring, surprised, wails of terror, where they floundered until something like flashies began tearing at them. Maybe they *were* flashies. The wails became . . . worse . . . then; like horses burning alive. Others flew on, little fazed by holes in their furry, membranous wings.

"Get away from that thing!" Stites roared at the 'Cat gunner when a higher-flying creature suddenly darted over the ship and released a large rock amid a flurry of Springfield and musket fire. The rock struck between the "Nancy" and the searchlight tower, barely missing the aft engine room skylights. It shattered on impact, leaving a dent in the deck and spraying sharp shards of stone. Stites realized that many of the creatures carried rocks, and others carried . . . something else . . . in each eagle-clawed foot. He finished shoving the 'Cat from the gun that had once been in one of the waist blisters of the old PBY and grabbed the handles himself. "Everything in naval gunnery's about shooting where something's *going* to be, Genius," he ranted. "If you haven't figured that out yet, you might as well strike for snipe—or go to work for Lanier!" he added as the ultimate insult. He wrenched the .50 around and crouched behind the sights just as he felt the deck shiver with multiple impacts. *The damn things are bombing us! With rocks!*

The 4.7-inch went silent, and a fusillade of small arms erupted from that position. Stites swung the gun aft and up and saw a trio of dragon birds coming in astern. These he could shoot directly at because they were making a beeline for him. He depressed the trigger. A stream of tracers from his gun and the one to port swept across the things, spattering gobbets of flesh and bone. Two dropped in the wake, but one bore in, crippled. It slammed into the aft deckhouse where the old three-incher would have been, and he felt another tremor. Immediately, 'Cats fired down on it from above, and his spine tingled as he prayed they had enough sense to watch for the depth charges in the racks. A quiver started at his neck and ended at his tailbone, but he shook his head when the stern wasn't blown off.

"Look out!" someone cried when a dragon bird actually lit on the searchlight tower and attacked the rail with its teeth.

"Shoot it, but for God's sake, don't hit the light!" Stites yelled. Lanier himself waddled from under the amidships deckhouse and hosed the thing with a Thompson. It squealed and tried to lunge at him, but it fell to the deck instead, flailing with wings, teeth, tail, and claws. "Son of a *bitch*!" It was the closest look Stites had had at the things and he suspected it must be light for its size, but it probably still weighed three or four hundred pounds. Its body and wings were a bright, fuzzy, bluish gray on top, and white-gray underneath. The head was almost orange, with streaks of purple-blue and yellow radiating from liquid yellow eyes. Oddly, the head colors were reflected in the tail plumage to a remarkable degree.

"Goddamn, creepy-ass . . ." He looked up. The dragon birds were having more trouble keeping up now, maybe tiring, and some began to fall astern as the ship accelerated past twenty-five knots, smoke gushing from her funnels. Faster ones still dropped things, however, but these objects made metallic sounds when they hit. There were screams from forward, and he saw a couple of 'Cats tumble off the amidships deckhouse. With a sick feeling, he realized one went into the water alongside. Another dragon bird swooped low and snatched one of the fallen 'Cats, a female, who shrieked horribly when the thing leaped back into the air, clutching her in its claws. She must have been too heavy for it, because it immediately lost altitude, though no one would shoot at it—until it dropped its screaming victim in the sea and frantically beat its wings. Probably everyone on the starboard side of the ship shot at it then, and it crashed into the water.

Stites snatched a 'Cat by the scruff of the neck. "Can you hit anything besides the goddamn ocean with this thing?" he demanded. The 'Cat nodded, and Stites flung him at the gun, snatching up his "personal" BAR. "Keep at 'em," he yelled, "but watch where you're shooting! They're starting to get on the ship!"

Maybe they were tired, or maybe that was just what they did, but more and more of the surviving attackers lit on *Walker* and attacked her crew on her own deck. Many converged on the bridge as if sensing that was the "head" of their victim. Stites glanced back at Reynolds. The aviator looked terrified, but he was holding his own, a 1911 Colt smoking in his hand.

"You got this, sir?" Stites asked. Reynolds jerked a nod. "Watch out for Spanky!" Stites yelled, pointing up at the auxiliary conn, forward of the dual-purpose gun. A pair of monsters had landed there, and Spanky was shooting his own pistol now. Stites aimed and fired a burst at the head of one of the things. It fell on the starboard propeller guard and vanished in the roiling wake. Spanky, or someone, apparently killed the other, but more were trying to land. "Watch him!" Stites yelled again, "and watch yourself! I'm going forward!"

"This just about beats *all*!" Kutas cried when a "dragon bird" threw something that ricocheted off the number one gun's splinter shield, then flared out for a landing on the fo'c'sle. The Bosun had run down there with his Thompson to protect two 'Cats who hadn't made it to cover and were trying to conceal themselves around the gun. The .30s up above were still chattering loudly, but either they had problems of their own or were afraid to shoot so near their shipmates. Gray ran at the thing, roaring like a demon to distract it from the helpless 'Cats. It whirled on him and snarled, and he fired a burst that sent it tumbling into the sea.

Matt ran to the aft rail and looked up and aft. They'd made a dent—a big one—in the terrifying creatures, and many had finally peeled off and headed back toward the island. But now the stubborn ones, maybe twenty or more, seemed intent on attacking the bridge. He leaned over the signal flag locker to see down on the weather deck below. One creature lay dead beside the base of the number one funnel. Carl "Boats" Bashear was carrying a 'Cat toward the companionway to the wardroom, and he almost slammed into Bradford who was apparently coming up to see what was going on. The Australian froze, despite Bashear's harsh bellow, and just stood there, staring around, enchanted.

"Get below!" Matt yelled. Instead, Bradford seemed to notice the dead creature for the first time and started in its direction. A dull shadow fell across him. "Damn it, Courtney," Matt roared, "get below!"

Bradford looked up, and that was all he needed to break his trance. Instantly, he whirled and chased Bashear down the companionway. The signal halyard ropes slapped Matt across the face and chest and sent him reeling back into the pilothouse, stumbling, and finally falling on his back. A dragon bird, still trailing the parted lines, landed in the cramped space where he'd been. Minnie squeaked and started to duck behind the chart house bulkhead, but she reversed course in an instant to try to drag her seemingly stunned captain to safety. She was half his size and just couldn't do it. Jenks shouted and ran past her, sword in hand. Slashing at the monster's face, he didn't see the wicked claw at the bend of its wing slash in from the left, across his shoulder, sending him sprawling as well. The thing hopped forward, squalling, trying to shake off the halyard lines. Matt, now kicking with his heels to help Minnie, fumbled for his pistol. The Colt came out, and flipping off the thumb safety, he emptied the magazine at the creature. It screamed and flailed more violently, but now Matt had time to stand. Inserting another magazine, he took more careful aim and shot the dragon bird dead with a pair of shots.

Another flared just above him, going for the fire control platform. He shot at it too, but what probably brought it down, almost on top of the other one, was a staccato of Thompson and BAR fire that sprayed blood all over Matt and the side of the chart house, and sent a cloud of downy fuzz drifting quickly aft. There were more shots from both guns, but Matt couldn't see the targets. He grabbed Jenks, and with Minnie's help, dragged the Imperial underneath the overhead.

"I'm fine," Jenks protested, "I'm quite all right!"

"You've got a pretty good cut there, Commodore," Matt said, peeling back the bloody coat and weskit beneath. Jenks had been slashed from the left shoulder, across his chest, and upward across his chin. The firing finally began to slack outside, and Stites and the Bosun crawled gingerly over the dead beasts clogging the space at the top of the ladder, pointing their muzzles at them as they crossed.

"You okay, Skipper?" Stites demanded anxiously.

"Swell. Commodore Jenks is wounded."

Gray pulled a field dressing from a small pouch on his belt and tore it open. Ripping an envelope with his teeth, he leaned down and sprinkled the contents on Jenks's wound.

"What's that?" Jenks demanded.

"Sulfonamide," grunted the Bosun. "We'll get you fixed up with some polta paste pretty quick, but who knows what kinda germs is smeared all over them devils. Better get started on 'em." Gray fluffed out a wad of gauze and handed it to the man. "Here, you're bleedin' like a stuck pig. Hold this on, there on your chest—that looks the worst—and keep pressure on it."

"Help me up," Jenks insisted. Together, they assisted him to his feet. "That was . . . extraordinary!"

"You said it," confirmed Stites in a loud voice. He shook his head and moved his jaw, trying to pop his ears. "Flyin' Grik! What about that?"

"Dragons," Jenks corrected, wincing, "but perhaps 'flying Grik' describes this group better," he acknowledged. "I've never seen anything like it. Never."

"Lookout," Matt said, "what's he see, Minnie? What are those damn dragon things doing, and what of the enemy fleet?"

"There no answer from crow nest, Cap-i-taan," reported the diminutive talker. "Spanky say Grik birds go 'way, fly back to island. He no shoot number four at them no more, you say so. Run low on time fuse shells."

"Of course. Tell him to cease firing and secure. Can he see the enemy?"

Minnie hesitated, listening. "They make sail," she said. "Warships get between us and transports, transports make smoke—maybe steamers—we too far now to see what tents do, but he think enemy going on transports."

Matt nodded. The enemy was moving. But where would they go? They'd done some serious damage, but not enough.

"Spanky say there even more flying Grik now," Minnie continued. "He send 'Cat up aft mast wit bin-oculaars. More flying Grik over enemy fleet, but not attacking *them*."

"Amazing!" Jenks said. "It must be true, then."

"What?"

"Think on it! Somehow the Doms have the dragons in their power! They command the beasts! I would've never believed it."

"What do you mean, 'in their power'?" Gray grumbled.

"Why, they've trained them somehow, of course! Perhaps from birth. That must be it."

"Makes sense, Skipper," Stites said. "Raise 'em from a chick—or whatever. . . ."

"Yes!" Jenks agreed. "And feed them, tend their wants, train them to consider you their masters . . . Amazing!"

"Yeah, but scary as hell," Matt said. "We were in the middle of maybe winning the war, and got chased off by giant flying lizards!"

"We can go back, Skipper," Kutas said gamely.

"Noo . . . As Spanky said, there're even more back there. We're going to have to play something new. We can't fight the Doms *and* those things," he said, gesturing at the corpses behind them. "The gun's crews would be sitting ducks." He looked at Jenks. "What kind of range do they have?"

"The dragons?"

"Yeah."

"That's an interesting question. They're rarely seen more than thirty or forty miles offshore."

"Guadalupe's a hell of a lot farther than that from Baja," Gray said.

"Indeed," Jenks agreed. "Perhaps a hundred and fifty miles. No doubt it was a one-way trip, straight out."

"Which means there almost had to be 'handlers,' or some kind of support for them practically due east."

"Which means they've been preparing for this a *very* long time," noted Jenks darkly. "I begin to fear there may be more than we bargained for, even on New Ireland. I *so* wish we could pass a message back to the Governor-Emperor!"

Ed Palmer had appeared on the bridge, staring wide-eyed at the dead, winged . . . things. He shook his head. "I still have nothing from Admiral McClain . . . sirs . . . or any of *our* ships either. We took a dogleg course, but they were supposed to come straight on to Saint Francis. Maybe they got caught up in the storm northeast of us, or it's interfering, but I'm thinking they should've been in range for us to hear *something* by now. Our transmitter's a lot more powerful, and I keep sending our position and intentions . . ." He held out his hands. "Maybe they're hearing us, but I haven't heard a peep back."

"We'll hear something in a few days," Matt said with conviction, "even if only from 'our' ships. *Simms, Tindal, Mertz,* and the oilers *are* on their way, even if McClain dawdled. They had their orders."

Jenks looked at Matt. "I'd like to apologize, Captain Reddy," he said.

Matt blinked. "What for? McClain's probably on his way, as he promised. Even if he is goofing around, it's not your fault. Besides, you probably saved my life when you went at that . . . dragon bird with a *sword*—and got cut up for it."

"That's not what I meant. I must apologize for . . . influencing you and your crew to take an unreasonable risk. You were right. They *did* know we are at war. They can only have trained dragons for the attack we withstood today, and they'd only have gathered at Guadalupe Island to prepare an assault on the colonies. I shouldn't have made you feel . . . compelled to follow outdated rules."

Matt shook his head. "Doing the right thing should never be out-dated, but in this war, the 'right thing' gets . . . blurry. Don't worry about it. It took us a while to get used to it too. Maybe it was easier because we were fighting a 'mean' war before we ever wound up here." He frowned. "We would've gotten a few more of their ships if we'd shot first, but not many more, and not enough to make a real difference. Only sinking the transports might have done that, and they were too well screened. The dragon birds made the difference in the end."

"What'll we do, Skipper?" the Bosun asked. "We gonna shadow the Doms, keep an eye on what they do, or make for Saint Francis?"

"Saint Francis. We know it's got to be their objective, even if we don't know their plan. Better to warn the colonies and help them prepare for as many contingencies as we can think of. Besides, we burned a lot of fuel today. Shadowing them will cost more—especially if they throw those . . . things at us again. For all we know, they've got them as tame as puppies, feeding them and letting them roost on their ships!" He stared hard at the dead creatures on the bridge, their blood beginning to con-geal in long, lumpy puddles on the strakes. "We'll have to do something about *them*."

"What?"

Matt sighed. "Right now, I have no idea. However they did it, the enemy has air cover and we don't, basically." He looked at Minnie. "Se-cure from general quarters, but maintain condition three . . . as always. Helm, make your course three, five, five, if you please. Two-thirds. Boats, get with Bashear and form a detail to clear my ship of these flying ver-min. I want casualty and damage reports as soon as possible." He looked around. "Does anybody know if the 'Nancy' made it through in one piece?"

* * *

Lieutenant Fred Reynolds sat on the deck, leaning on the light gauge "tub" encircling the gun position while its crew cleaned and secured it. His pistol was still in his hand, but the slide was locked back on an empty magazine. His eyes rested on the shattered head of one of the giant lizard birds that lay in the gap at the back of the tub and he shuddered. Suddenly, the exec, Spanky McFarlane, appeared, looking down at him.

"There you are, Reynolds!" he said. "I was starting to think one of those boogers carried you off!" He looked down at the creature at his feet. "Got this one, did you? Well done!"

Reynolds stood, a little shakily.

"Here, gimme that," Spanky said, motioning for the pistol. Fred handed it over, and Spanky released the empty magazine and stuffed it in a pouch on Reynolds's belt. Taking another, he inserted it, dropped the slide, and flipped the thumb safety up. He handed the pistol back. "Keep that handy," he said. "Damn things might come back."

"Aye, aye, sir."

Spanky looked around. The day was still cool, but his face glistened with sweat. "A hell of a thing. Listen, round up your crew chief—Jeek, right?—and go over the plane. It looks like it's mostly in one piece. Skipper wants it ready to fly as soon as possible." He noticed Reynolds's suddenly pale expression. "*Ready* to fly. You ain't going up with the sea like this. Send any of your fellas that ain't hurt to Bashear—you got any hurt?"

"Ah, I'll find out immediately, sir."

"Okay. Make sure they go to the wardroom, even if it's just a scratch. No tellin' what they'll catch from these nasty bastards." He kicked the dead beast. "Any others you don't need right away, send 'em to Bashear so we can clear all this buzzard bait off the ship."

"Aye, aye, Mr. McFarlane," Reynolds said to Spanky's back as the man moved on. He took a breath. "Okay, you heard him. Wounded to the wardroom." The crew from the portside gun had joined them, and he called out a couple of names. "You're with me," he said. "We'll satisfy the 'condition three' requirement. The rest, find Bashear. He'll tell you what to do." He saw Kari Faask gingerly making her way through the corpses on deck, past the departing 'Cats.

"You okay?" she asked.

"Swell."

A little hesitantly, she hugged him with one arm. The healing wound in her side was still stiff and painful. "You not *look* swell."

"I'm fine. You?"

"I was in comm shack, safe enough. Mr. Paalmer kept us all there. No weapons." She shook her head, and her eyes blinked loathing. "Them things sure *look* like flying Grik!"

"Yeah."

"We *fly* with them things?" Her tail twitched nervously.

"Maybe. We need to look the plane over."

"I hope it's busted."

Fred snorted and looked at her. "Me too."

It wasn't, at least not too badly. They discovered that, in addition to rocks, some of the "dragon birds" had been carrying and throwing cannonballs! This was further proof they were in league, in some way at least, with the Doms. A big volcanic rock had exploded on impact with the deck and sent some easily patched shards into the fuselage of the "Nancy," and a cannonball had punched a hole in the starboard wing, just forward of the aileron. Jeek said the hole would take a couple days to fix because it had damaged a stringer and the glue to fix it would take that long to dry—longer if it rained. Kari was clearly disappointed the plane wasn't wrecked beyond repair.

The rest of the ship hadn't suffered too badly. The heavy roundshot had dented the deck like giant hailstones but caused little damage otherwise. A 'Cat had been killed by one, and another had landed on Earl Lanier's foot, smashing two of his toes. He was hobbling around now, tormenting a single crutch far beyond its capacity and bellowing for somebody to get the "damn, stinking things" cleared away from around the galley "if anybody ever wants to eat again." Fred saw Tabby come on deck, look around, and seeing Spanky, rush to him and leap at him, enfolding him in a crushing embrace. *Awful lot of hugging on this ship today,* he mused, feeling a little uncomfortable. He wasn't the traditionalist some were—like Spanky. Fred was young enough that tradition hadn't yet seeped into his bones. But even he knew hugging just wasn't right on a destroyer. Spanky obviously agreed, because he glanced around self-consciously while he peeled Tabby off. Everyone knew he considered her like a daughter, but proprieties must be maintained. Spanky didn't scold the scarred Lemurian engineering officer, though; he just stood there, listening to her report on the leakage in the steering engine room, which Fred overheard was under control.

It wasn't all rosy. Six 'Cats were killed in the aerial attack, and three were "missing," including the lookout who'd been in the crow's nest. Doubtless, the "missing" were dead too. Nobody even saw what happened to the lookout. A few men and 'Cats had been wounded, but unless they'd been poisoned or got infected with something the polta paste couldn't handle, they'd be fine. The light nature of the injuries was confirmed when Fred saw Courtney Bradford on deck, apparently content to let his pharmacist's mate deal with the "scratches" while he defended a relatively undamaged specimen of the new enemy from Bashear's detail. Eventually, Captain Reddy himself came in response to Courtney's shrill cries of outrage and interceded on his behalf, saying, "Cut it up; learn what you can. I particularly want to know what it eats, and your opinion of its intelligence. But get it over the side before dark. Their guts can't be much different from Grik, and you've played with those plenty of times."

Courtney set to work, and Fred and Kari moved aft.

"We fly with those things, what we do?" Kari asked.

Fred shrugged. "We're faster, I think. We need to have a weapon, though—besides a pistol. Let's find Campeti or Stites and see what they have to say."

The storm in the west either dissipated or moved away, because the threatening clouds gave way to glittering stars when the sun finally sank into the sea. *Walker* churned north through increasingly quartering swells that maintained her sickening, corkscrewing motion, but she was no longer taking such heavy seas over the bow. The mood in the pilothouse was glum. Everyone knew they'd been on the verge of a momentous victory; one that might've even finished "this" war, at least for the time being, and allowed them to go "home" and get on with what many considered their "bigger business." To be deprived of that victory and chased away by animals—and very Grik-like animals at that—left some a little confused, thoughtful, and reevaluating their priorities. Most of *Walker*'s crew had fought in the Naval Battle of Scapa Flow, and it had been a bitter contest. Only a few had been ashore to see just how much like the Grik the troops of the Dominion behaved. Now a majority was beginning to realize that, regardless how different in some ways, this was the same war they'd already been fighting: a war against monsters bent on the destruction of people. That's what it came down to, in the end.

"What've you got, Courtney?" Matt asked when Bradford stumped up the stairs from aft. His clothes were bloody, but his hands were clean. Jenks was behind him, walking carefully. His wounds had been treated and he'd be fine, but the curative paste of the Lemurians had a slightly intoxicating effect.

"You were right," Bradford said. "Very Grik-like in most respects. The same, if even lighter hollow bones. A similar, though more colorful, downy covering. The wing structure is the greatest difference, but even the bones that support it look like radically elongated arm and finger bones! Of course, the musculature of the torso is different and more robust. I'm vaguely reminded of a pigeon." He shook his head. "The proliferation and adaptation of the basic form is quite astonishing! First we had the various 'races' of Grik. Then Mr. Chapelle's and Mr. Mallory's expedition to recover *Santa Catalina* and her cargo revealed an *amphibious* species. . . . Now we have one that flies!"

"You once said it yourself, Courtney," Matt reminded him. "On this world, Grik, or creatures like them, have risen to the top of the evolutionary heap."

"Yes, yes, I know," Bradford agreed with a frown. "Not only are they the most dominant life-form we've come across, they're even more physically adaptable to their various environments than we ever suspected." He glanced apologetically at the 'Cats in the pilothouse. "*Physically* adaptable," he repeated. "Like us meager humans, our Lemurian friends have had to, and been *able* to rely on *mental* adaptability to survive. Hand to hand, no human or Lemurian is a match for any of the . . . hmm . . . perhaps semireptilian?" He scratched his balding head.

"Courtney."

"Excuse me, indeed. As I've long maintained, we're no match for them physically, but we appear to have an advantage when it comes to our capacity for imagination. The enemy in the west has developed a competitive technology only with the aid of humans, past and present. Here, these 'flying Grik,' these 'dragons,' are the tools of our human enemy. They're a disconcerting weapon, but that's all they are. Our enemy here remains the humans that control them."

"Okay," agreed Matt, "so how does that work?"

Courtney nodded at Jenks. "The *dragons* have a similar brain capacity to other Grik. Perhaps slightly less, but not significantly. Still, greater than we've ever seen them demonstrate—with the exception of our own dear Lawrence and the rest of his people, no doubt. This is likely due to cultural imperatives and . . . well, their very physical perfection. Their lethality as predators has perhaps subdued requirements for imaginative thought. In other words, they're so good at what they do, they don't need to think about ways to improve!"

"Well . . . what makes Lawrence different?"

"I can only presume, as an island race, his people have had to imagine more efficient methods of survival than chasing prey and eating it. Their resources were limited, and they had to imagine and learn skills such as boatbuilding, fishing, even agriculture. The same may even be true of the 'jungle' Grik Mr. Silva discovered. It's possible Lawrence's people might have ultimately evolved along lines similar to those in the swamps of Chill-Chaap and become famous swimmers, but I believe they'd already crossed the figurative 'Rubicon.'"

"That's amazing," Matt said, truly impressed, "but that still leaves us with how do the Doms control their lizard birds?"

Courtney frowned, and his eyes suddenly reflected a horrible sight. "There's some training involved, certainly, but upon opening the specimen, I discovered . . . human remains." He stared hard at Matt, then at Jenks. "They feed them *people*."

There were gasps in the pilothouse. Courtney Bradford tried at times, but he really didn't know how to whisper. Invariably, his various dissertations were overheard and spread throughout the ship. It didn't really matter. Matt wanted his crew as well-informed as possible. "Scuttlebutt" often distorted things and made them worse. In this case, uninformed speculation would've probably sugarcoated the truth.

"It's known that the 'un-Holy' Dominion engages in blood sacrifice at the drop of a hat," Courtney continued, "as part of their 'native'-inspired perversion of the already rather . . . insistent . . . early-eighteenth-century version of the Catholic faith they brought to this world, but using people to feed those monsters . . . !"

"Makes perfect sense from their evil perspective," Jenks spit, his words slightly slurred. "Feed them the infirm, the sick, the wounded . . . perhaps the laborers they brought with them. Regardless, only able bellies are filled, and the priests probably manufacture 'divine' justifications!" He looked at Matt. "Do you think they'll be kinder to conquered peoples?"

"Relax, Harvey," Matt said. "We'll stop them somehow. We would have already, if not for their pets." He sighed. "Unfortunately, we have to assume they know that too. We can't count on their being idiots. What'll they do now that we've learned about their 'secret weapon,' but they know about *Walker*?"

CHAPTER 13

////// *Kaufman Field*
Baalkpan

en-*Hut*!" cried a shrill, Lemurian voice. The sound didn't echo in the hangar made of canvas and the oversize Baalkpan bamboo, but at least the building was tight enough to make it loud.

"Oh, ah, 'as you were,' by all means," replied Adar's voice in his carefully cultivated English.

"Thanks, Your Excellency," Colonel Ben Mallory replied, and his voice *did* echo—from within the wheel-well he'd somehow managed to cram an unlikely percentage of himself into. "Just a minute . . . and I oughta . . . Eeee! There! Now, if I can just get *me* outta here!" A pair of wrenches dropped to the hard-packed, concretelike crushed limestone floor, and Ben grunted and squirmed until he extricated himself. "Ahh," he said, wincing, as he stepped forward and straightened from his crouch. "Gimme a rag, Soupy," he demanded, his eyes clenched shut over hydraulic fluid and burning sweat. He held his greasy hands out, blindly.

Lieutenant (jg) Suaak-Pas-Ra, acting exec of the 3rd Pursuit Squadron, was similarly buried in the cockpit of the P-40E, with only his legs and tail visible. "Can't, sur," came the muffled reply, but somebody hit Ben in the chest with a clean cloth, and he wiped his face. He blinked.

"Wow," he said when he could see. "What brings the whole back row of the chessboard to my modest little abode?" Not only was Adar standing in the wide opening of the hangar, but quite a few others including Steve Riggs, Perry Brister, "Ronson" Rodriguez, and Bernie Sandison were with him. Those he understood. He was surprised to see Isak Rueben and several "high-up" Lemurians he recognized, but didn't really know, however. He didn't understand why Pam Cross and Sister Audry were there at all. *Wait, Pam's a nurse. She's probably here to check the new arrivals, and make sure the men they sent out to me are really fit to be here.*

Adar walked slowly around the big, muscular-looking plane that seemed to crouch menacingly in the still, sultry shade of the big building. As always, he wore what all the humans referred to as his "Sky Priest suit," despite his lofty status, but the star-spangled, purple hood was thrown back, revealing his gray fur and bright, silver eyes. He'd been there when *Santa Catalina* limped into Baalkpan Bay, and he'd watched the heavy crates removed from the dry-docked ship. He'd even been out to the infant airfield while it was still under construction and the fighters were being uncrated and positioned for assembly. But this was the first time he'd ever seen one of the "hot ships" in one piece. Even though he had no real grasp of what it was capable of, beyond what he'd been told, he could tell just by looking at it; by the sleek, animalistic, *hungry* lines, that it certainly appeared capable of more than he'd ever truly believed.

"It is magnificent!" he gushed. "Oh, it *is!*" He took a breath. "And how many have you managed to save, to assemble?"

"We have twenty, Mr. Chairman, that'll fly once we finish getting everything hooked up," Ben said as though he'd failed his task. "Plus one more we can fly with the landing gear fixed." He shrugged. "I mean to use that one as a trainer, if Bernie doesn't swipe it and stick those Jap floats salvaged out of *Amagi*'s hangar on it. Nuttiest thing I ever heard! A P-40 *seaplane!*" There were chuckles, and he looked wistfully at the fighter. "We *might* even cobble one more together, but no promises. It's not so much a matter of spare parts; we're actually pretty good there. As I said, we have engines, radiators, gauges, tires . . . you name it. But some of the airframes were damaged in fundamental ways we didn't expect just by looking at them. The crates must've taken a real beating, particularly those in the holds, and the crate bracings themselves actually torqued things around." He smirked. "The good news is, we'll have plenty of replacement tail assemblies, windscreens, control surfaces, and," he grunted, "rudder pedals. We're also using two pretty corroded fuselage assemblies for simulated flight trainers. Got 'em rigged in the trees to respond to stick controls!"

He looked at Riggs, then Ronson. "That was one little thing I was going to see if your guys could do: juice the instruments so we can do some night-flying training—without using one of our batteries . . . or busting a plane!"

Ronson grinned. "Sure thing, Ben." He looked at Riggs. "It'll be good training for the EM flight engineers, and you *can* use batteries! Home-grown ones! I don't know when we'll have anything like Bakelite, but we're doing good stuff with glass and ceramic, and we finally have batteries that don't weigh a ton."

Bernie looked at Ronson. "Just so long as you don't give us any more of those wood and brass 'box bombs'!"

Ronson cringed and cut his eyes back at Riggs. "So? I forgot there was zinc in brass! I'm an electrician's mate, not a metallurgist! Nobody got hurt!"

Ben laughed. "That'd be swell, so long as I don't have to use any of *my* batteries for the job!"

"So," Pam Cross suddenly asked in her heavy Brooklyn accent, "when're ya gonna fly one?"

"Well, it's been taking a while to get all the bugs ironed out," Ben defended, a little self-consciously. "I got almost two hundred 'Cats workin' on these crates and trying to learn how to fly 'em—without letting anybody fly one! Only guys with flight experience are even allowed into the training program, but"—he took a breath—"nobody but me, Lieutenant

Mackey, and those five other poor fellas that came in the other day on the 'Buzzard' have any experience at all in P-40s, and honestly, a couple of them have no business flying anything for a long time. The guys are *wrecks*, and not just physically. Karen says they shouldn't *ever* fly again! Those damn Japs . . ." He stopped. "Doesn't matter, anyway, I have to let the guys here have an equal shot, after all the work they've done."

"What about the ground crews?" Sister Audry asked. "Some enlisted men have also arrived from Maa-ni-la, yes?"

Pete was just as surprised to hear her speak as he'd been when Pam had.

"Yeah, they're doing okay, I guess. Sergeant Dixon, the one who showed up with Mackey, is a lot better now, and he's pretty much become the senior crew chief around here. He makes the new guys take it easy. Dixon's a gem. I don't know if we could've done it without him. All the planes came with instructions and I'd *seen* them put together before, but he'd actually done it."

"Where is he now?" Adar asked.

"Couple hangars over, doing the same as me and Soupy and these other guys." He patted the Curtiss green wing behind him. "About a thousand little 'final touches.' All the planes are together that are going to be, and thanks to the Corps of Engineer-'Cats Brister loaned me, we've got roofs over every one. But we've still got to finish checking out the hydraulic systems, which we were just doing here, and make sure all the connections are tight on the Prestone tanks, fill 'em up—and do the same for the oil tanks and Prestone and oil radiators, recheck the batteries, gauges, *triple*-check the connections on all three fuel tanks." He wiped his brow with his rag and grinned at Pam Cross. *Gosh, she really is pretty, looking at me like that!* he thought. *Too bad she's so stuck on that maniac Silva . . . or is she?* He blinked and looked at the others. "After that, we'll finally put the props on and do a preliminary run-up on the engines—we just got fuel a couple days ago." He stopped and looked at Isak Rueben. He knew the scruffy little guy was nuts; all the "Mice" were. He'd never forget watching them chain-smoke cigarettes, covered with oil from head to foot. . . .

"That reminds me. We have a problem with condensation in the fuel tanks. Too much humidity and heat, I guess."

Isak realized Ben was talking to him. "Uh, just hafta keep them tanks empty—er maybe plumb, brimmin' full, is all. Nothin' else for it. Drain off the damn water before you fill 'em . . . sir."

"Then you gonna fly?" Pam pressed.

"No. After we run up the engines, we'll double-check everything *again*, retighten any bolts we missed, or might've wiggled loose, and then we'll slow-time the engines. . . ."

"And fly?"

Ben grinned again. "Yes, ma'am. Then I'm going to fly each one of these beautiful crates myself!"

"Ha!" Pam yapped excitedly.

Sister Audry looked at the girl and smiled. Pam was an adventurous girl, a "free spirit," and she'd been concerned about her these last weeks since Dennis Silva didn't return. She'd been morose, uncommunicative. She was glad she'd suggested they come out to the field that day. Besides, she'd wanted to check on "the boys" who'd been through so much.

"By the Heavens," Adar murmured. "So many things yet to do! These P-40s are as complicated as any ship! And a single person will control them?"

"Yes, sir," Ben replied. "That's why we have to be very careful—and even then, no matter what we do, there're going to be crack-ups." He grimaced. "We're going to lose some planes, just in training, like we've lost some Nan . . . PB-1s. We're going to lose guys too."

Adar gazed at the plane. "It *is* magnificent," he said at last, "but I remain . . . uncertain that it—and the others—will be worth the time, effort, and blood that went into retrieving them and finally getting them into the air." He looked at Ben. "I know you disagree and I yearn to be amazed, to be wrong, but consider this: had all that has gone into these craft been applied to other things, more 'Naan-sees,' better, *different* planes we can build ourselves . . ." He blinked concern. "You yourself have said we cannot build others like these for some years, perhaps many. I fear the greatest weapon that ever was is of no use when it is spent."

Ben stiffened. "Would you have said the same about *Walker*?"

Adar looked at him sharply. "Of course not, but there's a difference. *Walker* has already saved our people many times. These craft of yours have as yet only cost us lives. Also, though we may be years away from building ships like *Walker*, we are not *many* years away. We need weapons *now*, and in the foreseeable future, that will carry us to victory against the Grik and our other enemies as well. Honestly, I fear . . . growing to rely on such complicated, potentially . . . transient advantages as these lovely aar-craaft, only to find them gone, used up, when we need them most."

Sister Audry frowned. "My dear Adar," she said, "I was not here during the terrible battle in the nearby bay, but I believe Colonel Mallory was."

Adar recoiled as if he'd been slapped. The old, battered PBY that Ben flew literally to pieces had probably done more, strategically, to save them than *Walker* had. Without it, they would've never known about *Amagi* and the Grand Swarm until it was much too late.

Ben's jaw was hard when he spoke through tight lips. "Soupy, which ship is farthest along?"

Soupy's eyes were wide. "'M' ship, a'course."

"Get Lieutenant Mackey and Sergeant Dixon. Ask them to bring their whole detail."

"What are you going to do, Colonel?" Bernie asked.

Ben looked at Pam, then back at the Acting Minister of Ordnance. "I'm going to fly, Mr. Sandison."

"This is ridiculous!" Adar insisted loudly over the sound of the rumbling engine. It had been running for an hour now, slowly taken and held through various rpm ranges and Mackey, in the cockpit, held out his fist, thumb upward. "I have already apologized as sincerely as I know how!"

"This isn't about that, Mr. Chairman," Ben said. "Not really. Sure, I was sore for a minute; then I realized you were right. It's time for you to look in the poke and see what you bought."

"She's already run longer than half the ships we sent up against the Japs in the Philippines!" Dixon yelled beside Ben, handing him a parachute. Ben considered the bulky pack for a moment, then shrugged into it. He'd need it to sit on if nothing else, and he wasn't going over the water. He had no plans of bailing out, short of the wings coming off. Even if the engine quit, he'd get the plane back on the ground in one piece—or die trying. "Just watch your mix, with this weird gas," Dixon added, "and don't take her too high!"

"Guns?"

"She's got two on board, just like you said. They *will* fire! I cleaned 'em, tuned 'em, and bore-sighted 'em myself. . . . You're up on those hydraulic chargers?" Ben nodded, and Dixon shrugged. "They won't be dead-on, but they'll put on a show. Soupy sent to clear everybody away from that banged-up barge down by the 'Nancy' hangars. Blow the hell outta that an' that'll show 'em!"

Ben gulped a cup of water somebody handed him and pulled on a pair of flight goggles, settling them on his forehead. With a nod at the gathered spectators, he ran to replace Mackey in the cockpit of the plane.

Mackey had throttled back to a rumbling idle and stepped out on the wing root. "Sure you don't want me to do it, Colonel?" he yelled with a grin. "I *did* zap three Zeros, you know!"

"Not on your life, Mack," Ben yelled back, slapping his shoulder. "No Zeros up there today. I'm only going to wring her out a little."

"Just don't wring her out too much!"

Adar watched anxiously with the others. He couldn't help but feel as if he'd forced Ben to do something he and the plane weren't yet ready for—and he deeply regretted his earlier insinuations. Ben was in the cockpit now, under the bright afternoon sun, and Lieutenant Mackey had trotted past those who were watching, which, by now, probably included every aviator and ground crewman in Baalkpan. Adar saw Mackey disappear into one of the hangars. Quickly, Ben put all the control surfaces through exaggerated motions, released the brakes, and gunned the engine. Immediately, the green and gray plane accelerated from a standing stop into what struck Adar as a foolhardy speed as it taxied away from the hangars, the tail twitching in short, erratic motions, and headed for the north end of the runway, a light, white dust cloud billowing after it. As the plane drew farther away, Adar was surprised by how rapidly the engine noise diminished.

"This is foolishness," he proclaimed aside to Perry Brister, but Perry shook his head.

'I don't know, sir. It *has* been months, and there's a war on. Maybe Ben needed a kick in the pants to get those planes into it before they all become 'hangar queens.' God knows he loves 'em like children. Besides, there's that other little matter we came to ask him about, and if this goes well, he's more likely to go along."

The P-40 vanished in its own dust cloud as it stopped and turned, facing south. For a few moments, nothing happened. A 'Cat raced up. "Maa-kee got him on raa-dio in other plane! He say 'all swell.' He just careful; check stuff more!"

Suddenly, the distant Allison engine growled deeply with an ear-splitting, feral roar that sounded like nothing Adar had ever heard. Maybe a chorus of a dozen "gri-maax," or "super lizards" might have come close. The plane hurtled out of the cloud, flaps down, tail already rising off the ground.

"There he goes!" Pam cried excitedly.

The hungry drone of the Allison reached a fever pitch, and about halfway down the bright airstrip, Ben's plane leaped into the air, already moving faster than anything most of those present had ever seen, short of a bullet. The landing gear dangled strangely beneath the wings, twisting, rising, disappearing into their wells one after the other, all while the plane clawed skyward at a shockingly extreme angle.

"Yes!" roared Dixon, his arms crossed over his head. "Yes, yes, yes!"

All around him, Adar heard wild cheering, and his own silver eyes became oddly unfocused.

"How often more must I apologize?" Adar laughed, grasping Ben by the shoulders and shaking him gently. "A glorious exhibition! Such speed, such agility!" He laughed again, almost giddy. "And that poor, poor barge! Ha! I doubt you left enough of it to build one of Ronson's battery boxes!"

"And that was with only two guns!" Dixon crowed. "Imagine what six would do—and it can carry bombs too!"

They were back in the shade of a hangar, the recently exercised aluminum steed still ticking as the heat transferred from her radiators.

"It wasn't *all* peaches and cream," Ben cautioned. "I spent more time

fooling with the mixture and throttle than just about anything else—
crummy gas!—and talk about a hog! I bet the spark plugs look like lava
rocks!" He shook his head. "She never cut out on me, but she *would* have,
eventually. We can't mix ethyl with the gas, so we're going to have to
figure out a way to *inject* it, or something. Jeez, did you hear that detonation when I first climbed out?"

"No."

Ben snorted. "I did!" He nodded at Adar's starry cloak. "And talk
about stars! PB-1s are swell—but I haven't pulled any *real* gees in a
while!" Mackey and Dixon laughed appreciatively.

"Still, a most successful, and . . . gratifying test, no doubt?" Adar
asked.

"Sure, for the most part," Ben agreed. "Showed us what we need to
fix, anyway. But mostly I hope it convinced you of the worth of my
planes!"

"It did that," Adar said softly. "So much so in fact that I'm persuaded
Mr. Riggs's scheme may have merit."

"What scheme?" Ben asked guardedly.

"As you know, Cap-i-taan Jis-Tikkar, 'Tikker,' harbors concern the
Grik, with Jaap aid, may employ flying machines of their own. Ahd-mi-
raal Keje-Fris-Ar shares that concern, as does General Aalden. The plane
that once bombed us here is still unaccounted for if nothing else, and the
Grik and Jaaps have had just as long as we to . . . advance themselves."

"So?"

"Arr-strips, just such as this, have been under construction at Aryaal
and Sing-aa-pore. Another builds on Andaman Island. Mr. Riggs wants
to put some of your planes there. In fact, once we secure enough of Saa-
lon, he wants them to go as far forward as they possibly can—even to the
extent of carrying and flying them off our . . . our carriers."

"What?" Ben looked at Riggs. "That's nuts! These aren't carrier
planes. They'd never take the stress of landing on a ship, or catching a
cable. Christ, even if we beefed 'em up enough to take an arresting hook,
they'd be too ass-heavy to fly!"

"I'm not talking about *landing* them on a carrier," Riggs said, "just
taking off from one. They'd fly their mission, then set down on land."

Ben scratched his beard. "Okay. That might work. . . . Mack says

Jimmy Doolittle did that with B-25s to bomb Tokyo! Drove the Japs wild."

"Yeah," Mackey agreed. "They didn't want us to know about it, but they couldn't help taking it out on us, so we knew something fantastic had happened. Gradually, the details seeped into the camp we were in. Cheered us up, despite the extra beatings."

"Just let me get the planes finished and crewed with good pilots before you throw an operation like *that* at me, for crying out loud!" Ben demanded.

"That goes without saying."

Ben eyed Riggs. "No it doesn't. *Say* it!"

"That was fun," Pam admitted as she and Sister Audry strolled back through the bustle of the Baalkpan trading district. They'd left the others, and after checking on the newly arrived survivors of the Japanese prison ship and tending a few small hurts, they headed back in the direction of the Baalkpan hospital. Even in spite of the war—and because of it to a large degree—the open-air bazaars had begun to thrive once more. There was a difference now, of course; there were fewer luxuries, and far more troops—some from distant lands—frequented there. Naked younglings still scampered about, eliciting laughter or chastisement, and the merchants and hawkers had grown more numerous, but most of the trade remained much as it had been, except there were more purveyors of fine blades—and gold had largely taken the place of barter as a basis of exchange. That was still odd, and the values fluctuated wildly as people became used to the new system.

"It was," Audry agreed. "Perhaps now you see that you needn't remain cloistered in the 'fem box' when not on duty?" she probed.

Pam's face fell. "I suppose. I just miss the big rat, ya' know?" she said, referring to Silva. "He shoulda' come home."

"There are other men," Audry reminded her. "And other women now as well, at last," she added with satisfaction, watching some dark-skinned former Respitans being led through the crowd, bearing a long, rolled-up fishing net. The women were mostly young and attractive, she noted, of that adventurous age most likely to strike out beyond the relative freedom, safety, and security they'd already found in Maa-ni-la. Nearly a hundred had reached Baalkpan so far, and though uneasy, they wanted to work. People stared at them, but there was no hostility, only curiosity and generally pleasure that the "dame famine" was over. Already, a few "old" destroyermen had been seen, in their best shoregoing rig, escorting an exotic beauty around the city, "seeing the sights."

"You might attend a dance at the . . .'Castaway Cook,'" Audry suggested, "without worrying about being pestered so much by men like Dean Laney!"

Pam chuckled, but it sounded forced. "I wrote Dennis that I'd *marry* that big jerk Laney, if he didn't come home . . . and he didn't. He doesn't care!"

Sister Audry sighed. "My dear, I grant you that sometimes it's difficult to fathom what Mr. Silva cares *most* about, but I've learned he does indeed care about a great many things." She paused. "He cares about you, for example, very much."

"Did he say so?"

"No, but he didn't have to. Have you asked yourself why he didn't return?"

"Sure, an' I know the answer too. He's gotta kill bad guys wherever the Skipper is!"

Audry pursed her lips. "You're more than half right," she conceded, "but I think, in his own way, Mr. Silva follows a calling much like Captain Reddy's: to protect those he cares about regardless of the cost to himself, in the only way he knows. He must destroy the threat. It is perhaps a simplistic approach, but most effective when successful. The Bible is full of examples."

Pam stopped and looked oddly at the nun. "You tellin' me that Dennis Silva's on a mission for *God*?"

"I consider it possible," Sister Audry replied with a straight face.

"You're *serious*!"

"God *has* chosen more unlikely tools," Audry said, realizing she was again being drawn into a subject she didn't want to discuss, largely because it remained unsettled—and unsettling—in her own mind. Silva had almost literally performed miracles on behalf of those under his protection, in his own singularly lethal way. She had witnessed them herself. There was often . . . disproportionate collateral damage, but the Old Testament was packed with examples where even God hadn't been terribly choosy about who suffered as a result of His actions. She shook her head. "Skip it, as you Americans say, but consider this: by 'abandoning' you, Mr. Silva has *freed* you to make a life . . . perhaps with one such as that Colonel Mallory? He also continues to protect you—and all of us—from afar, by 'smiting' those that might harm us before they can. He may not have consciously realized it at the time—though I constantly underestimate him—but he has given you a great gift; one such as these Respitan women now enjoy: the freedom to do as your heart desires . . . and the safety to exercise that freedom."

"Gee," Pam whispered, then snorted. "Dennis Silva, an 'Angel o' the Lord'! That's a laugh! Sister, you just don't *know* that lug like I do!"

Sister Audry smiled back at the now-grinning nurse. "Perhaps not," she conceded, "but *you* don't know him like *I* do."

"So," Pam continued, changing the subject, "what did Adar think when you showed up back here? I've noticed your 'congregation' continues to grow."

Audry laughed, and the sound was like musical chimes in the noisy bustle of the bazaar. "I think he was . . . discomfited. He is a dear creature and has responsibilities unprecedented among his people. I'm sure he was personally glad to see me, but the Church confuses him and even undermines his 'True Faith' to a degree he doesn't want to deal with just now." Audry smiled. "I try not to cause trouble, but the Word spreads of its own accord. . . . Perhaps that odd Mr. Bradford was right."

"'Bout what?"

"Oh, possibly a great many things after all; destinies, for example." She paused, and changed her tack slightly. "*Chairman* Adar is my friend, yet *High Sky Priest* Adar may have been less than pleased by my return!" She chuckled. "But I had only two other choices. I could have remained in Maa-ni-la, or gone to the Empire with Second Fleet." She sighed. "Sadly, despite my expectations—it has an even more varied population—Maa-ni-la was not yet the fertile ground for the Church that Baalkpan has become. I believe it more important to continue my work here, for now." She frowned. "After much prayer, I realized I couldn't go east, not yet. Even I see the diplomatic risks of extending my work into the Empire at this delicate time." Her voice grew determined. "I will *not* be the cause of further chaos there that might cost lives. I must—I *shall*—go there someday to help them understand the very real difference between the Word I profess and the vile dogma of the Blood Priests. As perverted as the Church has become under the Dominion, it desecrates many of the same trappings and symbols. It must be destroyed!" she declared fervently, her face reddening with rage. She caught herself and finally managed a small smile. "In any event, I suspect even were I to demand passage there immediately, I might finally overwhelm our dear Adar's forbearance!"

"In other words, Adar would rather you keep stirring things up here, where incidentally you're safe, than raise a stink beyond his reach to keep a lid on it?"

Audry giggled. "Essentially."

Isak Rueben clomped across the gangway to *Santa Catalina*, still high and dry in the Baalkpan dry dock.

"Foof," he said, contemplating the wasted day. He still didn't know why Riggs wanted him at the airstrip. *A skuggik would've known what to do about the condensation.* They'd talked a little about what to do with S-19 when she arrived, but he didn't know. He couldn't imagine any reason to leave her as a sub, and he'd said so. He wasn't a diesel man, but he could see putting her engines in something, and there was a lot of other stuff they could sure use her guts for. Bernie Sandison also wanted to know what else they could do to improve *Santa Catalina*'s firepower. They were making an "armored cruiser" out of her, hanging protective plating over her engineering spaces and building magazines to accommodate the 5.5-inch guns they'd installed. The four they'd used were the "last of the litter," and they'd been mounted in a casemate surrounding the single stack that allowed most of them to be brought to bear in any direction but directly fore and aft. Dual-purpose 4.7s had replaced the discarded guns that had been in the fore and aft tubs, and the tubs had been reinforced as well. The bridge had been armored too, and a fire control platform had been built on top of it. *Santa Catalina* would still be a creeper, but she'd be faster than a "flat-top Home," and nearly as heavily armed. Better for long-range work, except for the ten-inch gun sections. She might even get one of those—a twenty-foot section with the interrupted-thread breech! Interrupted-thread breechloaders were the next big thing Bernie was hot for—besides his constant tinkering with some kind of powered torpedo—as soon as they could rifle big tubes.

Still no reason to drag me off, he thought mopily. *I ain't Ordnance. Prob'ly just tryin' ta get me out an' around again,* he suspected. *Ever'body figgers a fella can't be happy 'less they's around other folks all the time. Must think I'm pinin' away without Gilbert an' Tabby around.* He snorted. He did miss them, like a brother or sister, but he wasn't pining. As far as he knew, to this day, nobody but Tabby—probably—knew he and Gilbert actually *were* half brothers . . . or quarter brothers . . . whatever. He sometimes got their precise degree of bastardy confused. They had the same mother, but different fathers; neither of whom ever married their mother. Isak didn't really blame either man; his mother had the face of a moose and the voice of a hog . . . but she'd been a good dame.

"Just me," he said to the musket-armed 'Cat sentry as he stepped aboard the ship. He flicked a salute aft and padded forward in the gloom until he stood on the fo'c'sle amid the anchor chains that came in through the hawseholes. The wood beneath his feet was no longer spongy and rotten; it was hard and new. Most of the old ship had been repaired, he realized with a touch of pride. Soon, decked out in all her new goodies, she'd be out of the dry dock and back in the war. *Well, in* the war, *anyway—a* different *war for her.* He sighed. *Santa Catalina* would probably also be the last "normal-size" ship in this dry dock. They were almost finished with a pair of new floating dry docks, like those they'd been building in other places. The new dry docks wouldn't last forever, but they were . . . portable, and they'd handle anything but a Home—or a carrier—and that was what this first, biggest, dry dock would be devoted to from now on.

He looked around. From where he stood, nobody was in sight. There was work underway aft, and on the adjacent dry dock wall, but no one could see him. His trip ashore hadn't been a complete waste. He'd had an opportunity to stop by and see his new "business partner," a Lemurian called Pepper, down at the Busted Screw. Pepper had been Lanier's mate in *Walker*'s galley, and the two had established the Busted Screw, or "Castaway Cook," during *Walker*'s resurrection and refit. Pepper ran the joint alone now, with Lanier away, and the place was usually jumping. For Isak's purposes, Pepper had cousins everywhere, including some involved in all the various projects—cousins who didn't care about human "habits," but more important, could keep their yaps shut. Isak had been engaged in an ongoing project he wanted to keep to himself. His stop by the Screw that day had left him in possession of the most recent "fruits" of that venture. Inconspicuously, he fished his tobacco pouch and a little hand-carved pipe from his pocket. With another look around, he stuffed the pipe and held a lit Zippo over the bowl.

"Ooo-hoo-ook!" He coughed when the first smoke entered his lungs. He blew it out and tried again. He still coughed, but this time it wasn't so bad. "Outta practice," he gasped—and took another puff. This time he didn't cough, and, with a dreamy expression, he let the smoke drain lazily from his nostrils. It was vile and raunchy beyond anything he'd ever used, even in the Philippines, but it could be smoked! He'd finally succeeded! He'd performed the greatest technological feat of the age! The yellow, waxy, Lemurian tobacco was almost universally chewed now, usually dried and mixed with something like local molasses, but up until now nobody had figured out a way to smoke it without becoming almost instantly, violently ill. "Yur-eeka!" he wheezed.

"What the hell are you doin' out here?" demanded a gravelly voice behind him. Isak almost squirted his pipe over the rail.

"Nuffin'," he chirped, trying to hide the smoldering pipe in his hand.

"Nothin' my ass," growled Dean Laney, drawing closer. "You been holdin' out on ever'body! You sneaked out here to smoke a cigarette you've been hoardin' all this time. What's the matter with you? There's fellas that'd choke you to death just to breathe your last, smoky breath, and if you don't share, I'll be one of 'em."

"I ain't smokin' no cigarette!" Isak stated, seemingly oblivious of the cloud around him in the dank murk.

"Like hell! I can smell it!"

"You can? What do you smell?"

"A cigarette, you freaky little dope! Give it over!"

"An' it *smells* like a cigarette?"

"Say, you're even squirrelier than usual tonight. Sure, it smells like a cigarette 'cause it is one. Maybe not a good one, but I don't care! Fork it over!"

Isak suddenly jammed his pipe under Laney's nose. "*There's* yer cigarette, you big, fat, lumpy turd!" he jeered, "'an that's the last whiff o' Isak Rueben's 'Patented Sweet Smokin' Tobacco' yer ever gonna get, if you lay one fat, turdy finger on me, hear? Ha! I'm goin' in the smokin' tobacco bizness. Cigarettes, see-gars, a nice arrow-matic pipe blend. Hell, I'll be the first tobacco magnet in the world!"

It's 'magnate,' you bonehead," Laney said, but he grabbed Isak's hand and held the pipe close to his face. "Damn, that smells good. How'd you do it?"

"No way! I tell you, and you'll swipe the process. If you think I done all this work so you can skim off the cream, you're stupider than you look."

"Watch that mouth!" Laney growled, his grip tightening on Isak's wrist.

"You watch yours, fatso, an' leggo my arm if you don't want my new comp'ny motto to be 'Heavenly Smokes for Ever'body but Laney'!"

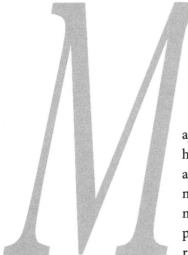

CHAPTER 14

////// *New Ireland*

ajor Chack-Sab-At *loved* horses. Before he and his mixed "division" came ashore at the New Ireland town of Bray the night before, he'd never ridden an animal in his life; not a brontasarry, a paalka, and certainly not one of the terrifying me-naaks, or "meanies," the Filpin cavalry used. He'd never had occasion to ride the first two, and he had no inclination to ride the latter. With his background as a wing runner of the People, he'd never imagined a reason to climb atop *any* animal before, but a Marine Major commanding almost two thousand troops needed mobility, and he'd been introduced to horses. He was entranced by the novelty of the experience. To sit upon so large a creature—that had absolutely no desire to eat him—and with which he could actually communicate after a fashion, gave him a feeling of warm benevolence toward the animal. He'd never understood the human preoccupation with "pets"; no Lemurian did. But though he was given to understand horses weren't exactly pets, he began to grasp the attraction of "having" a companion animal that could think for itself to a degree. He'd heard a great deal about "dogs" and understood humans were particularly fond of them, but none existed in the isles. There were small cats, which *did* bear a vague resemblance to his people but no more than the pesky forest monkeys did to humans (or again to his own people). He finally knew where the human "Cat-monkey–Monkey-cat" diminutive for his People came from but he didn't mind, despite the fact that he'd seen no evidence the little cats that roamed wild on New Scotland even *had* brains . . . but horses! He patted "his" animal on the neck.

He suspected by its twitchy responses to the distant, muffled booming that it was growing nervous. Chack doubted the hundred-odd horses attached to his "division" were alone in that. Many of his troops—virtually all the Imperials—had never faced combat. The first of his two regiments was composed of the remnants of his platoon from *Walker* and the Marine contingents from *Simms*, *Mertz*, *Tindal*, and the oilers. Some were hardened veterans, and he counted heavily on them to steady the two hundred completely green Imperial Marines attached to the regiment. The second regiment was almost entirely Imperial, but had a lot of the men who'd fought at the Dueling Grounds. All were "marching to the sound of the guns" in a sense, because the wind brought the heavy reports of the New Dublin defenses about fifteen miles east, over the Sperrin Mountains, and deposited the sound in such a way that it seemed to lie before them.

Chack knew it was an illusion, but there *were* enemies ahead, moving to resist "Major" Blair's assault on the "Irish" town of Waterford on the banks of Lake Shannon. Blair had landed four days before, south of the west-coast town of Cork, just as planned. The landing caught the inhabitants completely by surprise, and, after a short, sharp action, the town was in Allied hands. Blair was greeted as a liberator by the inhabitants, cheering and weeping with relief. Cork was a fishing village of indentured females, mostly, but several hundred "True Irish" Company troops and a contingent of Dominion "Salvadores" had been billeted there, going about their grisly "pacification, conversion, and reeducation" process. Hundreds in the town had already been slain and their bodies

carried away. This last act had been just as cruel and apparently irratio-
nal as the murders themselves.

In any event, the plan seemed to be working. Blair's capture of Cork
had drawn rebel troops from Easky, Bray, and Waterford down upon
him, and he met them with prepared positions in Cork and on both
sides of a pass through the Wiklow Mountains. Not only had he been
punishing the enemy severely, he'd drawn all attention other than that
focused on the fleet offshore of New Dublin, and Chack's division had
virtually strolled ashore at Bray. The reception there was similar to the
one Blair received except there'd been no fight at all. The "garrison" had
gone to Waterford in response to Blair's attack at Cork. Chack's most
immediate problem after landing had been convincing the locals that he
and his Lemurian troops weren't "demons" and were there to help—and
to keep them from lynching anyone suspected of collaborating with the
Doms. His division had swelled by several hundred "auxiliaries" who
knew the island intimately and who, regardless of their former leanings
or associations with the Company, were practically rabid to destroy the
murderous Doms.

Chack now had a great deal of experience with "plans," but he was
increasingly optimistic. Nobody knew what the enemy had at New Dublin. Doubtless, the bulk of the Dom troops and rebels were there, but
their attention was fixed for now, and Chack's scouts reported no effort
to force the bottleneck between the northern Sperrin Mountains and the
sea. As far as they knew, only whatever enemy troops might be in the
western "panhandle" city of Belfast were unaccounted for.

Major Alister Jindal, commander of the Imperial regiment and
Chack's exec, galloped up alongside the shorter 'Cat and stopped his
horse. Chack couldn't help but marvel at the man's horsemanship—and
the animal's willing cooperation.

"Good aafternoon, Major Jindal," Chack said pleasantly. He liked
Jindal, and the two had worked well together in preparation for this operation. Some Imperials still had reservations about the Alliance, and a
few were openly antagonistic toward the Lemurians in particular, refus-
ing to serve with them and unwilling to take orders from them under
any circumstances. Governor-Emperor McDonald couldn't fire them
all, but he could put them to use where their attitudes wouldn't be a

distraction. Jindal was a good friend of Blair's and perfectly prepared to accept Chack's more experienced command.

"Good afternoon, Major Chack," Jindal said, grinning. Chack had halted his horse under the shade of a massive tree of some kind; it looked much like a Galla, except for the leaves. Despite the wind that brought them the sounds of battle to the east, it was hot and sultry in the valley between the two craggy mountain ranges, and the dense forest harbored more than enough moisture to make the day oppressive. He'd been watching *his* division pass by. The Lemurian Marines wore one uniform, but probably represented every member of the Alliance. Some "artillerists" in the uniforms of various Army regiments walked or trotted alongside their paalka-drawn guns. The "tried and true" split-trail six-pounders were still moved by a single animal, but the new twelve-pounder field guns used a single stock trail and limber hitched to a team of paalkas. Horses pulled the Imperial artillery, and Chack considered that a waste. Even in the Empire, horses were rare, and paalkas were stronger, if slower. He foresaw a thriving horse/paalka trade.

Imperial Marines in their red coats with yellow facings marched side by side in column with Lemurian Marines in their white leather armor and blue kilts. Black tricorns and shakos contrasted with polished bronze "doughboy" helmets. The colorful nature of the force gave a festive impression, but there was no doubt it meant business. The Lemurian Marines had grown accustomed to war and the associated hardship and discipline. Even in this foreign land with its strange creatures and people, they knew what to do, even if the enemy was different. The Imperials didn't have the experience or training, but they were motivated. Nearly all the Marines, Lemurian and human, were armed with muskets; Imperial flintlocks and "Baalkpan Armory" caplocks were all brightly polished and glittered silver as they swayed to the marching cadence under the hot afternoon sun.

"It's a lovely sight," Jindal said, mirroring Chack's thoughts.

"It is," he agreed. "Lovely, stirring . . . and terrible all at once."

Jindal hesitated. "I'm . . . glad you're here."

Chack looked at him, surprised. His tail flicked alongside his right leg. That was one problem with riding horses. The saddle made his tail very uncomfortable, and he was constantly adjusting his kilt to maintain his modesty. Lemurians didn't care as much about such things as humans, but even among them, it was undignified to run around with one's "ass hanging out."

"I'm not," he said with a snort. "As you may have gathered, I consider this something of a 'sideshow' in a more important war . . . but it has become part of that war, regardless."

"All the more reason *I'm* glad you're here," Jindal said.

Chack barked a laugh. "Thank you for that. It's nice to be appreciated!" His tone grew somber. "And in truth, I don't mind it much. I've developed my own . . . dislike . . . of these 'Doms' and their Company rebel . . . tools."

"I can imagine!' Jindal blurted. Blair had described the action at the Dueling Grounds in considerable detail.

Chack's attention was diverted by a figure on a horse, racing toward them on the opposite side of the column. The animal jarred to a stop, and he was amazed to see Lieutenant Blas-Ma-Ar sitting atop as if she'd been riding horses all her life.

"Make way," she shouted, and forced the horse through the marching troops. Reining in before Chack and Jindal, she saluted.

"How did you learn to control that animal so?" Chack demanded.

"I practiced, sir," she answered simply. "Beg pardon, but scouts have encountered enemy pickets on the road ahead." She paused. "They could have brushed them aside, but they left them be, per your orders. They were probably seen."

"Any contact with Blair yet?"

"No, sir."

Chack considered and wished again they had the new field communications equipment First Fleet had deployed. Soon they would, reportedly with the arrival of *Maaka-Kakja*. They'd managed only about five miles the night before, and they'd pushed on early that morning with little sleep. So far, they'd made eight or nine miles that day, but with the heat and humidity, he wasn't sure his division was ready for a major pitched battle without some rest. "Let's have a look," he decided. "Stay back, Major Jindal, but push more scouts ahead on the flanks. We need to coordinate with Blair—and make sure there's nothing moving up on the left. We want to draw defenders out of New Dublin, but not many, not yet." His tail swished impatiently. "I do wish we had some 'air,' as Captain Reddy would say." He shook his head. "Not for a few days yet, according to the last reports, so we'll just have to muddle along the old-fashioned way for now." He looked around at the confining forest alongside the road. "Be ready to go from column into line," he said. "It will be hard, but do the best you can. The terrain should open up soon, closer to the town, I believe. If you have no word from me by then, deploy the troops at that point, regardless. But watch the flanks!" He nodded at Blas. "Come," he said. "Show me."

They trotted forward, Chack a little unsteady on his mount, parallel to the marching infantry and creaking guns. A sudden flurry of shots echoed in the woods ahead. Instead of dying away, however, such as would have happened if it had been just more pickets and scouts, the shooting intensified.

"It would seem someone has run into someone else," Chack quipped. He slowed his advance and looked around for someone to hold his horse.

"What are you doing, sir?" Blas asked.

"I want to go forward and see what's happening, but I don't want this animal shot!"

"Major, we're on the verge of a 'meeting engagement' as General Alden would call it. For the first time, we're stumbling into a battle we know almost nothing about. You must stay on your horse so you can move quickly from one place to another. That's why you have him!"

"But . . ." He looked at the horse. "*He* didn't volunteer to fight . . . did he?"

"Do paalkas volunteer?" Blas retorted. Chack started to reply that it wasn't the same, but Blas had already moved forward. The firing ahead continued to build; dull, thumping crackles of musketry. The troops around them on the road started to trot in response to orders shouted in two languages. The column began shaking out into a ragged line in the trees, facing south, and NCOs shouted and shoved men and 'Cats into position. Chack glanced behind him and saw the rest of the column had ground to a halt. *Blas is right,* he thought, patting the horse again. *I have to stay mounted and find out what's happening.* He urged the horse forward with his heels.

Musket balls *voomed* through the woods, *thwacking* into trees and causing a gentle rain of leaves.

"Major!" Blas called. She was leaning over in her saddle, speaking to an Imperial lieutenant.

Chack joined them, and the Imperial lieutenant saluted excitedly. The former wing runner had gained a reputation much larger than his stature, and sitting calmly on a horse with musket balls whizzing by only reinforced it in this man's eyes.

"Are you in command here?" Chack asked.

"No, sir. Captain Morris commanding Company E of the Fifth, and Company C of your own Second, sent me. They're in contact with the enemy!"

"I can *hear* that. What does he face and how did he come to be engaged so closely?"

"Their pickets fled and when we advanced, we ran into a blocking force on the Waterford road."

The musketry redoubled, and two thunderclaps stirred the brush and loosed more leaves.

"Six-pounders," Chack decided. "Ours. Your captain Morris must be fully engaged and at least partially deployed. What have we run into, and why were our pickets and scouts not between us?"

"The scouts were . . . elsewhere," the lieutenant admitted. "Captain Morris believes we face at least two companies, perhaps a regiment."

"Artillery?"

"None yet, but it will doubtless arrive soon."

Chack nodded. "Then we must displace them. They must've been expecting us, but maybe not this fast. If we give them time to dig in, this will be a costly fight." He looked west, toward the mountains he couldn't see through the trees. "And we have no contact with Major Blair—but he must see this fight; the rising smoke. . . ." He shook his head. "I didn't want this yet. I wanted to draw troops from in front of Blair but leave them confused about our movements, spread them out. That's over. The fight has begun. I won't ask troops to attack 'gently' to buy time with their lives." He looked at the lieutenant. "Tell Captain Morris that the rest of the regiment is coming up. I'll be there directly myself. In the meantime, he'll reinforce the companies now in contact and extend his left with an eye toward turning the enemy flank. If he sees an opportunity to do that before I arrive, he will, if he wishes to remain an officer. If the opportunity does not arise, the movement should at least weaken the forces in front of him—and that's where we will strike with all our might as soon as I join him."

"What of Major Blair?" Blas-Ma-Ar asked.

"He'll coordinate his attack with ours, I'm sure of it. We must push the enemy into the open around Waterford to gain the full effect from our artillery and mortars!"

The lieutenant saluted but stood there, waiting.

"What?" Chack asked.

"Uh . . . where will you be, sir?"

"Right here," Chack said. He turned to Blas. "Inform Major Jindal of this . . . change in plans, and return as quickly as you can. I don't want a battle in this oppressive forest. We must force the enemy out of it where we can see him—and kill him properly."

The Doms and "rebels" were eventually pushed out of their rapidly improving position by a combined frontal and flank attack. They held determinedly until the fixed bayonets of Imperial and Lemurian Marines drove them from their hasty breastworks. The almost-fanatical courage of Dominion troops had been proven before, but they suffered a major technological disadvantage in a close-quarters fight: their bayonets were "stupid." Their muskets were little different in function from those of the Imperials, but Imperial and "American" Marines used offset "socket" bayonets that slid on the outside of their weapons' muzzles. Doms used "plug" bayonets shaped like short swords. They were better tools for everyday use and could hack brush and cut meat and serve as large knives. When "fixed," however, they were inserted into the muzzles and held in place by friction. They usually had to be driven out. Firing a musket with one in place would rupture the barrel and likely injure or kill the shooter.

Socket bayonets with their triangular blades were virtually useless tools, but wickedly lethal weapons, and a musket could still fire when they were affixed. When the entire regiment under Chack's personal command rushed the enemy works, running, screaming through the dense trees and shot, bayonets fixed—then stopped and fired a *volley* into the terrified, waiting defenders—just enough broke and ran to crack the dam. Once that occurred, the remaining Doms had no choice but to run or die, and the crack gave way to a torrent. After that, the race was on.

The bright yellow coats of Dom infantry made fine targets, and many were shot as they fled. Chack's 'Cats and Imperials ran after them, shouting, shooting, stabbing at the fallen, and the woods grew dense with smoke even as the trees began to thin. The regiment had orders to halt at the clearing and regroup. Some, caught in the moment, continued chasing the enemy. Chack—still mounted and exhilarated by the experience of charging on horseback, despite having spent more time just holding on than slashing about with his Navy cutlass—shouted for the drummers to recall the overexuberant troops. The Doms were running away as fast as they could, oddly interspersed with monkeys of every size, blizzards of colorful parrots and other birds, and some other strange creatures Chack had never seen. The thundering drums were joined by Imperial horns, and slowly, most who'd continued their pursuit stopped, looked about, and realized how exposed they were. Quickly, they trotted back to the waiting ranks even as a battery of six-pounders rattled down the road, drawn by gasping paalkas, and deployed in front of the infantry. Soon, exploding case shot pursued the fleeing enemy, reinforcing their terror.

"Beautiful!" shouted Major Jindal, galloping up to join Chack. "Stunning! Yet another famous victory, Major Chack!" he gushed.

"It *was* exciting," Chack confessed, "but only the beginning. Look."

A wide plain, checkerboarded with ripening grain and other crops, lay between them and the New Ireland village of Waterford. It was a quaint, spread-out place, reminiscent of the economical architecture Chack associated with Imperials; but interspersed with the occasional classical planters or Company mansion Imperial aristocracy seemed to favor. Beyond the town, in the distance, the large amoebic shape of Lake Shannon sprawled around the settlement, and spread nearly to the water's edge was a sea of canvas tents that probably outnumbered Chack's and Jindal's force. Figure at least two men to a tent. . . .

"Anything from Major Blair?"

"Not yet. I've sent scouts farther upslope. Perhaps they've made contact by now. But the enemy stands between us." He paused. "I'm not sure we drew much of his attention away from Major Blair."

"We will," Chack promised. "Quickly, I want half your regiment and all your artillery up here. Leave two companies in the rear, guarding the approach from the north, and send the rest to the right and prepare to hit the enemy facing Blair on his right flank . . . Blair's left." Chack blinked, annoyed with himself for lecturing, but clarity was important. "Send a steady officer who will force his way to Blair if he must, and push hard when we advance!"

"I should go myself," Jindal said.

"No, if something happens to me, you must be here. We'll bombard the enemy before us, then advance across the entire front. That move should be unmistakable, and the enemy blocking Blair will have no choice but to defend his lines of communication and supply. I trust Major Blair to sense the proper moment and attack downhill, toward the town. Hopefully, your officer will have communicated this intent by then, but Blair should know what to do regardless. With luck, he may even catch them redeploying and add to the confusion. Ultimately, we should drive the enemy through the town and enclose him between us and the lake."

Jindal shook his head. "Marvelous," he confessed. "The scope of your planning . . ." He chuckled nervously. "The scope of this *war* is beyond anything I ever trained for!"

Chack blinked a sentiment Jindal hadn't seen before—not that he remotely grasped any of the Lemurian blinking yet. "For all your naval power, your people have little more experience at this kind of war than mine did not long ago," he said. "You'll learn, as I was forced to; as Major Blair has done. I was lucky to have good teachers, but the lessons have been . . . hard." He blinked something else. "Pray you never face a lesson such as Major Blair first endured; his might have destroyed a lesser person." He paused, then gestured around. "This fight is a *skirmish* compared to what this war has become in the west; compared to what it'll likely become here before all is done. Learn it well—however it turns out—because the most important points are these: plan for the best, but prepare for the worst, and every battle is won or lost in the planning, in the *mind*, before the first sword is ever drawn."

Jindal gulped and felt a chill. *A skirmish?* He was thoughtful a moment. "But this fight, your plan . . . will leave the enemy no avenue of escape. The rebels might surrender, but the Doms will fight ferociously if they can't withdraw!"

"Very good! You think ahead. What you say is more than likely true," Chack said. "It is in fact a . . . consequence of the 'best case' part of the plan. As a certain large . . . strange . . . man once told me, 'Any we don't kill today, we'll have to kill tomorrow.' You have your orders."

The first battery to arrive had long since ceased firing, but within an hour, twenty-four guns had wheeled into place at the edge of the forest. Most were Allied six-pounders, but four were Imperial eight-pounders—their standard fieldpiece—and six were the new twelve-pounders. A hundred of the highly effective three-inch mortars came forward as well, each weapon with a crew of two, and each section with a squad of animal holders, ammunition bearers, crew replacements, and its own paalka, heavily laden with ammunition for the tubes. The enemy was throwing up a new defensive line on the outskirts of the town and emplacing a battery of their own guns there. That would be the first target.

"The division artillery is ready in all respects, Major," Blas reported. To punctuate her words, the first Dominion piece fired and a cannonball struck the damp ground short of the Allied line, spraying dark earth in the air and sending the shot bounding into the trees.

"Commence firing," Chack said, and Blas wheeled her horse and raced off. Moments later, amid shouted and repeated commands, the mortars erupted with a staccato *pa-fwoomp!* and twenty-four guns belched fire and smoke one after the other from the left, and recoiled backward as the case and roundshot soared downrange. The Imperials didn't have case shot yet, and with their "nonstandard" bores, the allies couldn't share. The eight-pound solid shot got there first, retaining its velocity better, and geysered earth and fragments of the breastworks around the enemy guns. The case shot was lighter for its diameter and bucked more wind for the weight, but there was only the slightest hesitation before white puffs detonated above the enemy line, spraying shards of iron and copper down on the defenders. Then the mortars fell.

Some of the bombs landed short. The range had been only a good estimate before, and some of the late arrivals had little time to make the crude elevation adjustments on the simple tubes. Despite their simplicity, however, the mortars were amazingly reliable, largely due to careful weighing of propulsive charges back in Baalkpan and Maa-ni-la, and the steadily improving quality control on the projectiles themselves. Bigger mortars were in the works that would reach a mile or more, but even though nine hundred yards was stretching the limit of the current model, seventy or more of the bombs fell right among the enemy.

The rippling detonation of the bursting charges sprayed dozens of prescored fragments from each bomb, decimating the Dominion defenders with the effect of a point-blank musket volley. None of the fragments were aimed, of course, so there were fewer real casualties, but the very . . . impersonal, utterly random nature of the projectiles unnerved the enemy like no volley could. And more were on the way. Section chiefs called range corrections, and the second barrage was more precise. The delayed, rippling blasts reached them long moments after the weapons blanketed the enemy position with white smoke once again. A third hail of mortars left their tubes even as the fieldpieces erupted with an earsplitting, rolling roar. So far, there'd been only that one cannon shot by the enemy.

"It is practically murder," said the young lieutenant Chack had spoken to before. The man had suddenly joined Chack, Blas-Ma-Ar, and several other officers who'd gathered to "watch the show." He was riding a horse of his own now, and his uniform was rumpled; blood staining the yellow facings of his coat. Somewhere, back in the woods, he'd lost his shako.

"There was a time when I would've agreed with you," Chack said softly in the brief quiet imposed on the division artillery by the necessity of reloading. "My people long believed that to kill *anyone* was tantamount to murder, aside from the very rare duel. But Grik are not people; they're brutal animals—and no one would call killing *them* murder. In self-defense, we killed some of the Jaaps that aided them, and I admit I felt . . . unhappy about that. But still, it wasn't murder." Another stream of mortars thumped into the sky, and he looked at the lieutenant. "And the Doms started this war with as clear a case of murder as I've ever seen one species commit against itself. Perhaps war distorts perceptions—I'm rather new at it myself, you know—but is it murder to kill a murderer? I think not. It has more the feel of justice to me."

The lieutenant watched the mortars erupt among the enemy again. "But those are only soldiers, men like me. They follow orders. Their leaders are the murderers."

"Do you really think so? Would you have obeyed orders to kill civilians? Innocent, noncombatant females and their younglings?"

"Of course not!"

"Then there you have the difference, Lieuten-aant. Those we kill are 'only soldiers,' but they protect and do the bidding of their murderous masters. While the masters may be chiefly to blame, their soldiers—their tools—must be destroyed." Chack shook his head. "To kill them is not murder; it is war." He cocked his head. "And it is a *good* war. I feel . . . a sense of righteous vengeance, a desire to punish them for what they've done—and for my troops they've killed today. Do you not feel it? To fight a war without that . . . sense . . . must be a terrible thing. Perhaps *that* is what makes a murderer?"

"I feel it," replied the lieutenant, "but I do pity them."

"As do I. As must anyone who desires to remain a person." Chack paused. "Where is your captain?"

"Killed, sir. In the charge against the breastworks in the forest."

"Then you must take his place," Major Jindal said, rejoining the group. He turned to Chack. "The companies on the right have extended the line and made contact with Major Blair's command at last. There is . . . confusion there, but I believe all will be well. The enemy already seems to be reacting to our presence here, and a courier from the major indicated he may move more quickly than expected to take advantage."

Chack had suddenly removed his battered old helmet to listen carefully for a moment, ears erect and alert. Jindal had no idea what he could possibly hear over the pounding guns and mortars nearby, but Blas-Ma-Ar was listening too.

"Assemble your companies," Chack instructed the lieutenant, "if you think they have another charge in them."

"They do, sir."

"Very well. It would seem Major Jindal is correct. Blair is stirring! The division will soon advance!"

Blair unleashed his own mortars then, weapons no Dominion troops had faced until earlier that day. He'd been saving them since he arrived—

unless he'd had no choice—until this very moment. White puff-balls appeared on the now-visible flanks of the mountains to the west, popping soundlessly, the smoke streaming back uphill toward Blair's hidden force. The detonations became constant, creating a great, opaque cloud.

"The artillery will cease firing and prepare to advance with the infantry," Chack bellowed, his order repeated down the line. "The mortars will continue to target the enemy position to cover our advance. When the signal to 'cease firing mortars' is given, their crews will advance with their weapons to the next line and commence firing on the enemy camp, or anywhere the enemy gathers!"

Jindal reached across, extending his hand to Chack. "God be with you, sir," he said.

"May the Maker be with you!" Chack replied, grasping the offered hand. He looked at the lieutenant. "With you as well. Now see to your troops!"

The lieutenant saluted and galloped away, quickly followed by Jindal, who peeled off to the right.

"Now is an excellent time to dismount," Blas said, grinning and hopping down from her horse. "Not only for the beast's sake, but your own. Riding him in the open will make you both a target. Fear not," she added. "They will be brought to us if we need them!"

Chack clumsily stepped down from the saddle, his legs feeling strange. "Good advice, Lieuten-aant . . . and may the Maker be with you as well!"

Most of the 2nd (largely Lemurian) and 5th Imperial Marine regiments—eight companies strong—crossed the wide fields of a grain Chack didn't know amid a thunder of drums and behind a curtain of mortars. Some musket fire came from the enemy position, but it was ineffective across such a distance. There'd still been no more enemy artillery. Perhaps the guns were wrecked? The division advanced across a wide front with open files, four ranks deep. Furious firing erupted on the far right, where Jindal's companies slashed unexpectedly into the enemy flank, just as Blair's infantry struck the disorganized line head-on. The movement there was lost in the forest and beneath a growing fog of rising, swirling smoke. Ahead of Chack, there were still just the hasty breastworks.

They'd learned at the Dueling Grounds that the shield wall afforded some protection from Dom musketry, and they'd close files and use it here if need be. In the meantime, tightly massed troops only gave the enemy a better target. Three hundred yards separated the forces when Chack ordered the mortars to cease firing. The dirty white plumes were more impressive the closer they got, and by now they could even hear the screams amid the explosions. At two hundred yards, the barrage gradually lifted and for a time, all that was visible of the Dom position was a dark, hazy cloud drifting from left to right across their front. The sporadic musket fire gradually increased, forcing Chack to call his Lemurian Marines to the front rank to shield those behind. Balls struck their angled shields, ricocheting away with low, whirring moans. A man screamed and fell, just a few paces from Chack. Another fell without a sound other than that caused by a ball striking flesh. At one hundred yards, the Dom fire reached a fever pitch. They'd probably killed or wounded half the defenders, but there were more than enough left to take a terrible toll, and, despite the shields, men and 'Cats began falling with a wrenching regularity. Chack noticed the men around him literally *leaning* into the fire, as one would struggle against a gale, and he realized with surprise that he was doing it too.

They'd come far enough like this, he decided, unable to return fire. They'd pounded the Doms with their artillery and mortars, and now they were taking their turn. Much closer, and even the smoothbores of the enemy would be just as effective as the battered Krag Chack always carried. He unslung the weapon and affixed the long Springfield bayonet.

"Division!" he trilled in his best long-distance tone, only to hear the word race down the line, repeated half a dozen times. "Prepare to charge bayonets!" He was answered by an animalistic roar, and sixteen hundred glittering steel, two-foot spikes came down and leveled at the enemy.

"Remember to reserve your fire until you're right on them!" an officer shouted from some distance away. "It seems to rattle the sods!"

"Charge!" screamed Chack.

He'd faced more Grik charges than he could remember, and no matter how often he endured and survived the primal force of the Ancient Enemy—its wicked swords, short, thrusting spears, claws and ravening jaws—he still felt a shadow of the visceral horror that struck him the very first time. Implacable and remorseless as the Grik were, however, they attacked as a mob, a "swarm" as even they described it. General Alden had long told Chack that, daunting as their charges were, nothing could be more terrifying—to people—than a disciplined bayonet charge, executed by thinking, committed, *determined* beings. Chack had faced Dom bayonets, but not yet in a charge. He'd seen the effect *his* charge had at the Dueling Grounds . . . and he saw it again now. As usual in such matters, General Alden knew what he was talking about. Of course, Chack had added his own little twist that seemed to shake the Doms as badly as anything else: the point-blank volley before the clash that the Doms, with their plug bayonets, never expected—yet—and couldn't answer. The rippling blast was devastating, and delivered so close that even after their short sprint, the unsteady hands of gasping men and Lemurians simply couldn't miss. Then, with another roar that all but shattered the remaining defenders, the bayonets went to work.

Despite Lieutenant Blas-Ma-Ar's best attempts to stop him, Chack went in with the rest of them. He never fired the old Krag; the ammunition in its magazine was the "real stuff," not the hard-cast black powder reloads. It was precious for its long-range accuracy and utter reliability, despite its age. He went in with the bayonet just like *his* Marines and fought with a savagery that frankly unnerved a few Imperials, and an economical proficiency and precision that came only with the hard experience he'd gained. Through it all, his diminutive *female* lieutenant and apparently self-appointed "protector" fought alongside him with similar competence and equal vigor. That would later unnerve some of Chack's Imperials even more, when they had time to reflect on various things, such as their own attitude toward women—and the kind of combat that had taught Chack and Blas, and all the Lemurians, their skill. But more than that, if there'd been present any Imperial Marines who, despite the reputation Chack had gained at the Dueling Grounds, still clung to any concern or discontented notion that they were commanded by an "ape" or "wog," it vanished in the swirling smoke and bloody ground north of Waterford, New Ireland, that day.

* * *

The sky was purple, with long bloody streaks, when Major Blair found Chack in a large Dominion tent that was spared the firestorm that engulfed most of the enemy encampment when the mortars turned their wrath there. As always, Lieutenant Blas-Ma-Ar stood beside the brindled Lemurian while he sat on a bench, his furry torso bare, stoically enduring the stitches "Doc-Selass-Fris-Ar" applied to the dark, shaved skin over his left shoulder blade. Other wounded were in the tent, being tended by more "corps-'Cats" as even they'd begun calling themselves, and Chack seemed annoyed that Selass was bothering with him when others needed her attention more. In the middle distance, at the south edge of town, mortars still burst with their distinctive crackling thuds, and all the artillery of *two* divisions now thundered continuously, pulverizing the final works of the enemy along the shore of Lake Shannon.

"I'm heartily glad to find you in one piece, my friend," Blair said with a touch of reproach. "Or at least fit to be sewn back into one," he added.

Chack snorted. "You chastise me, when you creep along like a freshly hatched grawfish in the mud!" Chack pointed at Blair's leg. "You still limp from the wound you had at the Dueling Grounds! You hid that before."

Blair chuckled and patted his leg. "Actually, this is new. Courtesy of a Dom musket butt." He shrugged. "Perhaps not entirely new, then. The bugger hit me in the same blasted spot!"

"Do you need someone to look at it?" Selass snapped, her large eyes flashing.

Blair was taken aback, and wondered why she was so angry. Then it hit him. He suddenly remembered the rumors that she and Chack had a "history" of some sort; a history perhaps aggravated by her proximity, continued devotion, and Chack's betrothal to the distant "General" Safir Maraan.

"Um, no, not at all. It's just a slight ache."

"Then, as soon as I'm finished with this foolish person, you can take him off somewhere where he can hurt himself yet again—and I can resume treating others!"

"I just came here to check on the wounded. I never asked . . ." Chack began.

"Be silent!" Selass ordered. "If you speak again . . . I will sew your arms together behind your back!"

Chack said nothing more until Selass clipped the thread and daubed the wound with the purplish polta paste that would prevent infection. Even then, he didn't speak while he snatched his bloody armor from a hook and gathered his weapons. Only once he, Blas, and Blair were outside the tent and among his and Blair's waiting staffs—and the horses!—did he mutter, "I have always been respectful to that . . . spiky female. I can't imagine why she hates me so." Blas turned her head to hide the blinking she couldn't stop, but her tail twitched erratically. "What?" Chack demanded angrily.

"Nothing, Major," Blas replied, hiding her eyes under the rim of her helmet. "I'm just a lowly Marine. Selass-Fris-Ar is almost royalty, as our Imperial allies reckon such things. Her father is the great Keje-Fris-Ar, High Chief of *Salissa* Home, and ahd-mi-raal of First Fleet! Who am I to grasp the thoughts of one such as she?"

Chack growled with frustration, but went to his horse and patted the animal affectionately. He turned to Blair. "Come, it is time to finish this. The enemy here cannot escape and can no longer harm us." He remembered the sincere, confused sentiments of an Imperial lieutenant he'd last seen lying facedown in the bloody mud at the bottom of a Dom trench. "Perhaps we *are* doing murder now," he murmured, swinging stiffly into the saddle. Then his voice grew louder. "We must at least offer them surrender."

"*Pity* for the enemy?" Blair asked strangely as he and the others mounted as well. "This from the hero of the Dueling Grounds who was physically *dragged* from the fighting?"

Chack sighed. "Of course I pity them. Hard as it may be to remember at times, the Doms *are* people. They're not born evil. They *do* evil because they're taught to, forced to, *bred* to. . . ." Suddenly, Chack felt heat at the back of his neck, coursing into his head—along with a staggering revelation. "*Bred* to evil," he said again, a picture of Lawrence, cheerfully—and relentlessly—guarding Princess Rebecca from any possible harm springing to his mind. Lawrence wasn't Grik . . . but he was as much *like* them as Imperials were to Doms—or the remnants of the New Britain Company. Lawrence was no more different from the Grik than the evil Rasik-Alcas had been from Lord Rolak, his beloved Safir, or all the *good* People he knew. "Maker above," he whispered, "let us hurry and see if the enemy will *let* us save them."

"Very well," agreed Blair. "We must deal with them at any rate, and the less ammunition we expend, the better. The bulk of the enemy still infests New Dublin, across the Sperrin range. We must quickly prepare to threaten them there if the rest of the plan is to succeed—and every mortar bomb, roundshot, and musket ball we fire, not to mention the food to sustain us, must be brought over the Wiklow range from Cork, or all the way down the Waterford road from Bray."

The group started down the central avenue of the mostly undamaged town, moving through groups of people whose reactions to seeing them ranged from exuberant joy to resentful silence, depending on whom they'd supported. The latter were few, at least they appeared to be, and there were cheers when they reached the city center, already guarded by Marines, and Chack ordered the Company flag, the virtual banner of New Ireland, cut down from the pole in front of the Director's mansion. After that, he and the rest of his entourage rode purposefully on, toward the sound of the guns.

CHAPTER 15

///// *USS* **Maaka-Kakja**
Southwest of New Wales

aptain Lelaa-Tal-Cleraan angrily slapped the message form against her left hand, and Sandra Tucker looked at her with concern. She and Princess Rebecca, as well as several other *Maaka-Kakja* officers, had gathered on the bridge, forward of the comm shack to catch the latest news.

"What is it?"

"I don't know. . . . The issue on New Ireland grows more confusing by the hour!" She jerked her head to the side. "What seemed well in hand and going according to plan has apparently spun into the 'pot,' I fear."

"What's up?" asked Irvin Laumer.

"Yes, please tell us!" pleaded the princess.

"Yess! Goddamn!" echoed Petey—more crassly—peering around Rebecca's head from his perch on her back. Nobody paid his outbursts any attention anymore.

Lelaa glanced at the anxious group, all of whom she cared a great deal about.

"Majors Chack and Blair have reached their mountain pass objective and hold a good position on the ridge south of New Dublin. Sor-Lomaak and *Salaama-Na*, flagship of the bombardment element, heaps satisfactory abuse on the harbor defenses. . . . That much remains according to projections. But those defenses have not weakened in response to Chack's presence in their rear—and Dominion forces continue to sprout in . . . unexpected places. Apparently, there were far more troops at Belfast and Easky than ever expected, and they've counterattacked. The beachhead at Bray has been overrun, and the one at Cork is sorely pressed. An army—presumably the same that recaptured Bray, now marches south toward Waterford and threatens Chack's rear!" She sighed. "And now *Salaama-Na* begins to run short of ammunition—far in advance of the more intense covering bombardment that was planned."

"One would almost suspect that the enemy is as well versed on Major Chack's plan as we are," Brassey observed quietly.

"Indeed," agreed Lelaa.

"Somebody in the Imperial command must've squealed," Irvin snarled. "That's the only answer. They had to know what our guys meant to do before they even did it. How else would they know to place troops just so, and keep them quiet until the right—worst—time?"

"And where are they all coming from?" Sandra demanded. "The troops that took refuge there after the battle for New Scotland might account for the numbers Chack reported facing, but not many more than that. . . . There *had* to be more already there, or they're still coming from somewhere else nearby!"

"But where?" Lelaa murmured. She stepped to the chart table and peered down at it. Most Lemurians still called the charts "scrolls" even though those used by the Navy had none of the religious, cultural, or historic passages recorded by the prophet, Siska-Ta. It didn't matter. The term was almost interchangeable in the Lemurian-English patois that had begun to evolve—and Siska-Ta had never drawn scrolls of this region, anyway. Lelaa gauged the distance to New Ireland. They were just close enough to launch an air attack on New Dublin, but the planes would never make it back. They *could* set down at New Glasgow on New

Scotland, however, and if "Oil Can" prepositioned fuel there as they were supposed to . . .

"Pass the word for Lieutenant Reddy and Colonel Shinya," Lelaa said. "Reddy is COFO, for all practical purposes, though he's only once now flown a 'Naancy.' He's formed and organized the wing even better than I expected. No doubt . . . different from the way Colonel Mallory or Captain Tikker would have it, but the inexperienced chaos is at an end. I'll see what he has to say. As for Colonel Shinya . . . it seems we will need to land his troops. I would like his views on that."

Shinya and Orrin Reddy joined the group—with Dennis Silva and "Larry the Lizard." Lawrence apparently suspected something was up, because he came dressed in his Sa'aaran battle kit, to everyone's surprise. Oddly, Orrin and Silva had grown close over the weeks. That probably had to do with Orrin's youth and exuberance as much as anything. He was built much like his cousin, and though he'd begun to "put some meat back on his bones" after his ordeal, he'd never be a physical match for Silva. But his and Silva's personalities complemented each other, and Silva's fondness for his captain seemed to have extended to the man's younger cousin to a degree. "Maniacal giant meets fearless fighter jock," Sandra had commented.

Lelaa greeted them all but first turned to Orrin. "Lieutenant," she said, "please determine whether there actually *is* fuel, as well as sufficient facilities at New Glasgow to service our aircraft. If so, I have two missions for the Fourth Naval Air Wing. We'll immediately send the Ninth and Eleventh Bomb Squadrons to attack Dominion positions on New Ireland. They'll rearm and refuel for subsequent sorties at New Glasgow."

"What about the Twelfth?" Orrin asked.

"It remains here in reserve, as will the Tenth Pursuit. I want the Seventh Pursuit to scout the sea between New Wales and New Ireland"—she peered closer at the chart—"this Saint George's Channel, and determine if any enemy forces linger beyond our fleets. The Seventh will then proceed north of New Ireland, overfly the defenses at New Dublin, and determine the disposition of the enemy before also proceeding to New Glasgow. The pursuit ships will carry no bombs, so range should not be an issue."

"What targets for the bombers?"

Lelaa pointed. "The Ninth will overfly Belfast and Bray before turn-

ing southeast toward Waaterford. Its objective is to destroy enemy concentrations along that route, but to focus efforts closer to Waaterford if
necessary." She huffed in exasperation. "We just don't know what's *there*!
There is no direct communication with the interior! Regardless, the
Ninth should have the fuel to backtrack and hit any major concentrations they spot along the way if Waaterford remains secure."

"And the Eleventh?"

"The Eleventh will provide air support at Cork. They should be able
to coordinate with the naval forces offshore, either by wireless or signal
flags."

"Okay," Orrin said. "Sounds straightforward enough." He chuckled.
"Way simpler than some of the wild-goose chases FEAF sent us on in the
Philippines! Which squadron do *I* take?"

"None."

"Now wait a sec . . . !"

"Lieutenant Reddy," Lelaa began severely, "like it or not, you're something of an important person, through no fault or act of your own. You're
kin to our supreme military commander. Besides that, you're acting
COFO of the Fourth Naval Air Wing, not just another pursuit pilot! In
those roles, some responsibility is inherent. You must instruct our fliers
what to do, depending on what they find at their objectives. To retain a
'big picture' view, you must remain in wireless contact—with a scroll
before you—not romping off on your own, an individual combat pilot!"
Lelaa paused, deciding to toss the suddenly crestfallen young man a
bone. "Besides, if needed, you'll lead the reserve flights."

"Yes, ma'am, uh, Captain Lelaa," he replied.

"What do you need of me?" Shinya asked. He'd been studying the
chart with one ear tuned to the conversation around him.

"Your force may be needed to retrieve this situation. Where should
you land where you can best support Major Chack, while contributing to
the completion of the overall mission of liberating New Ireland?"

"What a load of crap," Orrin said as he, Silva, and Lawrence trotted
down the companionway from the comm shack where he'd just determined that New Glasgow at least *thought* it had everything they needed.

He gestured at a "Nancy" perched on its launch truck. "Flying those things is a cinch . . . and what's this crud about being 'important'?"

"Maybe it *is* a cinch; I wouldn't know. Scared ta death o' flyin' myself. But why do you want to? To fight, or just zoot around? Can't have gen'rals leadin' cavalry charges," Silva clucked. "An' you *have* wormed your way to the top of the flyboy heap." He stopped and shook his head. "That Cap'n Lelaa's got brains. She knows what she's doin'. You do as she says; go brief your 'Nancy' boys—an' don't treat it like a chore." Siva's scarred face turned uncharacteristically serious. "I know you're still new here, but these little guys, these 'Cats, are good people, an' they're in this fight in a big way." He shrugged. "You had a rough war. We all did. An' maybe this ain't *your* war yet, the way it is for me an' hisself, your cousin." He held out his big hands. "I ain't gonna wave no bloody shirt er nothin, an' I know how tough it is to go from hatin' Japs to gettin' along with Colonel Shinya." He snorted. "An' maybe I still have trouble now an' then thinkin' of him as a *good* guy—but I trust him, an' if you'll take anything from me, take this: he is a '*right*' guy."

He waved his hands. "'Nuff o' that. As you know, there's still plenty o' bad Japs, but your pilots—an' they *are* yours, like it or not—know you zapped a couple of 'em that were flyin' shit as far beyond a 'Nancy' as *Amagi* was beyond my ol' *Walker*. That's big joss to them. Hell, it's a big deal to *me* after seein' you Army guys get whupped on by them Zee-ros over Cavite. The point is, the little guys look up to you, an' they're fixin' to fly off an' risk their stripey asses on your word, with the stuff you told 'em rattlin' around in their furry little heads. So, if you're with 'em or not, you're their leader, an' just like them, you gotta follow orders." He grinned. "That's one of the problems with bein' a officer. Extra pressure to do the 'right thing'!"

Silva studied the contemplative, introspective expression on Orrin's face, then burped. "Besides, it's my experience that the best laid plans o' 'Cats an' men still foul their screws all to hell, 'specially on this goofy world. I bet you'll be flyin' before this is done."

Sperrin Mountains
New Ireland

Major Chack-Sab-At worked his way down the shallow black rock trench on a secondary ridge overlooking the sprawling city of New Dublin.

From what he saw, the city was about as big as Scapa Flow and the architecture was similarly alien to him: squat, blocky buildings with tile roofs and little color. Nearly everything was white and nothing stood on piers, as he was accustomed to seeing in Baalkpan. There were really big buildings along the harbor front, warehouses probably, and the Company headquarters in the center of the city looked like the Government House mansion of Gerald McDonald with its multiple stories and classical columns. Beyond, lay the harbor with its forest of masts and formidable defenses. Out at sea, *Salaama-Na* still held station, dwarfing countless Imperial warships and transports, fuzzy with the haze of the day and the occasional drifting cloud of gun smoke.

Chack's was a lousy position with a very exposed avenue of support and retreat, leading upslope to the grassy, craggy peaks behind. He'd chosen it because it *was* such a crummy spot, hoping to lure the Doms into coming up after him. An impressive force, perhaps three or four thousand men, had assembled on the flanks of the mountains below, but didn't seem inclined to do anything other than lob the occasional roundshot or volley of musketry. Suspecting that meant they were aware how close the force out of Bray was getting to Waterford, he realized he'd soon have to retire or risk being cut off and surrounded. No question about it, he wasn't facing Grik. This enemy was perfectly able to make detailed plans of their own—particularly when, as it seemed, they had advance knowledge of the one Chack and Blair had devised.

So, Plan A was in the crapper, obviously, but that didn't bother Chack too much. Something *always* went wrong, and he was preparing—he hoped—to do what the enemy least expected under the circumstances. As usual, his Plan B was risky; actually *more* so than usual, but that just made it even more unexpected . . . didn't it? The only real problem, besides the added danger, was that he had no direct communications with anybody other than a lengthy semaphore chain back to Waterford, over the Wiklow Mountains to Cork, and from there to the fleet offshore. Hopefully, Plan B had been transmitted to Sor-Lomaak by now, because he needed it to kick-start certain elements of Plan A all over again if he was going to have any support. If it hadn't, his only other option was to make such a ruckus that Sor-Lomaak would recognize the signal—and the opportunity—when it came.

A heavy roundshot struck the slope below the trench, showering the inhabitants with sharp, gravelly pumice and fine black dust. He spat dark mucus that had accumulated after hours of similar treatment. "Stay cool, Marines!" he cried. "They might hit us with shot rolling back down from above, but we'll just throw it back at them!" Tired cheers answered. *It's easy to stay cool,* he thought. *It's actually* cold *up here near the top of the range. And the troops have a right to be weary,* he reflected. They'd faced tough, unexpected opposition taking the heights. There shouldn't have been any Doms in the mountains at all, but that was what they'd encountered. No militia, no rebel troops, but Dom regulars! *Professionals,* he admitted grudgingly. That was when he first suspected a trap. It was reasonable to assume they'd gotten word of the Battle at Waterford back over the mountains, and some response was understandable, but they shouldn't have had the sheer numbers they'd responded with, both here and elsewhere. There could be only one explanation: there'd been more Doms on New Ireland than they ever knew; they'd been there longer than anyone considered possible, and the Imperial invasion had been expected.

Further treachery was the answer, but by whom? He blinked dismissively. It didn't matter at the moment. He'd been victim of treachery many times now, and humans held no monopoly on the practice. He looked forward to helping sort it out later—if he lived.

"Lieutenant Blas," he said, nearing her position in the trench.

"Major."

Chack looked at the sky. The sun was still visible over the mountains that trailed into the northwest. "Where is that Sky Priest, the lieutenant from *Mertz*?"

"Dead, Major, back at the town."

Chack sighed. "Are there any of Sister Audry's converts in the ranks?"

Blas blinked confusion. "Not that I know of. Strange buggers, them. Always either at you about your soul . . . or they don't make a peep." She considered. "Seen some Marines doing that funny thing with their hands. . . ."

"No matter. Where is Major Jindal?"

Blas motioned a little farther down the trenchline to their left. "That way, sir. Came by here just a few minutes ago."

"Thanks," Chack said, and moved on. Blas shrugged and followed him. She still considered it her job to watch over him—just as he'd once taken such good care of her.

"Major Jindal," Chack said, finally catching the Imperial, "any questions?"

Jindal paused uncertainly. "None, sir," he finally answered.

"Good. I . . . know it will be dangerous and the risk is high, but I see no alternative."

"Nor do I, except failure," Jindal agreed.

"We will not fail," Chack said, blinking certainty, "but given our situation, it's customary among many of my people, Lemurians—MiAnaaka—to perform a . . . prayer ritual, and to some, Aryaalans and B'mbaadans most notably, it's important that the sun be visible at that time." He looked at Jindal. "Your people use prayer as well, do they not?"

"We do, but our chaplain is upslope with Major Blair."

"Our priest is dead," Chack said, "so I will lead our prayer. It's a communal thing—I have never led before, but it's brief and I know it well. I just wanted to make sure you had no objection before I begin."

"Ah . . . no, I suppose not, as long as it's not terribly . . . unusual or . . . frightening."

Chack laughed. "It will not *scare* your men, I assure you, Major. I doubt those still with us are capable of fear."

Jindal chuckled. "I hate to disillusion you, Major, but I remain terrified!"

Chack grinned back and patted the man on the shoulder. He was near the center of the line and decided this was as good a place as any. He stood atop the gravelly heap thrown up in front of the trench within full view of all the troops lining the lower ridge, not to mention the enemy below. He faced the sun and spread his arms wide.

"Maker of all things!" he roared in that special tone peculiar to his people that let their voices carry a great distance. A few musket balls began kicking up small dark clouds around him, but they were well beyond the effective range of small arms. Even if one struck him, it would hurt a lot, but probably wouldn't do him serious harm. Roundshot was another matter, but it would take the enemy time to aim their pieces, and still the chance of a deliberate hit was remote.

Jindal was surprised to see a large number—most—of the Lemurians stand to join him, facing the west.

"I beg your protection," Chack continued, "for myself and my people . . . and these brave humans who fight beside us. But if it is our time, please light our spirit's paths to their Homes in the Heavens!"

That was it. Crossing his arms over his chest, Chack knelt in the gravel, bowing his head, and all the Lemurians who'd joined him did the same. Finished, they then slid back into the trench.

"That's all?" Jindal asked.

Chack nodded. "Yep. Would you like to lead your own men in prayer?" He huffed. "It might stir the enemy into an even greater frenzy, given their antagonism toward any faith but theirs, but their marksmanship is quite poor."

"Nooo," Jindal said reflectively. "I think your service was surprisingly appropriate for everyone. Some may wish to add words of their own, but that's customarily done in private, regardless."

Far behind them, beyond the pass they'd used to cross the mountains, artillery boomed and stuttered with a trembling thunder.

"Well," Chack said, "if Waaterford had fallen, we would have heard. Evidently, the enemy probes the pass with a flanking move. I think that's our signal to 'react' to him! Your bugles will carry better in this wind, and the enemy between us and the city will better recognize them anyway. Please pass the word to sound 'retreat'!"

The battered regiments on the ridge began to withdraw, back up the steep incline. Happy cheering rose from the plain below, as did round-shot and volleys of musket fire. Balls pattered around the men and 'Cats, and there were screams when a cannonball gouged through a group of Imperial Marines and bounded upslope.

"Keep movin', by Jasus!" bellowed a sergeant, "but by His holy name, I'll eat yer livers if I ever see ye run like this wi'out orders!"

"Halt beyond the crest!" came another shout. "Remember your orders! Re-form behind Major Blair's division!"

The sun was dropping quickly now; soon it would vanish beyond the mountains and darkness would descend. Chack hoped the sight of their enemy fleeing and the ensuing night would leave the Doms unprepared for what happened next. He himself was taken completely by surprise by what *did* happen then. He'd paused for a moment, trying to see the enemy in the gathering gloom, to gauge his reaction, when he caught a glimpse of a fleeting shape, then another, swoop past his field of view. Enough sunlight peeked between two distant crags for him to see a distinctive, light blue object pull up beyond the plain and silhouette itself against the still-bright sea. It was a "Nancy"! And then there was another, and another! Roiling pillars of fire erupted from the Dom position, and the cheers of a moment before turned to hideous screams that echoed against the mountains despite the wind and staccato detonations.

"Halt!" he roared. "Stop the retreat! Now is the time! *Now!* Jindal, where are you? Bugler!" He caught hold of a man still clawing his way upslope as if the noise from below were something directed at them. "Bugler! Sound 'recall and reform'!" Chack didn't know if there was a call for that, but recall should be sufficient. "Mortars!" he screamed upslope, hoping someone heard him. "Blair! Mortars, *now!*"

The retreating Marines, confused by the chaos and suddenly conflicting orders, began to pause. Many shouted at comrades still trying to do what they'd been told before. The night attack by the entire force had been carefully detailed and prepared, but now that was "in the crapper" too. There could be no delay; the time was at hand. Drums thundered on the summit above. Either Blair had heard Chack's cries, or he'd figured it out for himself—probably the latter. Flashes lit the uneven peak, and more than a hundred mortar bombs lofted into the sky, aimed for the carefully ranged enemy position. Airplane engines still rattled by below, followed by more mushrooms of flame, and Chack hoped they wouldn't hit any planes. Most of his Marines had stopped now, quickly re-forming to either side of him in the gathering twilight, lit by the inferno below. *Gasbombs,* he thought, and shuddered. He'd always hated fire weapons, and though nobody had a problem using them against Grik he knew there'd been talk of *not* deploying them against the Doms. *Well, talk is easy when all goes as planned.* Fortunately, the enemy hadn't known about, or had discounted the arrival of *Maaka-Kakja* and her Naval Air Wing.

"Chack!" came Blair's voice behind him, just as Blas appeared at his side. He turned to see his Imperial friend trotting toward him, his whole force advancing down the mountain to join Chack's and Jindal's troops. Mortars still thumped from the crest above, showering the plain below.

"Major Blair," Chack greeted him.

"I suppose if we must forever be reacting to things, it's better that they be advantageous distractions caused by *our* people for a change!" Blair laughed.

"I agree entirely," Chack said.

"See here, Chack," Blair continued, "your fellows have been hanging out here in the breeze all day. Won't you let my boys spearhead this advance?"

"By all means, Major Blair. Mine may still be somewhat confused at any rate. We'll advance as your reserve, but let us move quickly! We must hit the enemy on the tail of this surprise hard enough to break them; then they'll *have* to move more troops to stop us. That will give Sor-Lomaak his chance! Pray only he takes it!"

"He can't have missed the signal! Such a show!" Blair stopped and looked at the sky. A "Nancy" was burning, plummeting toward the sea. "Terrible!" he said.

Chack looked into the gray-gold sky in time to see another plane, its right wing shredded, spiraling down. A bizarre shape detached itself from the falling "Nancy" and darted off into the darkness. "Something is destroying our planes!" he said in alarm.

"What can it be?"

"I don't know, but those poor pilots have done their duty. We must do ours. Advance!"

USS Maaka-Kakja

"Something's taking out our planes!" Orrin Reddy said, entering the bridge from the flight comm shack that overlooked the flight deck. *Maaka Kakja* was the first carrier to have the separate compartment, as well as the first to have an alternate frequency capability. First Fleet would have it as soon as the new equipment was delivered or the more talented "signalmen" made the simple modifications to the equipment already deployed. Orrin had been listening on the new, dedicated "air" band.

"What is it?" Lelaa asked, blinking concern, looking up from a just-delivered fleet report.

"That's just it! They don't know! Some kind of flying things, like giant lizard birds, are jumping them out of the dark, and tearing hell out of the planes. Nobody ever said there were giant lizard birds on New Ireland! And why would they go after *our* guys? They can't even fight back!"

In the midst of his alarming report, Lelaa noted Orrin had used the term "our" a couple of times, for the *first* time, since he began performing the duties she'd set him aboard. She shook her head.

"How many have we lost?"

"I don't know. I've been trying to get them to make individual reports, but four for sure. Some may have lost their aerials, but others are damaged and don't think they can make Glasgow. I told them to try for the fleet, either north or south. If they're over the island, I told them to make for that big lake by Waterford—if they can find it in the dark! Damn communications! If we could get through to anybody, we could get the guys in the town to light some fires!"

"I cannot contact anyone in the town, but there are plenty of fires in Waaterford, Mr. Reddy. The enemy has begun his assault there, and I'm informed by the Imperial Navy off the coast that the remaining troops at Cork have moved to reinforce." She turned. "Pass the word for the signalmen to ask any Imperial commander they can contact what those 'lizard birds' are and what to do about them. If anyone expected them and didn't tell us, I want him *arrested*!"

"But . . . that'll leave the guys from Cork cut off with everybody else!"

"It may, for a time. Until we get there. You may have noticed we've increased speed." Her tail swished agitatedly. "That creature, that *mouse*, Gilbert Yaa-ger, *ordered me* to come to the engineering spaces and see the murder *I* was doing to *his* engines!" She sniffed.

Orrin stopped. "But . . . will we make it? I mean . . ."

"Of course. Even Yaa-ger allowed as much, reluctantly. We have never truly done a full-speed trial, and it's past due. He's merely protective of the youngling engines."

"Well . . . but we've got to *do* something!" Orrin insisted.

"What more *can* we do?" Lelaa demanded. "We can't send another air attack, it's long past dark. We will put Colonel Shinya's army ashore at dawn, and it will march to the relief of Waaterford. Major Chack has broken into the outskirts of New Dublin, and the Dominion troops that stopped him there were unable to prevent the landing of almost five thousand Imperial Marines in the harbor! One of the forts has been taken already." Lelaa paused thoughtfully. "Apparently the Dominion cannot use their 'giant lizard birds' against ground troops. I suspect the creatures don't distinguish friend from foe, individually."

"But what about Waterford?"

"The troops there, even with the reinforcements from Cork are in trouble," Lelaa admitted. "They amount to only a few hundreds and as your 'recon' flights suggested, they face several thousands. Apparently, there were *many* more enemy soldiers in Bel-faast than we expected."

Orrin was looking at the chart. "Almost as if they stuck them way out there knowing we'd ignore it."

"As I now suspect."

"My guys bombed the column, but it was still strung out, and it didn't do much good—no lizard birds got after *that* flight either. . . ."

"What are you thinking?"

"Captain Lelaa!" interrupted the signalman. "We get dope on 'lizard birds'!"

"What's the story?" Orrin asked.

"They not from here! They like 'draa-gons' Im-peer-aals hunt as food-sport critters, but these big draa-gons only ever seen in Dom country! They baad—attaack ships sometimes, but nobody ever know they do for Doms! They prob'ly here to pester ships, laand-een boats, up north!"

"Has Sor-Lomaak reported any such incidents?"

"Mebbee so," the signalman said uncertainly. "They go in with dark and gun smoke. Some few reports say see boat Maa-reens shoot at sky. Mebbe same monsters get planes, then jump on boats—nobody see good."

"They've been keeping the damn things at New Dublin!" Irvin Laumer said, hearing the last as he came onto the bridge.

Lelaa looked back at Orrin. "You were saying?"

"Okay, I *do* have an idea. First, I get every plane not already committed for New Scotland to make for the lake at Waterford. I take the Tenth Pursuit straight to Waterford now, no bombs, just gas—and weapons for the spotters! We refuel the planes that make it there and rearm them with mortar bombs—they're the same thing, anyway. That'll give us air over Waterford, and you can still support the landing with the bombers left aboard here, plus any that refuel and rearm at Glasgow!"

"Flying at night is too risky, especially now with those 'draa-gons' out there!"

"Captain, I probably have more night flying time than anybody on this world, next to Lieutenant Mackey. I can get there, and the rest of the squadron can follow me in."

Lelaa hesitated. "Are you sure?"

"Sure I'm sure. And besides"—he tossed his last ace on the table—"with the planes there, we'll have communications!"

"Very well, then. How will you defend against the monsters?"

"How many modern weapons are aboard?"

"We brought everything we had with us to get the submarine," Laumer said. "Two tommy guns, a few Springfields and Krags, and a couple of 1911s."

"That's it?"

"Afraid so. There were some Jap rifles and pistols left on *Mizuki Maru*, but Okada kept them."

"It'll have to do. Muskets with buckshot are probably just as good. The pursuit squadron will fly top cover for the bombers and try to keep the lizard birds off them. They won't need the best spotters, just the best marksmen."

"I can outshoot anyone here with a pistol," Sandra said suddenly from the opening to the bridgewing. Her new "orderly," Diania, stood beside her, the expression on her face betraying the contrast between knowing she probably shouldn't be there, and daring anyone to send her away. No one had noticed them till now, but they'd clearly caught most of the conversation.

"I'm sure of it," Captain Lelaa agreed, "but this time *I* command, and you cannot go. Besides some rather obvious reasons, we will likely need your medical skills quite badly very soon."

Silva suddenly popped his head around the corner, just above Sandra's. Diania instinctively recoiled. "Well *I* damn sure ain't goin'!" Dennis boomed. "Flyin' in the dark? With wingy Grik birds chasin' us? My beloved ass!"

CHAPTER 16

////// *USS* **Walker**

I t was still dark when *Walker* steamed into "Saint Francis" Bay in the wee hours of January 4, 1944, and they met nothing but a few brightly lit, anchored ships, probably waiting for the morning tide. They were not challenged by so much as a picket boat, and neither guns nor whistles brought them a pilot. Even when they crept through the shockingly narrow "Golden Gate"—with leadsmen on the fo'c'sle—beneath the guns of the twin forts situated on what should be "Fort Point" and "Lime Point," there was no challenge to their passage.

"They ain't got a clue," the Bosun snorted from the port bridgewing.

"He's right," Jenks declared disgustedly. "Low fruit, ripe for the picking. Obviously, the dispatch vessel we sent never arrived, but there's no excuse for this degree of complacency, ever. Had we been the Doms, the war would be over before those here even awakened."

"Well, you're the only one who's been here before," Matt said, lowering his binoculars. "You're our pilot. Where now?"

"The governor's residence is some distance south, beyond the North Point, in the West Bay portion of the city, but I believe our first stop should be Colonial Naval Headquarters just a few miles ahead, to starboard." Jenks fumed. "From the look of things, that will likely become *our* headquarters after I relieve the incompetent fool in charge there."

"It is disconcerting," said Bradford, "and rather ... achingly ... peaceful." He glassed the bay in all directions and saw sleepy, predawn lights everywhere. "Even now I can tell this may be the largest city we've seen; yet it slumbers so blissfully unaware."

"It's almost as big as New London and Plymouth together, on New Britain Island," Jenks said, "though not as densely populated. Less congested too. More space to expand. There, Captain Reddy"—Jenks pointed—"you can just make out that empty stretch of dock with the large buildings beyond. That's where the dispatch sloop would be had she arrived. We'll tie up there ourselves; there's no time to lose! Feel free to make all the noise you want. The guns of the fort will no longer bear, so we needn't worry about some fool waking up and touching one off in a panic. Perhaps we might at least awaken someone for your crew to throw their lines to!"

Matt turned to the bridge watch. "Take her in, Mr. Kutas," he said. "We'll sound general quarters and honk the horn, if you please." He chuckled. "Is there a specific window we should shine the spotlight in?"

The noisy tumult at the dock did arouse a reception. A few Imperial Marines were the first to arrive, milling about with their muskets, unsure what to do with them. An agitated naval officer finally appeared along with a trickle of sailors, but once they saw the utterly unfamiliar old destroyer, all they could manage was to stand and stare. Jenks held a speaking trumpet to his lips, and after identifying himself, demanded that those on the dock assist in securing the vessel. A few bold men scrambled forward and took the lines thrown to them—but then had trouble securing the lines after they saw the creatures that threw them.

"You there!" Jenks addressed the officer. "What's your name?"

"Uh ... Lieutenant ... uh, Daniels, sir, if you please."

"Lieutenant Daniels, who commands here?"

"The harbormaster, sir? The fort?"

"No. Who is high admiral here?"

"A . . . Admiral Rempel, sir."

"I must see him immediately. The very Empire is at stake!"

"Well, but . . . you see, he's asleep."

"Then wake him yourself this instant!" Jenks roared. "I'm here on behalf of the Governor-Emperor himself, and I'm the direct representative of his authority! Sound the alarm and have all officers gather in the Naval Headquarters conference room. If Admiral Rempel considers a few more hours' sleep more important than the safety of this city and the people here, he can take longer than the twenty minutes I give him to arrive." Jenks glanced at the large watch he pulled from a vest pocket by a chain. "Twenty-one minutes from now, he will be replaced."

Admiral Rempel, a short, obese man with the almost-universal mustache and a set of curly muttonchops, bustled into the noisy chamber with three minutes to spare. His face was red and his expression dour—until he saw the several Lemurians who'd accompanied Matt, Jenks, Spanky, the Bosun, and Courtney Bradford. The 'Cats were all members of the Captain's Guard and had come armed. No one wanted to take any chances the unpreparedness they'd witnessed was due to Dom or Company influence.

"What the devil is the meaning of this?" Rempel demanded when his surprise subsided and he regained his voice. "And what are those . . . creatures doing here?"

"Your attention, please," Jenks commanded, ignoring the admiral. "The Empire and the Dominion are at war, and have been ever since they recently perpetrated a dastardly, sneak attack against the Home Islands!" The room erupted with shouted questions, oaths, and excited conversation.

"Silence!" the Bosun bellowed. "Jenks ain't done yet!"

Harvey glanced at Gray and nodded ironic appreciation. "That's right," he said, "there's more." He took a breath. "At this moment, a most formidable force approaches here. It was to arrive tomorrow, but we . . . may have disrupted their schedule. Regardless, it's coming, with ships, infantry, and even trained dragons to attack from the sky!"

"Impossible!" someone muttered, but Jenks forged on.

"Not impossible. Fact. As of now, we don't know where they are or how their plans may have changed, but we have little time to prepare for whatever they mean to do."

"My God," muttered Rempel. "What will we *do*?"

"What do you have?" Matt asked.

"My apologies, gentlemen," Jenks said. "This is Captain Matthew Reddy. His is the lovely, fast ship tied to the dispatch dock. He and his crew, largely composed of the . . . unusual folk you see—'Lemurians'— are our allies in this war, and you may thank God for it. We haven't the time at present for me to detail all the ways they've already helped us. Suffice it to say they *will* be treated with courtesy, and Captain Reddy's word carries the same weight as mine; the same as that of the Governor-Emperor himself." He faced Rempel. "What *do* you have?"

"Why . . . there are two hundred Marines in garrison here, and half a dozen river steamers; gunboats you could say, but they're more suited to responding to the depredations of the local denizens than fighting battles. Other than that, there are a number of armed Company ships in port, and a few Imperial warships undergoing repairs."

"Immediately after this meeting, the Marines will take possession of those Company ships," Jenks said darkly, "and I need a full report on the disposition of the Navy vessels and crews. What of the militia? Every able-bodied man in the city is a member, if I recall."

Rempel glanced about. "True . . . but only the Governor may call up the militia and . . . he's not in the city. He's on a sport shooting expedition in the mast-tree forest."

"Sport shooting . . . after the creatures near here? Is he insane?"

Rempel fidgeted. "The greater beasts grow fewer near the city, but small game abounds."

"Regardless, the militia will be called in the name of the Governor-Emperor. See that the alarm is passed for a full mobilization! How many troops will that give us?"

Rempel's face had turned darker. "Some five thousand or so, if they all report. You must bear in mind that the militia is not a *professional* force by any means. Their personal courage and individual fighting skills are . . . sufficient, certainly, but they're not given to a high degree of discipline. An example is that some, more than a hundred, have already left against specific orders to scout some dubious reports by a brigade of trappers that arrived yesterday from the south. They brought wild tales of Dom troops coming ashore. . . ." His eyes widened. "I had no reason to credit the tale and considered it ridiculous, of course. . . ." He paused. "You don't suppose . . . ? Oh damn me, I had harsh words with the militia captain who wanted to investigate. I . . . ordered him not to go—the expense of an expedition!—but he went anyway, under threat of charges to strip his rank. . . ."

"Pray I don't do the same to you, Admiral Rempel," Jenks said. "Where did these reports put the incursion?"

Rempel stepped hesitantly to a map of the coastline on the inner wall of the chamber. "Here," he said, pointing at a bay about fifty miles south of where they stood.

Matt vaguely recognized it as Monterey. "How large a force did they report?" he demanded.

"Um, a dozen ships, perhaps a thousand troops—now see here, these trappers are notorious liars! Information is as much a commodity to them as the hides and ivory they bring to sell!"

"Are they in the habit of selling false information? What would that gain them?" Matt asked. Rempel didn't respond, and Matt studied the coastline during the uproar that ensued. "These can't be from the same force we tangled with," he said loudly, regaining everyone's attention. "It might arrive at any time, but allowing for the travel time of those trappers, it couldn't have gotten there *days* ago. This must be a separate force sent to establish a beachhead, maybe a base of operations. They might put the rest of their troops ashore there for a flanking attack while their Navy tries to force the forts guarding the bay. Maybe that's where they mean to base their damn lizard birds. We have to be sure about the range of those things; it might be crucial!"

"I say," said Bradford, "there wouldn't be any naturalists in the room at all?" A few hands tentatively rose. "Natural scientists" were fairly common in the Imperial Navy. "Splendid! Let's put our heads together and see if we can answer Captain Reddy's crucial question!" He looked at Matt. "Will these gentlemen miss anything important if they leave with me now?"

"Not unless they command troops or ships. Otherwise, what you come up with is of extreme importance."

"Thank you, Captain." He motioned at one of the officers who'd stood. "Please lead the way to a suitable chamber, preferably one where refreshments might be had!" Courtney Bradford followed half a dozen officers from the room.

"You believe the attack will come from two directions, sir?" Rempel asked Matt.

"At least two. They know we've seen them, their main force at least, but they'll probably assume we don't know about the landing at Monterey—that bay down there. I think those trappers have helped a lot because, based on their observations, we know the gist of their strategic plan. As I said, a direct attack on the forts and the bay, combined with an overland attack from the south. They'll even have most of their troop transports with them here so we'll think they plan to land infantry. Maybe they will, but my bet rides on that southern force, for the most part, coming up through the San Jose valley." He blinked at the blank stares, then turned to look at the map. "Oh. Up through here, the Saint Joseph lowland."

"If what ye say is true, sir," said a Marine captain, "an' we deploy in time, I've no doubt we can drub twice our numbers there, even wi' militia! 'Tis really their only avenue o' advance, an' we already ha' barricades there ta guard against maraudin' beasties!"

"What kind of 'beasties'?" Spanky asked darkly, speaking for the first time.

"Oh, we've some beauts, sir! Not so many as before, an' the bigger predators pervide excitin' artillery practice for the militia, so they've learned to keep scarce hereabouts, but we do nae massacre the big vegiticians—like monstrous great bloody coos, an' tasty as well. The barricades simply keep 'em from stompin' the city flat!"

"Okay," Matt said, turning to Jenks. "I recommend you command the land force here. Maybe some of your recent experiences will inspire a few alterations to the local tactics."

Jenks nodded, appreciative that Matt had spoken so delicately, but he was right. These people just didn't *know*!

"Deploy as quickly as possible with all the troops and field artillery you can get your hands on," Matt continued. "I'll send the 'Nancy' up at first light to confirm our suspicions, but for now, proceed as if our suspicions are fact. Take your Marines from the ship, and I'll also give you a few of my guys with modern, long-range weapons. A few Springfields knocking off some enemy brass at the right moment might come in handy." He looked at Gray. "Take the Bosun. *Walker's* already got Carl Bashear, and Gray'll just stomp around yelling at everybody—and you might need that!"

"But Skipper . . ." Gray began.

Matt shook his head. "It's going to get weird out on the water, Boats," Matt said, "but we're used to weird, and I've got the whole crew of *Walker* to 'protect' me. Harvey's never fought with any of these guys before, and he needs somebody he can trust to watch his back . . . and kick ass for him, if need be."

"Aye, aye, sir."

"The forts must remain fully armed," Matt went on. He looked at Rempel. "And vigilant. We'll also need to keep a reserve in the city. Otherwise, every ship and boat with so much as a swivel gun will prepare to defend the harbor mouth or join my ship in repelling the naval assault."

A number of officers in the chamber, including Rempel, had been listening with growing alarm. "Perhaps I don't understand," Rempel said at last, "but who exactly commands here? And how do you plan to face an enemy the size you described with only your—evidently—lightly armed ship, a few Company vessels, a Navy ship or two, and a handful of gunboats?"

Jenks pointed at Matt. "As for overall command, he's it," he said, "and any man who does not follow his orders instantly and to the letter will be *hanged*. Am I perfectly clear?"

There were sullen nods.

"And do not underestimate his ship. It's far more heavily armed than you think. Besides, we do expect reinforcements. A sizable portion of Home Fleet should be just over the horizon. We've had no communication with those elements—by means I'll explain later—but they're due anytime. *Walker*—Captain Reddy's ship—should be able to make quite a dent in the Dom warships if the dragons can be kept at bay. Some plan for that *is* crucial, but all is not as gloomy as it seems."

* * *

With the first light of the rising sun coloring the clouds overhead, Fred Reynolds and Kari-Faask lifted "their" PB-1B off the waters of Saint Francis Bay, to the incredulous amazement of those watching from the now fully alert forts and Naval Headquarters. Early risers in the city were equally astonished, but they didn't have time to ponder what they'd seen before the church bells began to ring. Despite the early hour, there were no services on Tuesdays, and an emergency was confirmed when the alarm horns wound up, beginning near the Southmouth fort and spreading outward from there. The alarm horns were an obligatory call to arms, and fishermen preparing for the morning trawl, shopkeepers, yard workers, bankers, farmers, and even female indentures (conventions were less restrictive on *this* frontier) dropped what they were doing, fetched weapons, and moved purposefully toward their assembly points. Some heard the engine of the "Nancy" and saw the plane circle back toward the mouth of the bay and quickened their step. They didn't know if the flying machine was hostile or not, but clearly something was up, and this alarm was no drill.

Walker shoved off from the dock, flying the Imperial ensign beside her own once again, as well as Imperial signal flags so no one would fire on her. Matt was taking Admiral Rempel to the main fleet shipyard across the bay. His ship was also towing barges full of Marines past the Company ships moored away from the docks. A barge was released near each vessel so the Marines could take it into custody. After that, the ships were to move to the Navy wharves for uparming and recrewing as necessary. Small swift sloops darted in all directions from the "Nav HQ" in search of the gunboats deployed around the bay, and one would go upriver to find the gunboat serving as the Governor's "camp yacht."

Jenks remained at HQ, commanding the Imperial land forces. In addition to the Bosun, Matt left him Sonarman Fairchild to operate the portable comm gear, and gunner's mates "Stumpy" and "Pack Rat." Both 'Cats had '03 Springfields and a full load out of twenty, five-round stripper clips full of smokeless .30-06. Gray had his Thompson. All were members of the Captain's Guard, but until further orders, they'd protect Jenks with their lives. Bradford also remained at HQ, ensconced with his new "naturalist" buddies, racking their brains to come up with some scientific or even anecdotal "dragon" repellant. So far, they hadn't come up with much.

The last barge released to secure a large Company steamer that reminded Matt of *Ulysses*, *Walker* turned for the primary colonial shipyard. Even from a distance of several miles, Matt could tell it was larger than all the yards in New Scotland combined. It made sense. There was plenty of timber here, and endless other resources simply not available in the Isles. Several ships were out of the water, undergoing hull repairs. Others were alongside the docks with men and women working in the tops. A few seemed to be taking on cargo and supplies. Almost a dozen ships, in various stages of construction, stood naked or skeletal on ways from which they'd ultimately slide into the sea. Matt realized then with absolute moral certainty that no matter the cost, this place must not fall. He looked at Rempel, standing behind and to the left of Kutas at the wheel.

"Don't fool with that, Admiral," he said, "if you please."

Rempel snatched his hand away from the engine room telegraph. "A most amazing vessel, Captain Reddy," he said sincerely. He pointed at the telegraph. "If that device does not lie, your ship is only making a third of her potential speed—yet she's already swifter than any ship I've seen."

"It doesn't lie."

Rempel nodded. He hadn't thought so. "How came you to be in the service of the Empire?" he inquired. He gestured about. "Your people and all these other . . . creatures?"

Kutas snorted, and Minnie chirped in shock.

"You misunderstand, Admiral," Matt said tightly. "I wish we'd had time to explain. We don't *serve* the Empire; we *saved* it from the Doms and its own homegrown traitors. Now we're allied for the purpose of destroying your enemies . . . and ours. As for the 'creatures' aboard, you can call 'em 'Cats, Lemurians, Mi-Anaaka, or Americans, but if you call them 'creatures' again, I'll have you thrown to the fish, and I guarantee your Governor-Emperor Gerald McDonald won't even blink when I tell him why."

"Then please accept my most abject apologies," Rempel gushed.

The yardmaster was equally impressed by the old four-stacker, but he was also sensible to the extent of the emergency on a level Matt doubted

Rempel had yet reached. "There're two steam frigates and a sloop of war now ready for sea," he reported. "Another frigate can steam, but her masts were sorely damaged in a recent storm and repairs aren't complete. They shouldn't be stressed."

"If she can steam, she can fight," Matt said. "Make sure all commanders understand they must make all preparations for getting underway immediately. We're sending some Company ships over to you, and we need them officered and crewed as necessary as well. Do whatever you like to them that you and the officers who'll command them think will improve their combat readiness. Oh, and under no circumstances will you leave any Company officers or officials aboard them. Elements of the Company are allied to the Doms, and we don't have time to sort out which ones are or aren't right now."

The yardmaster looked at Rempel, but the man said nothing. "Very well, Captain Reddy. It'll be as you say. Plenty of Imperial officers on the beach here, waiting for a ship."

"Good. Send each ship over to the Naval Headquarters area as it's ready. We'll muster the 'fleet' there."

"Yes, sir. Ah, sir? How long do I have? I mean, when do you need them?"

"We're waiting to find that out now. Did you see the flying machine that took off at dawn?"

"Yes, sir. Astounding!"

"It's our scout. Everything depends on what it finds, but proceed as if you have only hours to complete your task."

"Hours? God help me!" the man blurted.

"Let's hope so," Matt agreed.

"Monterey Bay" was just below, and Reynolds nosed the plane down and banked slightly left for a better view. Columns of smoke rose from the stacks of transport steamers; he counted sixteen. There were no warships. He was tempted to bomb them, but he had only two bombs on board, to save weight and extend his range. Besides, all the troops and supplies had probably been off-loaded. Better to stay high, quiet, and hopefully unobserved.

"Send to *Walker* that the transports are here all right," he shouted through his speaking tube. "A few more than reported, but still no sign of the main fleet. We'll swing out to sea a bit and head south."

"Wil-co!" Kari replied, and Fred grinned. A few minutes later, Kari's voice reached him again. "Mr. Paal-mer say 'Roger,' an' be careful. You hear that? Careful is *order*!"

"Yes, Mother," Fred answered, but despite his flip response, he meant to be *very* careful. Not only had he learned his lesson about being too aggressive on his bomb runs, but there were those damn giant lizard birds to consider. He didn't think they were nearly as fast as he was in level flight; they'd actually had trouble keeping up with *Walker* in a sprint. But he'd seen them dive like bats out of hell. He shaded his eyes and scanned the sky above.

There were plenty of "ordinary" lizard birds, and other flying creatures, but so far nothing bigger than gulls or pelicans. The midmorning sun made it tough to watch inland very closely, but what he saw of the "California" coast gave Fred the creeps. Beyond the bay, dense forests of mighty trees marched right up to the water's edge, teetering on the edge of sheer cliffs. He'd never flown over this coast "back home," but he'd seen it from sea level and it was utterly unfamiliar. The . . . wrongness of it all probably went a long way toward preventing the somewhat shocked disorientation and melancholy he'd experienced when he first saw the "Hawaiian" coast. Of course, he hadn't reached the San Diego area yet— his childhood home. He wouldn't either, not this trip. The PB1-Bs had better range than the prototype, about six hundred miles one way—but he had no intention of making this a one-way trip. He had just enough fuel to (probably) spot the Channel Isles in the distance before he had to turn back. He was surprised by the sudden relief that caused.

"Too bad these Imperials don't have a telegraph system," he muttered to himself. There were Imperial outposts at both "Los Angeles" and "San Diego," although they called them something else. A telegraph line would have given some warning if the Doms were in those places. A line of semaphore towers dotted the coast, but it had been cut at "Monterey." Of course, a telegraph line would've probably been cut as well. There was nothing like a pair of eyeballs on the scene. He was struck again by how people—of every race—chose many of the same ports here that folks had back home. The subject had been often discussed. Bradford or the Skipper (he couldn't remember which) once said, essentially, a good place for a harbor or a city was still a good place, no matter who or where you were. It made sense. He wondered briefly if any towns or settlements existed in any of the really stupid places humans had established them where he came from.

He shrugged and glanced at his gauges. He was flying at about three thousand feet. Fuel was . . . okay, but oil pressure and cylinder temps were nominal. The wind was currently out of the east, and the air was dry, cool, and refreshing. He looked in his mirror at Kari and saw her scanning the sea below with an Imperial telescope. So far they hadn't seen any ships at all, besides the Dom transports, and that was an ominous sign. He'd been told to expect quite a few ships and coastal luggers—if the ships were free to move. Apparently they weren't. That meant somebody was preventing them.

An hour later, they were nearing the extreme limit of their fuel, and sure enough, the overlarge, misshapen forms of the Santa Cruz, Santa Rosa, and San Miguel islands appeared hazy on the southern horizon. They'd *have* to turn back within ten or fifteen minutes if they wanted any return cushion at all, but they decided to push just a little farther. Fred used a lot of rudder, and Kari scanned as far forward as she could bring her glass to bear.

"I see some-ting," she suddenly announced excitedly.

"What?"

"Maybe ships between them two big islands! Yes, ships! Some smok-een, others not." She paused. "That them! It *must* be them!"

Fred still couldn't see, but he took her word for it. He glanced at his fuel gauge and cringed. "Well, we need a better look. Make a report with the position of the sighting, but we've got to get closer to make sure it's the enemy and not just a few Imperial ships snugged up, hiding from them." Soon, however, Fred could make out the distant shapes for himself. There were a *lot* of ships coming through the slot between the islands, and more were appearing west of San Miguel.

"Okay," he said a little nervously. "No luggers, just full-grown ships—and I see a few red sails. That confirms it. Make this report." He glanced at the chalkboard strapped to his right leg, comparing his calculations of flight time, air speed, wind speed, etc., with rough, remembered distances. Except for the looming islands, he'd had no real landmarks. "Ah, we're approximately two hundred and fifty miles, almost due south of Saint Francis. Probable enemy fleet sighted about fifteen miles southeast of our position on an apparent course of three, three, zero degrees!"

A large, dark, winged shape suddenly plummeted past the starboard wingtip, missing it by inches.

"Shit!" Fred screeched, his voice many octaves higher than usual. He looked up and saw many more shapes dropping toward them. "Get that off right now!" he shouted, pushing the stick forward and advancing the throttle to the max. "Then see if you can keep those devils off us!"

The sudden dive had left them less helpless, but the giant lizard birds had tucked themselves into an almost-perfect aerodynamic shape and were still gaining fast. Kari slammed out the message and ended it with a "Mayday! Lizbirds!" Then she grabbed one of the two shortened muskets stowed in the plane. One of the creatures was right above her, beginning to flare out and extend its claws. "You hold steady," she shouted. "I get this one!" She fired. The heavy load of buckshot impacted across the hideous thing's chest and throat, and with a croaking cry, it tumbled away. Kari pitched the musket into the compartment at her feet and retrieved the second one. The "Nancy" had begun to accelerate away by now, and the closest monster was maybe twenty yards back. She aimed as carefully as she could at its face and squeezed the trigger. Fire and smoke trailed aft along with two ounces of shot that shattered the thing's head. Kari began reloading the second gun but looked over her shoulder, forward, at Fred.

"What you do?" she demanded. Fred was leveling off, just above the water, but he pointed up. High above, another flight of the creatures was nosing over into the attack.

"I'm trying to get us closer to shore. If those devils knock us down, I don't want to land in the water! Too many flashies!" Ahead was a narrow strip of beach. On the one side were the near-vertical cliffs; on the other, a boisterous surf. He risked a look upward. "Here they come!"

Kari never got the musket reloaded. Even without the wild gyrations, buffeting, and evasive maneuvers of the plane, she was just too scared to make her hands obey the complicated orders she gave them. One monster plunged into the sea directly ahead of them. Another missed aft, almost tearing the tail off with its outstretched claws. The whole plane shuddered and nearly flipped into the sea when one of the creatures— that had to be lighter than it looked—slammed into the port wing and just clung there, slashing at the fabric with its teeth. Another lit right next to it and went for the blurry, spinning prop. With a horrifying *Splack! Smack! Whack! Crack!* the prop shredded the creature's head and sprayed blood and gore and shards of bone all over Kari. Of the prop itself, little remained but spinning stumps. Horribly out of balance, the crank likely sprung, the valiant little engine tore itself apart, and all Kari could do was hunker down and hope most of the pieces would miss her.

"That's done it!" Fred shouted, his voice tight with tension. The first beast had probably been torn apart by fragments of the engine, propeller, or its comrade, because it no longer tore at the wing, but the damage was done. Fred struggled against the loss of thrust and lift to coax the plane onto the beach, but they'd never make it. Forty or fifty yards short, the "Nancy" stalled, then pancaked into the surf. Kari screamed when a marching swell caught the tail and flipped the plane onto its back. There was a kaleidoscope of images: rushing bubbles and surging foam. Her eyes grew dim and her lungs felt as if they'd burst. Then, even through the seething waves, she heard the wing drag against the sandy bottom and with a terrible, rending crunch, the "Nancy" began breaking up.

"That was it, Skipper," Ed Palmer said, looking down. He stood in the curtained passageway leading to the wardroom from aft. "After that last 'Mayday,' nothing."

Matt merely nodded, but he thought his heart would break. Reynolds had been the youngest kid on the ship before the Squall, and he'd demonstrated buckets of guts more times than he could count, staying at his talker's post on the bridge throughout many major actions. Kari, a B'mbaadan and daughter of that city's greatest warrior, hadn't been a warrior by nature, but she'd been a sweet kid with her own share of guts, doing what she had to do. Somehow, Fred and Kari had become inseparable, and their friendship and devotion to a very dangerous duty had been an inspiration to everyone. If they had to go, at least they'd gone together. Matt didn't think either would want to go on without the other. Selass sniffed, and Matt smiled gently at her.

"Okay," he said gruffly, standing over the green-linoleum-topped table and peering down at the map laid out on it. Jenks was there, as were Rempel and several Imperial officers. Spanky, Selass, and Bradford were the only others from *Walker*. Gray had already left to join the militia so he, Stumpy, Pack Rat, and Jenks's few Marines could try to cram some of Chack's and Blair's tactics into their individualistic heads. "The . . .'Nancy' didn't report actually seeing it. They meant to overfly the lowlands on their way back here, but they did confirm the ships, so we have to assume there's an enemy column approaching from the south." He looked at Jenks. "You've got to stop it. I don't have any mortars for you, but you should have plenty of artillery—if you can crew it."

"We have enough professionals for the artillery," Jenks said, "but the militia will have to hold."

"They'll hold, if no one else will," Rempel said, somewhat antagonistically. "They're ill-disciplined, and their drill is laughable . . . but this is their home. They'll fight for it."

"Good," Matt said. "That leaves us with the enemy fleet. The forts should be able to keep most of it out of the bay, but if just one ship gets through, it can raise absolute hell with the infrastructure here; infrastructure we're going to need to take the war to the Doms. We can't count on the forts. We must at least whittle the enemy down before it arrives."

"Two hundred and fifty miles at last report," Jenks mused. "The wind remains in our favor to a degree, so they can't make best speed. Give them six to eight knots. That will put them here . . . day after tomorrow. Evening most likely."

"Yeah, no faster than their slowest ships, and in this case, their slowest are their most powerful. All the same, the wind could change and we need depth—behind us, I mean—to chase anything that gets past us. I think we should meet them."

"Chase? Meet?" Rempel said incredulously. "Are you mad? After great effort, we have the equivalent of four warships, not counting yours, to meet twenty-five or more!"

"Not four, Admiral, nine—*counting* this one. We've reestablished contact with elements of Second Fleet. *Achilles*, *Simms*, *Mertz*, and *Tindal* will arrive early tomorrow morning, along with a pair of oilers. They'd have been here earlier . . ." Matt's face clouded. "Let's just say I've no proof of treachery, but I'm awfully glad I gave orders for them to depart company from the rest of Second Fleet if they thought its commander was advancing too slowly. Evidently, your High Admiral McClain gave the impression he was dawdling."

"The Lord High Admiral!" Rempel gasped. "You don't suspect he's in league . . . ?"

Matt shook his head. "I honestly doubt it, but he wasn't enthusiastic about this mission from the start. I think he believed the threat overestimated." He snorted. "He preferred to relieve the Enchanted Isles. Evidently, he's strung out as far south as he can manage, to intercept any word from there. In the meantime, I doubt he'll be a factor in the upcoming fight."

"But still only nine ships!"

"Four are the finest anyone could hope for," Jenks stated, losing patience. "Three are entirely new and more than a match for any Dom ship of the line—and you forget *Walker*, sir."

"I do not! Though . . . honestly, I cannot see how she can be of any great use. Certainly she is fast, but she carries fewer guns than a brig!"

"That may be so, Rempel," Jenks said, "but they're unlike any guns you've ever seen. They can *destroy* ships like the Dom's—or ours, for that matter—from twice, *ten times* the range they could hope to respond!"

Matt winced. *I guess a little exaggeration never hurts when you're trying to bolster a man's courage. Twice the range, sure. Ten times? Not with black powder.*

"Indeed? Yet they are so small. . . ."

Spanky rolled his eyes but turned to Courtney. "Have you come up with any bug spray for them flyin' devils, Mr. Bradford?" he asked.

Courtney's almost perpetually cheerful, open expression contorted into a frown. "I'm not sure," he temporized. "They're not indigenous to Imperial territories, at least not specimens of such size and aggression, so little is really known about them." He brightened. "One of the officers I had the pleasure to meet is impressively knowledgeable about the local fauna! I thought *I* was a naturalist! There's so much I can learn from him. Fascinating, utterly fascinating creatures abide here! Some are even rather familiar to me, but others . . ."

"Courtney," Matt said dryly.

"Oh. Bloody hell! Of course," Bradford fumed, but inhaled to calm himself. "Based on my own studies, I feel comfortable stating that, for all practical purposes, 'lizard birds,' 'dragons,' *are* flying Grik! Their physiology is somewhat different, of course—their arms and fingers have become the framework for wings; the tails are longer and the plumage more specialized. They're also lighter for their size, but the corresponding flight muscles are greatly exaggerated." He looked at Spanky. "Your 'bug spray' analogy might be as good as any, strangely enough. Their lungs are immense, and they clearly rely on a great volume of air to sustain their prodigious cardiopulmonary requirements. . . ." He considered. "I don't imagine they could thrive for long in a smoky environment, for example. Set fire to their ships, and I doubt they could loiter above them. The smoke alone might well choke them, or at least tire them quickly." He shrugged. "That's all I have for you, I'm afraid—besides what you already know: they're vulnerable to gunfire, structurally and otherwise, and bleed rather copiously from any serious wound. Another drawback to their amazing 'power plant,' as it were."

Jenks was watching Matt's face. "Does that give you an idea, my friend?"

"Maybe." Matt glanced at his watch. "In any event, you should probably go ashore and start sorting out your 'army.' I expect the enemy to try a coordinated attack of some kind, but we all know how hard that can be. You had better be in position as early as possible." He looked at Rempel. "The 'fleet' will make all preparations for getting underway."

CHAPTER 17

////// *Grik East Africa*
Primary Industrial Site

General of the Sea Hisashi Kurokawa smoldered with anger as he stepped onto the dock from the deck of his stately yacht. His Grik protectors hurried after him, but he ignored them. Once again, he was being forced to do something against his will, before he was ready, and the results might well be catastrophic. Word had arrived on a few ships that managed to run the Allied blockade that Generals Halik and Niwa hoped to *hold* Ceylon after all. General Esshk still doubted they could; they now knew the Allied fleet had thoroughly invested the place and had deployed a variety of highly effective attack aircraft there. This news didn't come from Halik, but from the sole survivor of a supply convoy they'd tried to push through on the heels of the successful breakout. Lord Regent Tsalka seized on the notion, however, as a possibility that his beloved regency might be preserved, and he'd convinced the Celestial Mother to instruct Kurokawa to deploy his own as yet "idle" airpower to counter the enemy and ravage the Allied fleet.

Kurokawa objected as strenuously as he dared, citing the many obstacles to deployment: the craft weren't ready in the numbers he desired for a decisive blow, the crews were barely proficient, and even navigation would be a problem. He laid out his argument as carefully and respectfully as he could, even referencing the disaster that ensued the last time his advice was ignored, all to no avail. Esshk was on his side, as was the Chooser, but in the end it was Tsalka's argument that they must resist the conquest of Ceylon with every asset available if they hoped to save the sacred "Ancestral Lands" from the corrupting tread of *former prey* that won the day.

Kurokawa did manage to gain a major concession from the Celestial Mother. She understood his and Esshk's desire to prevent another disaster and valued their opinions. Therefore, if there was a "setback," only Tsalka would be blamed. Kurokawa was still enraged but managed to hide his temper—a skill he'd worked hard to master, and one that had served him well of late. He took the reversal with an apparent grace that visibly surprised General Esshk, but he'd secretly resolved to do everything in his growing power to ensure Tsalka took sufficient blame for any number of things to cost him his miserable life.

At least Tsalka hadn't insisted that Kurokawa's New Navy be involved in this fiasco, but likely only time and distance preserved it. That could have been a real disaster. The Navy he was building would soon be invincible, but upon learning of the threat from the air, he'd realized overhead protection was now essential, and his projected date for completion had been postponed accordingly. He slowed his pace and gazed out into the massive, artificial harbor and marveled at his own genius. Once his fleet was complete, nothing the ridiculous "allies" had, or could conceivably make, would be able to stop it. Certainly, there'd be losses. His machinery was crude and many of his ships might simply break down, but the rest—the best—would be impervious to anything but modern weapons. He looked at his flagship, which was undergoing topside reinforcement. Not since *Amagi* was lost had there been anything like her on this world, and he felt a thrill at the prospect of "taking her out" against the foe. It would be a very different meeting from the last one, he swore.

He growled and slapped his boot with his macabre riding crop. Damn Tsalka! Kurokawa had confidence in his fleet, but an unexpected combined attack would've been utterly irresistible, and he'd have had his own revenge at last! He paced the dock, watching the dronelike labor of the Uul, and hearing the harsh commands of his own Japanese officers as they instructed their overseers. He'd finally begun to forgive some of his old crew. Not *all* could have been traitors, he convinced himself, and they worked now with an apparently single-minded passion that mirrored his own. Perhaps they knew, with victory, a new order would emerge, and they wanted to be a part of it. Whatever the reason, most of his surviving "old crew" now worked with a will, and even if it was only to improve their own lot and not necessarily to advance the glory of Kurokawa or Emperor Hirohito, he was satisfied with what they'd accomplished on his behalf.

He left the dock, his unspeaking Grik close behind. The guards themselves signified a shift in his personal fortunes; they were there to protect him with their lives, not monitor or curtail his activities. They *belonged* to him. He managed a brief, snorting smile at that and worked his way quickly past the tightly constructed buildings holding the acid baths, trying to hold his breath the entire length of the structures. It was impossible. He finally took a gasping breath and inhaled some of the fumes. "Aggh!" he said, and worked his way upwind. Soon the smell was gone, and he beheld the dozens of massive structures built to protect his mighty flying machines from the elements. Only one craft was currently in view, and he stopped to marvel at the scope of this, his second greatest achievement.

"Magnificent," he muttered, a little wistfully. Turning, he stepped toward the office of "General of the Sky," Hideki Muriname, the last pilot of the old Type 95 floatplane that once bombed Baalkpan. The plane had been seriously damaged, and though it hadn't been cannibalized, Kurokawa was assured it could never fly again. They used it now as a pattern for gauges and other technical things Kurokawa had no interest in.

"General Muriname!" he boomed, throwing the door aside.

"Sir?" answered a small man seated at a large desk, blueprints scattered before him.

"You have orders." Kurokawa proceeded to explain the mission and the timetable.

"But"—the small man searched the room with his eyes—"that is madness! Such a distance! There will not be fuel for them to return against contrary winds! We will not only waste the machines, but all the aircrews we've worked so hard to form!"

Kurokawa allowed the outburst. It mirrored his own feelings, after all. Better to cultivate this man's goodwill—and animosity toward their "masters"—than slap him down. "Indeed," he agreed grimly, "as I argued. But their course is set. Do your best to consider alternate landing and fueling sites. Some will make it to India."

"But what of the others, destined for these even longer flights?"

Kurokawa sighed. "Doomed, I agree. I fear within a fortnight we will have to begin all over from scratch! Fear not, however. I have taken pains to ensure none of us will be blamed for failure or loss, nor will any of our people suffer—beyond those few who fly the mission. And who knows? Perhaps it *will* succeed, and ours will be the greatest share of glory!"

Muriname ignored the reference to glory, though he was relieved there'd be no more reprisals. "Must we send the entire fleet? All our trained crews?"

"Yes," Kurokawa said. "To hold back would be seen as courting failure, and if the balance of victory is perceived to have teetered on numbers, we *will* be blamed."

"I must keep at least two craft to continue training operations," Muriname stated. "Otherwise, it will take months to recover the most rudimentary skills. "Production will continue—it's only now reaching its stride—but we *must* keep training so the machines will have aircrews that can fly and maintain them."

Kurokawa frowned. "Of course. I'm sure Esshk and the Chooser will agree. Two craft should make little difference. But I must get the blessing of their vile empress, to protect our people."

"Yes, Capt—General of the Sea."

Muriname remained standing for some time after Kurokawa left. The new "Air Forces" had been his project since its inception, and besides the improved treatment he'd won for the Japanese engineers and other former *Amagi* crewmen in his "department," he was proud of what they'd accomplished. Despite the limitations and difficulties they'd faced pertaining to Grik physiology, not only had they built machines the creatures could operate, but they'd solved the difficult technological problems of power plants with simplicity itself: horizontal-opposed, two-cylinder, Reed valve, four-stroke engines that weighed only about one hundred thirty pounds, even made of iron. Lower rpm meant higher torque and reliability—and no need for a reduction gear. Muriname believed the things developed close to forty or fifty horsepower, while burning only about three and a half gallons of precious gasoline—they'd only just started to receive in quantity from the north—per hour.

Unlike the enemy, as far as he knew, they had naturally occurring rubber (or something so much like it as to make no difference) within the territory under their control, and they'd solved most of the other issues of large-scale production in the face of a labor pool with less intelligence than young children. Many of the "mass production" techniques pioneered by Kurokawa in the shipyards had been well applied, but the precision required for weights and shapes was far more critical for flying machines, and he'd noticed that, slowly, even his most unskilled laborers—those who survived—had begun to grasp more and more of what they were taught. Some were becoming quite competent, in fact, and a precious few could even comprehend how what they did *related* to other things.

The training aircrews were on an entirely different level; all were "Hij," or "elevated" specimens that generally exhibited levels of intelligence on a par with young adult Japanese. They were enthusiastic learners, and though insular and as slavishly devoted to their "Celestial Mother" as many Japanese youths were to their emperor, they demonstrated a hungry curiosity. He was beginning to form some rather radical ideas about their "allies'" society, and though he still loathed the Grik in general, he no longer hated them individually. He supposed he even felt vaguely *attached* to some of the aircrews! Regardless of the terrible waste of time, training, and resources, deep down, much of the sudden anxiety he felt regarding his orders stemmed from the simple fact that he just didn't want his students to die. He felt torn and confused.

Grik Ceylon

General Halik hissed and slashed at the map with his claws. "They are *monsters!*" he howled. "Each attack we send against them is savaged, and many turn prey!" He looked at Niwa. "Those who do are *not* destroyed, but they are so far gone, I fear they may never recover—or become useful for anything but fodder!"

"Give them time," Niwa said. "You've seen it before."

"But we don't *have* time! I want victory! *A* victory, *any* victory, to show General Esshk that Ceylon can hold. Only that will gain us aid!"

"That was not our mission," Niwa reminded him.

"It *becomes* mine," Halik snapped. "If I were . . . accustomed to failure, I would not be alive. Only victory in the arena deserves life!"

"But this isn't the arena, and we've accomplished the mission we were set—to engage and assess the enemy; learn how they fight and what they fight with. That was the greater mission. Saving Ceylon was never expected of us."

"I expect it of *myself*," Halik replied in a quieter tone. "I cannot help it. Despite my 'elevation,' I'm not—cannot be—dispassionate." He straightened. "Nor does it seem I have gained the wisdom General Esshk expected of me. I don't have the troops being bred and trained for defense, but as you said, wise offense can counteract that. I *know* it is so! I just can't . . . make it happen, and I chafe!"

"You still talk of attacking with your shield, as you did in the arena," Niwa observed, "but you know that sometimes a shield is just a shield, a tool to deflect a blow. Even your lowliest Uul understand this."

"Ha! You expect them to line up in the face of the enemy and deflect his lead spheres, arrows, cannon, *bombs*, with shields? They cannot stand that. They *will* attack, and nothing I can do will stop them!"

"And they are slaughtered."

"Yes."

Niwa sighed. He understood how Halik felt, and he felt *for* him. At some point, he'd finally stopped thinking of Halik as a *creature*, a Grik he somehow got along with. Maybe it was his isolation from his own kind, or perhaps it was the prestige of his position and his real power over the Grik of Ceylon. Maybe it was just the camaraderie of battle. Whatever the reason, he considered Halik a friend, and he couldn't help it any more than Halik could prevent suffering under his own burden. Oddly, Niwa wasn't even conflicted. He hated Kurokawa and had no real attachment to any of his "own" surviving people. Nor did he feel anything for the enemy other than a measure of admiration, even though he knew he had far more in common with them than any Grik. In spite of everything, they were the enemy. Halik, on the other hand, was honest, loyal, and brave. He was perhaps a true samurai in all the ways that mattered, and Niwa respected him for that.

"Then use your mind to shield them," Niwa suggested. "You already laid the groundwork for our 'surprise'; is it complete?"

"Not yet. Everything has happened so quickly, and the enemy moves like a machine! I never imagined anything like it. Now our front *collapses* to the south, and all we . . ." Halik stopped and stared at the map. "All we can do is take from one place and put it in another," he said softly. "The enemy will see that—their thrice-cursed aircraft—but they cannot see what we do in the dark!"

"That's true," Niwa said. "They occasionally fly at night, but they can't really see."

"They'll expect us to take from the highland front to reinforce the southern plains. The highlands are difficult country, and though they don't know it, that was precisely why we amassed such power there, emplaced your ingenious devices! But they won't come!" He paused. "Or will they?" Excitedly, Halik peered at the map. "They will watch us take forces from there to a place where *they* have made it necessary! The highland passes will appear to have been abandoned, while the plain grows more formidable! They *will* come where we want them, thinking it an empty road!" Halik snarled again, in triumph this time.

"Excellent," Niwa said approvingly. "But the movements must be convincing, and the troops and guns we leave must be well concealed."

"Of course," Halik agreed, "as well as the warriors we return there!"

"How do you mean?"

"As we both agree, they cannot see what we do at night. We'll move nearly *everything* out of the highlands! Prod them into attacking just as Uul will chase wounded prey! Under the cover of darkness, we put it *all* back!"

"Chancy," Niwa said, "all will depend on concealment and exaggeration—two things they will not expect of Grik, based on those they've met before."

"Indeed," Halik said with a self-satisfied gurgle. "We must see to it ourselves. The warriors we leave, those trained on the cannons, will have to hide—not an easy thing to achieve in itself—and . . ." He paused. "When we shift the warriors back to the highlands in darkness, we will fill the lines south of the city with the city's inhabitants themselves. Use the noncombatants."

"What will N'galsh say?" Niwa asked.

"He will wail as if being flayed alive. All his followers, merchants, artisans—his preparers of food!—all the privileged Hij in the city, along with their own little armies of Uul forced into the company of ungroomed warriors . . . !" Halik could barely contain his glee. "Perhaps we'll even *arm* them!"

Niwa chuckled himself. "The idea of N'galsh wielding a sword is amusing . . . but can he if he must?"

"Of course not, but if we fool the spies from the air, we will know it soon enough. The enemy will pause before the 'mighty force' we assemble before it, long enough to strengthen itself, while his lighter center force that slogs slowly through the mountains to the east will charge headlong into the trap! Once we destroy it, we'll attack the western force from the side, the 'flank,' as you say!"

"It could work," Niwa allowed, studying the map. "If we do it, it *must* work, because nothing remains if it fails."

"Yes," Halik agreed, sobering. "Either we achieve a great victory—or depart as originally planned. By then that might be . . . difficult!"

CHAPTER 18

////// *New Ireland*

The once almost-pacifistic Major Chack-Sab-At was a veteran of many battles now, but the wild melee that erupted in the darkened streets of New Dublin was something new in his experience. It was somewhat like the climax of the battle at the Dueling Grounds on New Scotland, except here it was on a completely different scale, sprawling through the congested streets of a large, unfamiliar city. He couldn't even tell which direction was which, because the smoke from guns and burning buildings hid the sky and blotted out the stars. Few of "his" Imperial troops had ever been to New Ireland before, and even fewer had been in this Company city. Most were as lost as he was in the confusion of this bizarre battle.

Blair's attack down the slope and across the field toward the city had succeeded far better than expected. The enemy positions had been devastated by the aerial bombing and mortar attack, and the remaining Doms were completely surprised when assailed through the smoky darkness by a force they'd been sure was withdrawing. They broke. Blair's regiments charged onward, yelling like fiends, flush with success— and lost all cohesion. The Imperial Marines weren't *real* professionals after all, Chack had reflected sadly, and he tried to round up as many clumps as he could when his own division went in, but when they continued advancing—while trying to maintain some contact with Blair— everything fell apart. By the sound, the seaborne assault had commenced with a will, likely catching the Doms attempting to respond to Chack and Blair's attack, as hoped, but now there was fighting everywhere, and Chack had personal control of barely a company of mixed "American" and Imperial Marines.

"The harbor's that way," gasped Lieutenant Blas-Ma-Ar, pointing vaguely over the top of a stone barrier that she, Chack, and the rest of his remaining command had been forced to shelter behind. The barrier formed a rectangle around the Company/Government headquarters building, and there were a lot more rebels or Doms within than Chack had Marines outside. "I can hear the monstrous, great guns still firing from one of the forts," Blas added.

"I'm glad *someone* can still hear something," Chack growled irritably. "This war gets noisier all the time."

"You *like* the exploding shells," Blas accused.

"They don't explode repeatedly next to my ears," he said. "And if our enemies ever begin using them, I'll probably like them less."

"General Aalden was right about the muskets, though," Blas insisted. "You can't poke a bow over a rock wall and loose an arrow without showing much of yourself!"

"A point." He looked around. Firing had resumed in the direction they'd come from, echoing dully down the narrow, debris-strewn streets, and he had no idea who was shooting at whom, or in which direction. It would probably not be a good idea to go back that way. "If they made their buildings up off the ground in a proper fashion, we could see more," he grumped.

"We can't stay here, Major. We must get back into the fight." Blas looked around. "We need a mortar—gre-naades. Something to raise the enemy fire so we can move." An errant roundshot, a big one, probably from *Salaama-Na* herself, crashed into the building before them and showered rocky fragments into the street. The strange but geometrically pleasing city was being systematically destroyed. Smoky dust filled the air.

"Major!" cried an Imperial Marine nearby. "Look there!" A door had opened across the street, and an arm was waving them toward it.

"A local?" Blas asked.

"Must be. It may be a trap, though," someone said.

"Not all here are rebels, surely," Chack speculated. He looked at the Marine. "Try to make it across. We'll fire a volley as you move, to cover your sprint!"

At Chack's signal, the men and 'Cats behind the barrier fired their muskets at the Company headquarters, and the red-coated Marine scrambled through the rubble and disappeared safely through the door. There was little return fire from the Doms. Several minutes later, a red-sleeved arm motioned from the door in the gloom, and Chack ordered the covering fire resumed. The Marine almost made it back before he tripped and fell, but he managed to scrabble back to safety with musket balls "vrooping" by above his head, or sending shattered rock over the top of the wall.

"Major," he wheezed, crawling up beside Chack, "it's a New Dubliner, all right. A cobbler." The man grinned. "He don't know what you Lee-mooans are, and he was a touch nervous, but he seen our red coats. He's a loyal man. Says his sons are watchin' the fight from the rooftop. Lots of locals are, all over the city, an' many're with us! The Doms've treated folk rough." He shook his head. "Anyway, a lot have risen up—that's one reason we're not takin' much fire from above. There ain't many of 'em armed, but those that are are tryin' to stay out of the way, on the roofs! They ain't fightin' much," he admitted, "just enough to keep the Doms down off their places, see, and not enough to provoke 'em as much against them as they are against us!"

"That's a larger service than they credit," Chack mused. "But are they not vulnerable to the flying creatures the Doms control?"

"They might be, but for the smoke. Seems the bloody damn things don't like it. Can't see through it, or breathe it, maybe. They don't know why. Anyway, all them devils are gone, or stayin' above the fight, says he."

"Does he know where our closest friends are?"

"Aye. If you'll look up, he has three stories. A fair view. There's maybe another company just two streets yonder!" The Marine pointed beyond the cobbler's establishment.

"Okay," Chack said, deciding. "Will you take me to meet your new friend?"

The Marine looked back across the avenue he'd just crossed twice. "Aye, sir."

"Good. Blas? Same procedure as before."

They both made it again, though a few balls came close, and they bolted through the door followed by splinters and powdered, gravelly dust. The "cobbler" was still in the dark room, standing behind a substantial wall. He started to move to greet them, then stopped, his eyes going wide in the gloom at the sight of the Lemurian.

Chack touched his battered helmet. "Major Chack-Sab-At, of the Amer-i-caan Navy and Maa-rine Corps," he said as pleasantly as he could manage. "Ally and friend of His Highness, Gerald McDonald. I am at your service, sir."

"By all that's holy!" blurted the balding, tall man. "The Doms said ye were demons, an' ye do look like one!"

"I hope we are demons to *them*, sir," Chack said, "but we're friends of the Empire."

"Well . . . that's good enough for me," the man decided. "If those bloody bastards fear ye, an' men such as this Marine obey ye, I'd wager ye're near a saint! How can I help?"

Chack quickly scanned the room. Shadowy objects were discernible. Shoe lasts, benches, stacks of leather, tools. "I'm told you can see the battle from above?"

"Aye."

"May I have a look?"

The man hesitated only slightly before nodding. "Aye, follow me." He opened a door that concealed a flight of stairs and retrieved a burning lamp from a step. "This way, if ye please."

Up the stairs they went, passing through the second-story living space. The third was much the same—possibly for the sons? Finally, the trio emerged on the roof, surrounded by a high continuation of the outside wall. Four young men greeted them with muskets, but turned them away when they recognized the cobbler. A middle-aged woman and a girl sat huddled to one side, wrapped in blankets head to foot, to protect them from flying debris. Chack didn't know if he'd ever seen such concern for Imperial females demonstrated by anyone other than Commodore Jenks—or Governor Radcliff on Respite Island. The reaction of the "sons" was similar to the cobbler, but he quickly assured them.

"Watch yerself near the edge," the cobbler warned as Chack started to look around. "I doubt the sods'll hit ye, but they might get grit in yer eyes!"

Chack nodded his thanks and began to absorb the Battle of New Dublin. The house/store/shop wasn't the tallest building in the city by any means, several being two or more stories taller, but it afforded an excellent view of the chaotic struggle. It was surreal. *Salaama-Na* had moved quite close to one of the forts with her great sweeps, and the two traded heavy fire like angry volcanoes locked in a hellish embrace. The Home had the advantage in firepower, but whether the great ship or the fort was more durable was anyone's guess. The other fort was a smoldering ruin, probably destroyed by a hit in its magazine, and Chack realized he must have missed its demolition during the bombing. He doubted it was constructed to protect against attack from the air.

The harbor glowed and pulsed with burning ships of all sizes, and buildings and warehouses all along the waterfront were in flames. Small flashes lit the night in all directions, like granules of gunpowder trickled in a fire, and he finally gained a semblance of understanding where the general respective lines were. A light gun barked in the street to the south and canister crackled down an alleyway amid foreign screams. *Must be one of our light six-pounders,* he thought. Bringing it down the mountains behind them would have been a nightmare. *I wonder how many there are?* Few pieces were firing anywhere in the city; the Doms must've had all of theirs pointing outward, and spiked them as they were overrun. The only other big guns still in the fight were those of the fort, a few light pieces firing inward that the landing Marines must have brought, and what appeared to be a Dom bastion of some kind far on the northwest side of the city. Guns from there belched fire in all directions.

"Maarine," he snapped, "what's your name, anyway?"

"Private Shmuke, sir."

"*Corporal* Shmuke, after I talk to Mr. Blair," Chack said. "I need you to contact that company fighting to our rear. I presume it's they who have the gun. Tell them to bring it up here to support us. We can't link up with anyone until we get past that building there." He pointed at the one they'd stalled in front of. "I assume that's this city's Government House?" he asked the cobbler.

"Aye, or at least it was. As ye may imagine, it was taken over by the Comp'ny several months ago when the Doms first started coming in," he seethed.

"Months?" Chack asked.

"Aye. Didn't anyone know?"

"No one who mattered, apparently," Chack said. "None of the shipping from here reported it, but it rarely touches at Scapa Flow. . . ." He paused. "Or anywhere I'm aware of except for New Britain Island, come to that. There's been . . . suspicion of late."

"Aye," the cobbler said, "an' naught but Comp'ny ships've been allowed to come an' go this past year!"

"That explains a lot," Chack murmured, "but not *why*." He looked at Corporal Shmuke. "Bring them up!"

"Aye, sir!"

"Corp'ral," said the cobbler, "one of my boys'll lead ye. Ye can get quite close moving along the rooftops. He'll know those ye meet, an' which dwellin's are safe to descend within."

"Thank you, sir!"

Another broadside thundered from *Salaama-Na* in the harbor and other Imperial ships had joined her at last, risking their comparatively thin skins in an effort to overwhelm the fort. The fort wasn't finished yet, however, and the night lit up with a terrible eruption as an Imperial "liner" disintegrated as a result of a lucky shot.

"Ye asked why," the cobbler said softly.

"Yes, sir."

"Many of us here, on New Ireland an' elsewhere, adhere ta the Catholic faith—the old, *true* faith some of the Founders brought with 'em. Even if it weren't for the Doms an' their perversions, the 'Old Church' is frowned upon. Its practice is legal, but grounds for revocation of citizenship. One cannot be an open Catholic an' vote for the court, so those of us who're honest to our God an' our emperor have no say. The *dishonest* sell their votes ta the Comp'ny. Some here, the 'rebels,' would have independence. Most would be happy just ta worship as we would. The Comp'ny, as separatist rebels, or for reasons of their own, p'raps hoped the Doms would help us gain independence and just be happy ta have us move a tad closer ta their way of thinkin'." He spat. "Madness, o' course. The 'Old Church' has nothin' in common with the filthy version the Doms advance—an' any fool could see they don't accept half measures. If they're in, they're in, an' the suffering here, especially after whatever transpired on New Scotland, has been enough to kill a man's soul. I an' me family've been lucky ta survive the 'cleansin',' an' me poor daughter's been hid ever since they arrived. Most females of childbearin' age . . . The sacrifices, ye see . . ."

Chack could bear no more. He hadn't really considered the lot of those on New Ireland who didn't support the new regime. He looked once more at the dying city. "There will be a reckoning for this, sir, I assure you. Now I must return to my Marines. You've been most helpful and kind."

"I thought you said your 'beloved ass' wouldn't fly!" Second Lieutenant Orrin Reddy shouted through the voice tube to his passenger, as the NC-1B "Nancy" achieved a cruising altitude of about five thousand feet. There were no lights on the plane—something that needed fixing—but his "passenger" knew enough Morse to confirm the other ships in the 10th Pursuit Squadron had converged on the orange exhaust flare from the lead plane's engine. Orrin hoped they wouldn't "converge" too close! He couldn't make out any details in his little mirror, but he suspected he'd see Dennis Silva's gap-toothed grin if it was light.

"*I* ain't flyin'; you are!" came the reply.

"I thought you were afraid to fly!"

"I am! That's why you're doin' it, damn it!"

"Well . . ." Orrin shook his head in frustration. "What difference does that make?"

"I ain't at the controls!"

Orrin started to ask at what point a maniacal gunner's mate in the Asiatic Fleet had ever controlled an aircraft, when something bumped into the back of his leg. "What the hell!" He looked down but saw nothing in the darkness.

"It's cold!" came a strange voice from within the fuselage/hull of the plane.

"My God, Lawrence! Is that you?" Orrin demanded.

"Course it is! Who else do you think could get in here?"

"But *what* are you doing in there? I *thought* this thing was heavy. . . ."

"Look, Mr. Reddy," Silva yelled. "I work for the Skipper, an' my job's to take care of stuff for him, you know, the gals an' such. Well, Miss Lieutenant Minister Tucker an' the Munchkin princess are safe as can be right now. They both think maybe you need a little watchin' over right now, you an' the Skipper bein' related an' all."

"That's bullshit!"

"Sure it is, an' I said so, but they *made* me come! It was a face-to-face, direct order!"

"But . . . what's Lawrence doing here?"

"He kinda thinks of himself as my sidekick, see? Sometimes I let him carry one of my guns."

"I ain't no sidekick!" Lawrence said.

"Hey, there's the moon!" Silva said, diverting the conversation. The bright orb, nearly full, had begun emerging from the sea. "Boy, it sure looks close! Hey! How come it always looks closer when it rears up than when it's right overhead, Lieutenant? I've always wondered that."

"You're kidding? Well . . . there's more atmosphere between us and it when it first comes up. It acts like a magnifying glass. . . . I think."

"So . . . it's because there's more air between us and it now than when it's straight up?"

"That's what I just said!"

"Then if you had a glass tank and filled it with compressed air, you could *really* see somethin', right?"

Orrin shook his head but didn't reply. *What a dopey question,* he thought. *Now it's going to drive me nuts!* He was glad to see the moon, though; it would make setting down on that lake in the dark a lot easier. He looked over his shoulder and saw the silhouettes of the rest of his flight. *Maybe we won't be as likely to run into each other either.* The silhouette of New Ireland had appeared as well, as the moon rose higher, looking like a mountain range surrounded by a sea of mercury. "We should see the southern elements of Second Fleet soon. Start keeping your eyes peeled, in case any of those damn lizard birds are waiting for us."

The four-cylinder engine droned companionably above them as the coastline neared and the dark shapes of ships emerged. On shore, northeast and southwest of Cork, a battle raged, with vertical slashes of fire in both directions pinpointing artillery emplacements. Occasionally, clusters of mortar bombs sputtered where observers must have spotted enemy troop concentrations. The ships weren't firing much, since all were Imperial vessels and had no explosive shells, but they'd probably rejoin the fight in earnest at dawn, once they could see what they were shooting at again.

"Anything on the horn I ought to know about?" Orrin asked.

"I can't make heads or tails of it," Silva confessed. "I ain't no spark catcher, but I can hold my own. Every time I start pickin' up a thread, somebody stomps all over it. Sounds like a mess, though. Everbody's screamin' for those swell new mortar bombs. Apparently, they're about all that's keepin' the bad guys back. Must be runnin' out."

"I'm not surprised," Orrin said. "This turned into a lot bigger fight than anybody expected, and all the artillery that fires exploding shells are with Chack and Blair, or left behind at Waterford." He looked down at the fighting around Cork as they flew above it. "They'll get more ordnance in the morning when that Jap colonel comes ashore—if they can hold that long." Orrin's tone revealed he still wasn't comfortable relying on Shinya. He liked and respected Sandra, Laumer, and Captain Lelaa (he'd taken to the 'Cats as quickly as anyone). He even liked Lawrence right off, but, of course, he'd never seen a Grik. In many ways, Orrin Reddy was still entranced and fascinated by this bizarre "Oz" he'd found himself in, and it sure beat the fate that awaited him aboard—or beyond—that hellish ship he'd ridden to this world. But no matter whose side he was on, Shinya was still a Jap.

Ahead were the Wiklow Mountains. Soon they'd cross them and view the valley beyond—and the lake that ought to be Pearl Harbor.

"This fight looks . . . even bigger," he observed a while later as they descended into the valley and neared what could only be the city of Waterford. A vast crescent of fire enveloped the northern part of the town, and Lake Shannon shimmered and glowed like a great puddle of blood. Bright flashes lit the valley, and crimson arcs of exploding shells fell on what had to be enemy positions, fired from the city and the mountains beyond. Cork was a holding action. Beyond the next range was the main Allied push, but here, the enemy had the whole campaign by the throat. If Waterford fell, each force would be isolated and vulnerable. From altitude, the battle resembled an inferno as the damp, but sappy forest burned almost everywhere. Immediately, Orrin Reddy changed his entire plan.

"Watch really carefully now," he instructed Silva. "That moon's a big help to us, but it'll help those flying creatures too!"

In the event, the entire 10th Pursuit Squadron set down on the placid, brightly lit lake without incident, and motored toward a pier where nearly a dozen other "Nancys" were tied. Willing hands helped secure the bobbing aircraft as the engines were cut, and weary, stiff-legged aircrews scrambled onto the dock.

"Where's HQ?" Orrin shouted.

"You not like it, sur," warned a 'Cat.

"Why?" He shook his head. "Never mind. Just take me there."

There was excited chattering he didn't understand, and he was quickly led through a maze of battered waterfront buildings to a long, low-slung structure that reminded him of an army barracks. Probably every one of his fliers gaggled behind him.

"What's the meaning of this?" demanded an Imperial officer as Orrin, Silva, and the leading edge of aviators burst into the building. Orrin was shocked by the tone, but also the level of chaos he beheld. At first glance, the activity they'd interrupted seemed to border on panic.

"Lieutenant Orrin Reddy, COFO of *Maaka-Kakja*, reporting," he said. He didn't salute, partly because he had no idea about Imperial rank devices, but also because his temper was rising.

"Very well, you've reported!" the officer said brusquely. "Now get out of the way! In case you hadn't noticed, we've a battle on our hands!"

"That's pretty clear from the air. What's also clear is a way to end it in a hurry!"

"Ridiculous! We're doing all that can be done with our meager forces here."

"You're not doing anything with the planes yet."

"Yes . . . well, I heard there was some scheme to use them in the morning for something," the man replied vaguely, "though I've no idea what possible use they might be. Freakish curiosities!"

"Who's in command here?" Silva demanded menacingly, taking a step forward. Lawrence squeezed in beside him, and his frightening visage and strangely colored armor were at least as disconcerting as Silva's sudden entrance into the conversation.

"Why . . . Commodore Luce came forward with the reinforcements from Cork. I suppose he's the highest in rank. . . ."

"So he's in charge?"

"I don't know as if you could say he's in *charge*, per se. . . ."

"Is anybody in charge?" Silva roared.

The Imperials visibly flinched.

"Uh, Major Blair was in charge of this element of the operation, though we've occupied an area originally designated for the Ape—Major Chack, I mean! Neither is here at present, so I command my forces, Commodore Luce has his, though his artillery is controlled by . . . someone else. Major Brighton has the troops that fled here from Bray, but his supply train security force is under Major Grimes."

"Nobody's in charge?" Silva roared again, but with a tone of furious incredulity. "Good Gawd a'mighty! What the *hell* kind of a way is this to run a war? You fellas haven't done much o' this, have you?"

"Perhaps not on this scale, but I assure you . . . !"

Dennis turned to Orrin. "Sir,' he said with more gravity than Orrin had ever heard him use, "as the senior officer on the scene who has the only f . . . lipperin' clue what the flyin' . . ." He stopped. "Oh goddamn, Lieutenant! Just rear up an' take charge o' this chickenshit outfit!"

"Jesus, Silva, I can't do that!" Orrin objected, his young face reddening in the lamplight.

"Of course not!" the Imperial practically squealed.

Silva raised the Thompson SMG he'd been holding innocuously by his side and yanked the bolt back. "Lieutenant Reddy, you're fixin' to *hafta* take charge after I shoot all these useless sons-o'-goats!"

"Just wait, damn it!" Orrin shouted. He spun back to face the Imperial "commander." "Look, I don't want your job and I sure don't want you fellows dead, but I do have a plan!" He pushed his way through the suddenly very quiet and attentive officers in the room to a map spread on a table. "The Doms are all around here," he said, drawing a crescent with his finger. "Some big fires are burning here"—he pointed again—"between the enemy and this little river, probably started by Chack and Blair's artillery."

"Yes," muttered another officer. "A great tragedy, all those trees!"

Orrin looked at the man and blinked. "Uh, okay. The thing is, those guns can't reach any farther. *We* can! *Maaka-Kakja*'s planes!"

"For what purpose?"

"We brought fuel for the planes that landed on the lake, but we don't need all of them for this. You pull all your troops back to the city, and we rig fuel cans with mortar bombs and drop 'em on the enemy! The whole valley north of the city will go up in a wall of fire, and the Doms we don't burn will have no choice but to pull back! By the time the fire simmers down, you should have reinforcements from the coast!"

"Madness!" cried the "tree" officer. "To burn the enemy alive! It's monstrous, simply monstrous! And all those trees! The beauty of the valley will be lost!"

"You're all nuts," shouted Orrin in return. "You'd rather lose the battle and get nailed to a post—and maybe lose the whole damn war—than kill the enemy and burn a few trees?" He looked at Silva. "I should've let you shoot 'em!"

"Still can," Silva said.

"Now, now!" cried the first Imperial. "This *is* madness! We're all on the same side, by Imperial decree. I will respect that. You have your own command, so please do as you think best with it! I'll pass the word to Commodore Luce and the others! Just leave us."

"I need some mortar bombs," Orrin insisted.

"As do we all. I don't know if any can be had, but if so, you'll have to get them from . . . oh, blast! I still can't remember his name! The artillery gentleman! Now, if you don't mean to shoot us, please leave us to fight our battle!"

Orrin turned without saluting and strode out the door, followed by his fliers. "Silva," he said sharply.

"Sir?"

"Take a detail and get me some mortar bombs . . . I don't care how you do it."

"You bet! C'mon, Larry, you fuzzy little salamander. Let's go get some bombs!"

Half a dozen 'Cats followed Silva and Lawrence into the noisy, fiery night.

"What we do now?" another 'Cat asked Orrin.

"Let's go see how many planes we can gas up enough to do the job, and still have enough fuel to burn the Doms out of this place!" He looked back at the HQ. "This joint's even more screwed up than things were back in the Philippines when the Japs came! I didn't think that was possible!"

Within an hour, Silva returned with almost forty bombs; Orrin had eleven planes with tanks topped off, each with two five-gallon gas cans slung under it's wings. They hadn't figured out a way to secure the bombs to the cans in a way that would ensure the contact fuses were pointed down when the ungainly weapons were dropped, so they decided to try something like what Orrin had heard First Fleet did in the west, except in this case the observers would toss a couple of bombs at the same time the pilots yanked a release lanyard on a gas tank. If they hit close enough together, swell. Some would, certainly, and their next pass with their second cans would connect the dots. Orrin knew "real" incendiaries were now in production at Baalkpan and Maa-ni-la, but they wouldn't have them here for some time.

"I'm almost surprised that crazy-assed Imperial gardener hasn't sent troops to stop us," Silva said as he propped his and Orrin's plane, and then sat down in the observer's seat when the engine caught and farted to life.

"Me too," replied Orrin, shouting over the sudden rumble of engines up and down the dock.

"Watch where your giant shoes go!" Lawrence suddenly protested from within the fuselage.

"Well, move your damn lizardy face out from under 'em!"

"Lay off, you two!" Orrin said. The moon had dulled behind the smoke, and there was less visibility on the lake now. "I need to concentrate—

and you do too! Don't forget, there're still some other 'lizardy' things out there!" He paused. "Besides, why'd you bring Lawrence *this* time?"

"What, you wanna *leave* him back there with that buncha dopes? I doubt any of 'em has ever seen his type before. Hell, they'd have 'em on a leash—or in a fish tank—by the time we got back."

"Just as well," Orrin said. "After the stunt you pulled, I'm not sure we *should* go back! Listen, as soon as we're up and get some altitude, send a report to *Makka-Kakja* about the mess here, and what we're going to try."

"Okay," Silva responded doubtfully, "I'll try. They may have trouble readin' my writin, though!"

"Just do your best," Orrin directed. "Use the 'air' frequency. You'll have a better chance of getting through that mush offshore." With that, he advanced the throttle and the "Nancy" accelerated across the water.

Once they were airborne and the rest of the pickup squadron, mostly from the 10th Pursuit, had formed on them, Orrin banked wide around the valley to the south of the lake, almost to the sea. There, the sky was clear and the bright moon was almost overhead now. He circled to the east, near the Sperrin Mountains, and tried to view the battle for New Dublin, but all he saw was a bright glow on smoky clouds beyond the craggy peaks. He steadied up on a northeast to southwest flight path that put the greater enemy concentration directly ahead.

"We're first," Orrin shouted back. "The rest of the guys'll try to lay their eggs just beyond ours, and then the next plane's in succession! It's gonna be tough in the dark. Hell, it'd be tough in daylight, but there's not much else we can do. If we leave it to those rear area . . . *gentlemen* at their supposed HQ, your Jap buddy'll have to fight this whole campaign all over again."

"He may be a Jap," Silva returned, "an we ain't exactly 'buddies,' but if he has to start over, I guarantee *his* campaign—with *our* guys—won't be anything like this one! These New Brits ain't like our Marines, but they ain't bad soljers, I hear. I can tell you their Navy men are damn good—but their Navy's kept 'em from havin' to fight a big land war before, an' except for that Blair fella—accordin' to Chack—they don't much know how." He looked over his shoulder at the glare beyond the mountains. "An' which it looks like ol Chack an' Blair are stuck in pretty good. *Chack* damn sure knows how to fight!"

"Yeah, well maybe we'll have a look after we're done here." Orrin nodded back toward the lake. "As I said, maybe we ought not go back there. Now hang on!"

Suddenly, the nose pitched down and the plane aimed for the edge of the now-much-larger fire burning on the enemy's left flank. Orrin's warning had really been just a figure of speech, because Silva couldn't hold on with a ten-pound bomb in each hand. The "Nancy" hurtled downward, and if it hadn't been for the sudden fusillade of musketry crackling toward them, it would've been frighteningly difficult to tell how low they were getting.

"Get ready!" Orrin yelled. Musket balls began striking the plane. "Now!"

Silva pitched his bombs just as the plane jolted to starboard with the sudden lightening of the port wing. He was pressed back into his seat as Orrin pulled back on the stick and applied full throttle, but still managed to keep his eyes on the general area where their "ordnance" fell. "Who-eeee!" he roared when two small flashes ignited a mushroom of orange and black. Myriad trees and limbs were silhouetted, many already adding yellowish wisps to the fireball. "That was a good-un!" he cried as the plane continued climbing, banking east over the city and out of the haze already lingering over the enemy position. Another fiery eruption extended the fire a little southwest, and Silva whooped again. There was nothing more for several moments beyond a few probable mortar bursts, long past the time for the next two planes to drop. Suddenly, the sky spit a spiraling meteor that spun out of control and impacted almost a quarter mile past the last explosion. It detonated with even greater force than their own bomb had done—just as another "Nancy" suddenly blew up a little beyond where the first had fallen.

"Two of them must've run into each other," Orrin said stiffly. Even as they watched, the new flames leaped back the distance toward the first. Evidently, the drops had been good; they just hadn't ignited. They did now. Tall, sappy trees became instant torches, swirling flames coiling around them and pointing at the sky. Another plane dropped its payload, then another. Orrin was sad about the pilots he'd just lost, but damn, the rest of the "boys" were pasting them!

"Okay, one more run!" he commanded. "Send it, if you can." He circled around, out of the growing haze of smoke to the southwest, and tried to line up on the procession of strengthening fires. *It must be hell down there,* he thought, but then tried not to think about it. They took more bullets on this run, and Lawrence squeaked when a ball tore through the hull and exploded some of his tail plumage, but they made their drop without serious injury to the plane or themselves. The gas didn't burn this time, but a plane behind them connected fuel to the flame, and the whole thing went up in a quickening rush. Orrin was probably only imagining the screams he thought he heard over the engine and the wind rushing by.

"Jesus," he muttered, looking down. The Dom artillery flashes had all but stopped, and the semicircle of encroaching fires had become a cauldron of flame. Somewhere in the midst of all that were hundreds— *thousands* of men who'd had absolutely no idea what was coming, how to deal with it, or even how to take cover. They'd never been attacked from the sky before. He felt a little sick. In the dark days before the Philippines fell, the few remaining American planes had been forbidden to tangle with Zeros. They could outrun them or dive away, and that was what they'd been told to do, to preserve their planes for recon and ground attack. Mixing it up with the nimble Japanese planes was a losing proposition. Therefore, he'd strafed and bombed his share of landing craft and troop columns—but that was different. They were Japs, they'd attacked his country, and they were after *him*. He felt protective of "his" pilots now and he mourned those he'd lost, but this still just didn't feel like "his" *war* yet.

Below, the flames grew more intense as the prevailing east wind curled around the flank of the Sperrin Mountains and blew them northwest. He began to see why the "tree officer" had been so concerned; the conflagration was growing and threatened to consume the entire valley in a sea of fire. Well, that was tough. He'd come to save people, not trees, and the increased fire from the Imperial positions showed that "his" side was taking advantage of the situation and pressing the Dom survivors back toward the blaze. Their reserves, caught on the other side of the advancing firestorm, were abandoning them and starting to flee up the Waterford road. Soon, those left behind would have to surrender or die.

"Our work here is done," Silva shouted in the lofty tone of some satisfied warrior prophet. "Let us go across the mountains!"

"You think we ought to take the rest of the flight?"

"I dunno. They're as likely to be welcomed as hee-roes as shot, I guess, an' they was just followin' orders. Then there's them giant lizard birds to consider."

"Right. Tell 'em to set back down on Lake Shannon and await further orders. If they don't hear from us in a couple of hours, they're on their own. If they can't get any reception, they can take a plane up once an hour and try to contact *Maaka-Kakja*. Otherwise, they can still support the ground elements here, but don't let the boneheads push 'em around! We just won their damn battle for 'em," he added grimly.

Silva sent the message, and the two men and Lawrence turned northeast for the pass Chack and Blair had crossed to New Dublin.

"Have Major Jindal bring his company up even with us, on those parallel streets to the right, then move up several more . . . sections? Blocks! Several blocks, and wait for us to do the same! Oh, and watch for people on the roofs! Ask their aid in spotting enemy concentrations. They've been most helpful."

"Aye, sir," said Shmuke, and he trotted off with his squad.

The "mystery company" they'd joined near the Company HQ was one Jindal put together much like Chack had. It even included some of Blair's men. No one had been prepared for urban combat like this. The only good thing was that the Doms apparently weren't very good at it either; and even fractured as they were, the allies were pushing from all directions while the enemy had little choice but to contract toward that heavy bastion in the northwest of the city.

That didn't mean the fighting had gotten easier. The first thing Chack and Jindal accomplished together—with the help of the light six-pounder an industrious Lemurian artillery crew had brought forward—was the capture of the holdouts in the Company HQ house. Several double-shotted loads collapsed the south-facing portico, and a final round of

double canister preceded a bayonet charge by the two companies of
'Cats and men. The fighting in the rubble of the entrance, and then
through the corridors of the building, had been savage but ultimately
futile for the defenders. Some surrendered—rebels and Company men
for the most part—and were dragged roughly into the street where
Chack and his Marines had been pinned down.

"What shall we do with them?" Jindal had asked, still breathless after
the fight. Chack saw the cobbler and his sons coming from the door he'd
entered earlier. More "rooftop militia" appeared as well, from other
doors and buildings.

"We can't take them with us," Chack said. "You, sir," he addressed
the cobbler. "We must move on. We have wounded, and perhaps twenty
prisoners here. Can we leave them with you?"

"Aye," said the cobbler. 'We'll do whatever we can for your wounded."
He'd looked hard at the prisoners, some he likely knew. "We'll take care
of *them* as well."

That was almost two hours ago, and Chack and Jindal had finally
linked up with the Marines who'd taken the port facilities. Most of those
had moved east and southeast toward the still-unconquered fort. Its
guns had finally fallen silent, but it hadn't surrendered. Apparently, Blair
was moving north, going for the bastion, but much was still confused.
Many enemy troops were still encountered in what had to be Blair's rear,
and clumps of Marines were swept along as Chack and Jindal advanced.

"Jindal's on the move!" came a cry from above. Chack had sent a few
Marines to augment the rooftop militia and help form a verbal semaphore system.

"All right, take your positions," Chack ordered. As often as not, when
one element moved forward, enemy troops ran out in front of the other,
trying to flank the first, or just get out of the way. Chack never knew
what their intent was, and didn't care. The idea of receiving or giving
quarter still struck him as odd. Sure enough, dark forms appeared in the
flame-lit streets, scurrying around a corner and heading in their direction.

"Make ready!" Blas-Ma-Ar cried beside him. The growing gaggle of
Doms tried to slow their advance, suddenly aware of their mistake.

"Fire!" Chack yelled. The booming volley echoed down the rubble-strewn avenue and men fell, or clutched themselves, screaming. Others bored in. In the flashes, Chack saw the uniforms of these men and recognized them as "Blood Drinkers," the elite, special force of the Dom Army, commanded by their "Blood Cardinals" and sworn to their twisted "pope." *They* wouldn't ask for quarter. "Bayonets!" Chack yelled. "At them!" He lunged forward himself, his old Krag lowered. His hatred for the "Blood Drinkers" rivaled his hatred for the Grik. Even badly outnumbered, this group of Doms sold their lives dearly, but none were left for Chack to kill when he reached the melee.

Blas grabbed him from behind. "Quit that!" she seethed forcefully. "You get killed, who'll take over here? Not me! Our guys would be okay, but you think these Im-pees do what *I* say?" She snorted. "Not goddaamn likely! I'm just a dame to them, a forrin 'ape' dame to some! We still win this fight if you're dead?"

Chack almost laughed at the little female shaking him by the arm— then remembered a time when *she'd* been shaking, under entirely different circumstances. She'd been through a lot and come a long way. And she was right. Suddenly, as often happened in the midst of battle, he thought of his love, Safir Maraan, impossibly distant. *She* wouldn't be holding him back; he'd be trying to restrain *her*—but that was what kept them balanced. She'd been born to this, but he'd come to it late and without her influence, or more properly his need to influence her, he chased it like an addict. He suddenly missed her so intensely, he felt almost ill.

"I . . . will try to refrain from impulsive acts, in future, that might leave you with the burden of command," he said.

"Daamn well better," Blas muttered, blinking rapidly as she released him and turned away.

"Females," Chack grunted. "All right," he said, raising his voice. "Wounded to the rear. The rest of you, let's move up to that next street crossing. Major Jindal may be about to give us more business; I hear firing from his direction!"

"That's not Jindal!" came the voice of a Marine on a rooftop. "That's one o' yer bloody flyin' machines! There's a dragon latched onto it, an' it's comin' down! Somebody's shootin' one o' them fast shooters at it!"

Almost at that instant, the plane staggered overhead, aiming for a bayside park a few blocks over. A grotesque, winged shape was plummeting away from it, but another was underneath, clutching its tail.

"Continue the push," Chack said. "I'll rejoin you shortly. If any still live when that craft comes to rest, I must hear their news and observations at once! Anyone who questions Lieutenant Blas-Ma-Ar's orders will regret it! Half a dozen volunteers, with me!" He looked at Blas, and his eyes and tail flashed irony, confidence, and fondness simultaneously in the pulsing lights of the citywide battle. In an instant, he raced off in the direction the "Nancy" disappeared, followed by a mixed group.

"Hold up!" cried a 'Cat in the "point" position of the squad, flinging himself against a plastered corner as white, dusty chunks erupted around him. He slammed back against the wall as several more musket balls whizzed past. "A dozen—red on coat fronts; more 'bloody boys,' work their way to plane!" he said.

"Did you see it?"

"Ay, te plane busted up, one wing tore off—hit tree, I tink. Lizard bird still 'live, but busted up too!"

"Did all the Doms fire?" Chack demanded.

"Ah," the point 'Cat blinked furiously. "Ay, most."

"Then at them!" Chack yelled.

Not all the Doms had fired, and one of the two Imperials in Chack's squad went down as they rushed the "Blood Drinkers" with the disconcerting Lemurian battle shriek Pete Alden had once compared to a "Rebel yell." Almost on top of the frantically reloading Doms, they all planted their feet and fired directly into them, then leaped forward with their bayonets. The elite troops almost never surrendered, but these never even had a chance to decide. All were killed while either still doggedly reloading, or reaching for bayonets. Chack twisted his Krag and dragged his own sixteen-inch steel from the chest of a writhing man and snapped his gaze toward the wrecked plane, when a mournful, hissing wail caught his attention. The lizard bird had been flung against some other trees beside a nearby circle of benches in this apparent "park" area, and it was quickly stumping back toward the smoking wreckage, dragging a shattered wing and leg. It used its other folded wing like a foreleg, though, and its progress was surprisingly swift. In an instant, it was between them and the broken "Nancy," its jaws agape, protecting its "prize."

This was Chack's and his squad's first real look at one of the things, and it did look shockingly like a big Grik, with thicker, oddly colored plumage—and, of course, wings instead of arms. Chack's squad was furiously loading its muskets, and the thing, seemingly convinced they didn't mean to challenge it, turned its attention back to the plane. Chack opened the bolt of his Krag enough to ensure there was a round in the chamber, and raised it to his shoulder. Just as the beast peered into the rear opening in the fuselage, where the observer sat, a rapid burst of yellow-orange flashes *tat-tat-tat*ted from within, and the "flying Grik" collapsed backward, flailing and flopping with a spastic energy that only lifeless creatures seemed capable of. Chack lowered the Krag and sprinted for the plane. "Two with me!" he shouted. "The rest of you, keep a careful watch! Others will have seen the crash!"

Reaching the warped, wingless wreckage, he saw a practically shaven head, followed by a pair of massive shoulders, a Thomson SMG, and then mighty arms pried themselves through the relatively small oval opening like a brontasarry emerging from an improbably tiny egg. The head swiveled, exposing a blond beard and black eye patch. A good eye focused on Chack, and the brow above it arched.

"Goddamn snakey-bird bastards!" Dennis Silva grumbled. "*This* ain't my fault!"

"Dennis!" Chack was utterly stunned. He'd heard of Silva's recent exploits, but the last time he'd seen his friend was before the "Second Allied Expeditionary Force" left to secure Aryaal and B'mbaado, and finally invaded Singapore. That force was now collectively referred to as "First Fleet," and so much had happened since. . . .

"It's me in the battered flesh, Chackie! Are you gonna stand there starin' and chewin' yer cud, or help me outta this junk heap before I have a hydrophobic fit?"

Except for a few ugly cuts, Silva emerged relatively unharmed. Quickly, they practically tore the plane off Lieutenant Reddy. The man was unconscious but alive, and they carried him to a group of trees and laid him on the grass. Lawrence was banged up, but not too badly. They'd found him in the nose of the plane, under its pilot, where he'd tumbled during the crash. He limped a little from smashing the control stick and rudder pedals with his hip, but he quickly busied himself removing their weapons from the wreckage.

"What about the wireless set?" Silva demanded loudly, checking Orrin's pulse.

"It's 'usted," Lawrence cried back, his voice muffled. "You 'recked it 'ith your idiot ass!" Despite his aches, Lawrence was *very* happy to be on the ground, in one piece.

"Okay . . . burn the wreck. Don't want the Doms getting a good look at it!"

"Ay, ay, *General* Sil'a!" Lawrence retorted.

"Our little lizard is growing up," Chack said fondly. He was surprised how glad he was to see them both. He stooped. "This is the 'Reddy Cousin' the reports mentioned?" he asked, looking down at the unconscious man. "Doesn't look like him . . . to me."

"Me neither," Silva said. "Not much. But he's a good'un—in different ways. We need to take care of him."

"Of course. The area behind us is mostly secure now. Take these troops and escort him back to the harbor. You will meet Imperial Marines and possibly shore parties from *Salaama-Na.*"

"Nope," Silva said as the ruined "Nancy" began to burn and Lawrence limp-trotted back with weapons on his shoulders—and a long object in his hands.

"Send these other fellas. I done all I can in the Air Corps. I ain't been in a *real* fight in a while. I'm with you." He suddenly noticed what Lawrence had. "Oh nooooo!"

"What?" Chack asked.

"The war's lost! My be-loved 'Doom Whomper' is busted!" The giant flintlock rifled musket he'd made from a turned-down 25-mm antiaircraft gun barrel from sunken *Amagi* had broken at the wrist in the crash. He shouldn't have brought it, not for this fight, but it had saved him so many times in such a variety of ways, he never knew when he'd need it. It was his lucky charm.

"You can 'ix it," Lawrence said. He seemed equally affected.

"Yeah . . . well, bring it with us," Silva said. "You can still sling the big part, an' stick the buttstock in the shootin' pouch!"

"Why I gotta carry it?" Lawrence demanded, suddenly less concerned.

"I gotta wag this Thompson an' this heavy bag o' magazines," Dennis retorted. "Not to mention my cutlass, bayonet, an' pistol. You don't even need a sword—you got them claws."

"I broke one!" Lawrence complained.

"Woop-te-do. We get in a fight, you can set my poor rifle down—gently—an' pitch in. Till then, you wag it . . . or I won't let you go huntin' with me no more!"

Lawrence fumed but slung the broken weapon and heavy pouch that went with it.

"This reunion is swell," Chack said, "but we must get out of here." He motioned toward the now furiously burning "Nancy." "Besides, we still have a battle. We must finish it before the enemy comes over the mountains behind us."

"I agree on all counts," Silva said, "but don't worry about the last. Shinya's comin' ashore at Cork, an' maybe Easky in the mornin', with four nice, fresh, well-trained regiments, chompin' at the bit. He'll have more air too. There ain't nothin' on this whole shitty island he'll even notice bustin' through. An' as for the bad guys attackin' that Waterford burg"—he shrugged—"me an' the lieutenant, an' a few other planes pretty much took care o' that, I figger."

"What did you do?"

Dennis chuckled. "Wasn't my fault . . . mostly. Wasn't even my idea." He nodded at the motionless man and looked at the squad that would carry him out. "You take *good* care o' him. Like I said, he's a good'un!"

CHAPTER 19

////// *Central Highlands*
Grik Ceylon

olonel "Billy" Flynn was riding one of six paalkas, drawing a battery of light six-pounders on split-trail "galloper" carriages near the front of the column of his 1st Amalgamated. He still liked "Flynn's Rangers" better, and through persistent repetition, he had enough people using the term that he was confident the moniker would stick. He had two more batteries of light guns along, one in the middle and another at the rear of the column. Looking back at the winding snake of Lemurians, he was proud of what he'd accomplished and what they'd achieved. They might not be Marines, or the Six Hundred, but he'd put his thousand-'Cat regiment up against any Army unit anywhere, especially with their new rifled muskets. Soon, they'd even have breechloaders, and he couldn't wait. Since they'd been among the first to get rifles, they'd probably be the last to get the "Allin-Silva" conversions, however.

He guessed it was inevitable that he'd wound up "back" in the Army. He had good leadership skills and remembered by heart the infantry drill manual he'd been taught. For a while, Captain Reddy used him to help create a new manual that was applicable here. He'd modified and simplified the original in his head and unconsciously substituted a number of nautical terms and commands here and there, but it seemed to work okay. The new book—the first printed on this world with movable type—was titled *Flynn's Tactics*. He wouldn't admit it, but that "honor" actually embarrassed him. Ultimately, his manual set the stage for his getting his own regiment, and the irony of his command wasn't lost on him. He'd made corporal in the 77th "Melting Pot" Division during the Great War, and now he had the "Amalgamated," another "melting pot" of people from every Lemurian Home they were known to inhabit, mostly uniformed alike now, and many from places still trying to stay out of the war.

A good example of that was the nominal commander of his newest— if possibly temporary—company: Lieutenant Commander Saaran-Gaani, the brown-and-white-furred former exec of USS *Donaghey*. He was one of a few, but growing number of troops recruited from the Great South Island that *really* needed to be in the war. Not only was it a vast land with many resources, it was fairly well populated in the warmer north. He hoped 'Cats like Saaran could take their stories home and get their various Homes, or "city-states" on board. The allies needed the Great South Island much like the Brits and French needed the U.S. in the "last" war.

Billy's contemplations were disturbed by a more immediate concern—his ass. He *hated* riding palkas. With their broad backs, it was probably about as comfortable as riding an elephant. He tried to sit as he'd seen folks do in movies, riding camels and such, but the damn palka's rolling gait and this unpredictable terrain made that almost suicidal. Therefore, whenever he was "aboard" one, he was perpetually doing the splits. He'd ride only a little while more, he decided; just long enough to give his knees and ankles a rest. He'd been a submariner too long, and honestly, he had some joint issues. Some of that likely stemmed from the near-scurvy he and the others experienced on Talaud Island while marooned for the better part of a year. He'd heard the island had blown itself apart, and though he was saddened by the loss of life and the damage to their Fil-pin allies, he was glad the island was gone.

"Somebody stop this goddamn thing," he finally growled. "I've had all the 'rest' I can stand." The Lemurian mahout stopped the beast by a means Billy didn't see, and he slid gingerly down the animal's flank, to be assisted to the ground by Captain Bekiaa-Sab-At. "Lemme go," Flynn protested.

"Very well, Colonel, but if you break a leg or ankle in these rocks, you'll have to ride a paalka all the time."

"Yeah? Well, sorry, Captain. I didn't mean to snap. Just mad at my own worn-out carcass. Walk with me a little, wilya?"

"Of course."

It was beautiful here; the mountains rising on either side of the valley, the heavy timber composed of something like ferny pines. It was cool, and for once the mosquitoes weren't that bad except at dawn and dusk. Even the "Griklets," the feral youngling Grik that dogged the column all the way up from the southern coast, screeching at them, throwing sticks, rocks, and feces, and occasionally even attacking, had finally laid off.

It *did* stink, though.

The valley they advanced through had been packed with Grik just a few days before, but after Alden's breakthrough on the coastal plain, recon had reported the enemy abandoning the rough terrain to reinforce the southern approaches to the industrial heart of Ceylon; the area between "Colombo" and the natural low-tide causeway connecting the big island to the "Indian" subcontinent. The stench left by the departed Grik "Army" still lingered heavy in the valley, however. Grik didn't use slit trenches, and the reek of their dung was all-pervasive. Billy wondered how on earth they avoided epidemics. Maybe they didn't and just ate their dead. The stench of rotting flesh was strong as well.

Saaran joined them, wearing a bandanna over his face. "If this is what it smells like when the Grik leave, I'd hate to be in a confined place like this valley when they were here! I thought it was bad on the Sand Spit when we were downwind of them."

Flynn's brow furrowed. "Stink wouldn't be the worst thing about being in a place like this!" he said, looking up at the wooded flanks of the mountains. "I wish we had comm down in here." He glanced at his watch. "Another twenty minutes or so before our guardian angels check on us," he added, referring to the four-plane flight tasked to watch over the long, winding column. "Anything from the flank pickets?"

"Just Grik . . . excrement, Colonel," said Bekiaa. Her tail swished. "They abandoned a lot of their artillery, though. Orders from Colonel Grisa of the Ninth Aryaal behind us is not to destroy the guns, we might use them. Even if we don't, they'll certainly be easier to salvage on their carriages."

"True." Flynn rubbed his jaw. "Look, maybe I'm paranoid, but it wouldn't be the first time the flyboys missed something. They have to key on movement like the rest of us, and it's a lot harder to see when you're moving yourself."

"The Third Maa-ni-lo Caav, under Cap-i-taan Saachic, scouted the whole area carefully this morning, and their . . . me-naaks did not alert," Saaran reminded him thoughtfully, "but with the scent so thick, they may not have." They used a vaguely similar, if smaller—and much more agreeable—version of "meanies" on the Great South Island to track game, and Saaran was familiar with them. They weren't "pets" per se, but they did respond to affection and familiarity. Saaran respected the larger beasts' capabilities but had no desire to befriend one.

"Yeah, but this valley is just too good a place to put a cork in the bottle—hell, the Grik *were* here!" He shrugged. "I feel sorta like I'm on the conn tower of the old S-19 in the bottom of a big trough with all the hatches open."

"I agree," Bekiaa said, a little edgy. "As you say, something stinks here—besides the waste. But the pickets move all the way to the crests"—she pointed north and south—"and see no movement."

"Hmm. I hate to string the poor guys out that far, where those damn Griklets might gang up on 'em, but signal the pickets to drop over the crest—in pairs—and see what they can over there."

"We might not hear shots, or even see the puffs of smoke," Saaran reminded him. "They certainly won't be able to signal us visually."

"Then they'll just have to haul their asses to where we or other pickets *can* see or hear 'em if they spot anything," Billy said. "Pass the word back to Grisa that he might want to do the same." He looked back as far as he could see. His and Grisa's regiments were fully committed to the valley now, but the rest of the division wasn't yet. Was that good or bad? Both the Amalgamated and the 9th Aryaal were well trained, and the 9th was a hardened, veteran force. If this was a trap, could two thousand stand against whatever might be assembled against them? It occurred to him with a chill that if his instincts were correct, the Grik thought they could handle the entire division!

"Okay," he said, a little tentatively, "I want another runner to suggest to Grisa that our two regiments go from column into line, act like we smell a rat. If the Grik are up to something, maybe that'll prod them into showing us what it is. If they attack down one of these slopes, we can funnel the follow-on regiments in behind our lines."

"What if they attack down *both* mountains?" Bekiaa asked.

"Then we're screwed . . . but maybe the rest of the division can block the valley behind us, and we can retreat back to them." He shrugged. "Prob'ly nothin', anyway, just a superstitious old pigboater!"

They continued to advance a short distance until Grisa's reply arrived. Apparently, he was superstitious too and fully endorsed the scheme. If nothing happened, the worst that would occur was perhaps an hour's delay in their advance.

"Just a few minutes until the planes," Flynn said, as much to himself as to Bekiaa who remained beside him. "If we do poke a hornet's nest, maybe they'll see it before it hits us." He raised his voice. "Rangers!" he yelled, followed by other shouts up and down the column, crying out to their various companies or batteries. "Halt! Action left! Column into line by files . . ." He waited while his command was relayed and the appropriate drum cadence rumbled. "Execute!" (He'd always thought it was stupid to punctuate a command with the word "march"—particularly when troops were already marching.)

Despite the rocky, uneven ground, NCOs scampered out to the left, looking back at the troops, and the column of Lemurians that had been marching four abreast transformed into a battle line facing southwest, two ranks deep.

"Batteries! Action left!"

The "Gun 'Cats" wheeled their palkas to the right until their pieces were even with the infantry line; then the beasts were halted while the long, twin shafts were unhooked from either side of them. The animals were then moved to what was now the "rear," where they were joined by more palkas pulling similarly hitched ammunition limbers. The new twelve-pounders had single, "stock trail" carriages that hitched directly to the limbers, which were in turn drawn by a pair of palkas, but they'd been considered too heavy for the rough mountain trails.

In moments, thirty-six guns in six batteries were crewed and pointed up the slope of the mountainous ridge to the south, and two thousand Lemurians from the 1st Amalgamated and 9th Aryaal stood prepared for battle. Colonel Flynn studied the crest through his binoculars, but so far, there'd been no response to their maneuver. In the sudden near silence, he heard the sound of approaching planes.

"It's about damn time!" he said as the four-ship formation swooped low over what had been the head of the column, and obviously seeing its deployment, banked left and climbed to investigate the flank. "This is probably all for nothing," he admitted sheepishly to Bekiaa. "Everybody always says I give those Grik bastards too much credit for brains, but I spent some time talking to Rolak's pet, Hij Geeky . . . or whatever." He swatted at a mosquito. "He ain't a genius, and he's weird as hell, but he's no dummy, you know? Anyway, maybe I'm bein' a dope, but I didn't last this long. . . ." He stopped. A tiny, distant puff of smoke drifted up out of the trees; then another. "Pickets, I bet," he murmured. Several more puffs appeared, but they never heard the sound of the shots over the diminishing engine noises. The planes must have seen as well, because they banked further, aiming for the crest of the mountain just west of Flynn's Rangers. Barely an instant after the "Nancys" cleared that crest, the entire top of the mountain seemed to explode as hundreds of gouts of flame stabbed upward, shrouded in dense gray-white smoke. Two of the planes instantly crumpled and fell. One spiraled down, out of control, and painted a smear of orange fire and greasy black smoke on the skyline. A single ship staggered on, trailing smoke.

"Sonuva bitch!" Billy yelled, just as the thunderous reports of the enemy weapons began to reach them. They would echo in the valley for some time. "I wish for once I didn't have to be right about how shitty a thing can turn! What *were* those things?"

"I would say they were either cannon on the extreme opposite slope, or they have something similar to our mortars for firing a heavy load of canister straight up. Either way, the range cannot be great," Saaran said.

"Great enough," Flynn seethed. "I hope that one plane is able to report, because whatever did that wasn't here this morning. The Cav would've seen them." The sporadic musket fire from the retreating pickets was diminishing. Either they were breaking contact—or being wiped out. "And whatever the hell else is up there all of a sudden." He looked around.

"Colonel!" Bekiaa suddenly cried, pointing at the mountains to the north. There were small puffs of smoke there as well!

"That . . . ain't good, huh? I bet this is how Custer felt."

"How is that, Colonel?" Saaran asked.

"Like pukin'."

"Who is Custer?" asked Bekiaa.

"A dead idiot," Flynn said. Suddenly, the thunder echoing in the valley took on a different, more strident tone, with the power and malevolence of a typhoon sea. He'd heard this thunder before, just prior to the Grik assault on the south wall of Baalkpan. It was the mind-numbing, terrifying sound of thousands of Grik, roaring, screaming, pounding weapons on their shields. He shook his head, as if trying to clear it. "Except we ain't gonna be dead idiots, see? Not if it kills us! We might still wind up dead—and I can live with that—so long as we're dead heroes! I didn't quit my sugar boat and join the Army to be remembered as the biggest military dunce of the war!"

"What shall we do?" Saaran asked, thrown a little by Flynn's contradictory comments.

"Rangers!" Flynn roared in response. "From line into column to your left . . . execute!" Immediately, the nervous and confused, but motivated troops, re-formed their column, facing the direction they'd come.

Bekiaa had echoed the order like all the other company commanders. Technically, Saaran was senior, but here on land, they both knew who was really in charge of "their" company. She looked at Flynn. "What are we doing?"

"We're going to run back there and double up with the Ninth, facing north. Then, if I can get Grisa to agree, we'll try to ease back and form an arrowhead-shaped front with the First B'mbaado deploying from what will then be our right, and the third Sular extending Grisa's left flank to the mountains. Eventually, as we suck the devils down, we'll fall back into a continuous line and the other regiments behind us can reinforce as necessary! We'll get 'em into a stand-up fight on our terms instead of givin' them the ambush they wanted!"

Bekiaa glanced at the timber-cloaked mountains, wondering how far down the slopes the hidden enemy had advanced. "If we have the time," she said, her tail swishing nervously behind her.

About then, more huge billows of smoke shrouded the opposing mountains as maybe a hundred guns commenced an erratic fire.

"That's right, Captain. If we have the time." Flynn raised his voice once more. "Artillery will return fire at the enemy smoke, then retire behind the infantry. Spike your guns if you can't move 'em. Rangers! At the double time . . . march!" He saw Saaran begin to whirl and follow his company. "Saaran!" he shouted, and the brown and white 'Cat turned.

"Sir?"

Heavy roundshot began falling in the valley, followed by the heaviest rumble yet. Most fell short, but some was unnervingly close for a first attempt. Shards of rock and clouds of brown-black dust exploded from the iron spheres when they struck and bounded visibly on.

"Get your blotchy Navy ass out of here!"

Saaran blinked with fury.

"Don't even start," Flynn warned, "you're the bravest 'Cat on the island! But in case that plane didn't make it, or transmit, I need you to take the word, personally, to Queen Maraan that we're about to have a hell of a fight on our hands!" The first trickle of sprinting, howling Grik finally appeared at the edge of the woods about four hundred yards to the south. The artillery that hadn't already limbered up, nearly half, fired into them and the forest beyond, the guns jumping against their springy trail shafts and rolling backward—where impatient hands waited to hitch them to palkas. "Tell her I think we've set the hook pretty hard, and a little help would be appreciated. Also, unless the flyboys have been making up fairy tales, the fact this bunch is here probably means there ain't really doodly in front of General Alden, no matter what it looks like! Got that?"

"Ay, ay, sir! If you . . . insist it must be I who goes!"

More roundshot struck, some among the artillery palkas, and the huge beasts screamed shrilly in agony and terror as some were sprayed with rock or iron fragments and others were simply shattered. A red mist flecked Saaran's white fur.

"I do! Now git!"

With a lingering glance at Bekiaa, Saaran raced off.

"If they send any more planes up this way, tell 'em to watch their ass!" Flynn yelled after him, then looked at Bekiaa. She and several of her company, all sailors or Marines from TF Garrett, remained with him as the rest of the company trotted away. Flynn looked at the "Gun 'Cats," still wrestling with maybe a dozen guns and their wounded or balky animals.

"Leave 'em, fellas!" he shouted. "Spike 'em and go!" A solid mass of Grik was now descending as if being poured from the tops of the mountains. Crossbow bolts flew thick.

"If you don't want to be a 'dead idiot,' Colonel, I recommend we do the same," Bekiaa said sharply.

"Oh, all right. Just tryin' to be the last, like in the movies, you know? We're all gonna be heroes outta this one!"

"I for one cannot 'live with being a dead hero,' and the 'last' ones here are not going to survive."

Flynn looked at the few remaining Gun 'Cats, utterly fixated on saving their weapons, oblivious to orders or danger. "Say, I bet you're right. Let's get the hell out of here!"

"Just what the hell's going on up there?" General Pete Alden demanded angrily.

"It's . . . confusing still, General," Lord General Rolak replied. The overall commander and some of his personal staff (he'd temporarily swiped Alan Letts to lead it), as well as the division commanders of Task Force West (TFW), were under the protection of a field tent as a coastal squall lashed the plain around them. Those leaders included Rolak, General Rin-Taaka-Ar of the 1st Marine Division, (1st and 3rd Marines, and the 1st Battalion, 2nd Marines, with the 4th, 6th, and 7th Aryaal attached) and General Taa-leen of the 5th "Galla" Division, composed of the 5th, 6th, 7th, and 10th Baalkpan, as well as the 5th and 6th B'mbaado. Rolak was in charge of this oddly shaped I Corps. Outside, other staff, as well as some of the regimental commanders and a security company from the 1st Marines, stood stoically watching in the rain.

"Well, get it unconfused, fast!" Pete demanded.

"We're trying, sir," Alan said. Pete's borrowed "chief of staff" looked pretty rough. He hadn't slept much over the last few weeks, and it was beginning to show. He had his "combat experience" now, and he'd learned an awful lot about logistics in the field. When this campaign was over, he'd decided to return to his old job in Baalkpan. Not because he couldn't take it; he'd finally proven to his own satisfaction that he could—despite the daily assaults on life, limb, fair skin, and sanity. But he'd seen just how important it was for him to start a real, live, staff college. This war was growing beyond what a meager handful of talented "logistics types" could handle, and they needed more support personnel even worse than they needed more troops.

"Something big popped in front of Second Corps; something recon didn't detect. Only one of our air patrol ships made it back, and it was shot to pieces. No radio, spotter dead. The pilot said it was as if the whole mountain 'shot at them' all at once."

"Artillery?" Rolak asked.

Alan shrugged. "My guess is something more like mortar tubes stuffed with junk, by what the pilot said. Anyway, he also saw 'swarms of Grik' jumping right up out of the ground and running to the attack."

"They must have been camouflaged, so the recon flights and scouts didn't see 'em. Damn, I never would've thought it!"

"Hij Geerki has hinted that, after the Battle of Baalkpan, some in their leadership developed . . . radical views," Rolak reminded him.

"Sure, but he didn't know what they'd do, or even if they'd get to live," Pete growled. "I guess they did. That damn 'General Esshk,' at least."

"So it would seem."

"What else do we know? I mean, now that some Grik have conjured up an imagination, what's it going to cost us? What kind of crack have Second Corps and Safir-Maraan got their tails stuck in?"

"Reports are just now coming in from her HQ," Alan said, reading a dripping message form passed to him by an aide. "Oh crap. They nearly got sucked into an ambush . . . here," he said, stepping to a damp map laid out on a table under the dripping canvas above. "In this pass, or valley—whatever it is. Pretty high. Anyway, somebody must've smelled a rat, because the first two regiments, the Amalgamated and the Ninth Aryaal, deployed about the time the recon flight got hammered. The combination of those two things must've tripped the trap the Grik must've hoped would catch the whole division, maybe the whole corps." His brows arched. "Lucky. Anyway, those two regiments pulled back and formed with others behind them to create a division-size front across the valley, with fairly secure flanks. General—Queen—Maraan's moving up now to support what's shaping into a knock-down drag-out."

"Enemy numbers?"

"Best guess is twenty-five to thirty thousand. You know how it is— it's not as if you can count 'em when they're all gaggled up." Alan watched Pete's expression morph from shock and horror to concern, and finally, tentative confidence. They'd faced worse odds before; II Corps apparently had a good position, and nearly all its eight thousand troops carried muskets with bayonets. Some had rifles. It would be a hell of a fight, one for the books, but the Corps should survive.

Pete swore and stared hard at the map. "Okay, I can see that . . . but why? And where'd the bastards come from? I mean, recon this morning showed about as many Grik in front of us as would be there if those attacking Second Corps had come down. Hell, our spotters *saw* them come down!"

" 'Why' is obvious, General," Lord Rolak grumbled, his old eyes also exploring the map. "To strike a decisive blow. Their attacks on us have delayed our advance but have nearly bled out the forces opposing us . . . and still we advance. Their 'straa-ti-gees' have changed, even improved in terms of maneuver, but the 'taac-tics' remain much the same. They cannot cope with our training, discipline, and modern weapons in an open-field contest." He blinked a Lemurian shrug and added a human one for emphasis. "They try something different . . . significant in itself, hoping we'll grind to a halt and lick our wounds—further delay our push on Colombo. They fight for *time*, and that's another . . . *straa-ti-gee* I would never have credited them with."

"That *is* significant . . . if true, and I'm inclined to agree it is. Damn. I *hate* smart Grik!"

"Perhaps *too* smart for their own good," Alan mumbled.

"What?"

"Okay. I'm just a supply guy, remember, but if we're right about *why*, then we have to figure *how*. Our planes combed this joint from top to bottom, and we've had a good idea where all their major troop concentrations are, or where they were headed, for a while. As of right now, all they have unengaged is a really big wad up north around that land bridge that splits Palk Bay from the Mannar Gulf, see? I'd bet my last Navy pencil they don't have what it takes to pull what they did today against Second Corps—and still keep what they've got in front of *us*."

"But it is there!" General Taa-leen interrupted. "The fliers watch constantly. They bomb! They see!"

"Maybe they see what the enemy wants them to," Alan said softly. "Throughout our advance, we've only ever seen a few 'civilian' Grik— besides those . . ." He shuddered and took a breath. He *hated* the young, feral Grik. A pack had ganged up on him while he was alone at night, using the latrine! Only his 1911 had saved him from a terrible and ignominious end. "Those Griklets," he said, finishing the thought. "But we know they exist. They've either been rounded up and herded before us, or refugee'd out on their own. Anyway, where are they?"

"You think whoever this sneaky Grik commander is, has dumped them in with his warriors facing us, to swell their apparent numbers?"

"I do."

"I'll be damned," Pete said, staring at his friend. "You really do!"

"I said so, didn't I?"

"Rolak?"

The old Lemurian warrior stared out at the Marines surrounding the tent. The rain was passing and the sun already glared down.

"I have to agree with Mr. Letts. His reasoning is sound, particularly in light of what has transpired today. It would seem the enemy commander *is* clever, and that bodes ill for the future, but fortunately for us here, now, his army cannot match him. I believe we have a grand opportunity."

Pete grunted. "Yeah . . . I hate it for more reasons than I care to name, but I guess it does make sense. God help us if we're wrong."

"God help us if we're *right*, in the long haul," Letts said. "They've always had us outnumbered, but our noodles gave us an edge—even if we're making up most of what we do as we go. Cancel that advantage and . . ." He shook his head.

Pete glanced at the wide-eyed aide who'd brought the message. "Send to Admiral Keje," he said. "Request the whole damn fleet move up and start hammering Colombo. All air to focus on the Grik formations in front of us and in the city; firebomb the hell out of them! Hold back enough to assist Second Corps in the valley, if requested, but remind them there're some scary plane-swatting weapons there. Maybe in front of us too." He looked at the faces around him. "Return to your commands, bring everything up! Lord Rolak, you and Alan stay here. There's not much to plan; our standard 'march up and piss 'em off' play ought to do it, but we need an order of battle and to make sure everybody has what they need."

"Okay," Alan said, praying *very* hard they were right after all. "When do we start the dance?"

Pete looked at his watch. "Dark in nine hours. If 'General Grik' isn't stuck all the way in with Second Corps, he might try to move something back. If he does it in daylight, we can cut him up from the air, once he's in the open. We can't stop him in the dark, so . . . we need to make sure he has nothing to come back to before the sun goes down. We'll have to hustle, but everything's nearly in place now." He looked up. "We go in two hours. Start the bombardment in one. Ships offshore now will begin simultaneously, and the others can join in as they arrive."

"Some won't be here for hours, General," Alan said.

"That's okay. Reasonable care should be taken to avoid the docks and manufacturing facilities we've pinpointed from the air, but the latecomers'll still have plenty to shoot at. I want Colombo—the disgusting, puss-filled sore it is on *this* world—turned into a gravel pit."

"Ah, should we pass the word to try to take any prisoners?" Alan asked.

"What for? We don't eat *them*! Oh never mind, I know what you mean. Orders are don't kill any Japs you see, and try to catch a few honchos in fancy clothes so we can find out more about 'General Grik,' and what else might be up. Besides that, take *no* risks to secure prisoners! In other words, don't kill 'em if they throw themselves at your feet, but for God's sake, cut their claws and bind their jaws—and kill 'em anyway if they twitch while you're doing it."

General Halik snarled with fury and literally flung the abject messenger away from him, drawing his sword as he did so.

"If you kill messengers that bring ill tidings, soon you'll have none willing to bring you any, ill or good," General Niwa said mildly. "Your messengers are not Uul, after all. They are . . . fairly valuable."

"N'galsh, that . . . traitor! . . . has fled the city with the cream of the cadre we've spent these long months forming! He didn't even *test* them against the enemy—he just took them and ran away!"

"Can you blame him? Honestly? He's no general. I told you one of us should have remained behind."

Halik and Niwa were standing near the crest of the highland range overlooking the cauldron of death the valley below had become. Both were filthy and a little scorched by a firebomb that landed nearby earlier in the day, destroying several large guns and roasting their carefully trained crews. Unlike the first such weapons they'd seen deployed in the south, these detonated on impact. The enemy revised and adapted their tools so quickly!

It was late afternoon now, and even Halik had long since wished he could end this battle. He wouldn't have started it at all, if he'd been able to properly communicate with the forces on the northern slope. He'd been forced to rely on rote memorization of the "plan," based on "you see this, you do that." Even now, few of his Firsts of a Thousand (Niwa called them colonels) were willing to exercise initiative, even if they could. Now, having insisted Niwa accompany him here, he'd compounded that error by insisting he remain by his side. Had it been nerves? Insecurity? Halik suspected so. This had been his first real test, and he'd wanted the Japh with him . . . but then he'd ignored almost all his advice! He wasn't really angry at the messenger, or really even N'galsh. N'galsh had done the only thing he knew to do. Halik was angry at himself.

"You speak truth, General Niwa," he said, sheathing his blade and staring at the smoke-choked abattoir below. He couldn't see much from where he stood, but even after the long hours of fighting, the enemy guns still thundered as frequently as they had all day, and the stutter of their "muskets" only wavered when the diminishing horde fell back out of range. Even then, curiously, some of the enemy small arms continued firing—and taking a toll—far beyond what he knew their own new "muskets" were capable of hitting anything. None of his "special" warriors armed with the things were down *there*, of course; they remained an elite guard for him and Niwa, but after their first blooding in the south, and what he'd seen here, he knew they were the future of this war.

"Call them back; end this," Niwa said softly. "They're not yet what we would make of them, but they're *becoming* good troops, General. None I've seen have run as prey, even in the face of that impenetrable wall of fire. They *are* beginning to revert, however, and many are bunching up rather badly. The enemy planes will likely return, and their mortars . . ."

"Yes, yes! I know all that! It's just . . . hard! In this one day, we've lost everything! With a single 'plan,' all is undone!"

"No, my . . . friend. Nothing is undone. As I've said many times, we've accomplished our mission here. We learned about the enemy, and he's learned little new of us. Even more important is what *we've* learned about us! It's long been an axiom among my . . . species that one often learns more from failure than success; more from defeat than victory. Not least among those lessons, I think, is that defeat is possible, even likely, if one has never seen its signs before."

"There are 'signs' all around us!" Halik snorted.

"Indeed. You've seen much that doesn't work today: too rigidly adhering to a plan, assuming that plan is too clever for the enemy to divine, overconcentration of command—all these and many more you won't do again—if you and some portion of this army live to fight another time." He put his hands behind his back. "General Halik, there are . . . some things . . . General of the Sea Kurokawa admires about your Uul. He admires what he calls their 'discipline,' their willingness to do anything they're told, within the context of their understanding. Tell them to charge into certain death and they do—because few have any real concept of death, what it means, and that it will happen to them. They are told and they obey. We once watched hundreds dive into the water to assist with repairs to *Amagi*, my lost ship. They were torn to shreds by the fish. They finally managed the simple task set them, but *hundreds* died to accomplish what might have been achieved with no loss had any real thought been given to the assignment. Kurokawa believed that was discipline, but it wasn't." He paused. "I don't know if you're ready to discuss what I think it *was*, but it wasn't *discipline.*"

He pointed down at the battle. "Those . . . creatures and their Americans have true discipline! They move and fight as a team, like a machine—and not the way your laborer Uul behave, with no thought or understanding of what they do. Our enemy, each and every one of them that performed that admirable maneuver to evade your trap, knows what is expected of them, knows they can die—they are as intelligent as you or I, it seems; yet even though they're likely terrified, they do their duty. *That* is discipline! The contrast between that and your average Uul couldn't be more striking.

"Now we've begun to form troops with a measure of understanding for what they do. Some are even *afraid*, I think; yet they don't 'turn prey,' as you put it. They begin to *know*, as you once did, yet still they *do*. We must preserve that!"

Halik hissed a long sigh, looking to the west where a great column of smoke rose above Colombo. "I will end this, if I can. Some will not retreat; others *will* turn prey at last, once they show their backs to the enemy. . . ."

"Perhaps." Niwa stared down at the milling, dying army. "Perhaps not. If so, you can't help that. Save what you can."

Halik raised his voice. "The horns will sound the 'gathering' call!" He listened as his order was obeyed and the horns boomed along the crest, answered by others on the far slope. Almost immediately, the Grik horde, savagely depleted, began to stir; to disengage.

"See?" Niwa said with satisfaction. Greater, stricter "horn" training had been one of his own contributions. The horns not only told the warriors what to do, they gave them direction and ensured them that "someone" was watching over them, leading them. The sound of the horns gave them something to cling to when they were confused. "They've learned *that* well enough. Their obedience to the horns has become even stronger than their urge to attack—or break!"

"What now? Will the enemy pursue?"

Niwa glanced at the sun nearing the horizon. "I think not. He's been mauled as well. He'll expect us to move to the relief of the city, and if it has truly fallen as the message suggests, he'll move to intercept us. I recommend we retreat north, as quickly as we can. We may have time to destroy some of the factories and other facilities, but I submit our greatest imperative is to save as much of the Army, this one and that to the north, as possible; to prevent a rapid enemy advance across to India. The factories may be here, but the things that feed them are there. You must decide on which side of the land bridge to try to stop them. Once that's done, you must also decide if we should stay, or if it's time to leave at last, to pass what we've learned to others."

"It will be as you advise," Halik hissed. "I will decide that last question when the time comes."

"Jesus, they're pullin' back!" Colonel Flynn gasped, pausing his attempt to pound a stuck "Minie" bullet down the fouling choked barrel of his Baalkpan Arsenal rifled musket. A few of his Rangers also paused to look, to *realize* what he said. They'd never had a chance to throw up a proper breastworks, but they'd improvised one during the battle with the bodies of the Grik dead. Those with shields had tried to protect the firing line from the hail of crossbow bolts, but the killed and wounded in almost every engaged regiment approached thirty percent. Naturally, the Rangers and the 9th Aryaal had been hardest hit, being in the center, and the 1st Amalgamated had been forced into close combat with their slightly slower-loading rifles. Flynn vaguely suspected there'd always be a place for the "buck and ball" smoothbores as long as the fights remained such close-quarters affairs.

The Grik had paused about two hundred yards away after their most recent rush was blunted. Even they had to rest a while, though their attacks had been unnervingly well coordinated for a change. Their ranks remained disorganized, but they seemed to have adopted the concept of successive "surges" that allowed those most closely engaged to fade back and be replaced by others at the point of contact. This allowed them to keep the pressure up far longer—and more exhaustingly—than ever before. The change was a . . . chilling development. Finally, they'd pulled back en masse beyond what they must have considered "musket shot," apparently to sort things out a bit. They weren't out of range of the new rifles—or canister from the artillery, of course. For the last ten minutes, the Grik just stood there and took it as if unsure what to do while the battered II Corps obligingly poured it in. Flynn had been wishing for the hundredth time he had one of Hij Geerki's "recall" horns, when suddenly the things began to thrum in the valley, and the massive Grik swarm began obediently withdrawing.

He was stunned. Never had the Grik just backed away from contact— never. In the past, they always either fought until they died, or ran. This was completely new. Alden hadn't reported seeing anything like it during his march up the coast.

"Jumpin' Jehosephat! They're licked!" Billy paused, his eyes widening. "And they *know* they're licked! Goddamn! Let 'em have it! Pound 'em! Don't let 'em just *walk* the hell away!" The firing around him redoubled, and he tamped the misshapen projectile the rest of the way down the barrel. Putting a copper percussion cap on the cone at the breech, he thumbed the hammer to full cock, aimed into the departing mass, and fired. The recoil of the weapon wasn't really all that bad— unless one had already fired it a couple of hundred times. His shoulder felt as if somebody had been whacking it with a baseball bat. "Mortars, damn it! Hit 'em now, while they're bunched up!"

"We're out of bombs!" someone hollered. "More are on the way, but we have none now!"

Flynn swore and looked around. "Corporal, gimme some water!" he cried to a 'Cat hurrying by with a bucket. The corporal paused while Billy threw some salty-tasting water at his mouth with the floating cup, then spat some down the barrel of his rifle. "Ghaa!" he said, spitting out the foul remainder. He plugged the muzzle of the weapon with his finger and tilted it in a seesaw motion so the water would slosh back and forth in the bore. "Musta been an artillery sponge bucket!" he said, spitting again and pouring the black water from his rifle onto the ground. He placed a piece of cloth over the muzzle and ran it down with his jag-shaped rammer head. Withdrawing the rammer, he stuck it in the ground at his side, and the now-soggy, blackened cloth fell away. He popped two percussion caps and blew down the barrel, then snatched another paper-wrapped cartridge from the box at his side and tore it open with his teeth.

The firing around him was diminishing, except the artillery, which was now shooting the lighter spherical case—he could tell by the report. White puffs cracked and blossomed over the retreating enemy, spraying shell fragments among them, but still they moved away—as a mob certainly, but a *controlled* mob.

"It is over, Col-nol Flynn," said a familiar voice behind him. He turned and quickly saluted Safir-Maraan, throwing most of the powder in his cartridge at his face. Self-consciously, he wadded the torn paper around the bullet and dropped it back in his cartridge box.

"Aye, uh, General," he said. Regardless of her various other titles, on the battlefield, she was "general" first. "It looks that way," Billy added. He reached up and pulled the helmet off his head, revealing his thinning mat of sweaty red hair. He started to slick it back but was shocked to see how badly his hand had begun to shake.

Safir took a deep breath and almost gagged herself. The stench of the morning had grown exponentially worse with the addition of the mangled corpses all around and the fog of smoke that clung near the blood-drenched ground. Her normally resplendent silver-washed armor was stained with red turning to black, and her black cloak was torn and tinged with shiny reddish patches. Knowing her, she'd probably been right up on the line with a musket and bayonet at some point, Billy thought. Not the best place for a corps commander!

"But they retire in . . . I think you say 'good order'?" she said huskily, holding her hand over her mouth. "Oh, surely this is the stench of the unlighted void! I barely noticed it before." She fumbled for her water bottle and took a long swig. "Odd, the things one perceives immediately after these 'new' battles—at least I've found it so," she almost whispered. She composed herself and gestured toward the retreating Grik. "I do not like to see that."

"Me neither," Billy agreed, stunned to see even an instant of weakness from the indomitable Safir. "It was a hell of a fight, but we'd turned the corner—even if there *was* a bunch more than I thought at first. Sorry about that. It's hard to count 'em when they're all wadded up. Anyway, any battle in the past, we would've about wiped 'em out. This *retreatin'* crap, instead of just runnin' away, gives me the creeps."

"I feel 'creeps' as well," Safir admitted. "We must report this immediately." She looked at him. "Thank you Col-nol," she said sincerely. "I admit, I didn't know what to think of you and your Amaal-gaa-mated before today. You are a strange man, originally from a *very* strange craft! But your and Col-nol Grisa's regiments likely saved my entire corps today when you 'smelled a rat,' as Lieutenant Saaran-Gaani put it. You have my most profound appreciation."

"More like 'smelled a turd,' General, but thanks. How's Saaran? He never came back. We have to come up with a portable wireless we can use on the march! It would still be line o' sight, but we wouldn't have to send runners up and down the line!"

"Yes. I see no practical way to use wire as we did at Raan-goon! They say we will have better baater-ees and wireless sets soon." She blinked a shrug. "Saaran is lightly injured, but fine. He tried to return, but tumbled from the back of a paalka!"

Billy laughed, then sobered. "I lost a lot of good guys today."

"As did we all."

Bekiaa-Sab-At finally gave the belated order for the nearest artillery to cease firing, and its example was soon followed by the other batteries up and down the line. She stepped wearily up beside Flynn and also exchanged salutes with Safir Maraan. Bekiaa looked terrible—again—and this time she had a Grik crossbow bolt buried between the twinbones of her left forearm. She'd refused to leave the front. "Shall we chase 'em?" she asked.

"No," Safir said reluctantly. "They outnumber us still. I estimate now that we engaged upward of forty thousand today. Even if we've killed half the vermin, they could still overwhelm us in the open, in the dark, and we suffered sorely as well. No, we will consolidate the line and stand down those who were most heavily engaged. I've already sent cavalry to scout the high flanks, but I do think it's over. Here." She looked at Billy. "Tend to this stubborn Maa-reen female . . . and your Flynn's Raangers! We will need you all again!"

* * *

"We've got the city, Admiral," Alden said when Keje-Fris-Ar entered his tent, now erected inside the original Grik defenses.

Keje was in his martial best: his new white Navy tunic and blue Marine-style kilt. The polished, chased, copper scale armor he'd always worn in battle was fastened *over* the tunic, though, and he still wore his old helmet. He also had standard-issue leggings and a web belt with a 1911 Colt holstered on one side and his old "skota" or "working sword" hanging from the other. He looked like a short, armored Navy bear.

"Splendid news, Generaal Aalden," Keje replied. "When I got word that you desired the fleet to shift our fire to the north, I suspected as much and promptly came ashore! I hope I do not intrude."

"Of course not!" Pete grinned. "This is a big deal, sir. The first time we've ever kicked the bastards out of one of their own provincial capitals! At least, Rolak's pet Grik claims that's what Colombo is. The little creep even acts excited for us, if you believe that!"

"I cannot fathom the Grik mind, Generaal. Even Lawrence has . . . exceedingly odd notions, and he is not Grik. Perhaps Hij Geerki is sincere, but I could not care less. Your victory here today, and Queen Protector Safir Maraan's victory in the highlands are the greatest acts of the age! They will be recorded in the very scrolls!"

"Those scrolls of yours are going to get mighty long if we keep adding to them at this rate," Pete said less enthusiastically. "We need to keep a history of this war, damn straight, but your 'scrolls' are sacred—and these battles today were an unholy mess. You know the details of the battle in the mountains?" Keje nodded. "Yeah, well, that was a real fight," Pete continued. "This here was mostly just butchery once we broke through the first couple of countercharges. Rolak was right. General Grik filled his ranks with civilians; fishermen, artisans, builders, farmers—most were a buncha fogies by Grik standards. More head crests, like officers have, than we've ever seen before. A few females too, apparently, though you can hardly tell by lookin' at 'em. Fatter, no crest, that sort of thing. Same teeth and claws."

"Have any been found like Lawrence's 'Great Mother'?"

"No. Thousands of eggs left in joints like chicken coops, probably laid by the regular Grik broads hereabouts, but no big mama." He looked away a moment. "I ordered all the eggs smashed. The few prisoners we took so far didn't give a shit. You know? That part still gives me the heebie-jeebies. Wild Griklets runnin' loose all through the woods, and nobody gives a damn about the eggs. Hell. According to Geeky, they used to eat the little buggers when they hatched. He doesn't know why they're takin' over the jungle."

"But you did secure prisoners? Any of account?"

"How should I know? Word is—again through Geeky—that the city manager, or whatever the hell he is, hauled his ass outta here with the 'special warriors,' whatever the hell that means. No word on General Grik, the guy in overall command. Maybe he knocked himself off like all the rest we've come across. Hope so. He's no Napoleon, but he was startin' to bark up some of the right trees."

"Naa-po-leon?"

"Skip it."

"What is the situation now?"

"Pretty much unchanged from my last wireless report. Victory in the mountains, but those forces didn't come back here as I'd hoped. We were waiting if they did. General Maraan says they *disengaged* and retreated in an *orderly fashion*! Must've headed north."

"I would wager that is where your 'General Grik' was."

Pete sighed. "Probably so. His stunt almost worked, you know? I can *hope* his bones are smashed under one of the goofy buildings they build around here, that First Fleet knocked flat. At least for a while." He held up his hand. "I ain't going to *count* on it, just *hope* it!" He grinned.

"You are pleased with the fleet's gunnery?"

"Oh, you bet. Naval Air did a great job too. Whatever they used to knock those planes down this morning wasn't here. They must've cobbled 'em together in a hurry and taken them all. Bet we see 'em again, though, so the Airedales need to watch out. Anyway, like I said, the city's knocked flat. Grik don't go in much for fancy digs. Mostly adobe, either kind of sensible multistory, rectangular structures, or like . . . I don't know, domes, I guess. Not much reinforcing. There're a couple of exceptions, big buildings made of stone. You clobbered a couple; the forts overlooking the harbor, but there are more that didn't take such a beating. Look like temples or something." Pete shook his head. "I have some squads going through those, rooting out some *really* wild lizards, but maybe we'll find something useful. I'll send another squad with Geeky once the holdouts are hacked out. Wouldn't want anything to happen to the little shit; he's the only interpreter to the other Grik we caught."

"Yes, and not only those, but the ones being held in Baalkpan all this time! How many did you take alive?" Keje asked.

"Altogether?" Pete's expression turned to stone. "You know, I gave strict orders that nobody risk his life to take prisoners. Most think that *seeing* a Grik is too risky to let it live, and you know, I'm fine with that after the hell we've had trying to take 'em in the past. Some of the Manilos and Sularans actually went out of their way to capture a few in 'fancy dress,' like I sorta asked." He took a breath and let it out slowly. "I'll *never* do that again." He looked at Keje. "They captured *nine*, all civvies, who might've been willing to fold anyway, like Geeky, but the warriors defended 'em or killed 'em themselves. I'm pretty sure they killed more Grik here today than we did! As soon as it went in the pot, it was as if they had orders to kill every one of their own people they could catch! It cost me almost *thirty* good troops to capture—hell, *rescue*—nine of those lizard bastards. Regardless of what we might learn from 'em, it ain't worth it, and I'll never ask it again! Kill 'em all; that's what they'd do."

Keje said nothing for a long moment. He knew Pete was angry; so was he. *Nine* out of a city of thousands! But he also knew the Marine would see reason . . . if they ever *needed* prisoners again. "So . . . how do you think we should proceed from here?" he asked.

"There's still fighting in the northern part of the city, so I don't know how much of the industrial works we'll get—whatever it is—but there're fires even farther north, farther than our deepest penetration, so it looks as though they're wrecking what they can."

"Hmm. Further evidence this 'General Grik' has escaped, I fear," Keje said.

"Well . . . yeah, maybe so."

Keje looked out at the ruined city in the dark. Some parts burned brightly while others smoldered like coals in a fire. "We must pursue," he said simply. "We have a chance to annihilate them in the northern plains before they cross the land bridge to Indiaa."

"You got it, Admiral," Alden said. "That's what I was going to suggest. We need to finish rooting this dump out, but we can handle that and be back on the move in a few days. If you head north along the coast, bomb or shell anything you see, then park your ships to cover that low-tide causeway. . . ."

"If the water is deep enough . . ."

"Well, sure. Anyway, we can sweep up behind you, guided by the 'Nancys,' and maybe we can catch 'em between us, out of hope, out of gas, out of supplies and artillery, and hopefully by then, out of their goddamn minds!"

CHAPTER 20

////// *New Dublin*

he battle for New Dublin raged furiously throughout the rest of the night as the Doms fell back toward the bastion in the northwest part of the city. Chack, Silva, and Lawrence rejoined the companies pushing north with Jindal, and after a brief meeting when Silva told them what they'd seen from the air—and Lawrence squirmed under the amazed scrutiny of strangers—the push resumed with a better idea of what they faced. More and more townsfolk, either honestly rising to aid in their liberation or cynically taking what appeared to be the winning side, swelled Chack's and Jindal's ranks to the point that they finally reestablished communications with Blair's larger force on what had become the allied left. He'd known they were coming through the coastal suburbs and palatial estates of the elite by the numbers of Doms—and their sympathizers—streaming past his own right toward the bastion. When the flood became a trickle, he knew the linkup was at hand, and he and his staff met them as the moon began to fade in the brightening sky. The entire allied line was finally reestablished among the affluent—and far less congested—homes southeast of the bastion between the mountains and the glimmering, graying sea.

"We meet again, Mr. Silva!" Blair said, extending his hand.

"We do?" Dennis asked, clasping it, and shaking vigorously.

"Well . . . yes. I was but a lieutenant of Marines at the time, but we met at a quaint dining establishment in Baalkpan before I sailed with Commodore Jenks and the squadron bound for the west."

"Zat so?"

"Perhaps you'll remember later," Blair said uncomfortably. He saluted Chack. "A most interesting night. I'm glad you're well, sir. I apologize for the . . . disorganized nature of the assault."

"I'm glad *you* made it, Mr. Blair. And as for the confusion"—Chack blinked—"my Marines have never fought a battle like this before either."

"Yeah," said Silva. "More like a drawn-out street brawl in Olongapo—with no SPs—than any battle *I* ever saw."

"What's the situation here?" Chack asked.

"The enemy has skirmishers in the dwellings ahead, but the greatest threat is that they've massed their artillery on this front of the bastion."

"If we could flank the fort, they'd be at our mercy," Chack observed.

"True, but we can't move along the cliffs on this side of the mountains. The slopes are bare and within range of their guns. They would see the movement and merely shift their batteries accordingly. And even if we could embark enough troops on ships in all this chaos to get beyond the fort, we'd have to take them nearly to Bray—which is in enemy hands—before we reach a suitable place to land them."

"Mortars?"

"Most of the crews brought their weapons up to the edge of the city, hoping to support our movements, but we had no contact with them through the night. They showed admirable initiative, and would have saved us if we'd been repelled," he admitted, "but their utility now is questionable. They're low on ammunition, and they haven't the range of artillery. If we move them close enough to drop their bombs into the bastion, they'll be slaughtered."

"We can try to get air support," Chack suggested.

"Uh, maybe," said Silva. "Lieutenant Reddy, the pilot of the plane that brung me and Lawrence . . ." He saw Blair's surprised expression. "Yeah, he's the actual cousin of 'Himself,' if you can imagine." He chuckled. "I guess it's a small world, even when two of 'em get mashed together. Anyway, he'd know what we can get and how to do it, but I ain't got a clue."

"Semaphore back up the mountains and down to Waterford?" Jindal suggested.

"Maybe," Silva allowed, "but everything at the lake looked like a mess to me—before we might've sorta made it a little worse," he added cryptically. He saw the others stiffen. "Don't worry, I reckon the Doms in the valley are the least o' your concerns, and the garrison there should be safe enough, but things were already a goose pull at the command level even before . . ." He grinned. "I *like* that Lieutenant Reddy. He has a elegant approach to fightin' I can appreciate!"

Chack's tail swished with . . . nervous anticipation, but Silva didn't elaborate.

"Anyway," Dennis resumed, "we might get word to Sor-Lomaak, who can holler at Cap'n Lelaa, an' maybe she can sort it out. But what about them flyin' Grik? Is there more of 'em? Where're they roostin'? Tough to bring more planes in when they might just get knocked down."

"I can't answer that," Blair said. "We've taken few prisoners and none would speak. The loyalists we've asked never saw them before last night, so it's doubtful they 'roost' in the city. Yet further proof this . . . treachery was planned and begun long before the attack on New Scotland! The question of where all these Doms and their support elements have been preparing still remains, however."

"Oh." Silva shrugged. "As for that, I got the word before we got tangled up with them Grik birds. Cap'n Lelaa sent a recon north, and several Dom ships was seen steamin' toward here outta the west. She figgered they were troopships, from your folks' description of their warships still bein' under sail. She recalled them scouts to be armed an' sent to sink 'em! What's west o' here where the Doms might stage up?"

"The India Isles?" Blair speculated. "A couple are substantial, but not particularly suited for habitation. They're rarely visited."

"Sounds ideal," Silva agreed. "They use 'em for a stagin' area for here. If there's anything left on 'em after this fracas, just park a couple ships there an' starve 'em out."

"Indeed, that seems the most likely explanation," Blair said, "and the best way to eliminate the problem . . . there. We still have our problem here, though."

"Why not just starve these creeps out too?" Silva asked. "I mean, you said yourself we've about got the boogers bottled up in that fort. Leave 'em to rot."

Chack was surprised by the relatively passive suggestion, considering the source.

"No," Blair said, determinedly. "They've invaded our country, and we're only beginning to learn the extent of the atrocities they committed here in the name of their sick Church! They've 'sacrificed' hundreds of people, mostly women, and not even most were indentures! Most were daughters of citizens! We must destroy them root and branch so any here that sympathize with them will learn the cost of treason!"

"I agree," Jindal growled with no less intensity.

"I as well," said Chack, less eagerly but with equal determination. "We have a much wider war to consider. Our forces cannot be tied here waiting for the enemy to starve." He looked at Silva. "I've faced these 'people' before, and they fight with near the same determination and fanaticism as Grik. Unlike Grik, however, their fanaticism is based on thought and teaching, not instinctual rote. They do as their priests demand of them *believing* it is right! As long as they hide behind those walls, we must keep sufficient forces here to protect against an attack from within, and they *are* smart enough to plan an attack to coincide with our moment of least preparedness. They might inflict heavy casualties before they're stopped, and may even raze the city completely. Worse, they won't care if all die in the attempt, because the leaders of their faith assure them they'll be gathered into paradise at the very instant of death!"

"So these 'padres' o' theirs are like Hij gen'rals, er somethin? What's the top dog look like?"

"Like those that attacked Scapa Flow, a 'Blood Cardinal' is present, and would be their overall commander," Blair said. "His vestments resemble their flag: a red cloak with a barbarously shaped gold cross embroidered upon it. Their headgear is ostentatious, but its shape is different from one to the next. The descriptions I've heard of the one here makes it sadly clear it's not that damned 'Don Hernan,' who orchestrated the plot on New Scotland. He must have fled east, back to their lands after all."

"What would happen if he got bumped off?" Silva asked casually.

Jindal snorted. "Who knows? He'd never expose himself to harm, I'm sure, but 'Blood Cardinals' are reputedly immune to 'earthly injuries'! That's one reason we'll hang the bastard for all to see when we catch him. That might go a long way toward undermining the foundations of their perverted teachings!"

"Don't they ever just, you know, croak?"

Blair snorted this time. "Oh no. To attain 'godliness'—and I *do* mean they're semideified!—Blood Cardinals must mutilate *themselves* to death! For your average Dom, it's enough that they 'die in pain at the hands of another' to enter paradise!"

"Do they really do it?" Chack asked, amazed. He knew more than Silva, but hadn't known that.

"Their 'popes' sometimes do, when they're old and sick. I'm sure they're drugged silly at the time. Usually, those like the chap here, or Don Hernan, are simply laid out for viewing *after* they've suddenly been 'called to the heavenly embrace.' I suspect they're mutilated after a natural death."

"Wow," said Dennis. "Huh. I bet them Dom soljers'd flip if they seen their head witch doctor spattered by a cannonball!"

"A lovely thought, and likely correct," Blair said, grinning, "but as I said, he'll be well protected—and better protected the longer we wait to finish this!"

Chack looked at the Imperials, then studied the condition of the troops gathered round. "We must destroy them *now*, while we have the momentum, before they have time to consolidate and improve their defenses!"

All during the conversation, the guns in the bastion continued a steady fire, demolishing houses and shops on the ground separating the two forces. The air was filled with white dust and gray smoke from shattered masonry and rampant fires. A few buildings remained standing, probably full of observers, but it was clear the Doms were making a killing ground that would be difficult to cross.

"Big guns for a fort not designed to protect a harbor. What are they? Eighteens? Twenty-fours?" Dennis suddenly asked.

"Twenties," Blair said, and Silva blinked at the odd, non-"British" standard bores.

"Watcha got in them forts Sor-Lomak's fellas took?" he asked.

"Thirties . . . but many will be damaged and none will bear!"

"So? Look, Chackie here knows you ain't gotta prod me to fight, but a great hero o' mine once said, 'Never send a man where you can send a bullet'! How long would it take to bring them thirty-pound whoppers up?"

"Considerable time, I'm sure," Blair said, "but they *would* outrange the enemy batteries and negate their efforts to improve their defenses— once we started battering them down! Mr. Silva, I've heard a . . . great many things about you, but the accounts have neglected your tactical value!"

"Oh, he's a *taac-ti-caal* wonder, gentlemen," Chack said dryly. "Just pay no heed to his . . . straa-teegic suggestions!"

"I'm too modest to crow," Silva proclaimed grandly, looking at Lawrence, who stood there with the broken Doom Whomper. The artillery duel he'd proposed would make a hell of a show, but he intended to send a few well-placed bullets of his own. "Say, anybody in this dump got any glue?"

Colonel Tamatsu Shinya strode into Waterford at the head of his column of Lemurian troops late that afternoon, still staring in wonder at the forest of blackened, skeletal trees surrounding the surely once-picturesque lakeside town. His eyes quested upward occasionally, searching the sky for "dragons," or "Grik birds" as the fliers called them in their reports. Nothing flew, not even the blizzards of parrots and small, indigenous "dragons." There was nothing in the air but smoke.

It had been a grueling day. First, they'd come ashore under stiff fire from Dom positions on either side of the beleaguered town of Cork, where the pitiful remnants of the garrison had managed to hold through the night, despite gloomy expectations. The survivors were overjoyed to see them and the mighty USS *Maaka-Kakja*, as her massive form resolved itself offshore in the light of the breaking day. Another Imperial ship of the line had joined her in the night, and added her guns to *Maaka-Kakja*'s as she shelled the enemy positions. Air strikes from the great carrier and the planes she'd recalled from Lake Shannon quickly disrupted the Doms and rebels investing the town across the Belfast and Easky roads. Unable to stop the landings, both forces withdrew as the crack Lemurian regiments streamed ashore. Imperial Marines disembarked from the newly arrived ship of the line, under the direct command of the one-armed Sean "O'Casey" Bates, who'd come to represent the Governor-Emperor himself. As soon as the enemy pulled back, Bates went aboard *Maaka-Kakja* to greet Rebecca Anne McDonald, his long-lost princess. It was a tearful and touching, if brief reunion, between the child and her onetime fugitive protector and guardian, but Bates quickly returned to shore to oversee his troops and the reconsolidation of the defenses around Cork.

The Imperials remained there while "Shinya's Division" pushed over the Wiklow Mountains and saw firsthand the results of the previous night's action in the valley below. None had seen the valley before except the local scouts who led them, but by all accounts what had once been a beautiful, green, sprawling land of old-growth timber, now more closely resembled the bristly black back of a rhino pig. Miraculous pockets of green remained in freakish clumps or lines where the vagaries of the vortex had spared them, but most was now a charred, smoldering landscape as far northwest as the eye could see. Denser smoke still choked the sky in the far distance, fed by the awesome firestorm Lieutenant Reddy's air attack the previous night had sparked. Nothing could have survived in the path of the monster the fire became, and Shinya doubted any of the Doms that came so close to retaking Waterford had lived.

They'll be lucky to save Bray itself, he thought, *unless the rains come to its rescue or the wind shifts back on itself.* Shinya was . . . horrified by the sheer scope of destruction, and suspected their allies would be none too pleased, but he knew Captain Reddy's cousin and Dennis Silva—of course Silva had been involved!—had done the only thing they could to ensure the forces fighting in New Dublin weren't cut off from Cork, or attacked from the rear. That didn't mean he was unaffected by what he saw. Tamatsu Shinya had viewed many horrors in this terrible war, and though the dead valley couldn't compare to the countless dead people he'd seen, it struck him in a visceral, almost-prescient way that deeply disturbed him.

Adding to that discomfort, all the long day he hadn't known what became of Reddy and Silva after their flight to check on the situation at New Dublin ended with a terse "bats outta hell" sent by Silva's erratic Morse, and he'd been surprised how concerned it made him. They'd lost so much in this bizarre war, but he'd come to truly believe Silva was indestructible. And there was the issue of Captain Reddy's cousin to consider. The captain had become such a source of moral strength to the western allies, not to mention these new ones in the east, some of that . . . aura . . . had been bound to rub off on his cousin to some degree, he supposed. How much was uncertain, but with Captain Reddy so far beyond help or even communication, and his fate utterly unknown, the possible loss of the young aviator so closely connected to his "clan" had caused a notably chilling effect aboard the ship beyond what he would've expected. It was . . . odd. Adar was unquestionably Chairman of the Grand Alliance, but whether he realized it or not, or even wanted it, Matthew Reddy had become "royalty" of a sort, and that status extended to his "family."

Finally, shortly before, a courier arrived from Cork on horseback with the latest intelligence via Sor-Lomaak, describing the battle at New Dublin and the evolving situation there. Included was a brief statement that Reddy, Silva, and Lawrence had survived the downing of their plane. Reddy had been taken to *Salaama-Na* with a concussion, but Silva and Lawrence had vanished into the swirl of battle. Shinya was relieved but still disturbed. It looked like the battle in New Dublin might require a costly frontal assault to finish, and he was anxious to get there and see the ground for himself. He was tired, his division was tired, and they had a long, long way to go.

"Halt there, I say!" cried a hoarse, officious voice.

"'Imp-ees' coming, sur," the company commander walking beside him said—belatedly.

His Springfield rifle on his shoulder, Shinya had been walking, almost oblivious to his immediate surroundings. He was so focused on the scope of the desolation, he hadn't noticed the procession of dusty, smoke-blackened Imperial officers riding toward him from the edge of the ruined town. "Thank you for the warning, Captain," he said wryly. "Have we no pickets to the right?"

"Only friends to right . . . Nothing to left," the 'Cat said.

Shinya watched the Imperials bring their horses to an ashy, dusty stop. "Perhaps you have not learned human expressions well, Captain," he said. "I'm not convinced these men are necessarily friends." He raised his voice to the new arrivals. "I'm Colonel Tamatsu Shinya. I would speak to the person in command here. If none of you are he, please lead me to him, bring him to us, or get the hell out of our way. We have a battle to join."

"The battle here is quite over!" the officious voice declared, allowing Shinya to put a face with it. The man's expression seemed more annoyed than relieved by that.

"Excellent. Then we'll continue on to find another," Shinya snapped. He kept walking.

"To what purpose? To further destroy this land?" the man snarled.

Shinya waved the column on but stopped himself. "It's been a long march already today—after a predawn landing and a short fight that began it. I'm weary. It was my understanding this battle ended in victory, for which you should be thankful. The Dominion does not treat those they conquer with kindness, true? Rejoice that the fighting here is done and you still live."

"But . . . that madman and his flying machines destroyed one of the most beautiful—not to mention strategic—resources in the Empire! This valley is almost sacred to those who live within it, and the timber is essential to the shipbuilding industry!"

Shinya looked around. "No one lives here now, and there are other forests in the Empire." He waved about him. "These trees will still make fine ships; they're only scorched on the outside."

"Damn you, sir!" raged the officer. "Have you no compassion? No understanding of the tragedy here?"

"Damn *you*!" Shinya roared, his eyes darker than the blackened trees. "Have *you* no understanding of the word '*war*'? I desire words with the *commander* here, not fools. If you can't produce such a specimen, I'll be on my way—anticipating the day you and I meet again on the Dueling Grounds at Scapa Flow!"

"I command here, Colonel Shinya," another officer announced firmly, after a brief hesitation. "As of this moment. Run along now, Colonel Meems. Perhaps I can convince this belligerent gentleman not to murder you in front of your children, come the next 'Meeting Day' Sunday!"

The officious officer whirled his mount and galloped away, followed by another, amid a rising, gray cloud, leaving four mounted men.

"Major Gladney, at your service," the "commander" said, dismounting. "Of the artillery. Meems is an excitable fellow, where his trees are concerned. He has holdings here. Please, I brought maps when I saw your column. We have recent news of the fighting across the Sperrin range, and I think I can show you some pathways your infantry might use that will place you well to support our friends. The paths are quite steep in places and utterly unsuited for artillery, but men or . . . your people . . . should be able to negotiate them in daylight."

"Thank you, Major Gladney. I'd hoped as much." Shinya paused, looking at his tired troops marching by. "Can these trails be found in the dark?"

Gladney was taken aback. "I suppose, by one who knows them. I could not recommend it, however."

"Nevertheless, there will be a good moon again tonight, and we must move with haste."

"You're talking about a march of thirty miles—as the parrot flies!— over two rough, high ranges without stop!"

"We will stop . . . now and then. I may not make it with all my troops, but I'll certainly have my Marines. They have . . . practiced marches such as this."

Gladney shook his head. "Very well. I'll see that you have guides."

Sunday, January 8, 1944

"Well, well," Silva said, staring through an Imperial telescope with his good eye and stifling a yawn. "I figgered it was gonna be a helluva show. Glad we got here early for a good seat, hey, Larry?"

All night, the big guns in the bastion and the heavier ones the allies dragged forward from the ruined forts flared and snarled thunderously at one another, jetting white, orange, and yellow fire from vents and muzzles amid sparkling streaks of tiny red embers. The bastion was taking a pounding, as was the entire city most likely, but the Doms simply couldn't give as good as they got. They were more concentrated, engaging well-placed and dispersed targets, and the weight of metal alone left them at a disadvantage enough to smother them eventually. That fact didn't seem to discourage them, and they did their best to match the allies shot for shot. Silva had to wonder just how much ammunition had been stowed in the bastion. The Doms had to know they couldn't last long under such a storm of iron and must've decided to use their artillery to cause as much damage to their enemy—and the city—as they could before their guns were silenced.

"Are you sure our guys know we're here?" Lawrence asked nervously when a heavy roundshot struck the building on the ground floor below, crashing through the volcanic rock wall and sending pumice and plaster dust swirling up the stairs into their second-story overlook.

Silva turned and spat a yellowish stream of "tobacco" juice that missed Lawrence's clawed hand by inches. "*Course* they know, dummy! You think I'd lie here all comfterble an' ser-een, careless o' danger, if our fellas didn't know we was in what the Doms'd expect to be a prime target for *our* guns?"

"Yess!" Lawrence hissed darkly. "That *was* one of '*our*' guns!"

Silva shrugged in the gloom. "So? With all that flashin' out there, some poor gunner was prob'ly seein' triple. 'Sides, it might raise suspicion if they didn't shoot at this shack once in a while. It *was* an observation post, after all."

Six Dom corpses kept them company in the building that had once been a drying house for a wheelwright. The Imperials made good wheels and the place was full of them. There were probably thousands of spokes and felloes of all sizes, and hundreds of hubs. Five dead Doms were downstairs where they'd been killed by Silva's Thompson when he and Lawrence burst in upon them, utterly unexpected. A sixth man had fled upstairs, but Lawrence caught him from behind and tore out his throat before he could leap from the window they now stared through.

"I wonder why the ene'ee doesn't shoot at us," Lawrence said. "It's not as if we send any signals. They ha' to think we're here."

"Naa. What would we do if we was them dead Doms? Run back 'n forth 'mongst all that iron an' shit out there? Make a light? They prob'ly had 'em here for daylight spottin', or to holler if we was doin' somethin' . . . like we did. Now, quit bein' a weenie!"

Dawn began to break at last, and the cannonade slowly tapered off. It was as if each side yearned for a look at what they'd done to the other. Then, by some unspoken, mutual consent, all the guns on the north side of New Dublin gradually fell silent. Sunday was a holy day to all present, except Lemurians, and perhaps no one wanted to be first to resume the killing under the bright sun creeping above the eastern sea and displaying for all to view what that terrible night had wrought. Dark smoke towered into the sky from a large percentage of the city, rising above the mountains and joining a purple-brown haze moving west. Dennis, and likely the rest of the allies, caught their first real glimpse of the "dragons" then, spiraling high above on rising thermals in the clear air to seaward. There weren't many, maybe half a dozen in view, and they weren't nearly as scary in the daylight—at least to Dennis, who'd seen far more frightening things. They *did* look like big Grik, though, with longer, more feathered tails—and broad, almost batlike wings, of course— and he knew if Lieutenant Reddy had been able to see them they'd have never brought his "Nancy" down. One of the creatures approached the battlefield from upwind and swooped down to light on a corpse, savagely tearing into it. Where the body was, it had to be a Dom.

"Eww. Not particular about the menu, I guess," Silva said. "Flyin' Griks, all right. Nasty bastards. Can't even tell whose side they're on down here!" He blinked. "Hey! Maybe they *can't* tell, with everything so mixed up. I wonder what good they are? They would'a had to already be here before the Doms ever saw a plane! Maybe they use 'em for goin' after ships or somethin?" He shrugged. "Get a load o' this, Larry! Your lofty relations got shitty table manners!"

"Not relations!" Lawrence snapped. "You're a 'right guy,' Sil'a, usually. You're also an asshole!"

"Well, this world is so screwed up, I guess it's up to me to balance the scales," Dennis replied philosophically. He continued to watch the creatures kiting lazily above. "Not real energetic this mornin'," he muttered to himself, "and they don't seem to care much for smoke. Every time one gets close to any, he veers off, soon as he notices it. Huh."

The "cease-fire" persisted, and it started getting hot in their upstairs lair. Eventually, a distant church bell tentatively rang, then another. Still the Doms didn't fire.

"I'll be damned," Silva said. "I was hopin' for somethin like this!" He was peering through the telescope again, adjusting the length to sharpen the focus.

"What?"

"Everbody's takin' a break from the killin', for a prayer meetin'! Since that didn't poke the Doms into shootin' at the 'heretics,' maybe they'll have a 'God *save* my murderin' ass, 'cause I'm fixin' to *die*' meetin' of their own!" He shifted his view to the steep mountains beyond the enemy stronghold, refocusing and examining, then returned it to the bastion. Quite a few guns had been dismounted, their carriages shattered, and the walls were largely battered to rubble. There were probably still more than two thousand men inside, some near remaining guns and others milling around. Corpses had been piled in heaps, and the yellow-and-white uniforms of Dom "regulars"—"Salvadores" he'd heard them called—and the yellow and scarlet of the "Blood Drinkers" were spattered and smeared with blackening red. He stiffened when a group, not nearly as soiled as most, emerged from what looked like a companionway in the ground, near the most heavily reinforced portion of the structure.

"Yes indeedy! That goofy-lookin' devil's *gotta* be ol' Bunny Crap hisself!"

During the night, Silva's name for the Blood Cardinal had changed many times. First, it was simply "B.C.," but that didn't seem right for a lot of reasons. Finally, he'd taken the initials and expanded them in numerous ways, ultimately settling on "Bunny Crap" with a vigor Lawrence didn't understand. Of course, he had no idea what a "bunny" was. Maybe their excrement was particularly notable?

Silva hefted the Doom Whomper and inspected the repaired wrist in the growing light. The brownish glue hadn't quite set, but the joint seemed firm. He'd also wrapped it tightly with about a thousand turns of fine, strong thread. It *felt* as if it would hold. A bunch of dust and other debris had stuck to the tacky glue saturating the thread, but the weapon was otherwise spotless. "Gimme my pouch," he ordered. Lawrence handed it over. Dennis removed a "paper" cartridge. (Although the allies had "real" paper now, the cartridges were a kind of early "industrial" grade, unfit for writing on, made from pulped, pressed "linen," and waxed when assembled.) He tore it open and poured the powder down the barrel. Then he opened a small wooden box he'd made in one of *Maaka-Kakja*'s shops, expressly for protecting a dozen "perfect" bullets from deformation—particularly of their relatively fragile "skirts." He chose a pair of the massive, prelubed projectiles and laid one aside, then carefully inserted the other into the muzzle. Drawing the rammer, he seated the bullet down the long, 25-mm barrel until it rested firmly against the powder charge. Removing the rammer, he handed it to Lawrence.

"You hang ready to hand me a cartridge, that other bullet, and the rammer quick, you hear?"

"I hear."

Dennis nodded and raised the frizzen of the old Imperial lock he'd lovingly tuned, picked the vent with a hammered bronze pick that dangled by a thong from the triggerguard, and poured a dash of finely ground priming powder into the exposed pan. Closing the frizzen, he retested the edge of the flint clamped in the jaws of the gooseneck-shaped "hammer," or "cock," with the tip of his finger. "She's all set," he said softly, easing closer to the window and sitting down. He'd spent some of the night erecting a sturdy rest for the long, heavy barrel, and he'd placed a wooden chair where it would support his right elbow. Carefully, he settled in.

"You sure you can shoot that long?" Lawrence asked, his eyes flicking from Dennis to the distant target. "*I* never saw you shoot *that* long! Four hundred 'Cat tails . . ."

"Just shut up, wilya?" Dennis growled. "I shot it this far enough times to mark the sight," he added, flipping up the sight slide and easing the aperture up. "I ain't done it since then," he admitted, "but I ain't had to. I know it'll do it . . . I know *I* can do it. That's what counts. Now, I'm gonna start concentratin'. Things might fuzz up, and ol' Bunny Crap's just a red blob in this sight. You get that glass and tell me everything you see!" He pulled the hammer back all the way and squeezed the rear trigger until it clicked.

Lawrence raised the brass telescope and peered through it, adjusting the length to suit his vision. The device fascinated him. He couldn't use human binoculars, but the telescope worked just fine. "He's the guy dressed in the red sail, right?" he asked.

"Yeah. Real fat booger with a goofy white hat. There's other guys in red capes, or whatever, but they got helmets on."

"Okay. I got hi . . . he. He's going through the soldiers, touching they, raising his hands o'er they . . . I think he's going to get on a wrecked thing so they see he easier."

"Swell."

"You still got he?" Lawrence asked.

"I still gottee," Dennis mocked.

Lawrence's crest twitched upward, but he said nothing for a moment. "You . . . don't think this is . . . incorrect to your soul, to . . . *ass-assinate* he like this?"

The brow over Dennis's eye patch arched slightly, while his right eye continued staring fixedly through his sights. "Uh, nope."

"It . . . gi's I a strange . . . sensation. . . ."

"You ain't gettin' cold flippers on me, are you?" Silva demanded. "We've killed lots o' fellas together that had less of a chance than fatso over there."

"Yes . . . in war, in 'attle. Close. This 'eels . . . sneaky—like hunting, though not to eat. You should not hunt thinking, *knowing* things."

"It *is* sneaky, you nitwit! But I ain't gonna *eat* him. He's like a shiksak, see? You kill 'em to keep 'em from killin' you or people you care about. Some things need killin' just because they're bad, and there's folks the same way. *Bad* folks that need killin'—an' damn sure don't deserve a 'fair fight.'"

"Shiksaks don't know they're 'ad."

"Which makes me feel more regret killin' *them* than that fat bastard over there! Look, you know me. I'd rather walk over there and knock his brains out with a rock, but I don't expect all them other fellas around him would let me. I'm told he's the . . . shiksak's head around here. If you cut a shiksak's head off, the body might flop around a while, but it ain't near as dangerous. In this case, if I take the 'head' off, the 'body' could do the same thing for a while, but it won't necessarily die. Maybe . . . not all of it really *deserves* to die. Lotsa times, the body only does bad things it needs killin' for because the head makes it . . . see?"

Lawrence sighed noisily. "Sorta. Now I think sad to kill . . . 'ody, and not just head!"

Silva grunted. "Well, that won't do. Look, war's a hell of a thing, and there just flat ain't any rules like we think of 'em otherwise. You try not to kill folks that don't have it comin', but the bottom line is to protect those that matter to you. Period. The enemy's gonna try to do the same thing—and somebody's gotta lose. That's the deal, and it's our job to make sure it ain't us and ours doin' the losin'. Now, we been sittin' here most o' the night waitin' for this, and we better not screw it up. I gotta concentrate, an' if you won't spot for me, then get the hell outta my sight."

"I'll s'ot," Lawrence said quietly, and refocused his glass. "Okay, he's on wreckage, still talking. He's standing still—exce't his hands. Looks like all now gathered to see . . . To hear. They kneeling, looking down, all exce't 'unny Craph. He's looking down too now, still talk . . ."

Lawrence jerked when the mighty roar and physically stunning overpressure of the Doom Whomper took him completely by surprise. He almost dropped the glass, but he managed to steady it just in time to see most of the Blood Cardinal's head erupt in a crimson explosion that launched large chunks of flesh, bone, and other matter in all directions—and sent the ridiculous white hat tumbling high in the air. The bloated body beneath the red blast instantly collapsed and rolled from its perch.

"I thought you only see red thing!" Lawrence cried.

"So?" answered Silva, his voice strained.

"You knocked his head . . . gone!"

"No shit? I was aimin' pretty much 'center of blob.' Musta shot high."

Lawrence looked at him then and saw Dennis still sitting, a slightly stunned expression on his suddenly bloody face. The Doom Whomper remained in his hands, but the wrist repair had obviously failed under the intense recoil of the weapon, folding the buttstock back on itself within the frayed and shattered coils of thread. Something, most likely the hammer, had struck Silva under his right eye as the gun traveled backward, opening a long gash. Dennis shook his head and blood pattered the dusty floor around him.

"Damn. Busted my favorite gun again." He looked at Chack, his eye now clear. "We better get the hell outta here! Nobody else is shootin' just now, and they'll have seen our smoke. Remember what I said about cuttin' a shiksak's head off? I bet its whole, floppin' carcass is about to land on top of us!"

Lawrence's bright eyes bulged. "You didn't say carcass could *choose* where to land!"

Dennis gently kissed his broken weapon and laid it on the floor. "So long, Doll. I'll be back for ya!" He snatched his Thompson and the belt loaded with his pistol, cutlass, bayonet, and mag pouches that he'd removed for comfort during his shot, and hustled Lawrence toward the stairs. "Well . . . maybe it won't, but you know how them shiksaks are! They tend to flop toward what killed 'em even after they're dead! Don't forget your musket—might need that!"

"Batteries, commence firing! Fire at will," Chack roared down from the crumbling rooftop on which he, Blas, Blair, some of their staffs . . . and others . . . had assembled.

"What in blazes are *they* shooting at?" Blair demanded. "All morning, not a shot, then they grow irked at that one structure? Madness!"

"That 'structure' is the one Chief Silva asked us to avoid demolishing last night," Chack reminded him, his tail swishing irritably, "while he was repairing his giant musket. He and Lawrence must've secured it, and now they have managed to . . . *do* something exceptionally annoying to the Doms. You may have heard Silva has that effect on people?"

The "grand battery" the allies began assembling the morning before now included almost thirty big guns, plus all the field artillery with its explosive case shot Chack and Blair could bring down from the Waterford pass. From their hastily formed, then carefully reinforced positions roughly a thousand yards or "tails" (handy how that worked out so closely) from the "Dom" bastion, Chack's batteries opened fire in ones and twos, but soon the entire line hammered at the enemy from within an impenetrable white cloud of continuous, earsplitting thunder and dazzling, lightninglike flashes. Smoke billowed across the shot-churned, devastated "no-man's-land" that had evolved between the positions, and drifted west toward the base of the more extreme slope that still lay under a blanket of lingering gun smoke caused by the long duel. Despite the improved visibility daylight afforded the enemy, Chack was amazed to see, from his elevated post, almost the entire remaining Dom artillery target the nearly lone-standing structure both sides had thus far largely ignored. The building was very rapidly disintegrating under the combined hail of iron.

"Whatever he did," Blas said, "'irked' seems a weak word. It means 'a little pissed,' yes? They pissed a *lot*!"

"I certainly hope your strange friends have made their escape," Blair said, "but whatever they did to attract such fire, our guns are now slaughtering theirs with virtually no reply." He looked meaningfully at Chack. "And the enemy's attention is suddenly quite fixed."

"Very well." Chack looked at Blas and motioned her to join the "partisans" who'd brought them one of Colonel Shinya's exhausted "Maa-ni-lo" Marines, along with a squad of the first Imperial Marines he'd found when he wandered into a command post near the waterfront a few hours before. "Assist that Marine in his task, Lieutenant," he said. "He has earned the honor."

The Marine, a corporal by the stripes on his kilt, blinked appreciation, but waved at the locals. "Thank you, sir, but this is *their* Home."

"Well put," Chack agreed, nodding. "Corporal, would you assist Lieutenant Blas-Ma-Ar in showing the loyal citizens how to fire the signal rockets Colonel Shinya sent? Major Blair, I'm going to join my troops. I suggest you remain here."

Blair smiled. "Major Chack, if I thought it necessary for *anyone* to remain behind, I'd insist it be you . . . but we've *all* earned this!"

Chack grinned, his sharp teeth shining in the sunlight. "Very well, Major. *Lieutenant Blas* will remain and direct the reserves, if any are needed." He glanced at the furiously blinking female. "*She* has 'earned' the rest!"

* * *

"Rockets!" Lawrence said, staring into the sky from the debris-choked culvert where they huddled, scarcely a hundred and fifty yards from the wheelwright's shop being systematically pulverized. Fewer Dom guns were firing now, however. "'Retty rockets!"

Silva looked up at the sputtering, dissolving flares. "Those're *signal* rockets, you imbi-cile!" he shouted. The sudden thunder of drums couldn't compete with the allied guns, but it bled through between re-ports. "Attack's a'comin'!" he announced gleefully. Then his abused ears heard *other* drums, more distant, resonating against the mountains. "Ha-*ha*! I *knew* that Jap couldn't stay outta this!" He removed the twenty-round stick from the Thompson, blew dust off of the rounds clustered at the top, and slid it back in with a *shklak*. "C'mon, Fuzzy, let's try to get back in this fight before it's all over!"

Lawrence looked at the cap under the hammer of his musket. "You think it's nearly o'er?"

"Yep . . . if it ain't already! Let's go!"

"Ain't 'uzzy!" Lawrence grumbled, and the two of them bounced up amid a cloud of plaster dust and ran and leaped toward the middle of what had once been the exclusive "Company" district of North New Dublin where nothing of the desolated houses and shops still stood higher than Silva's knees. That was where the center of the advancing ranks would pass.

"It" wasn't *completely* over for some. Now almost surrounded, the Doms in the old bastion had no chance. The grueling, almost thirty-hour bom-bardment had taken a terrible toll on lives and nerves, and the "regulars" and rebels had been ready to surrender with the coming of the day and the realization they were all alone. The city burned and smoldered be-neath the smoky sky and against the incongruously achingly beautiful landscape beyond. Reinforcements weren't coming; there was *nothing* on the coast road from Bray but refugees fleeing the only direction they could from a wall of fire that encompassed all the vast valley of the is-land. The entire host Don Alfonso and the Bishop of the Seven Relics led down the Waterford road had surely been consumed by the flames of the hell they'd marched into. Even Bray would probably burn. Nothing re-

mained on that now-desolate, virtual plain between the stronghold and
the enemy in New Dublin, and nothing could *possibly* remain of the
grand plan to advance the "Modo de los Santos" and take this place for
themselves, their leaders, and the greater glory of God.

Into this outpost of ruin, misery, death, and defeat, Cardinal Don
Kukulkan de los Islas Guapas, newly appointed Ruler of the Conquest
and Saver of Souls, emerged into the hot, bloody day and went among
the shattered men of the garrison. Few were unmoved by his gesture and
most honestly expected him to Purify himself before them and release
his soul into God's embrace. Perhaps that was his ultimate intent, but
first he began to pray. He prayed that the men of the garrison would
enter paradise boldly, each with a long tally of the unclean heretics
they'd cast into hell. He prayed their families wouldn't suffer excessively
due to their sacrifice, and if they did, that God and the saints would
readily accept them because of it—in some capacity at least. He'd just
finished this last plea on behalf of the doomed men around him, the men
he was condemning with his words, his charge, his *edict* not to yield,
when his head blew up.

At first, there was shock and, frankly, superstitious awe, until an ar-
tilleryman cried that the cardinal had been *shot* by a distant, hidden
marksman. That announcement created pandemonium because it just
wasn't possible . . . was it? Regardless, the artillery commander shook off
the dreadful implications of the event and summoned the wits—or
whatever it took—to order all his guns to fire on the indicated building.
That galvanized all the troops into action of some sort, and they'd begun
reverting to their training . . . when the barrage suddenly resumed. Dominion soldiers, rebels, fugitive family members, all were caught in the
open when heavy roundshot and high-velocity shards of stone slashed
them apart. Case shot exploded over the fort, scything into flesh and
bone with red-hot copper fragments and musket balls. The hail of death
was unrelenting, and the screams competed with thundering guns and
bursting case. The garrison would cast no heretics into hell; hell had
found them there, within their demolished walls.

Then the apostates formed for their final assault, not only from the
southeast, but from the *west* where no troops could possibly have gathered! The artillery commander, who'd somehow survived the onslaught,

saw this, and his confused mind finally crystallized around a coherent thought: surrender. He raced for a pair of blood-spattered breeches that had been blown nearly off a corpse, yanked a mangled leg out of them, and cast it away; then he began tying the morbid garment to a rammer staff. A "Blood Drinker" cut him down with a sword. Outraged, the artillerymen fell upon *all* the Blood Drinkers, joined by the regulars who dared to brave the maelstrom. The elite, holy guard of the pope himself all got their most fervent wish when they were shot, stabbed, and torn apart by their own countrymen. Only then did the white flag wave above the bastion.

"All that beautiful music, then somebody called off the dance!" roared an unhappy voice behind Tamatsu Shinya. He was standing on the rubble of what had been the southwest wall of the bastion, thinking dark thoughts, and staring down into a pulverized cauldron of mangled flesh. Men and 'Cats moved through the carnage, coughing on the dust they raised and occasionally retching at the stench. They were searching for signs of life, but there were few survivors after the majority of the shell-shocked defenders had been led or carried from the fort. In spite of himself and the scene he viewed, a corner of Shinya's mouth quirked upward, and he turned. Dennis Silva stood grinning at him, Lawrence by his side. Both were filthy, and Silva had an ugly wound on his face.

"You have contrived to cheat death once more, I see," Shinya said.

"Good to see you too, Colonel. I'm fine. Thanks for askin'." Silva gestured around. "You missed a good fight." He paused. "In the city the other night, I mean. This was just killin'."

"I heard you had a hand in that . . . again."

Silva waved modestly and kicked a bronze gun tube, half-buried. "Shucks, it was nothin'." His expression turned serious. "You musta seen Chack?" Shinya nodded. "Good. He was lookin' for you." The grin returned. "You mighta missed the fight, but I sure was glad to see you come marchin' across that field, yonder. How'd you get there, and so damn fast?"

"A quite dreadful march, I assure you," Shinya said ruefully. "And still too late."

"Don't worry. There'll be plenty more fights in this war, and you can't miss 'em all! I've decided to retire from the battle-winnin' business. Folks are startin' to whisper that maybe I'm hoggin' all the glory." Silva shook his head. "Spread the joy, I always say."

Shinya chuckled. "If I had not spent so much time around you, and Americans in general, I might think you were serious." It was Shinya's turn to shake his head. "You will never retire—and you will never die . . . my friend. The day may come when you no longer breathe or live among us, but you will *never* die."

For a moment, Dennis said nothing. Suddenly, he stuck out a grimy paw. "Say, did you just call me 'my friend'?"

"I did."

"Didja mean it?"

Shinya took the offered hand. "Yes. Yes I did, if you've no objection."

CHAPTER 21

///// *Off "Monterey" Bay*

SS *Walker* and her "squadron" of three paddle frigates and a sloop exchanged signals and rendezvoused with *Mertz, Tindal, Simms, Achilles,* and the two practically "clipper" rigged oilers sixty miles offshore beneath a warm, benevolent sky, upon a placid sea. Commander Grimsley of *Achilles* had been acclaimed commodore of the "detached" Second Fleet squadron by the 'Cat captains on the other ships due to his knowledge of the waters. Besides, Jenks's former exec was well liked and respected—and he'd definitely seen more action. He was also smart enough to grasp the qualitative differences between his ship and those of the "Amer-i-caan" 'Cats, and they'd discussed tactics based on those strengths and weaknesses many times during the long voyage.

Walker made a beeline for the oilers like a hungry wolf pup to a teat, and hoses were rigged across and pumps engaged to fill her grumbling bunkers. At Matt's orders, the frigates took their turns at the other oiler.

They probably had sufficient fuel, having topped off a few days earlier, but like any destroyer skipper, Matt remained obsessive about fuel—particularly when they were this far from home. *Achilles* could replenish her coal bunkers locally, and the oilers retained a sufficient reserve to see the rest of them all back to the Isles, but what if something happened to the *oilers*?

While fueling was underway, the air between the gathered ships virtually sizzled with messages, plans, and reports. Matt and *Walker* learned of the opening stages of the campaigns for Ceylon and New Ireland, at least to the extent they'd progressed before distance interfered with communications. They also received the love and best wishes of certain persons attached to TF *Maaka-Kakja*, via Respite to Scapa Flow.

Matt sat in his chair in *Walker*'s pilothouse, gazing sightlessly out the windows at the fo'c'sle. Sandra never strayed far from his mind, and he yearned to speak to her, see her, hold her in his arms. Absence doesn't always really make the heart grow fonder, but in his case, it certainly did. . . . But at the same time, he knew a crossroads had been reached. The "Dame Famine" was slowly fading, and the primary obstacle to their "relationship" had finally, essentially passed. But that very relationship had left a kind of scar, a fundamental wound that was difficult to understand or explain. They'd suppressed their love, hidden it, then downplayed it so long, it had become a damaged, *inconvenient* thing, and as much as it had been a source of strength to them both, it had also harmed them in subtle ways. It had been so long, and so much had happened to them both since they'd seen each other, he knew they'd both changed.

A heat flashed across his shoulders and up and down his back. He'd made a fateful decision regarding that relationship; one he might regret for any number of reasons, maybe for the rest of his life. But things simply couldn't go on as they had—for both their sakes. Sandra might not agree, and she'd undoubtedly suffer either way, maybe even more than he would, but he'd made up his mind. Ultimately, the choice would be hers as well, of course. She'd already suffered, and she'd invested so much of herself into what they had, he *would not* force his decision on her, but for himself, he knew it had to be. He sighed.

"Signal the fleet," he said quietly. "All ships will advance at ten knots in line abreast on a course of one, two, five degrees. Ten-thousand-yard intervals. *Tindal* will screen to landward, *Mertz* to seaward. Double all lookouts, report any and all sightings. When *Tindal* opens Monterey Bay, she'll enter in company with *Achilles* and destroy all enemy shipping. No boarding, just stand off and sink 'em unless they strike their colors. Direct those that choose to surrender to drive their ships hard aground; we don't have time to fool with them. *Tindal* and *Achilles* will then rejoin the fleet, and if contact hasn't already been made with the enemy, we'll resume our advance to meet him." He rubbed the young stubble on his chin, suddenly missing Juan. "Tabasco" was a fine steward, but it had taken Matt a long time to let Juan shave him. Tabasco wasn't ready yet, and he was back to performing the chore himself. Despite his terrible coffee, Juan had spoiled him badly.

"Make sure all ships confirm receipt." He looked around at the faces on the bridge, saw their surprised blinking or arched eyebrows, and wondered if his voice had sounded as normal as he'd thought. "All ahead one-third, if you please."

"Sea's getting up a little, Skipper," Spanky observed unnecessarily, coming on the bridge at 0400 with the morning watch. "Even 'Cat's'll have a hell of a time seeing anything out there with this overcast."

"They know what to look for. There are—were—steamers with the Dom fleet. They'll be throwing sparks."

Spanky grunted. "Like 'our' Imperials? Hell. It looks like the Fourth o' July out there. Wish they'd go to oil."

"I'm sure they will over time," Matt replied absently.

Spanky looked at him with concern. "Did you get *any* sleep?"

Matt grinned. "No, and neither did Tabasco, I'm afraid. He makes better coffee than Juan, at least."

"Poor devil," Spanky clucked. "He needs to learn to stand up to that grubby bastard Lanier. Juan knew how to do that! I saw Tabasco down in the galley, building sandwiches for the bridge watch, and Earl was giving him fits. One of these days, one of his 'little monkey' mess attendants is gonna beat the hell out of him—and he'll probably wonder why! If I see it, I won't say a word unless they're killing him. Earl's a turd, but he can cook. I can't choke down 'Cat food. Too spicy."

Matt chuckled. "You'd better encourage some of those mess attendants to learn to cook something you *can* eat, besides sandwiches. One of these days, Earl's liable to catch something over the side that'll pull him over and eat him! Did you see what he caught just while we were tied up at Saint Francis?"

Earl Lanier was a fiend for fishing—and fish—and he'd sampled the denizens of nearly every port they'd touched. Just about anyone would've eaten many of the things he caught, but sometimes he brought things aboard that nobody even wanted to *know* were in the water. A couple of times, he *had* nearly been snatched into the sea.

"Yeah . . . he's not going to eat *that*, is he?"

Matt shrugged.

"Aggh! Damn thing looked like an inside-out squid stickin' out of a boot . . . with pinchers!" He yawned. "What's the dope on *Achilles* and *Tindal*?"

"They're coming back out. They got eleven transports. Eight chose to beach. Not as many as Reynolds reported seeing before . . . we lost contact. A good haul, but I wonder where the others went?"

"Home? Maybe to get more troops?"

"Maybe."

"Lookout reports 'spaarks' off staar-board bow, Cap-i-taan!" Minnie suddenly cried. "Bearing two four seero, relaative, may-be five t'ousand yaards!"

Matt glanced at his watch. He'd been allowing *Walker*'s crew just a few more minutes of precious sleep before what promised to be a busy day. "Very well. Sound general quarters. Signal to all ships, 'enemy in sight,' and give the position."

All the Imperial ships had closed *Walker* before the sun went down since, except for *Achilles*, they had to rely on visual signals. Those were flashed now, by lights to port, and 'Cat liaison signalmen would interpret the Morse. *Walker*'s unnerving general alarm gurgle-screeched into the night, and Spanky stepped to the shipwide comm.

"All hands, draw small arms and man your battle stations! Man your battle stations!" he said with infinite calm. "I repeat, draw small arms and man your battle stations. This is no drill."

"*Mertz* has 'enemy in sight' now," Minnie reported. *Mertz* still screened to seaward. "Her cap-i-taan says enemy fleet, many ships, on course, seero, one, seero! Range to him, two t'ousand yaards. He asks turn about and open range until 'daylight make gunnery . . . praac-tic-aable'!"

Matt chuckled again. "I'll bet he does! Vey well. Tell *Mertz* to beat feet, but maintain contact. Remind her of the dragons! Be prepared to clear the deck if necessary. Have our lookouts skin their eyes for anything moving toward us, and tell *Achilles* and *Tindal* to hurry!"

"Ay, ay, Cap-i-taan!"

Matt looked at Spanky. "We're liable to have company too. My guess is, they expect some of the transports to join them, so they won't think much of sighting us if they do, but if any sniff too close, the jig'll be up. You'd better run along to the auxiliary conn. Stop by engineering and tell them to expect some frisky maneuvering today. I do *not* want my ship shot to pieces halfway around the planet from a dry dock!"

"Aye, aye, Skipper!" Spanky said, grateful he'd been *ordered* to see Tabby before the fight. "I'll . . . see you later, sir."

"Spanky!" Tabby said, surprised to see the diminutive officer enter the forward engine room under the circumstances. "I mean, Commaander McFaarlane! How . . . good of you to drop by. Good mornin', sur!"

"Tabby," he said, and nodded at the others in the compartment. "Fellas," he added. He looked back at Tabby. "Everything okay in your division, Chief?"

"Condensers are staartin' to choke up again. We'll be sayin' so long to freshwater showers." Spanky cringed. It would be fire hoses and naked bodies on deck, then. That had never been a problem in the "old" Navy, but with nearly half the 'Cats aboard being female, and *very* "human" in the pertinent parts . . . He cleared his throat. "Listen, this might be another 'Scapa Flow' today, so keep your eyes on the ball."

"Won't be no 'Scaapa Flow' with you an' the Skipper in charge," Tabby said confidently.

"Hey now, that wasn't Frankie's fault . . . and don't speak ill of the dead."

"Ain't speakin' ill. He was a swell guy, just not good Skipper."

"Well . . . anyway, *the* Skipper says to be ready for some fancy moves . . . and be careful down here! Seems like every time there's a fight, my poor boilers and engines get the worst of it. Not to mention my snipes." He looked at Tabby. Her burn scars remained but were fading well, and her fur—though short and thin like all Lemurian snipes—was filling out. He *did* love her, in his way. He smiled and gently squeezed her arm, watching her eyes begin to glisten. "I'd better scram," he said brusquely, taking his pouch from his pocket and stuffing a chew in his mouth. He offered it around and was surprised when a 'Cat water tender tentatively took a few leaves. "Well . . . fine. Just don't be spittin' on the deck plates!" he warned. Every snipe in the space had seen *him* do it a hundred times.

The day dawned gray and cloudy, and brisk enough that deck apes—'Cat and human—gladly wore shirts for a change. A few lookouts and fire controlmen even donned peacoats. The whole Dom fleet loomed to seaward, their numbers impossible to gauge due to their relative congestion, sailing in multiple columns. The Allied force, minus *Mertz*, was shadowing them inshore, and apparently *hadn't* raised any alarm so far. *Walker*'s profile was shielded from view by *Tindal* and *Achilles* as soon as they rejoined, and the sky began to lighten. Now, Captain Reddy stood beside his chair, staring out at the Doms through his binoculars and trying to determine the number of warships. He was almost sure there were twenty or more, ranging in size from ships of the line, or "battleships" as his crew increasingly called them, to the heavy frigates or "cruisers" Doms preferred. There were at least that many transports, maybe more. Few of those were steamers this time, and that made it hard to tell.

On its face, the impending battle seemed a terribly lopsided affair, as bad as when the old Asiatic Fleet faced the Japanese. Essentially, each enemy warship mounted forty to eighty guns, and each "class" was larger than its Imperial counterparts, but Matt's little fleet had some advantages. His "American" frigates, or "DDs," were screw steamers and much faster than the enemy, particularly with the Doms beating to windward. They mounted fewer guns, but they were larger, with a significant range advantage. If they could avoid crippling damage, they could stand off and pound the Doms largely at will. *Achilles* didn't have much range on the enemy; neither did her Imperial sisters. Matt planned to use them as a rear guard, to snap at the enemy's heels and destroy any transports that broke from the line and tried to run south with the wind. The allies also retained the element of surprise, since none of the enemy had come snooping after all, obviously thinking them to be the transports they expected.

Even as Matt watched, however, flocks of dragons lifted from some of the transports within the Dom formation, headed for *Mertz*—still all alone up ahead. *So they do let the damn things aboard their ships,* Matt realized with surprise. *Well, at least we know where they come from—and where they are.* That would help. Soon, he'd release *Tindal* and *Simms* to charge up the enemy flank, and *Achilles* and the other Imperials to steam for its rear. The Dom warships couldn't turn toward *Tindal* and *Simms* without charging straight for shore; a very bad move for dedicated sailors. He kind of hoped they'd turn away, though he didn't expect them to. A lot could be gained in the confusion following such a maneuver. As currently disposed, all they could really do was maintain their course and slug it out, and lonely *Tindal* and *Simms* would actually *control* the terms of the engagement. Given enough time, ammunition, and luck, there wasn't a hell of a lot the Doms could do about it—without their damn dragons. That left the final Allied advantage: USS *Walker*. She'd be in the fight from the start, and exposed to considerable risk, but the dragons were her priority opponent.

"Warn *Mertz* to prepare for air attack," Matt instructed. "Looks like fifty or sixty of the devils are inbound for her position, if she hasn't seen them yet. We'll need to let them get right on her before we make our move, but holler if they manage to do worse than chew ropes or dent the deck!" For this part of the action, *Mertz*'s crew would have to abandon their exposed guns and take what the dragons dished out for a while.

"Ay, ay!"

For some time, nothing changed except the weather, which continued to worsen. The sea developed a genuine chop, and the wind rose, shifting several degrees back and forth. Matt was afraid the enemy would be forced to tack and that would change his initial deployment plan, but it shouldn't make that much difference.

"*Mertz* says draa-gons are attacking now, much as before with roundshot, but the wind makes them drop too low to do bad damage," Minnie reported.

"Very well," Matt replied, almost distractedly. "All units will increase speed, *Mertz* too. Make the damn things work to keep up with her!" *Mertz*'s top speed under steam in seas like this was probably only ten knots, but every little bit helped, and the dragons were flying into a twenty-knot headwind. That ought to wear them out. "Achilles will join the Imperial squadron and lead it up on the enemy rear. *Simms* will take her place as our screen. As soon as the Doms get wise, *Simms* and *Tindal* are on the loose—weapons free—and we'll pull our little stunt!"

Someone in the Dominion fleet apparently caught on fairly quickly, most likely when they saw what appeared to be two steamers overhauling their starboard flank considerably faster than any transport should be able. Signal flags raced up halyards on several of the closest ships, and when there was no response, they fired a few guns for emphasis. Matt didn't see the flags or hear the shots. The screening ships blocked his view and *Walker*'s blower, pounding hull and rumbling machinery more than absorbed the distant reports, but a signal from *Simms*'s Morse lamp was sufficient.

"Execute," he said simply, and the word was passed to every Allied ship by wireless or signal flag. "All ahead full," he added a few moments later. "Main battery will stand by for surface action port, explosive shells. Inform Mr. Campeti he may fire when ready. Somebody hoist the battle flag, if you please."

The vibration in the deck strakes beneath their feet intensified, and the blower roared. *Walker* went from plodding through the swells, to a virtual leap forward, and the sea boomed across her fo'c'sle. 'Cats on *Simms* and *Tindal* cheered lustily as she left them behind, her twin screws churning the sea behind her fantail. Their cheers redoubled when they saw the oversize ensign rise to the top of the old destroyer's foremast, standing out straight and taught in the stiff wind, her many battles embroidered on the red and white stripes. Those on *Walker* cheered their consorts in return when other large flags broke and streamed above them, and *Simms* and *Tindal* altered course to close the range to the enemy. The old Japanese alarm bell, turned salvo buzzer, jarred loudly against the bulkhead, and three bright flashes lit the drab day, illuminating the expectant faces of the gun's crews stationed around a 4-inch-50 on the fo'c'sle, another on the amidships gun platform, and a 4.7-inch dual purpose on the aft deckhouse. Their line of sight was clear now, and Matt moved to port and stared through his binoculars at the enemy still more than two miles away. Campeti had been drilling his crews remorselessly and now that they had the tables of fire adjusted for black powder, the guns were actually more accurate, if shorter-legged, since velocity variations were less extreme. Of course, regardless of the ammunition, *Walker* still had her single, greatest combat advantage: gyro-stabilized fire control that allowed a pitching, rolling, racing ship to hit an equally lively target.

Matt grunted in satisfaction when two of the three shells struck a battleship on their first salvo. The explosions of the bursting charges weren't very big and wouldn't have caused much damage against a modern warship, but they blew quite satisfactory holes in wooden ships, little matter how stout and thick, because they naturally penetrated *while* exploding. Of course, the enemy also relied on bringing large quantities of bagged powder from their magazines to the guns. Powder that was immune to the passage of solid shot, splinters, or virtually any hazard they might face in battle—except random and energetic flashes of fire. What began as something resembling fireworks going off within the distant ship, even as her gunports began to rise, rapidly accelerated into a catastrophic detonation that *everyone* heard over the wind, distance, and sounds of their ship. In an instant, all that remained of a once-mighty vessel—and possibly five or six hundred human beings—was an expanding cloud of smoke and falling debris.

Those on the bridge stood almost stunned for a moment, but Campeti's roar of "Next target, next target! Match pointers, goddamn it!" on the fire control platform above snapped them out of it. They'd blown up enemy ships before, but rarely before they were fully immersed in the fight—and never with so many *humans* aboard.

Matt turned to the bridge watch, his face hard. "They started this, so they asked for it," he grated. "I'm not happy about it either, but I'm *satisfied*, and I'll stay that way if we blow every one of 'em out of the water!"

The salvo buzzer rang again, and three more tongues of fire snarled at the enemy and jolted the ship as *Walker* continued her dash to get around in front of the Dom fleet.

"Hello the bridge!" came a cry from aft. "May I come up there, please?"

"Courtney! I thought you stayed in Saint Francis!" Matt said, surprised.

"Well, I didn't. I may have made an extra effort to stay out of sight, so you wouldn't force me to, but I am, indeed, here! I'm the acting surgeon after all, and I have my duty," he reminded him piously. "May I join you?"

"Yeah, I suppose. But since you're here, I expect you to do your duty without whining. If we take a hit, you're off to the wardroom!"

"I shall vanish instantly, sir! Vanish!" He peered out at the Doms. Another salvo boomed, and he worked his jaw to pop his ears. "So we're engaged in yet another unequal fight," he observed cheerfully. "How exciting! Shall we see more of those dreadful but fascinating flying creatures?"

"I think you can count on it," Matt said, watching another salvo launch water spouts around one of the lead "cruisers." Only one shell hit the ship and it didn't explode, but it must have struck somewhere near the wheel, because the ship suddenly fell off, beam on to the wind. It did manage a stuttering broadside in *Walker*'s direction, but every shot fell randomly short.

The whole right side of the enemy formation suddenly erupted fire and smoke at *Simms* and *Tindal* as they eased ever closer, but that fire had no greater effect. The two Allied DDs held their fire.

"It must be terribly frustrating for them," Bradford commiserated. "I mean, I doubt any of those men over there had ever heard of *Walker* before we waylaid them at Guadalupe, and there they stand, directly into her fire with no hope of a meaningful reply. You can despise what they represent, but you must honor their courage."

"Theirs is the courage of the Grik, Courtney," Matt snapped.

"It's not! They're . . . misguided. Criminally so. They're doubtless coerced by their faith, and by our standards, even evil. But they must sense fear and understand their danger." He shook his head. "Their courage is real."

"I don't know. After meeting that weird 'Blood Cardinal' bastard, Don Hernan, I wonder if it's only that they're less afraid of us than they are of him and his kind."

"Perhaps. Pity we never caught him. I suspect he now sits happily at the feet of his 'pope' . . . perhaps as a footrest?"

Matt barked a laugh. "That would be a sight, with all his puffed-up dignity!" He shook his head. "I doubt it, though. He's probably on New Ireland. Maybe Chack's already killed him!"

"A happy thought!"

The salvo buzzer rang.

Walker finally passed around in front of the Dom fleet, still keeping her distance on a course of two, eight, zero, mauling its ships practically at will. Roundshot, probably fired by heavy bow chasers, moaned by or plunked into the sea close aboard, shrouded in massive splashes. Courtney was as good as his word and promptly left the bridge when a pair of lucky shots staggered the ship. At this range they didn't penetrate, but they did open seams and cause leaks. *Mertz* reported that the dragons had all dropped their loads, causing some damage to her decking and a few gun carriages, but little more. As Matt had predicted, they'd started shredding her rigging. The ship and her swarm of attackers were visible from the crow's nest now, and the report said the distant struggle looked like a flock of "regular" lizard birds picking at a floating fish.

"Make your course three, three, zero, Mr. Kutas," Matt said. "I hope those flying Grik remember what we did to them the other day and still hold a grudge. Let's see if we can get their attention." The salvos still flew hot and heavy to port, and the enemy van was losing its cohesion. Two more ships had been utterly destroyed by *Walker*'s fire, and gouts of smoke billowed southward on the landward side of the fleet as the firing between it and the two Allied DDs grew more furious. *Achilles* signaled that she and her consorts were finally bringing the Dom rear under fire. Matt began to grow concerned that the enemy might wear and turn on the Imperial squadron. He didn't think they would, not yet anyway, but if they did, *Achilles* and the other Imperial frigates wouldn't last long. He had to be ready to respond quickly if that occurred.

"Cap-i-taan!" Minnie cried. "Commodore Jenks signals on small wireless we left him that the Dom Army is attacking in force! They is a lot of them, maybe five thousands. They not have much artillery, though, and Jenks does. Artillery has kept them at arm's reach for now, so Bosun an' his rifle militia can kill them well! He holding. He ask how we do?"

"Tell him we're holding too."

"That all?"

"That's all. For now."

More splashes rose around *Walker*, falling ever shorter as she steamed farther from the Dominion fleet—toward *Mertz*.

Bradford clomped back up the stairs aft, waving away questioning faces. "No injuries. Nothing *serious*, anyway. Just the usual cuts and scrapes, bumps and bruises you always see whenever large numbers of people scamper about on a vessel this small, handling heavy shells and manipulating large objects designed to pinch hell out of anyone coming near." His bushy eyebrows rose as he stared off the port quarter. Several ships had begun to burn, and a number of warships had turned toward *Simms* and *Tindal*, regardless of the risk. The pounding they'd been taking simply couldn't be borne any longer. "Can't say the same for those poor buggers, I'm sad to say."

"No," Matt said, "but our guys are about to get it if they don't pull ahead. Signal *Simms* and *Tindal*, 'Full ahead, remain to windward of the enemy.'"

"Ay, ay . . . Cap-i-taan!" Minnie passed the word, then paused, listening to her earpiece. "Lookout says, 'Draagons come!' Signal from *Mertz* says they leave her be now." Minnie cocked her head. "Says some real tired draagons roost on ship! They shooting them!"

"Swell," Matt replied. "Have *Mertz* rejoin *Tindal* and *Simms* at her best possible speed! She's finished playing bait, and I think her sisters are going to need her!"

"Here they come!" Kutas said, peering up through the windows.

"Secure from 'surface action port'!" Matt cried. "Stand by for air action, aft! Helm, give us a gradual turn to course two, four, zero! Reduce speed to two-thirds."

"What exactly are you planning?" Bradford asked.

"I'm playing a hunch you gave me. Those devils have *got* to be getting tired, all of them. At the same time, they're going to hate giving up chasing something. If they really are like Grik, they can't help it! So . . . we let 'em chase us, farther and farther away from their 'base' ships, hopefully staying just out of reach as long as we can. Shooting at 'em the whole time ought to keep them stirred up. . . ."

"But what happens when they catch us? They might, you know. Then we'll have half a hundred of those vicious things romping all over the ship! We won't be able to man the guns, and go back and assist our friends!"

"You let me worry about that. I have a surprise for them based on something else you said."

"Oh dear," Courtney mumbled. "I certainly hope, whatever it was, I was right!"

Staring astern, Spanky stood on the aft deckhouse, striking his signature pose, hands on his skinny hips.

"Bunch of 'em," Carl Bashear said, taking a chew from Spanky's tobacco pouch. A virtual cloud of "dragons" had gathered in their wake, beating their wings and gaining quickly. "Look kinda aggravated," he mumbled around the mouthful of leaves.

"Yeah. A Grik charge in midair," Spanky agreed. "What a hoot." He looked at Finny, serving as his talker. "Marksmen to the stern. Inform the captain we're about to engage . . . aerial targets." Chief Gunner's Mate Paul Stites had the "number four" 4.7-inch gun. Spanky scowled at him. "Don't miss. We're running low on those Jap time-fuse shells." He raised his voice so he could be heard by the crews of the 25 mm's in the tubs just forward. "Antiair . . . lizard batteries, in local control, commence firing!"

Matt was looking aft around the chart house, trying to see the effect of the fire. Tabby was on the ball; only the faintest wisps of smoke smeared the tops of the funnels, and the 4.7-inch and 25-mm guns still ate "smokeless" Japanese shells they'd salvaged from *Amagi*. Even many of the marksmen still had '03s. That left a better-than-average view of the terrifying creatures flying up *Walker*'s skirt. Matt still had trouble seeing them clearly through his binoculars, as the creatures tended to group together, and the flying mass became a wild flurry of motion in his Bausch & Lombs. He got indistinct impressions: furry, bright-colored bodies like the ones before, grasping talons and ferocious, golden, reptilian eyes. Every mouth was open, revealing rows of teeth unlike the Grik—thinner, longer, more curved—the better to snatch prey from the sea or sky. They were not shrieking, however. Over the sound of the guns and rifles, he couldn't tell if they made any sounds at all. His brief glimpses at their faces left him with a growing conviction they were gasping for air.

"All ahead full!" he ordered.

The deck trembled, the blower roared, and the bow lurched out of the sea between the streaming troughs. The pitching eased a bit as the ship practically leaped from swell to swell. Still the monsters gained. If anything, they seemed to be gaining more rapidly. Maybe they knew they had to board *Walker* or die, at this stage, and they were giving it their all. Its fuses set shorter and shorter, the number four gun fired rapidly, the dark explosions erupting closer and closer to the ship. Shattered dragons staggered in the air or plummeted lifelessly into the sea. Pom-poms blatted at the creatures that lunged ahead and tried to board on the flanks, perforating wings and shredding bodies. Muskets started firing, joined by a Thompson and a BAR. Even more monsters fell, still reaching desperately for the ship. Spanky fired at a dragon swooping over the aft deckhouse with his pistol, and a couple actually lit on the platform, causing a wild melee of shots, slashing teeth, and a fusillade of flung shell casings. More clawed their way onto the fantail, their tongues literally lolling with exhaustion. They were easily shot—with extreme care, considering their proximity to the depth charge racks.

"All ahead flank!" Matt shouted remorselessly. Realistically, most of the dragons were probably already doomed. They'd never make it back to their ships, and their only hope was to land on *Walker*—but *Walker* was even faster now, making almost thirty knots on three boilers for the first time in . . . Matt couldn't remember how long. She was just a little faster than the wind now, perfect for his purposes. It was time. Kari Faask and Fred Reynolds were on his mind when he gave his next order:

"Make smoke!"

Tabby had been waiting. Raw fuel gushed into the boilers at a far more prodigious rate than they could ever burn it all, and Jeek and the rest of his flight crew activated the on-deck smoke generators with grim satisfaction. In moments, impenetrable black columns of thick, sooty smoke piled into the sky and streamed aft, slowly spreading into the wind. In many places, it swirled on the ship itself, under the bridge and through the galley space beneath the amidships deckhouse. Men and 'Cats choked and coughed, holding T-shirts over their faces. The giant lizard birds chasing the ship with their final breaths fell into the sea as if they'd been switched off, and in less than three or four minutes, a gasping Spanky called the bridge and reported that all the "air-lizards" had "splashed."

"Very well," Matt said with vengeful satisfaction. "Secure from flank. Secure from making smoke. All ahead full."

"Cap-i-taan Reddy!" Minnie squeaked. "*Tindal* has lost her rudder and got tangled with a Dom baattle-waagon! They try to board! *Mertz* steams to her aid, an' so do *Achilles* an' another Imp-ee ship!"

"I told them to keep their distance!"

"They try—but lose rudder!"

"Okay. Send to *Simms* to stay the hell out of there, whatever she does. Try to get *Achilles* to break off. We're coming as fast as we can!" He scanned the now-distant battle with his binoculars. "Still too many!" he murmured, then lowered the glasses and stepped to the bulkhead where the shipwide comm microphone was mounted. He twisted the switch. "Well done, *Walkers*!" he said, and waited for the relieved, triumphant cheers to dwindle. "Now, all hands resume 'surface action stations'! We still have a battle to finish!"

Walker dashed back toward what had become a chaotic, sprawling brawl with a bone in her teeth, shouldering aside a mounting swell. The transports had turned, possibly making for Monterey, but Port Admiral Rempel aboard *Perseus* was leading two more of the Imperial Frigates in a determined attack against them. Matt was frankly surprised by that. Rempel hadn't struck him as a particularly bold fighter—and maybe he wasn't, since the transports were only lightly armed—but he was pressing his attack with sufficient gusto to prove he had no sympathy for the enemy. *Tindal* was in a bad way, almost dismasted, her bowsprit snared in a Dom cruiser's foremast shrouds. Despite her loss of control, she was still driving forward, keeping the link as rough as possible to prevent boarders from swarming across. Her guns still vigorously pounded other Dom ships that ventured too close.

Mertz had almost joined her, orange flashes stabbing out either side, smashing mighty hulls, and utterly disrupting enemy attempts to close or even maintain formation. She'd become the focus of the Dom's attention, however, and even as she plowed forward, she was being viciously mauled. To the south, *Achilles* and the rig-damaged frigate *Hector* slashed their way through damaged and undamaged Doms alike, guns thundering and paddles churning. It was a terrible, inspiring sight. If the Doms hadn't been thrown into such disarray, largely due to their initial formation and inability to alter it with any precision, the four allied ships in their midst would already be floating debris. Matt reflected yet again how lucky they were that the Dominion had elected to start this war before fully "modernizing" its warships.

"Pass the word to Campeti," Matt shouted as *Walker* drew to within a mile of the fight. "Concentrate fire on those battleships working over *Tindal* and *Mertz*. It looks as if the remaining cruisers are peeling off to protect the transports. Get that big devil twenty-five degrees off the starboard bow! She's stern on to us, but she's giving *Mertz* hell!"

"He acknowledge!" Minnie cried, and moments later they all heard Campeti's bellow above. "Surface target, bearing one four zero; course zero, zero, five; speed six knots! Range . . . three nine five zero! Guns one, three, and four, match pointers!"

"On target!"

"In salvo, commence firing!" The salvo buzzer rang and a mere instant later, all three guns boomed, and the smoke quickly vanished to leeward. Even over the ship noises, the "Shhhhhh!" of the shells was audible. Three splashes erupted just aft and short of the big enemy ship. "Up fifty!" came the cry. "Adjust left zero zero five degrees!"

"On target!"

"Fire!"

Three more shells screeched away, and all must have crashed through the vulnerable stern of the Dom ship before detonating against something substantial. There was a series of flashes, and, once again, another huge Dom ship of the line vanished amid an expanding cloud of smoke and a blizzard of splinters and larger fragments.

"New target! Range . . ."

Matt quit listening. Campeti was good—maybe as good as Greg Garrett. He concentrated on conning his ship through the tumult ahead. *Mertz* was closing on *Tindal* now, starboard guns flailing the port bow of the liner *Tindal* embraced, smoke streaming from her perforated stack in half a dozen places. The liner spat back, chopping further at *Mertz's* mangled rigging, but most of the shot flew aft of the target and battered a wallowing, dismasted hulk beyond her. Soon, *Mertz* would add her boarders to *Tindal's* and they'd have a chance to turn the tables on the Doms. For just a moment, Matt glanced at Tabasco, standing out of the way beside the chart table. The 'Cat steward had brought his pistol belt to the bridge, with his Academy sword hanging from it. *No,* he decided. Much as he'd have liked to, joining a boarding action wasn't *Walker's* job. Not his job. Not this time. For now, he had to be content with destroying as many Dom ships as he could, and a stationary *Walker* was bound to attract too much fire—and far too many holes. No one aboard his ship had anything to prove, and *Walker* was much safer and far more effective underway. His decision was punctuated by a series of hammer blows pounding the port flank of his ship, and he rushed to the bridgewing, followed by Bradford. A ship of the line had suddenly turned and presented them with a full broadside.

"Get that son of a bitch!" he roared up at Campeti.

"Surface action port!" Campeti bellowed in reply. "Guns two and four engage that battlewagon at zero three five in local control! Range, uh . . . eight hundred! Commence firing! Portside twenty-fives assist!" He paused for only an instant. "Guns one and three maintain fire control connection! Target bearing one eight five! Range two thousand! Match pointers!"

"Make your course zero, four, zero!" Matt shouted as soon as the salvo buzzer rang and the gun on the fo'c'sle boomed and bucked.

"Sero, four, sero, ay!"

"Damage control reports one shot penetrated aa-midships deckhouse, an' one punch through guinea pullman," Minnie shouted in her high-pitched voice. "Two spring plates in aft engine room! They prob'ly skate in. Casualties to waard-room!"

Matt looked at Bradford, who'd been uncharacteristically quiet since they "bug-sprayed" the Grik birds, and sighed. "You have work, Courtney."

Bradford nodded. "Indeed. As do you." He waved about. The numbers two and four guns opened fire, as did the port twenty-fives.

"Yeah. We won't board anybody, but it looks like we're back in the pool with the flashies again, fighting both sides. No choice. I'll do my best to spoil their aim."

"God bless you for that, Captain Reddy," Courtney murmured, and vanished down the ladder aft.

"Lotta iron flyin' around amongst all that, Skipper," Norman Kutas said matter-of-factly, nodding ahead toward the densest concentration of enemy ships. *Achilles* and *Hector* were in it now, smoke gushing from their guns.

"Yeah, and we're bound to catch some," Matt agreed solemnly; then his lips quirked into a grin. "You're not worried about something spoiling your boyish looks, are you, Norm?"

The badly—and often—scarred First Lieutenant chuckled. "No, sir. I'm way beyond that, but I feel everything that hits this old ship in my bones."

"Me too, Norm," Matt agreed. "So let's do our best to avoid as many hits as possible."

"Fancy footwork ain't gonna save us from everything, Skipper."

"No, but right now good people are dying, and the enemy's in disarray. We'll race through, shooting up whatever we can while avoiding as much return fire as we can manage."

"Then what?"

Matt shrugged. "We turn around and do it again until our friends are safe and every Dom out there is on the bottom of the sea."

CHAPTER 22

////// *Above Ceylon*
January 17, 1944

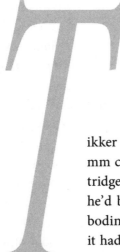

ikker scratched his ear around the highly polished 7.7-mm cartridge case thrust through a hole a similar cartridge once shot through it. Sometimes it itched, and he'd begun to associate that with a superstitious foreboding. He looked around. Everything seemed fine, and it had been a swell day for killing Grik. The "Nancy's" engine rumbled healthily above and behind, and they hadn't been hit by any Grik "shot-mortars" when they bombed the hell out of a retreating column earlier in the flight. It was windy, and the plane bounced around a lot, and the sea to the west showed white teeth, but they should be able to set down safely in *Salissa*'s lee. All in all, it was a glorious day, and he didn't know why his ear was bugging him. A shout from aft shattered his sense of well-being.

"How come you don't go down and let me shoot more Grik?" Captain Risa-Sab-At, commander of Salissa's Marine contingent, demanded sharply.

"I don't *see* any more," Tikker snapped. "They've had enough. They abandon Saa-lon!" He pointed down, behind them, where *Haakar-Faask, Naga, Bowles, Felts, Saak-Fas,* and *Clark* were spraying grapeshot across the rocky, mushy land bridge to India proper, gnashing the remnants of the Grik host trying to cross in daylight with the ebbing tide. The Allied armies were rapidly advancing to chop up what remained of the enemy on Ceylon, and those stranded by the tide would likely be annihilated.

"Then let's go kill some of those trying to cross the sand!" she demanded.

"Right! We'd probably be hit by our own ships, if we go low enough for you to shoot them with that musket! Besides, we're low on fuel!" Tikker was growing beyond annoyed. Risa had been cooped up on *Salissa* throughout the campaign, and she'd begged him to take her on this patrol. He'd reluctantly agreed when Admiral Keje just as reluctantly gave his blessing. They both knew how anxious she was to get in the fighting, *any* fighting, particularly after hearing of her brother Chack's—and Dennis Silva's—latest . . . adventures on New Ireland. She'd spent the flight taking potshots at Grik during their bombing runs. At first, the shots surprised and alarmed him. Then they became annoying. He'd told her that if she flew with him, she had to perform all the duties of his spotter/wireless operator, and she'd readily agreed. Once in the air, however, she'd "spotted" all right, trying to get him to dive in on every lost Grik they saw, and he'd quickly determined she barely knew Morse. Except for the column they'd chopped up, it had been a wasted patrol. He hoped the other three ships in his flight had made better observations.

"So," he said, trying to make conversation and lighten the tension he felt. Risa was a "dish" after all, as the Amer-i-cans would say, and, despite his present aggravation, he actually kind of liked her. There were those pesky rumors about her being "mated" to Silva, and he didn't know what to think of that. She didn't seem to be pining for the big chief gunner's mate, however, and he wondered if he had a chance. He never would have before the war, but now? To say things had changed was a vast understatement. She was just so damn *intense* sometimes! "What are you going to do? Did you really put in for a transfer?"

"Yes," she shouted back through the voice tube. "To a line regiment. I want to stay on this front and kill Grik, of course, but I'll go east if I must."

Where Silva is, Tikker thought glumly. "There is *Salissa*!" he said, pointing west-southwest. The mighty ship was anchored a few miles off-shore, with *Humfra Dar* a thousand tails beyond her. Both massive "car-riers" were screened by a squadron of "DD" frigates under the command of Jim Ellis. It was a heady sight that banished his gloom. Never had so much combat power been assembled in one place, and soon *Arracca* and *her* battle group would arrive. Tikker grinned and turned toward the ships and began his descent.

"Must we return?" Risa asked. "This has been . . . fun."

Tikker grinned and was glad Risa couldn't see his embarrassed blinking.

"Yes, fun," he admitted. "To a degree."

Once they reached her, he circled *Salissa* while his squadron mates set down in the water between her and the shore and were recovered. It would still be bumpy there, but the winds were largely blocked by the bulk of the massive ship. Finally, it was Tikker's turn. He lined up on the calmer water, fighting the crosswind that would buffet them until they neared the sea, and reduced power. Down they swooped, and he heard Risa shout with glee. Just fifteen feet off the water, he was preparing to cut power even further, when a massive waterspout erupted directly in his path and something tore through the nose of his plane, slashing him along the left forearm. Without thought, he pushed the throttle to the stop and leveled off. More splashes rose, seemingly at random through-out the area of the anchored carriers and their screen. An explosion sud-denly rocked Cablaas-Rag-Lan's USS *Scott*, and the new frigate coasted to a stop, her fo'c'sle bathed in flames.

"They're bombs!" Tikker muttered wonderingly, looking at the sky as he pulled back on the stick. "Bombs!" he shouted. "They're bombs, Risa!"

"Yes!" she shouted back. "Bigger than ours! But where are they com-ing from?"

"They can only be shells from a mighty ship, like *Amagi* herself or bombs dropped by aircraft!" He frantically continued searching the sky and the horizon. Nothing!

"What's that?" Risa yelled.

Tikker turned and saw her pointing almost straight up. He followed her gaze. *No! That's impossible,* his mind shrieked. High above, *very* high, higher than he'd ever flown, thirty or forty massive objects drifted lazily, seemingly effortlessly, eastward. They were long and fat and looked like the "scum weenies" that Laan-yeer, the cook, was always trying to make people eat. They were clearly flying but had no wings!

"Send . . . flying . . . *scum weenies* are attacking!" he shouted back at Risa.

"I . . . I'll try!" Risa yelled back as Tikker put the plane in the steepest climb he thought it would handle. He was above the splashes now, and could actually *see* bombs hurtling down. At that moment, several things happened at once. A strangely formed engine, prop still slowly turning, dropped into the sea, followed by a woven wood contraption of some kind, filled with shrieking Grik. He had no time for the oddity of the sight to register before a bomb erupted directly in the path of another, lower plane, also trying to pull out. The "Nancy" staggered through the spume, but its left wing clipped a wave. Tikker watched in horror as the plane cartwheeled across the sea and literally disintegrated. In the next instant, before he had the slightest opportunity to recover from that awful sight, the horizon before him pulsed with light. A colossal, fiery pyramid of smoke and flame vomited upward and outward from *Humfra-Dar,* flinging debris, burning planes, unrecognizable fragments, and *people* through the air like smoldering motes.

"*O Maker!*" he cried. For an instant, he was too aghast to even remember what he'd been doing. How could one bomb . . . and then he realized. It hadn't *been* just one bomb. The 5th, 6th, and 8th Bomb Squadrons of the 2nd Naval Air Wing had been next in the rotation. They'd been on the flight deck, loaded with bombs and fuel . . . "O Maker," he whispered, "guide their path." He tried to jam the throttle *past* its stop, then yanked back on the stick again, blinking furiously through the tears filling his eyes. He had to get up there, where the "flying weenies" were. What he'd do—if he did—he had no idea. The "Nancys" still had no weapons besides bombs, and Tikker was out of those. Risa had a musket . . . Behind him, Risa-Sab-At said nothing.

Baalkpan

Bernard Sandison was a happy man, and he whistled erratically as he walked briskly from his small office in Adar's Great Hall down the damp, crowded street to the expanding complex past the "Navy Yard" that comprised his "division." Occasionally, he paused and watched a group of "dames," newly arrived from Maa-ni-la, being led on tours of the city. Quite a few had wound up working for him in the ammunition factories, and he was admittedly more than a little sweet on a couple. He restrained himself, however. No sense in committing himself so soon when new "drafts" arrived almost daily now. Besides, they all wanted to work and were so willing to please, he wanted to make sure he wasn't taking advantage of them during this initial, vulnerable time. They'd been virtual slaves in the Empire, and the transition to free citizens with all the rights, benefits—and responsibilities—involved was difficult and confusing for most to adjust to. Not all the guys were so conscientious, and he scowled. Dean Laney was probably the worst at "making the most" of the situation, and Bernie meant to have a word with Riggs about that yet again. Laney was such a jerk.

His expression softened as his thoughts returned to other things. The news on all fronts was good—or at least not bad—and he felt that was largely due to his herculean efforts (and those of all the great people he had working for him in Ordnance). He was still mad at Silva for going AWOL, but the new "Allin-Silva" conversions were coming along nicely. A regiment's worth of the "kits," consisting of barreled actions with calibrated sights already installed, as well as cast conversion hammers, were now ready for shipment. The next batch would be ready in half the time, and he expected that to improve even more as production hit its stride. Once the "conversions" arrived at the front, troops in the field could simply install the new barrels and hammers themselves in a few minutes' time, and then send their old barrels back for lining and alteration. It was an elegant solution that would cause no downtime at all. He'd have preferred the .45-70 cartridge for ballistic reasons but settled on what was essentially a .50-80. The extra powder would help make up for the larger diameter, and that diameter would mean the weapons would only be a little heavier than the .60-caliber smoothbores. What extra weight there was would help tame the heavier recoil. He considered it an ingenious compromise, if he did say so himself. No more smoothbore small arms were being made in Baalkpan.

He'd finally solved the problem of making small cartridge cases too, which made him particularly happy. In this, he'd been assisted by a Lemurian bowl maker who applied his own methods to the task. Bernie had no idea how it "should" be done, but what they did was cast brass case heads at the base of a large, thin disc. The case heads, with primer pockets already formed, were clamped in new specialized lathes with a precision template and a long, thin "live" center in the tail stock. After that, they simply spun the lathe and formed the disc into an appropriately shaped tube. The cool thing was, they could make .30-06 and .45 ACP on the same machines since the heads were identical. They just cut the .45s off shorter. Other machines made .30-40 for the Krags, 6.5 for the Japanese rifles salvaged from *Amagi*, .50 BMG, and some other calibers for the few civilian weapons found on the first visit to *Santa Catalina*, but most were dedicated to the new .50-80 cartridge. They'd started out making a few hundred shells a day; however, as production expanded, machines were built, and workers trained, they'd be making tens of thousands a day very soon. Of course, then the shells had to be loaded.

The .50-80s would always be fed black powder for pressure reasons, but Bernie's team had finally created suitable nitrocellulose powders for the remaining "modern" firearms. The testing had destroyed a Krag and split a 1911 at the ejection port, but now they had the formulas and loads down to the point that the weapons functioned properly and trajectories matched the calibrated sights. New, fixed ammunition was coming out of Baalkpan Arsenal for the first time. Bernie wasn't satisfied with that. He was still improving the explosive rounds for the four-inch-fifties and the salvaged Japanese guns, as well as the mortars and bombs. They were still stuck with muzzle-loading, smoothbore artillery for the foreseeable future, but he was making progress toward rifled guns, and ultimately, rifled breechloaders. He was even close to testing new torpedoes at long last. That would make Captain Reddy smile, he knew. He frowned. *Captain Reddy may not smile when he finds out about some of the other "projects"*

Adar's got me working on. But Adar's Chairman of the Grand Alliance, and it makes sense to have the stuff, even if we never use it, Bernie supposed. *And it's not as though we can transmit to the Skipper—and even if we could, other folks would know. . . .*

He avoided a mud puddle and hurried on.

The other "divisions" hadn't been idle, he confessed to himself. New ships were coming off the ways, some with bolt-on armor protecting their engineering spaces. They'd finally located and literally hoisted shattered *Mahan* from the waters of the bay, using two Homes to place her on one of the new floating dry docks. Now the debate raged as to whether they should rebuild her, or incorporate her machinery in new construction. The latter seemed to be the consensus regarding S-19. She was so badly damaged—and nobody but Laumer and a few others really *wanted* a sub. Riggs and Rodriguez had made electric arc searchlights to replace the one *Walker* lost and equip new ships with the simple, powerful lights. Based on the USAAF SCR-284 sets that came with the P-40s, Riggs was also on the brink of completing real-voice radios.

Yes, things were going well and Bernie was happy, but that happiness came with a measure of anxiety. It seemed every time they got an edge, the Grik came up with some way to negate or match it, and he couldn't help wondering what they had come up with in the equally abundant time they'd had to plot and scheme. He snorted. *Whatever it is, they'll be hard-pressed to match us this time!* Through the crowd, he caught sight of Riggs and Rodriguez making to cut him off. *Speak of the devil,* he thought. Despite the heat of the day, he felt a chill when he noticed their expressions.

"C'mon, Bernie!" Riggs said urgently. "We're headed for the Great Hall."

"I just came from there! I have work. . . ."

Without a word, Riggs thrust a sweat-darkened message form into his hand.

FROM KEJE-FRIS-AR CINCWEST AND CMDR FIRST FLEET X
TO ALL STATIONS X
SUBJECT GENERAL ALARM X
   AT 0855 THIS DAY A LARGE FORMATION GRIK REPEAT

GRIK DIRIGIBLES REPEAT DIRIGIBLES ATTACKED FIRST
FLEET WITH HEAVY BOMBS FROM HIGH ALTITUDE ESTI-
MATED 15000 FEET X

SEAPLANE CARRIER HUMFRA-DAR DESTROYED WITH
ENTIRE 2ND NAVAL AIR WING MINUS SQUADRONS ALOFT
THAT WERE RECOVERED ABOARD SALISSA X FEWER
THAN 300 SURVIVORS X RESERVE CAPTAIN GERAN-ERAS
AND COFO LT CMDR ALFRED VERNON USN MISSING AND
PRESUMED LOST X SERIOUS DAMAGE ALSO SUSTAINED
TWO DDS X MINOR DAMAGE SUSTAINED SEVERAL AUX-
ILIARIES X

NO EFFECTIVE ANTIAIR EFFORT POSSIBLE BUT CAPTAINS
JIS-TIKKAR AND RISA-SAB-AT DESERVE NOTICE FOR
CLOSE INSPECTION AND DESCRIPTION OF AIRSHIPS AS
WELL AS SENDING ONE OUT OF CONTROL WITH MUSKET
FIRE X NUMEROUS OTHER ENEMY CRAFT DESTROYED BY
INEXPERIENCED HANDLING X EXAMPLE: RAPID UNCON-
TROLLED ASCENT AFTER DROPPING BOMBS APPARENTLY
CAUSED CATASTROPHIC STRUCTURAL FAILURE AT LEAST
SIX (6) GRIK ZEPPELINS X

DESCRIPTION GRIK ZEPPELINS: APPROXIMATELY 100 TAILS
(YARDS) LONG WITH 4 TAIL-MOUNTED CONTROL SUR-
FACES AND 5 HORIZONTALLY OPPOSED TWO-CYLINDER
ENGINES X COMMODORE ELLIS DESCRIBES AS "STUMPY
VERSIONS OF ACRON OR MACON" X

MAJORITY OF SURVIVING AIRSHIPS RETIRED 345 DE-
GREES RELATIVE OUR POSITION TOWARD MAINLAND X
SOME CONTINUED ON BEARING OF 115 DEGREES POSSI-
BLE TARGET ANDAMAN X

DO NOT REPEAT DO NOT ASSUME THIS IS ONLY RAID X
MAKE ALL PREPARATIONS FOR ATTACKS SINGAPORE

ARYAAL BAALKPAN X JAP ADVISOR KUROKAWA MUST BE
INVOLVED SO REMEMBER JAP AFFINITY FOR COORDI-
NATED AIR ATTACKS X
CINCWEST SENDS X

"Oh my God!" Bernie breathed. "Zeppelins! It makes perfect sense,
though. No Grik's ever going to sit in the cockpit of a proper plane.
Look, you guys go ahead! I'll run out to the airfield and give Mallory the
dope! We can't let those bastards hit us *here*! Not now!"

"Relax, Bernie. We're hardwired to Ben's CP from the comm center.
He's already got the word and says he can get four ships in the air if he
has to. He'll have them armed and prepped just in case the red rockets
go up. Everybody's watching the sky, and we've already diverted a squadron of PatWing One 'Nancys' on a training flight. More planes'll be up
within the hour."

"Okay, I'll come with you," Bernie said, relenting, but then his face
turned ashen as he stared toward the Great Hall. Red rockets arced from
under the boughs of the Sacred Tree, and others flew skyward from Fort
Atkinson and several other designated OPs. "Shit!" he said as the popping sounds of the rockets reached them and general alarm bells began
clattering across the city. High above, barely visible in the west-
southwest, a jumbled school of what looked like giant fish emerged from
the late-afternoon haze.

"Son of a bitch!" Riggs swore. "I didn't *really* believe they'd come
here! No way they're the same ones that hit First Fleet! How many of the
damn things can they have?" He paused. "Okay, guys. Do *not* go to the
Great Hall! The last thing we need is everybody under one bomb! I'm
heading back to the comm center!" He looked at the two men. "Go wherever you want, but split up! And pass the word to anybody you meet:
take cover!"

Kaufman Field
Baalkpan

Ben Mallory dropped his coffee mug on the table in the shade when the
alarm bells began ringing and the rockets popped over the city. The cof-

fee spilled across the table and dripped on the ground. "Jumbo!" he shouted at a tall, still-emaciated lieutenant who'd recently arrived from Maa-ni-la. The man had supposedly been a good pilot despite his regulation-busting six-foot-two frame, but he was still in no condition to try out for the P-40s. "Get over to Flight Ops and warm up the radio!" They had one of the spare radios configured for ground use, with a hand crank and dynamo. He looked at Soupy, Mackey, and "Shirley"—the shortest female 'Cat in the Air Corps—and the only other person besides himself and the previous two yet qualified in the P-40E. They'd all been gathered in the shade, waiting, since the first alert. "Let's do it," he said a little nervously. "If they're popping rockets, the damn things must be in sight!"

Together, the four fliers, two human and two 'Cats, ran to the four planes parked two by two out on the strip. Ben leaped onto the trailing edge of the port wing near the fuselage of the plane now sporting a big white cursive M painted on the cowl, and stepped into the cockpit. He immediately flipped the battery switch on and reached for the primer handle with his left hand, unlocked it, and pumped it vigorously to give the engine a good gulp of fuel. Still pumping, his right hand found the starter switch under the throttle quadrant and flipped it from Off down to Energize. The high-pitched, dynamo starter wound up and Ben realized he hadn't been counting the priming "shots" he'd sent the big Allison V-1710 in front of him. If he'd given it too much, there'd likely be an induction fire.

"Crap!" he growled aloud. *What a "newie" mistake!* Of course, he *was* a "newie" when it came to a combat scramble! Thinking the number felt about right, he locked the handle with a twist and pushed the throttle forward about an inch. The dynamo had reached a fever pitch. "Clear prop!" he yelled, moving the starter switch to Engage. The plane shook violently when the clutch grabbed, and the three-bladed Curtiss electric prop began to turn. The engine chugged, popped, and then several loud blasts blew soot out the exhaust stacks and the big prop blurred. Quickly, he pushed the mixture to Auto Rich, released the starter switch, and jockeyed the throttle. "C'mon!" The Allison blatted up to 900 rpm, let out a string of explosive farts, then stopped firing. "Goddamn crappy gas!" he shouted in frustration, unlocking the primer pump again and waiting for it to refill while the prop windmilled down. He jammed the handle forward, eased the throttle just above idle, and the engine finally caught and roared to life. It hadn't rained in two days, and a white cloud of dust erupted and gushed aft of the plane.

He buckled the lap belt, looking left and a little behind at the ship beside him. Soupy's engine was alive, beginning to behave, and the 'Cat was looking nervously around, bouncing up and down on his cushion and parachute, trying to settle himself. Ben's ears reddened when he saw Lieutenant Mackey in his mirror, looking back at him. Mack was grinning, his engine running smoothly. The prop on Shirley's ship was still turning on its starter, and Sergeant Dixon trotted out where Ben could see him, shaking his head and waving them on. Mallory nodded irritably and stirred his stick, then lowered the flaps. They'd learned from experience to take off side by side, a little staggered—and try to leave the dust-spewing, chip-throwing strip as quickly as they could. Mackey, as tail end Charlie, would wait until the dust settled. Someday they'd have a grass strip, but in the short term, "paving" and rolling the crushed limestone and coral they had plenty of was easier than grading, filling a billion stump holes, rolling the soft earth—and then waiting for grass to grow. Ben held his brakes for a brief mag check and listened while the others did the same, then pushed the throttle forward. The plane didn't move!

Damn it! The chocks! He pulled the throttle back to idle, cursing his jitters, but saw a 'Cat emerge from under the right wing, the triangular blocks from the left main already in his hand. He made a "hold on" motion, and pulled the right chocks from under the plane by the rope connecting them. Pitching the bundle of wooden blocks aside, he came to attention and saluted with a toothy grin. Ben grinned back, relieved, and returned the salute. Glancing at Soupy again, he briskly pointed down the strip.

The 'Cat nodded back; Ben shoved the throttle forward in a fluid motion and the Allison roared. The sudden noise and wind blast painfully reminded him he'd made another "newie" mistake. He'd neglected to don the leather helmet, headphones, and goggles still on his lap! Oh well, that would have to wait, but the noise was *physically* painful. He fed in a little left rudder as the plane accelerated, and he brought the tail up. Now he could see the strip in front of him when the P-40's long nose leveled out, and he danced on the rudder pedals to keep it straight. Another quick glance showed him Soupy still beside him and not lost in the growing dust cloud.

The plane got light on the gear and he eased back on the stick, lifting off and accelerating. The "Nancy" hangars by the river were getting larger, but he waited a moment longer to make sure his ship wouldn't bounce. Satisfied, he tapped the toe brakes to stop the spinning wheels, depressed the gear handle locking pin, and pulled the lever up. His head bobbled like a gobbler in a turkey shoot so he could keep track of his surroundings and watch the multitude of gauges, and he squeezed the hydraulic pump switch low on the stick that both raised the landing gear and allowed him to milk the flaps while the ship gained more speed. He confirmed that the strange landing gear position indicator was telling the truth when the left main completed its rotation and clunked into the port wing, followed moments later by the starboard, and the Gear Unsafe light went out. Now, with everything up, he had to resist the temptation to lift the nose and go straight at the enemy. He needed speed first; then he'd claw for altitude. He pushed the throttle past the established thirty-five inches of manifold pressure and immediately a loud *glackering* sound reached him even over the buffeting wind and now almost-agonizing exhaust. "*Goddamn* crummy gas!" he yelled again, unheard even by himself. He backed the throttle down half an inch or so, and the detonation quit. *Guess we'll have to settle for what we've got,* he thought, finally closing the canopy and muffling the terrible noise.

Airspeed passed 190 as he roared over the river at a hundred fifty feet—just enough to clear the highest trees on the other side. At 220, he pulled the nose up about thirty degrees, and the altimeter needles spun as he shot upward. The airspeed was holding and he trimmed her up. Finally he had a chance to put his helmet on. That helped a lot. He could actually hear himself think. Climbing through five thousand feet, his speed started bleeding and he advanced the throttle. The manifold pressure had been dropping about an inch per thousand feet, and now it came back up—but the engine started clattering again! If the detonation continued, it could overheat the engine, burn a hole in a piston, or— according to the manual—even blow a cylinder head off the block! He'd honestly never considered the possibility he'd have to climb this fast, this high, on this world for any reason, but he wasn't even half as high as the bizarre gaggle of Grik airships looming ever closer to Baalkpan.

I've got to get up there! he raged. He had one trick left, something he hadn't tried since that first, short flight when he was trying to impress Adar. He shoved the mixture control into the manual, Full Rich position. This was usually an emergency setting for low altitude when the auto feature failed due to a ruptured diaphragm in the controller. Normally, it would flood the engine or foul the plugs, but . . . *What the hell. In this situation, the Devil's gonna take the hindmost!* He was almost surprised when the detonation quit. He pushed the throttle forward and still didn't hear any clatter. A grin formed, and he eased the prop control back to 2,600 rpm. Not only did the engine still sound happy, but there was a definite increase in thrust. He raised the nose slightly and the speed settled at 160. Satisfied at last with his ship's performance, he activated the Bendix hydraulic gun-charging system. His plane was armed with only two guns, but it had extra ammunition. None were incendiary rounds since today they'd been loaded for more ground attack training.

They were lucky to have any bullets to train with at all and wouldn't have if Bernie hadn't solved the ammo issues. As it was, they had one precious tracer for every six rounds. Those damn Grik zeps *had* to be filled with hydrogen . . . didn't they? A tracer ought to light that . . . shouldn't it? One way or another, their fifties would shred them, he was sure. He held the Squeeze to Talk switch on the throttle knob to report what he'd done to overcome his detonation issues and called "Tally ho!" on the Grik airships, just now beginning to move over the city. There had to be twenty or more.

"All right, you lizardy bastards! Let's see how your balloons stand up to flasher fish!"

Mack had joined on Soupy's left wingtip, and the three P-40Es scorched across the sky and plunged into combat. If the Grik dirigibles had been a surprise to the allies, Ben's new toys came as a very rude shock to the enemy. One of the strange airships appeared in Ben's excellent (but according to Mack, dangerous in a crash) gunsight, and he fired a burst into the thing. Both his guns responded, and the target immediately seemed to become misshapen. One of its engines fell off and became entangled in

some sort of netting that covered the craft. The red tracers bored in, smoking white, and what began as a blue flicker above the odd "gondola"
erupted into an orange torrent of flame, and the craft sagged in the middle
as the fire raced fore and aft. Soupy's voice reached him through his earphones, screeching with glee as two more zeppelins gushed flames. Ben
shredded another himself as the planes blew through the ragged formation that scattered before them like terrified, lethargic fish. They *did* look
something like fish, Ben thought as he avoided debris that both rose and
fell. They weren't perfectly cylindrical but had an oval cross section. He
briefly wondered what advantage that shape might provide.

There was no time to ponder that; dark objects began falling from
the survivors of the first pass, plummeting toward the city below, and
all three planes climbed slightly and stood on their right wings to tighten
their turns for another strike. "Reduce speed!" he ordered. "We have to
spend more time shooting! Did anybody see anything that looked like
weapons on those things?"

"No weapons I see!" Soupy answered. "Look at that one! And that
one! They go up! I chase?"

Ben watched as several airships almost rocketed higher into the sky
as their bombs tumbled away. "No, leave 'em for now. They've already
dropped their bombs, and they're probably goners, anyway. Look at the
junk falling off them! They can't take that kind of upward acceleration!
They get high enough, their gas bags'll crack 'em wide-open! Concentrate on the ones with bombs!"

The formation had completely broken with that first pass, and the
Grik were now flying in all directions, dropping their bombs as fast as
they could. Ben destroyed two more in rapid succession, then stitched
another that had already dropped, but had apparently dumped enough
gas to prevent a catastrophic climb. He made sure it went down in flames.
No sense in letting any "smart" ones survive! Mack torched three in
quick succession, and Ben could only marvel at the guy's gunnery skills.
He'd already learned the man was a hell of a pilot.

"They make for shipyard!" Soupy squealed, tearing into another zep-
pelin that was dropping right then but maintaining its altitude . . . at
least until its aft end bowed under a torrent of fire. "We eat them up!"
Soupy yelled. "This big skuggik shoot!"

Ben was turning again, lining up on a pair of airships heading for the airstrip, when he happened to glance down. He gulped. Smoke was rising all over the city like malignant gray-black toadstools. "Shut up!" he shouted. "Maybe we're eating them up, but they're pasting our goddamn *Home*! Quit crowing and *kill* them!"

"Colonel," Mack's voice sounded. "You're not going to believe this, but something just dropped out of the sky and knocked a hole the size of a baseball in my left wing! I'm losing fuel."

"Okay, Mack, set her down. You've done a swell job. Soupy and I can handle the rest of these freaks. Looks like just a couple left, anyway. Over."

"Wilco, Colonel. You guys didn't do too shabby yourselves. I'll see you on the ground!"

"Roger, and out!" Ben said, opening up on the last two airships he could see, even as their bombs dropped away. One ship lit off, and it was close enough to its companion to ignite the gas it was venting. The combined fireball was enough, finally, to make Ben whoop. "Anything else, Soupy?"

"No, Colonel. Nothing near our level. A few still high up, but pieces falling off, so watch out!"

"Yeah. Don't want a whole engine falling on us! Let's scout around a bit, all the same. There may be stragglers, or even another whole batch behind this one."

"Ah, Roger, but if that's true, I better get more bullets!"

"You shot yourself dry?"

"Not completely."

Ben sighed. "Okay. We'll touch all the bases and head for the barn. The rest of PatWing One ought to be up by now. Maybe they're looking in the right direction this time—up!" It had occurred to him that the attackers *had* to have flown over at least a few of the patrol ships, and their pilots simply hadn't imagined anything flying higher than they did.

"Colonel Mallory." Jumbo's voice suddenly came through Ben's earphones. It sounded strained. "This is Kaufman Field Flight Ops. Be advised, a few bombs hit the strip and there're some craters. There's a clear lane, and we'll mark the damage, but just . . . be careful. Over."

"Roger, Kaufman Field. Soupy? Go ahead and take your ship down.

Mack's dust should be clear by the time you get there, and yours'll be gone by the time I come in."

Ben flew a little longer, enjoying the responsive fighter and his sense of accomplishment. He'd finally fought his first real air action, and although the targets had been sitting ducks, the threat had been real and the stakes enormous. It was a big deal. Only a couple of the enemy could have escaped, and only if they'd gained control of their airships before they came apart, high above. Even then, where would they go? He was pretty sure this part of the Grik blitz had been a suicide mission. He couldn't imagine they'd have the fuel to return after what had to be one of the longest flights in the history of this world. He looked down. The damage below looked bad, and fires started by the bombs and fallen airships blazed vigorously here and there. The shipyard seemed to have been spared, but it looked like at least one of the zeppelins had gone down right near the airstrip. Other than a corner of the Ordnance complex, it looked like the worst hit were civilian areas. *Of course, damage always looks worse from the air,* he consoled himself.

Finally, he turned for home, descending rapidly. He'd been right. The damage did look worse from higher up, where the smoke clouds broadened and made the fires look worse than they were. There was damage, sure, but he was proud they'd prevented far worse. Gear down, flaps down, he brought his "M" plane fluttering (and *blatting* loudly, still Full Rich) in over the airstrip. The dust had settled, but smoke was thick. At least the new craters had been well marked with red flags. Then, just as Ben's tires touched the crushed, packed strip, and his own dust cloud bloomed behind, he saw that what he'd taken for a burning airship wasn't an airship at all, but one of his precious P-40s lying twisted and scattered, the main portion of its corpse on its back, beyond one of the relatively small rock-filled cavities in the strip. Stunned, he let his plane roll nearly to a stop, then stood on the brakes. Letting off, he gunned his engine and turned toward the wreckage.

Black smoke still roiled skyward, but the fire had largely burned itself out. All that remained were the charred bones of a plane. He killed the Allison, slammed his canopy back, and stood in the cockpit. He couldn't tell whose plane it had been . . . until Soupy ran up and leaped on the wing beside him, his furry face wet with tears.

"Jumbo say he touch down just as bombs hit," Soupy almost moaned. "Big smoke, big dust." He shook his head, blinking. "He say even if he go full throttle then, he still hit hole. He screwed."

Jumbo, Sergeant Dixon, Shirley, and many more began gathering around Ben's plane, and he removed his helmet and dropped it on the seat. Stepping out, he saw many tears—but none on Sergeant Dixon's expressionless face. The man seemed to notice the scrutiny and managed only a shrug.

"Mack was a swell guy, Colonel," he said roughly, "but I can't *tell* you how many times I saw this exact same scene in the Philippines before the Japs caught us. So *many* swell guys . . . An' then with all that happened on that goddamn Jap ship . . . I just . . . I ain't got any tears left, ya know? I've *bled 'em* all out." He turned to the others, 'Cats and humans. "An' I won't cry a tear for you neither, *none* of you! I'll help keep these planes going until every last one is gone, because there's a war on and . . . Here we are. Beats where we *were*. But I'll spit on the bones of the next bastard that dies—and takes a good ship with him—'cause if he's dead, he ain't killin' those Jap-Grik bastards that just killed my friend!"

With that, Sergeant Dixon wheeled and stormed off in the direction of the hangars. Jumbo started to follow, but Ben called him back. "Leave him be, Lieutenant. I guess we all know how he feels. There's not a soul here who hasn't lost *somebody* in this damn war. Now we've lost somebody else. We'll bury him in the old Parade Ground Cemetery, beneath the Great Tree . . . and pray we *all* don't run out of tears before this war's done."

////// *Scapa Flow*
New Scotland
Empire of the New Britain Isles

*I*t was Sunday, February 13, 1944, by the New Britain calendar when Governor-Emperor Gerald McDonald observed USS *Walker* steaming slowly toward the mouth of Scapa Flow. He'd been staring through his telescope in the "observatory" atop Government House all morning, anticipating the landfall, and he'd even taken his breakfast there. Others were with him, anxiously drinking cooled tea in the warm breeze that ruffled curtains and papers through the large wide shutters.

"There they are, at last!" he announced triumphantly. "Coming straight in! The glass is fixed upon them!" With some difficulty, he stirred from his chair—brushing off Ruth McDonald's assistance—and heaved himself up on his crutches. "You needn't mother *me*, my dear," he said, glancing with a smile and thankful wonder once again at Princess Rebecca, the daughter who'd been returned to them at last.

She'd grown so much, in so many ways, and he sometimes had difficulty believing she was really back. "I get quite enough of that from your child—not to mention that tyrannical individual Captain Reddy forced upon me!"

Selass-Fris-Ar blinked disdain and harrumphed in a very human fashion. She hadn't been just a nurse to the Governor-Emperor, of course. Most of her time was spent dealing with the horrendous casualties of the New Ireland campaign, but she did check on him every day. Today she'd lingered longer than usual.

Hobbling aside, Gerald McDonald's eyes rested on Sandra Tucker. "Would you like to have a look, Minister?" he asked softly.

Sandra stood, exhausted but full of nervous energy. She'd been even busier than Selass. First, she'd chased after Shinya's division as soon as she was allowed, arriving in New Dublin with most of *Maaka-Kakja*'s medical division just as the fighting in the city came to an end. She'd grown accustomed to war and all its associated horrors: the wreckage of ships, cities, and the combatants themselves. However, she hadn't seen anything like New Dublin since the Battle of Baalkpan. That the majority of the dead and wounded were humans had come as a shocking reminder that not only Grik were savages. The devastation of the once almost-idyllic city was nearly complete, and people crept among the ruins like tentative, curious specters. She'd been particularly horrified to see so many people hanging from tree limbs or anything else that was handy. While treating some of Chack's wounded in a central square, she'd asked a man and his sons, cobblers by trade, about it. "Damn Dom collaborators!" had been the simple response. She doubted if any "rebels" who'd helped subjugate the people of New Ireland would last very long. Since then, there'd been the usual, endless procession of maimed bodies for her to attend.

Now she managed a thankful smile for the Governor-Emperor. "Yes, please," she said mildly to hide her anxiety, and peered through the large brass contraption.

As always it seemed, when *Walker*—and Captain Matthew Reddy—returned from action, the poor old ship looked like hell, and her heart jumped into her throat. Once again, *Walker* was streaked with rust from her long voyage, and her slightly rumpled shape and ragged superstructure testified to the beating she'd taken at the climax of the fight as she'd battled to save her consorts. In the end, there'd been no choice but to risk herself to the enemy guns, and she'd taken quite a thrashing. Only her speed and careful handling saved her.

"Oh, Matt," Sandra whispered sadly. She couldn't see him yet, couldn't make out any of the figures on deck, but she already knew he was alive at least, and she also knew, somehow, he'd be staring back at her. Cheering erupted outside again as news of the arrival began to spread. The city had been wild with excitement after the old destroyer drew near enough to send a report of the terrible Battle of Monterey Bay and of the fierce but short series of actions south of Saint Francis. Costly lessons had been learned in each battle, doubtless by both sides, but for now there was victory—and a breathing spell for the first time since the war exploded on the Imperial Dueling Grounds. There'd be sadness when details of the fighting and the cost became known, she knew, but for now, there was joy.

Two undamaged Imperial frigates, detailed by Commodore Jenks from a late-arriving element of Home Fleet, escorted the wounded ship. Battered as she was, it was obvious to Sandra that *Walker* was creeping along for the benefit of her companions.

She stepped back from the eyepiece. "Thank you, Your Majesty," she said, eyes glistening. "I think I'll go down to the American dock in the Navy Yard now."

Rebecca had moved to the glass. "As will I," she said softly.

"As shall we all!" Gerald proclaimed. "It's the very least we can do!"

For a while, it was like a reunion of old friends at the "American" dock, but the gathering quickly became a crowd. *Salaama-Na* was there, undergoing repairs after the pounding she'd taken from the New Ireland forts, and *Maaka-Kakja* had arrived two days before, the "mop-up" of New Ireland complete. The island was swamped with Lemurian sailors and Marines on liberty, much to the genuine delight of the populace, and the two massive Lemurian ships dominated the harbor and dwarfed all other vessels there. Not everyone was present, of course, and two of the most keenly felt absences were Fred Reynolds and Kari-Faask. They'd become very popular in the fleet, New Scotland, and on *Walker* in particular. But the reunion was still jubilant because many of the others hadn't seen one another in a long, long time.

Added to the commotion of greeting was the presence of the royal family, hundreds of female yard workers, and many hundreds of people from the city itself, come to pay their respects. In the midst of it all, USS *Walker* (DD-163), swayed gently at her moorings, the sea lapping soothingly at her dented plates. Battered and bruised, she'd protected most of her people . . . most of them . . . and again that had been a major achievement. Her blower sighed contentedly and smoke wisped lazily from her aft funnel. Someone had finally begun painting her victims on the side of her port bridgewing, and the collection was as bizarre as it was lengthy. Everything from Japanese planes to Grik ships (nobody remembered how many of *those* she'd destroyed) to the now acceptably coined "Grik birds" were represented. And, of course, there was *Amagi. Walker* lay there at rest, beneath her battle flag and canton fluttering at the jackstaff above her bullnose, proud, confident, and far more than she would have ever been on the world where she was made.

Princess Rebecca was first to meet Matt when he descended to the dock, sprinting ahead of everyone else. She clasped him in an embrace that startled him but also melted his heart. At the same time, he was a little disconcerted by the strange, semiwinged . . . creature . . . drooped across her shoulders that looked skeptically up at him.

"Thank you," Rebecca said, wetting his shirt with her tears, "for everything. You *did* come for us, as we knew you would, but then you not only saved my father, but my country as well. I'll never forget it!"

"Forget it!" Petey screeched. "Goddamn!"

Sandra was next, but after only a quick embrace she and Matt were forced to focus on the endless stream of greetings and congratulations. Still, they remained glued together, side by side, the mere presence of the other after so long and so much renewing their souls. They shared a strange new tension, however, an almost-sickening, floating sense that regardless of their attachment, something . . . fundamental was about to change. Both knew they had much to discuss, officially and otherwise. From an official standpoint, Matt's stormy expression when he saw the gathering of dark-skinned *human* females—in USN T-shirts, dungarees, and Dixie cups—arrayed behind a woman Sandra introduced simply as

"Carpenter's Mate, Steward Diania," promised a lively debate, and Sandra had blithely ignored it. If 'Cat "girls" could serve in the Navy, so could the human variety as far as she was concerned. She knew she'd win that one, eventually. She had no idea how their "personal" discussion would go.

Happy greetings occurred all around, and 'Cats scampered excitedly on and off the old destroyer, dispensing with ceremony. But each one saluted her flag. Matt caught a familiar loud voice and saw Juan Marcos leaning on a crutch, his left pant leg pinned up. He was berating Tabasco and Earl Lanier in Tagalog, a language nobody except maybe the few Philippine Scouts who'd survived their hellish ordeal in *Mizuki Maru* understood. He was glad for Juan that there were other Filipinos now, but he was also very worried about that Japanese destroyer, still apparently on the loose. *Mizuki Maru* had finally steamed after her, but there'd been no word. And, of course, he'd heard about his cousin Orrin, still on New Ireland. He wasn't flying again yet, but he was in charge of rooting out the last of the Grik birds. Fortunately, there'd never been many on the island. Their surprise appearance in the dark had been costly, but Orrin had developed tactics to lure them from their hiding places and destroy them. Matt smiled sadly. Thank God the kid was alive, but it had apparently been a bad war for the Reddy clan back home. Juan's jabbering continued unabated. Poor Tabasco kind of slunk back, but suddenly, to Matt's amazement, Earl Lanier stepped forward and picked Juan up off the deck and held him in a greasy, furry-armed, stinky embrace.

"I'm glad to see you too, you goddamn, crazy little Flip!" he rumbled.

Eventually, the horde dwindled. The Governor-Emperor was tiring, and he invited all the senior officers to join him at Government House and dine early. There they could debrief at greater leisure and in more comfort. Unexpectedly, many crew and Marines from *Walker* and other "Lemurian-American" ships flocked along. The officers' gathering would be on the wide veranda of the residence, but no one had prohibited the growing party on the grounds surrounding it. Some Imperial officers and officials seemed shocked and dismayed by the familiar way the human and 'Cat Americans behaved around their officers, and several suggested they dine inside, away from the revelers. Princess Rebecca gave them a steely glare, and even the Governor-Emperor dismissed the notion as he and the other Allied leaders assembled around a long, narrow table on the broad porch.

It's the Lemurian way, Matt recalled with a small smile, remembering the times he'd made landfall among the People. He took his indicated seat to Gerald's right at the head of the table, with Sandra at his side, and noticed that Ruth McDonald sat with her husband. He'd never seen that before. He wondered if their influences were beginning to take root and whether they'd ultimately be appreciated or resented. Right now, the expanded Alliance was on solid ground.

There was no ceremony, no speech, no "official" greeting, and Matt was thankful. He *was* surprised, but suspected Sean O'Casey (Bates) had probably advised against it, knowing him and his people the best. The Governor-Emperor began the "proceedings" simply, by leaning forward and saying something to Courtney Bradford. The Australian cupped his hand behind his ear, and the Bosun abruptly stood, facing the crowd.

"Pipe down, you bunch'a' goons!" he bellowed. "The brass is tryin' to decide whether to give you medals or throw you all in the brig!"

Sean Bates rose as well. "There'll be fine, great barrels o' beer available soon on the north porch. Do enjoy it there, fer the time bein', ta the extent allowed by yer officers! This *is* a celebration, an' there'll be music an' dancin' at dusk, but we must have a wee chat before then." Amid cheers, the vast majority of the partyers made their way to the other side of Government House, and Bates nodded at Gray with a grin. "Now I'm His Majesty's Factor, er 'chief o' staff,' I reckon, I've learned ta reward wi' beer, rather than berate wi' roars!"

"That might work ashore . . ." Gray muttered as the two sat down, eliciting laughter.

"I beg your pardon, Your Majesty," Courtney said. "What was your question?"

"What did you think of the fauna in the colonies?" Gerald repeated more loudly.

"I had little opportunity to explore, I'm afraid, with all the bothersome battles. I did see a few fascinating specimens after the sea fight ended and we joined the shore action." He paused, and his wild brows fairly bounced with excitement. "One beast we saw was simply *titanic,* but the locals paid it little heed!" He sipped tea, cooled by ice brought from *Walker.* "Of course, by then, it was more a general chase. Commodore Jenks and Mr. Gray"—he nodded at the Bosun—"had already won the fight."

"Those locals are damn good shots, and even Silva'd appreciate their humongous rifles!" Gray said with actual admiration. "We never saw any o' their 'Grik birds'—they must've all been after you, Skipper—an' Chack's probably right about 'em not havin' enough sense to use in a pitched land fight. Anyway, once the Doms found out their fleet was beat, they retreated south faster than our artillery could keep up. They left most of theirs, but we needed our guns because they still had us outnumbered pretty bad." He took a gulp of tea himself. "We didn't take many prisoners," he added. "Mostly wounded they left behind. I'm told if they try to walk all the way back to the Dominion, most won't make it, though."

"True enough," Gerald agreed soberly. "I once visited the borderlands, back when Harvey Jenks and I were both 'squeakers' aboard the old *Zeus,*" he reminisced. "The country they must cross is quite dreadful, full of terrifying beasts." He looked at Captain Reddy and smiled crookedly. "But since my attempt at preliminary pleasantries has been so successfully redirected, we may as well get down to it. Tell me, what do you think about the situation concerning Governor Dodd and Lord Admiral McClain?"

Matt considered. "The admiral's no traitor; he simply disagreed with our strategy. He made no secret of his belief the Doms would strike at the Enchanted Isles. The problem is, he *understood* our strategy and knew what was expected of him. His tardiness cost us more casualties than we would've taken with the force we expected, and nearly cost us the battle. All here had already agreed what the consequences of that would have been. Jenks was right to relieve him in your name."

Gerald nodded. "Indeed. Of course. A sad necessity."

"On the other hand, it looks like Governor Dodd *did* turn. He was 'missing' throughout the crisis, gone 'camping' or 'hunting,' I'm told. A search was unsuccessful and revealed no evidence his party fell prey to predators. The militia there—damn fine scouts—don't think he went anywhere near where he said he'd be, but went south toward the Dom landings instead. The consensus is he retreated with the beaten enemy."

"I thought I knew Dodd," Gerald lamented, shaking his head. He looked at Chack and Blair. "It seems sure we still have high-placed traitors here as well, who passed nearly our entire plan to the enemy. They must be discovered!" His gaze returned to Matt. "And though Dodd was always a 'Company man,' I never believed him capable of treason. Clearly, we still have our hands full on the home front."

"That's what it looks like."

"Aye," Bates agreed. "Jenks'll have his hands full in the east as well, sortin' out the colonies an' tryin' ta take the fight ta the Doms. They'll go fer the Enchanted Isles now for sure."

"Most likely," Matt agreed. "At least he should have the ships to stop them now, with what we left him. Frankly, the Dom 'ships of the line' are almost useless. Good thing for us they started this war with last generation's Navy! I guess that's all they thought they'd need. The transports are fairly new, *built* for this war, but their fighting ships are twenty or thirty years old. They're still dangerous as hell if you get close to one, but with enough steamers, you shouldn't have to. Sooner or later they're going to put engines in them and that'll change, but for now? We captured a couple, once they were helpless. Dom sailors and regulars aren't all crazy, at least. I recommended Jenks put some of their heavy guns on the steam transports we took. He's 'CINCEAST' now by the way, if you've no objection, Your Majesty."

"None whatsoever. He's earned it. He'll need troops, however."

Matt looked down the table at Tamatsu Shinya and Lelaa-Tal-Cleraan. "Troops *and* air cover. What do you think, *General* Shinya? *Admiral* Lelaa?" He'd received the reports of their activities several days out. Lelaa blinked rapidly and would have blushed if she could, Matt was sure.

"*Maaka-Kakja* and her battle group will go where they're needed, Cap-i-taan Reddy," Lelaa said.

"Shinya?"

"May I have Chack?" Shinya asked.

"Well, no, you can't," Matt said, his brows furrowing. "He's going home with me and *Walker*." He glanced at Sandra, then looked at Gerald. "My ship needs a refit like she can't get out here—yet. Besides, things are heating up in the west, and while the Dom Navy might be on its heels for now, we haven't heard a peep from the Grik Navy in a while. They build fast, Your Majesty!"

"You can say that again, Skipper!" Spanky muttered, several places down. Tabby sat beside him—in a real uniform, thank God—and as an officer, it was appropriate she be present. None of *Walker*'s destroyer-men doubted why she'd chosen to sit next to Spanky, however. "About the refit, I mean," he added. "And things *are* heating up. I almost popped my cork when we got word about the zeppelins! I mean, well . . . shit!"

Matt nodded grimly. What Spanky didn't elaborate on was the rest of their reaction when they "got the word." The Ceylon operation was a success, but they'd had it almost easy out here compared to First Fleet. *Humfra-Dar*, *Tolson*, *Revenge*, Geran-Eras, Pruit Barry, Clancy, Jamie Miller—not to mention the *thousands* of soldiers, sailors, and Marines the campaign cost—and there was that "new" Grik general Rolak's pet Grik had learned about, questioning the survivors at Colombo. . . . *Walker* needed to go home for a lot of reasons.

"I mean to escort *Salaama-Na* as far as an island we call 'Wake,'" he said. "I can't remember what your charts call it. We need another comm relay. After that, I may have another short stop to make, but ultimately"—he looked fondly at Chack—"*Colonel*-Bosun's Mate Chack-Sab-At deserves to go home—and on to fight the Grik. I'm . . . sure he's been sorely missed."

Matt didn't notice, but Sandra saw Selass sink down slightly in her seat. She pursed her lips, sad for her friend and her hopeless love. She cut her eyes at Matt. "And what's this 'short stop'?" she asked, suspecting he meant to visit the Great South Island "on the way" home. It was a trip Courtney had long been pressing. There were many potential allies there—and just as many wonders for Mr. Bradford to explore. Or maybe he wanted to chase that Japanese destroyer.

"Just a minute," Matt asked her, looking at Shinya. "Do you mean you won't take the job if Chack's not with you?"

Shinya blinked. "What? Oh! Of course I'll take the job! I thought that went without saying! I just wanted Chack along, that's all." He paused. "I *should* take as many Imperial troops as possible, of course, and I'd like to recruit some of these 'colonial scouts.' I do think it's time a few

Imperial troops went west, however," he prompted. "Our Lemurian allies have given much on this front."

Gerald nodded gravely. "Your point is well taken, General. Our 'Army' is growing quickly, but it's still small. Do you think a regiment would suffice for now?"

"Yeah, under the circumstances," Matt said. "Our friends know you're stretched. A regiment now, with a promise of more, would be sufficient and appreciated. Our losses in Ceylon have been heavy."

"Have you anyone in mind to command this force, Colonel Chack?" the Governor-Emperor asked.

"Ah, yes, sir. Majors Blair and Jindal."

Gerald laughed, looking at the two men in question. "Blast it, you can't have them both! I've just relieved half the officer corps of the entire Imperial Marines! Useless bureaucrats! Hmm. Major Blair's already faced these Grik of yours, but Major Jindal could use the experience, and perhaps your tutelage? I shall consider it."

"What 'little trip'?" Sandra insisted again.

Matt took a deep breath and looked at her. He'd been hoping for a better, private time, but those were likely to be rare in the few days he planned to tarry in Scapa Flow. He rubbed his forehead and glanced around the table at the people there, all friends, most practically *family* in a sense. "Well, I thought a little vacation might be in order, just a few days. I know this place called Respite Island. Good people, beautiful weather, lots of secluded places you can actually *swim* . . ."

"What *kind* of vacation, Captain Reddy?" Sandra sternly pressed, and Matt looked around again, almost helplessly this time. He saw the grinning faces and knew he was blushing. He was in *hell*. "Oh, well . . . I don't know. The . . . honeymoon kind, I guess," he finally mumbled.

Sandra was struck speechless. Not as much by the implication of what he'd said, but by seeing Captain Matthew Reddy, honored hero, *fearless warrior*, afflicted with the timidity of a schoolboy. "Taking something for granted, aren't you?" she finally managed, and immediately cursed herself. *What kind of dope am I?*

"No, he ain't, Miss Lieutenant-Minister Tucker, with all due respect!" boomed a voice nearby. She spun in her seat and saw Dennis Silva leaning on one of the porch columns, a mug of beer in one hand, the bent barrel of the Doom Whomper in the other. It was all he'd managed to salvage of his precious weapon from the shattered remains of the wheelwright's shop, and he'd moped around with the thing ever since, waving it like a bloody shirt or using it to menace Dom prisoners. Now he was back to form. Lawrence peered out from behind him, crest rising in a kind of cringe. The amused tension around the table broke and erupted into laughter.

"Not about *you*, anyway," Silva added. "There's one small bookkeepin' chore to settle first, though. Since I ain't yet been ree-leeved o' watchin out for you an' the Munchkin princess"—he glared at the child—"who says I'm stuck pertectin' her for *life*—dooty permittin'. I'm still sorta yer guardians, so to speak. The way I figger it, Skipper's either gotta let me off the hook or ask my blessin'!"

"Ask my blessin'!" Petey demanded insistently, and Gray had had enough.

"Silva! Ain't you got *any* decency or respect? Even a *sliver*? You're the most outrageous, immoral, degenerate . . . !"

"Don't forget 'debauched'!" Courtney added gleefully.

"Yeah, that too. And . . . other stuff! Can't you even let the Skipper and his dame have a tender, private moment without stickin' yourself in it, damn you?"

Silva gestured around, grinning. "Ain't exactly private, Bosun, and I don't think he wanted it to be, deep down. He thinks he needs *our* permission to be happy, you big rotten-hearted toad!"

Gray blinked and looked at Matt, who sat staring into Sandra's eyes.

Finally, Matt looked around one last time and stood in the sudden, total silence. "You're right, Silva," he croaked, then cleared his throat. "You're right," he repeated more normally. "Even now, I think my crew deserves a say. Partly because if I marry her, it's not as if she can accompany us on extended cruises anymore, and her fine advice and counsel have been invaluable in the past." He looked down at Sandra. "That's what bugs me most, I think. As this war drags on, I'll probably have even less time with you if we . . ." He stopped, seeing her feelings reflected in her damp eyes. "Chief Gunner's Mate Silva," he enunciated clearly. "Request permission to marry Lieutenant Sandra Tucker!"

Amazingly, Silva's almost-taunting grin re-formed itself into as gentle a smile as his battered face could manage. "Permission granted, Skipper."

"Very well. You stand relieved."

Silva dropped his mug and snapped a sharp salute. "Aye, aye, sir. I stand relieved."

Sandra stood beside Matt as the applause began, and feet stamped the porch beneath the table. "Are you sure this is what you want?" she asked.

"Aren't you?"

She hugged him. "Of course," she whispered into his chest.

"Good, because this is the only thing I've really wanted, for myself, for the better part of the last two years. Sure I'm sure."

The "Sea of Jaapan"

izuki Maru plodded slowly north by east into the cold sea and biting wind northwest of what should have been Kyushu. "Lord" Commander Sato Okada grimly scanned the sea ahead with the binoculars they'd found on the ship during her refit at Maa-ni-la. Occasionally, his gaze swept east, despite his efforts to prevent it, and he viewed the unfamiliar coastline of his homeland with a sense of loss and betrayal. He'd come to grips with the "way things were" and accomplished great things, he thought, in the "shogunate" he'd established. There'd been few illusions of democracy, aside from the willingness of other communities to join, but he thought he'd set up a system whereby the peoples there might be ruled in a benevolent way. With that rule came responsibilities, however, and now he was hunting members of his own race for what they'd done to the Lemurians who'd adopted him—and placed themselves under his protection. Whatever national commonality he'd once shared with the people, the *animals*, who'd perpetrated the massacre near Yokohama, was more than eclipsed by the atrocity they'd committed—and his duty to destroy them.

"It is still a beautiful land," he whispered to the other Japanese officer beside him, another member of *Amagi*'s crew rescued from the Grik at Singapore. There were six such men aboard *Mizuki Maru*, in addition to the cook/deserter who'd brought them the tale of horror. The cook was still just a cook. He had no desire to leave his galley at all. There he could surround himself with the familiar and perhaps pretend nothing had really changed. The largely Lemurian crew that came to him for meals had to be a constant reminder that such was not the case, but he persevered, sometimes teetering on the brink of madness, but there was always hot food for the furry crew who, despite their coats, were unaccustomed to the damp cold that blew at them out of the north. It was winter, Okada knew, but only those Lemurians from his new home understood. His colony had been one of the northernmost outposts of the People known, and only the hardiest tried to subsist there. Some had even seen snow; a rare novelty. The "Navy" 'Cats that augmented his crew had no experience with snow, or even cold for that matter, and the farther north they steamed, the more miserable they were.

"Anything on the radio yet, Lieutenant Hiro?" Okada asked the officer beside him.

Hiro shook his head. "Nothing yet, Lord."

Mizuki Maru had been broadcasting terrified entreaties for someone, anyone to answer them, to tell them where to go, to assure them they weren't alone in a terrible world gone mad. Okada could only guess that the destroyer *Hidoiame* and her tanker had come this way, and he had nothing tangible on which to base that guess. He assumed his . . . enemy would scout the Japanese coastline, ensuring there were no others of their kind, before venturing afield into the greater unknown. He wasn't sure he'd have done that himself, after a couple of brief explorations, but it was his only hope for a quick encounter. The trail had gone quite cold, and if *Hidoiame* wasn't near Japan, he had no idea where next to look. So the radio calls constantly dangled the bait of another ship, swept as they were to this world, but a "supply ship" with plenty of food and ammunition aboard, and no idea where to take it. Okada was confident that if his enemy could hear him, he wouldn't be able to resist for long.

"What will we do, Lord?" Hiro asked.

Okada grunted. "We'll continue north through the Sea of Japan until we hear word, or we're stopped by ice. If there's no ice, we'll steam down the Pacific side of the home islands. . . ." He paused. "And keep looking. We'll put in at Yokohama, visit our people, and replenish supplies, then proceed southeast of the Fil-pin Lands, wailing our heads off all the while. I still believe we should concentrate on areas *Hidoiame* might hope are populated by others such as us—castaways from our world to this. After Japan itself, the more populous regions of Imperial expansion would seem most likely. We shall loop south around New Guinea and head back up along the Malay Barrier toward Baalkpan and Aryaal. Perhaps we'll hear word of a sighting if she's gone into those seas." He looked at Hiro. "If we don't find her by then, we must assume she either went east into New Britain territory, or has . . . somehow communicated with that madman, Kurokawa, and turned west toward the Grik."

"What if she encounters the Allied fleets?"

"Actually, I'm confident they will destroy her, if one of their"—he grimaced—"*our* capital ships is present. It will be costly, but I only truly fear her torpedoes."

"Indeed," Hiro said nervously.

The speaking tube from the radio shack whistled, and Hiro stepped over and spoke into it. "Bridge. Lieutenant Hiro speaking."

"The murderers have taken the lure, my lord," came the tinny voice. "They want to talk to our captain."

Okada leaned toward the tube. "I'm on my way."

"We are the *Junyo Maru*, my lord," the radioman reminded Okada when he entered the compartment. *Junyo Maru* was a ship *Hidioame* would be familiar with, and she was a dead ringer for their own.

"Of course." He took the microphone. "This is Captain Okada of the *Junyo Maru*. I cannot express my relief at finding countrymen here in this . . . wrongful place!"

"I am Commander Kurita of the Imperial Japanese ship *Hidoiame!*" a terse voice crackled in response. "Now that we have established communications, please cease screaming your head off for all the world to hear! We are not alone in this place, and there may be enemies listening! We have monitored what sound like coded *American* transmissions, so send no more open radio messages. Any further communications will be via coded CW, understood?"

"Understood," Sato replied. Grinning, his radioman patted the codebook the fools had left on the ship when they abandoned it, obviously expecting the ship to sink, or if it didn't, no one would ever make use of it. Evidently, they were more concerned about that now. "I'll put my radioman back on," Sato said. "Please instruct him on what frequency you wish to use, and tell us where to find you!"

Okada handed the transmitter back to the radioman and stood back while the man finished the conversation. A few minutes later, the code-groups began coming in. A Lemurian striker versed in Japanese started transcribing what the radioman wrote, the codebook in one hand, a pencil in the other.

"They did not give their exact position, Lord," the 'Cat announced a short while later. "They merely ordered us to steam for Sapporo. Do you know where that is?"

"Yes," Okada said grimly, picturing the geography in his mind. "I would wager that is where they have made their base, for now. Ishikari-Wan should make a good, deep anchorage, even here. I suspect it will be cold, my friends, but they made no mention of ice. That is a relief."

"How long until we reach that place?" the Lemurian striker asked.

"A week, at this pace. Perhaps a bit longer. We'll have them anxious to see us! In the meantime, we will prepare."

A Cave
Somewhere in the Holy Dominion

Lieutenant Fred Reynolds tried to open his eyes, but they felt glued shut by some thick, rough, gooey substance. He couldn't wipe them with his hands because they were roughly bound behind his back, so he blinked repeatedly, trying to clear them. It did little good. He could see a little, not that much was visible in the damp gloom of his underground "cell." Torches guttered meagerly in a passage beyond the iron bars that isolated his little alcove from the cavern beyond, and occasionally, he heard what sounded like distant, echoing voices.

He was beyond miserable; naked, cold, covered with filth and reeking mud. He couldn't remember when he'd last been given water. Every part of his body hurt, but his shoulder was still the worst. He suspected his collarbone had broken when the "Nancy" flipped in the surf, and his heel might be broken too. In any event, he'd almost drowned before Kari dragged him out of the sea and up on the beach. She's been injured too, he remembered, pretty badly, and he didn't know how she'd managed. All that had happened to them after the crash had become little more than a vague blur.

Neither of them had been in any condition to resist when the Doms came for them. Fred was pretty sure he'd been unconscious when they arrived. It didn't matter. He'd lost his pistol in the crash, and didn't have the strength to fight them. All he remembered was being carried, slung on a pole like a dead hog, for what might have been minutes or days. At some point, he'd been carried aboard a ship in the darkness, and the next he knew, he was here. He'd probably been drugged. He knew they'd taken Kari too, but he hadn't seen her since. He prayed she was alive.

The voices in the passageway became louder, and he expected a visitor at last. *Maybe I should pray Kari's not alive,* he reconsidered, remembering what he knew of the Doms. New torches flickered, adding their light to the darkness, and forms appeared, moving toward him. A lock clanked, and a barred door swung open with a damp, rusty groan.

"Fetch water, fools," said a mild voice that contrasted with the perfunctory order. "This man is ill, hurt! He cannot be allowed to die before given a chance to atone! To be purified!"

"At once, Holiness!" came a nervous reply in thickly accented English, and a dark form retreated.

Fred was grateful he'd get water at last, but chilled by the other comments. Torches were placed in sockets and others lit. There was plenty of light now, but his sight remained blurred.

"Poor creature," the soft voice whispered again, and a red-robed figure bent and gently wiped the goo from Fred's eyes with a soft cloth. "Better?"

Fred nodded, seeing a face at last. It was dark skinned, pleasantly solicitous, with a salt-and-pepper mustache and chin whiskers.

"What is your name?"

Fred cleared his throat. "Frederick Reynolds. Lieutenant, junior grade, serial number . . ."

"Your given name is sufficient for God to know you, my son," the man consoled. "I am Don Hernan de Devino Dicha, Blood Cardinal to His Supreme Holiness, the Messiah of Mexico and Emperor of the World by the Grace of God. It pleases him—and myself—to offer you sanctuary from the wicked, damned heretics whose orders placed you in contention with God Himself. But God is merciful, my son! You may yet achieve grace in His eyes, and your soul and life be saved!"

Don Hernan! He'd heard that name. *Oh, Jesus, help me!* he begged. Water finally arrived, and he was allowed to drink, but not too much. "How—" He broke off, coughing. "How did you get here?" he asked.

"You know of me!" the Blood Cardinal exclaimed. "Most excellent, indeed!" He shrugged. "It was a simple thing. I merely took passage on the very ship the heretics sent to 'warn' their illegitimate colonies of the hostilities they initiated. Her captain is a child of God."

So, that explains a lot. There was no point in arguing who'd started the war. "Where's Kari?" Fred managed. "What have you done with her?"

Don Hernan blinked. "You mean the animal captured with you? It has a *name*?"

"Of course she has a name! And she's no animal! Where is she?"

Don Hernan shook his head. "Such a tone! I forget sometimes that the unenlightened are known to form deep attachments to their pets." He peered intently at Fred. "It lives, for now. I've considered putting it on display, as a curiosity. That might still be done if it dies, of course. The creature is a menace, dangerous to handle, even with its sharp nails and teeth removed! I *should* have it killed and stuffed."

"*No!*"

For the first time, Don Hernan's voice rose. "You shout? You demand? *Of me?*" Visibly, he calmed himself. "The creature's fate, as is your own, is up to you. You must be purified, of course, but your suffering thus far has doubtless earned you *some* measure of grace." Don Hernan made a sour face. "I confess the sin of arrogance. I badly underestimated your

'Captain Reddy' and his iron steamer. Our efforts to bend the small dragons to our will have been lengthy and tedious. Their potential facility is great—as you and your marvelous flying machine have proven—but a decade of preparation and great expense was lost in a single day to Captain Reddy and his stratagems. Not to mention his remarkably swift and unexpectedly powerful ship." He paused. "The ship we can counter," he said confidently, "but continuing the small dragon project seems of dubious value—except of course for having brought us *you*. They *do* appear effective against your flying machines!" He hesitated and smiled. "Which *brings* us to you!"

"What do you want from me?" Fred asked, already fearing the answer.

"Flying machines, of course! And instruction in their use. Give me those things, and you will not only live—with your pet by your side, I presume—but you will become a wealthy and respected Child of God, a convert to the Holy Church, and a beloved citizen of the Holy Dominion! More you could never ask nor earn!"

Fred started to say he knew nothing about building airplanes, only flying them, but decided that might not be the best idea just then. "And if I refuse?" he asked instead.

"You and your pet will both be skinned alive . . . to begin with." Don Hernan shook his head sadly. "And regardless of your . . . suffering, your very soul will be destroyed and you will never see God." He paused as two men entered the alcove with a brazier of coals and assorted irons. "Think on it for a time. We will talk again." He turned to leave.

"But . . . W-what the hell is *that* for?" Fred cursed, his tone shrill.

The Blood Cardinal glanced back. "Just something to pass the time, to *help* you think. Besides, even should you choose wisely, as I expect, you must first be purified for your conversion." He gestured at the two men. "They will call me when you have decided . . . and they are positive you are sincere."

South Africa

Lieutenant Toru Miyata was alone in the vast wilds of southern Africa. A strong cold wind blew directly in his face from the south, leeching his strength and seeping into his bones. He was still struck by the irony of the weather, given where he was, but irony barely registered anymore in his starving, pain-filled, cold-numbed mind. Things had gone pretty much the way he'd always expected, he supposed, even if the sequence of events hadn't. Umito wasn't the first to die, after all. Even in his weakened state, he'd been more resilient than the Grik to the cold of the high plateau they traversed. One of Bashg's "elite" Uul warriors was almost immediately eaten by something barely bigger than itself, despite the firearms and swords of his companions. Toru didn't know what the thing had been; the creatures of this land were different from any he'd seen, and he could barely even think of anything to compare it to. Maybe a combination of a furry crocodile, a giant sloth, and a koala bear. The thing had looked more ridiculous than menacing, but it made short work of one of Bashg's best "troops."

They remained on the alert for the creatures after that, but no others were ever seen. That didn't mean there weren't other threats, even more dangerous. That was probably why they didn't see more "Koala-diles."

Another of Bashg's Uul was just simply dead one morning, presumably of the cold, even though it couldn't have dropped much lower than forty degrees during the night. It made its bed too far from the large fire they'd maintained, and the relatively "advanced," but still imbecilic creature probably died completely unaware of its danger. No Grik, as far as Toru knew, was accustomed to cold, and that was one of the things he and his companions were counting on; secretly why they'd suggested this colder, higher altitude route, ostensibly based on its directness. Grik weren't reptiles and actually had better insulation than humans, but Toru supposed, like most birds, they just didn't like the cold and avoided it as a species. Therefore, the weather took a toll on them. The temperature had been similar to that of a Japanese fall, for the most part, so Toru and his companions weren't terribly affected, but even in their heavy coats, the Grik shivered almost uncontrollably—and were always hungry.

Bashg's remaining warriors butchered the chilled corpse of their former comrade to augment their already dwindling rations because, after only two weeks, they'd flown through the provisions meant to last two months and had resorted to eating whatever they could catch. For all intents and purposes, halfway to their destination, the expedition had ground to a halt. Even Bashg no longer seemed to care about the mission, though he still talked of "resuming" the trek once they were "rested." Despite his supposedly superior intellect to his underlings, instinct now prevailed. He was just as cold and hungry as the others, and all he wanted to do was sit near a huge fire.

Aguri and Toru hunted, trying to find food with their trusty, but rather underpowered (for this world) Arisaka Type 38 rifles. That last morning they'd struggled through knee-deep, frozen grass, across what should have been a tree-covered plain teeming with game, but which was now a glistening, frosty steppe. Some snow had even fallen during the night, and they were both confused by that. They knew the weather on this world was different, and they counted on it to aid them now, but they didn't understand why it was. They saw a few creatures from a distance, but all were bigger than they wanted to attempt with a 6.5-mm projectile. One of the beasts seemed impossibly huge, and they watched it quite a while from a careful distance. It looked something like one of the brontosaurus-type creatures they'd seen before, but it was bigger and covered with long, thick, shaggy fur. Unlike its apparent cousins, it was solitary as well, with no great herd for company or mutual protection. Toru was no biologist, but everything about the creature just seemed wrong and out of place—at least until he saw it eat.

The thing's head was shaped like a bony spade at the end of a powerful, but oddly shorter than "normal" neck. It moved slowly through the thick grass and light snow, shoveling it aside with its head in wide, sweeping motions and heaping the grass into large piles beside it. For a time, it then stood still, eating the dark, lush, still-greenish stuff it harvested.

"Look at that!" Aguri had said. "*He* has plenty to eat. I wonder why he's by himself?"

"Maybe he's an old bull and doesn't like company. Maybe something got the rest of his herd and he's the last one left," Toru said.

"Or maybe he's just grumpy, an outcast from his kind," speculated Aguri.

"Outcast . . . like us?" Toru chuckled darkly. "Come," he said, standing from the vantage point where they'd watched the monster. "Let's get back. We won't find anything today. Perhaps the snow has everything curled up in a warm bed."

"I doubt it," Aguri said. "I'm sure they're used to it."

"I don't know. I don't know much at all."

"Neither do I. That's why we're here, Toru."

"Well, let's get back, anyway. I don't like leaving Umito so long with that pack of jackals."

"How much longer must we remain here?" Aguri asked. "Umito can't last, and those Grik could never catch us if we fled."

Toru nodded. The timing was just about right. They no longer needed the Grik to carry supplies—there weren't any left. Also, only four Grik remained; each far more weakened by hunger and exposure than the Japanese sailors. "We must wait a while longer. Umito still lingers, and though he has begged me to, I will not leave him until he has joined his . . . impossibly distant ancestors." He paused. "You know what will happen to him even then, and we must not allow it. As soon as Umito passes, we will slay the remaining Grik and then move on—get off this damn plateau. It must be warmer at the lower elevations near the sea, agreed?"

The three men had grown close, and Toru didn't expect an argument from Aguri. There was none. As they'd known all along, a confrontation with their captors was inevitable. It had always been a matter of timing. As it turned out, the *exact* timing of their plan was a little off, as were the circumstances that precipitated it. When they trudged back to their camp, they discovered their Grik "allies" frantically devouring their—hopefully already dead—friend, and as quickly as a brain can comprehend a thing the eyes try to tell it, everything suddenly changed.

"Aaieeee!" shrieked Aguri, and charged down the slope into the little bowl where their camp lay, bayonet thrust forward before him. All he saw was the spattered blood on the snow and the mangled shreds of his friend dangling from savage jaws.

"No, Aguri!" Toru yelled, bringing his rifle up. One Grik sprang at Aguri, and he and the other man both shot it. It went down, writhing, but another reacted just as quickly. Toru worked his bolt—too slow!—but Aguri lowered his bayonet with a roar and buried it in the creature's chest up to the handguard—where it stuck. Toru shot a third Grik, still wolfing down gobbets of Umito as fast as it could, and the creature merely collapsed atop the scattered, unrecognizable corpse. But there was still Bashg.

The Grik leader approached Aguri from an angle, leaving Toru without a clear shot. Realizing Aguri's bayonet was jammed, Bashg plucked a coal from the fire with his claws and held it to the slow match on his musket until it sputtered and smoked. He slid aside the plate covering the priming powder in the pan. "This work now. Less stomachs, lots eat!" he said, almost excitedly. "Us go quick now, do orders!"

Frantically, Aguri released the bayonet from his muzzle and tried to chamber another round, looking at Bashg. Toru was running downslope. Bashg must have realized the fight wasn't over after all, and before Aguri could raise his rifle, he squeezed the lever on the bottom of his gun. The glowing match descended, lit the charge, and a huge, bloody hole appeared on Aguri's back as the heavy ball exited and whirred away.

"Stu'id," Bashg said, surprised. "Lots eat already." He saw Toru approaching. "Stu'id Jaaph," he said. "No di'rence. Just us now."

"No," Toru snarled, aiming at Bashg's head. "Big difference. Just me."

Now, almost ten days later, Toru Miyata was alone. He had a compass to guide him, but it had snowed nearly every night since he lost his friends, and the daytime sky was gray and gloomy. He just didn't understand the weather, and it was taking a toll on him, despite his dwindling supply of fire-dried Grik flesh. He thought he knew roughly where he was and he should've crossed the frontier of the "others" by now; however, he saw no sign of habitation, and he didn't know how many more miles he had in him. Still, he'd escaped Kurokawa and ultimately the Grik themselves. Despite losing his friends, at least he was free. Unfortunately, if he didn't find other friends soon, or if this damnable weather didn't break, he was doomed.

He was roused from his stumbling, exhausted stupor by a terrifying screech and the sound of heavy beasts running toward him. Panicked, he looked toward the noise, knowing his moment of inattentiveness had cost him his life. His panic turned to amazement. Four men, mounted on *horses*, galloped to a stop before him, rifles slung on their shoulders.

"Blimey!" said one bearded horseman. "It's a man!"

"*Ja*," replied another. "A dead one, if we don't get him quickly to shelter."

"Blimey," the first muttered again. "Looks like a Chinaman or somethin'. Wonder where he's from."

"Perhaps we may find out, if we save him," came the bantering reply. "He must have quite a tale to tell."

"I do," Toru suddenly croaked, splitting a lip. "The world's at war, and the Grik will soon drag you into it."